W9-DEJ-417

MOM'S MAIN MAN

SANDY STEEN
Some Kind of Hero

She needed a hero...and he was happy to oblige

VICTORIA PADE
Cowboy's Kiss

*She was gorgeous and her kid was cute,
but no way was he letting them on his ranch...
or into his heart*

Relive the romance...
Two complete novels
by two of your favorite authors!

As a youngster growing up in the wide-open spaces of the Texas Panhandle, **Sandy Steen** loved storytelling—everything from tales about her family's pioneer history, to movies and, of course, books, books and more books. From that early beginning, her love of storytelling found its way into almost every corner of her life, including such jobs as writing descriptions of new houses, speeches and advertising copy. It was through one of those jobs that she met a published writer who suggested she try her hand at writing a romance novel. She's been at it ever since.

Victoria Pade is the bestselling author of numerous contemporary romances, six historical romances and two mystery novels. She began her writing career after leaving college to have her first daughter. That daughter was seven years old and there was a second daughter before Victoria had her first book accepted for publication. Her first four novels were historical romances. But the exit of her husband and the urge to do more contemporary writing, exploring the kinds of problems she was facing, inspired a switch. Contemporary romances are still where her main interest lies, although she's enjoyed veering off the path into two more historical romances, as well as into mystery writing.

Sandy
Steen

Victoria
Pade

MOM'S
MAIN
MAN

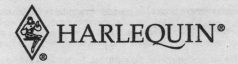

HARLEQUIN®

TORONTO • NEW YORK • LONDON
AMSTERDAM • PARIS • SYDNEY • HAMBURG
STOCKHOLM • ATHENS • TOKYO • MILAN • MADRID
PRAGUE • WARSAW • BUDAPEST • AUCKLAND

If you purchased this book without a cover you should be aware that this book is stolen property. It was reported as "unsold and destroyed" to the publisher, and neither the author nor the publisher has received any payment for this "stripped book."

HARLEQUIN BOOKS

by Request—MOM'S MAIN MAN

Copyright © 2001 by Harlequin Books S.A.

ISBN 0-373-21721-8

The publisher acknowledges the copyright holders
of the individual works as follows:
SOME KIND OF HERO
Copyright © 1996 by Sandy Steen
COWBOY'S KISS
Copyright © 1995 by Victoria Pade

This edition published by arrangement with Harlequin Books S.A.

All rights reserved. Except for use in any review, the reproduction or utilization of this work in whole or in part in any form by any electronic, mechanical or other means, now known or hereafter invented, including xerography, photocopying and recording, or in any information storage or retrieval system, is forbidden without the written permission of the publisher, Harlequin Enterprises Limited, 225 Duncan Mill Road, Don Mills, Ontario, Canada M3B 3K9.

All characters in this book have no existence outside the imagination of the author and have no relation whatsoever to anyone bearing the same name or names. They are not even distantly inspired by any individual known or unknown to the author, and all incidents are pure invention.

® and TM are trademarks of the publisher. Trademarks indicated with ® are registered in the United States Patent and Trademark Office, the Canadian Trade Marks Office and in other countries.

Visit us at www.eHarlequin.com

Printed in U.S.A.

CONTENTS

Some Kind of Hero
Sandy Steen

_____ Prologue _____

"WHAT YOU NEED is a woman," Wynette Dickerson informed her friend, and part-time employer. "Correction. What you need is a wife."

Jared Markham didn't even look up from strapping on the standard issue holster and Glock 40, now riding comfortably on his right hip. "If you're going to start in about that magazine again, forget it. Even if I did need a woman, I sure wouldn't go looking for one in the want ads."

"It's not the want ads." Wynette, a friend, the waitress at the Pecos Café in Alpine, and the woman who had washed and cleaned once a week for Jared since his wife had died two years earlier, propped a hand on her bony hip. "And before you get your back up, there's absolutely nothin' wrong with puttin' an ad in one of these." She held out a copy of _Texas Men_ magazine. "Why, my cousin Lerlene's friend answered a personal ad in the _Alaska Men_ magazine, and first thing you know, she was off to Anchorage to get hitched."

"I'm happy for her, but that doesn't mean—"

"This," she waved the magazine in the air, "is a bona fide publication. On the up and up. Strictly legit. And if you ask me—"

"I didn't."

"Now, there you go. That's exactly your problem.

You never speak up for yourself. Not about somethin' personal anyway. You've kept to yourself too long. You need the comfort and softness a woman—a good woman—can offer, and as far as I can see, you're either too shy or too stubborn to go find one on your own.''

Jared adjusted the holster, and the leather creaked as if in protest to the unnecessary handling. The truth was, he did need a woman.

And the admission swamped him with guilt.

How could he even think about another woman when Amy had been gone barely two years? Two lonely, desolate years. Two years of feeling as if his empty, barren soul would never again be nourished by love. How could he even contemplate the idea of marriage, much less the actuality?

But the fact was, he *had* been contemplating the idea of marriage. Actually wrestling with the idea was more appropriate. Ever since the incident on Santiago Peak.

"You haven't been the same since they hauled you down off that mountain." When he glanced at Wynette, she shook her finger at him. "And don't you try to deny it."

"I'm not denying anything." Jared headed for the front of the Victorian style house and the small parlor he had converted into an office. Wynette followed, stopping in the doorway.

"How long has it been since that business on Santiago Peak?" she asked, leaning against the doorframe. "A week? Two weeks?"

"Fifteen days."

"And you been walkin' around here with a hangdog

look on your face ever since. I know you think I'm a real buttinsky, but I just wanna see you happy."

"Plastering my private life all over the pages of a damned magazine won't make me happy," he snapped.

There was a long pause, before Wynette replied, "Well, excuse me, I was just tryin' to help. You don't have to bite my head off." Then she pushed away from the door and left.

Jared sighed, knowing he had been a real jerk. Wynette was a good friend and didn't deserve his foul mood. A mood that basically stemmed from the fact that she was right. He hadn't been the same since the incident. The fact that even now he preferred to think of what happened as an incident rather than an accident was an indication of his denial. Probably because the word *accident* implied the unexpected, a mishap, something he had no control over.

The lack of control, the pure happenstance of the situation, was what had finally made him see himself, and his life in the harsh light of reality. So much of the time that had passed since Amy's death scarcely caused a ripple in his memory, yet he remembered that night on Santiago Peak with startling clarity.

He had gone into the foothills of the Del Norte Mountains after some hunters who'd been illegally tracking desert bighorn sheep. The hunters had eluded him, slithering over the unforgiving terrain in the darkness like invisible snakes. Frustrated at having lost his quarry, he had started back toward his truck, mumbling some uncomplimentary words for the hunters...and not paying attention to where he was walking. The toe of his boot caught on a length of exposed root, and he went ass-end over teakettle down fifty yards of mountainside. A rookie, tenderfoot kind of thing to do.

Reacting instinctively as he tumbled, he had made a desperate grab at a huge boulder hoping to stop his bone-jarring descent. But for the second time that night his judgment was bad. The slab of rock wasn't firmly embedded in the ground. As he grabbed hold, it gave way and brought a rock slide with it.

The boulder literally chased him down the hill. Half rolling, half sliding, he came to an abrupt stop when his body slammed into a rocky outcropping at the bottom of the hill. The sixty-pound-plus boulder come to an abrupt stop against his left foot.

Because he had landed facedown and at an awkward angle, he had lain trapped for three hours before Tucker Weiss, the second game warden assigned to Brewster County, had found him. Thanks to sturdy boots, he had emerged from the accident basically unscathed with the exception of a badly bruised ankle. Physically he was okay. But something emotional— maybe even spiritual—had happened to him while he lay on that dark mountainside. For the first time in two years he had come face-to-face with his loneliness.

The reality that he had no one.

His parents were dead. His only brother lived in Wyoming, and years passed between their visits. His friends, mostly other game wardens he had befriended over his eight-year career, were scattered across the state.

No one was waiting for him to come home.

If he had lain on that mountain for three days instead of three hours, no one would have been worried. And if he had died...

Yes, there would have been some who grieved, but his passing wouldn't have left an empty place in anyone's life.

The reality of his aloneness had been a cold, horrifying shock. He could still remember the fear clutching at his heart, so powerful he felt as if he couldn't breathe. Lying there in the darkness that fear, once recognized, had crystallized. He loved his work, and he was proud to be a game warden, but he didn't want to end up with nothing to show for his life but a bunch of fellow officers standing around his casket talking about what a great guy he had been. Until that night, Jared hadn't realized just how much he had isolated himself since Amy's death, how much he had truly missed sharing his life with a woman.

Strangely enough, it wasn't the major things that he missed. It was the thousand and one little intimacies that he remembered about sharing his life with Amy. The moments when he would hear her softly humming in another room, or the way she used to touch his cheek once in a while. That last moment right before she drifted off to sleep and whispered, "Sweet dreams," or the first moment she opened her eyes to a new day, smiling, eager to kiss him good morning. Her gentle manner that never failed to soothe him. She was his anchor, the calm at the center of any storm life threw his way.

As he waited to be rescued, knowing he wasn't in life-threatening danger, Jared realized that he had sealed his pain inside of himself like some kind of morbid shrine to his late wife. A painful, private shrine where only he could worship. He had sealed himself off from life. And in doing so, he realized that his heart had become as isolated as the part of Texas he was sworn to protect.

In his job, good instincts could mean the difference between life and death. And that night, every instinct he had was telling him that he *had* to change his life.

Even now, days afterward, he was still struggling with knowing change was necessary, yet not knowing how to accomplish it.

With a weary sigh he raked his hands through his thick blond hair, then went to find Wynette and offer his most sincere apology. Hell, maybe she was even right about that magazine. That admission in itself proved how desperate he was. Still, even though it was certainly an unorthodox method of starting a relationship, the more he thought about it, the more he realized it might be his only realistic approach. After all, it would solve his main problem. Namely, that there weren't many women in the sparsely populated Big Bend area, and he had precious little time to go courting.

What could it hurt? Besides, Jared thought, as he headed to the kitchen to find Wynette, he probably wouldn't get more than a handful of responses anyway. What were the chances of finding the kind of woman he could spend the rest of his life with—a million to one?

1

GAZING OUT THE BIG bay window in his kitchen, Jared watched the early morning sun spill over the Glass Mountains, and wondered if the isolation of his job had finally affected his mind. Change, and a need to end the loneliness was one thing, but what he had done was beginning to feel more like insanity.

Advertising for a wife.

What kind of man gets a wife from a want ad? And what kind of woman answers such an ad?

At least he hadn't come off sounding like a complete jerk in the magazine, and it had painted a picture of him as a man of old-fashioned, but not outdated values, strong morals and a deep and abiding respect for women. And it stated the most important traits for the relationship he was contemplating—honesty and self-reliance. Any woman answering his ad knew where he stood, and what he was looking for.

Raising a cup of steaming black coffee to his lips, he glanced at the old metal milk carrier on his kitchen table, stuffed to the brim with responses to his ad. Over a hundred letters from women looking for...for what? Love, security, steady sex? Jared had read them all, and had been amazed, even shocked to discover that there were so many women anxious to jump into a relationship, sight unseen. And downright stunned to discover many of them spoke freely of their need for a physical relationship. Very physical.

At age thirty-one, women's lib and the sexual revolution weren't exactly foreign concepts, but he had to admit he had been totally unprepared for the candor and borderline pornographic explicitness some of the women had expressed in outlining their likes and dislikes. One thing was for sure. After wading through his mountain of correspondence, he knew he had been out of the dating loop too long to ever be glib and charming, or any of the other things these women seemed to want.

Out of all the letters, he had found only three that sounded even remotely as if they'd been written by someone he might be interested in. Now all he had to do was call the women, and possibly arrange a meeting. Yeah, that's all he had to do.

Jared set his coffee cup on the counter and reached for the phone, then stopped.

He couldn't do this.

It just wasn't his nature to call up some strange woman and make small talk, then ask her if she wanted to come size him up while he was doing the same to her. He just couldn't do it.

Once again he gazed out the window at the mountains, watching the last traces of the night's purple shadows fading before the sun. They looked so majestic, so strong. He had always found great solace in their beauty, great strength in their majesty. And though he considered them as no less powerful, since the incident at Santiago Peak he had seen them in a different light. For perhaps the first time in his life, Jared had identified with their solitude. He was a solitary creature in need of warmth, companionship. He didn't want to stand alone against time like a mountain.

So what were his alternatives? The sameness he had grown pitifully comfortable with since Amy died. A lonely sameness. That wasn't an alternative. It was a death sentence.

No, he *had* to do this. He had to pick up the phone and call these women. He had come this far. Losing his nerve now was silly.

"No guts, no glory," he mumbled, jerking up the receiver. His hand shook as he dialed the first number.

Forty-five minutes later, Jared hung up from his second call. So far he was batting zero.

The first woman, a twenty-nine-year-old dental hygienist from San Angelo, had been appalled at the description of how remote his home was, and how self-sufficient she would have to be.

"You mean you really don't go into town except for once a week?" she had asked. Followed shortly by, "Do you mean it's literally forty miles to the nearest restaurant? What do you do for entertainment?"

The second candidate wasn't much more receptive. The thirty-five-year-old divorcée with a soft southern accent had asked, "You mean you actually go around hunting poachers? With a gun? How could you do that?"

The thought of a third rejection was enough to make

him give up on the whole idea. But, he had come this far, and there was only one candidate left.

"What the hell," he said, dialing the number.

STANDING BESIDE THE pay phone in the hallway outside her rented room, Shannon Kramer stared at the number scribbled on the piece of paper her landlady had just handed her. The piece of paper that might be her ticket to eventual freedom, or back to an intolerable existence. It was a risk. Maybe this was the man in the ad, or maybe it was a trap set by her ex-husband.

If only she wasn't so desperate. If only she could have come up with any other way to keep herself and her daughter out of danger. God knows she had tried everything she could think of: changing names, hair color—hers, and Lily's—padding to make herself look pounds heavier than her usual willowy build, even dressing herself and her daughter up as males. None of it had worked.

Hal always found them.

Her ex-husband's network of survivalist good old boys worked like a trap where she and Lily were concerned. They were everywhere. It was almost as if he had his own personal army of spies. Whenever, wherever she and Lily surfaced, eventually they were spotted, and the news got back to Hal.

And the last time he tracked them down, he had almost strangled her to death when she refused to tell him where she had hidden his daughter. He would have succeeded if her burly ex-bouncer landlord hadn't arrived, and taken a hand. He did succeed in issuing a threat. While the landlord kept him pinned to a wall awaiting the police, Hal had vowed he would hunt her down. There was no place she could hide, he promised. No person she could trust. He told her that she and Lily belonged to him like everything else he owned, and if he couldn't have them, no one would.

Shannon could remember that horrifying, bone-chilling moment as though it were five minutes ago instead of five months. There had been so much venom in his voice. So much hate. She never doubted for an instant that he meant every word. She hadn't waited to press charges. Instead she and Lily had gone as far underground as they could. But it wasn't far enough. She had begun to think it would never be far enough.

Then fate had intervened, or maybe one of her many prayers had been answered. Either way, the day she had happened across a copy of *Texas Men* magazine, and Jared Markham's ad while waiting in a bus station, she had decided he was exactly what she needed. His home was remote, he made infrequent trips into the city, and his job required him to be gone a great deal.

Money and nerves worn almost to nothing after playing Hal's freakish game of hide-and-seek for over a year and a half, Shannon had taken one look at the ad, and felt her heart leap for joy. She knew she couldn't take much more of the continual stalking. Every day, every hour was an eternity spent looking over her shoulder, scrutinizing every stranger. She was constantly on guard, jumping at shadows while trying to pretend to Lily that she had everything under control. That everything was going to be just fine.

Who was she kidding? Nothing would ever be fine again until Hal gave up on them. And she knew that would never happen. Hal was as desperate to find her as she was to stay out of his grasp.

So, she had no choice. Either this man, this Jared Markham was the real McCoy or he wasn't. If he wasn't, she and Lily would continue running. Shannon dialed the number.

THE PHONE was picked up on the first ring. "Markham."

"Hello," Shannon said nervously. "Could I speak with Jared—"

"Jared Markham. Yes, I'm, uh, Jared Markham," the man said. He sounded as nervous as she was. "Is this Shannon Kramer?"

Despite the fact that Shannon had written the letter in good faith, she figured the odds were at least a thousand to one that he would contact her. Now that her plan had suddenly gone from concept to reality, her heart rate jumped and her nerves tingled partly from excitement, partly from fear.

"Hello," Jared said again. "Are you still there?"

"Yes, I'm...I'm here." She licked her dry lips, and knew a sudden, intense craving for a cigarette, despite the fact that she had abandoned the habit almost six years ago.

"I have the right Shannon Kramer, don't I? You answered an ad in *Texas Men* magazine?"

"That's me. I mean, yes. You've got the right Shannon Kramer." She reminded herself that he was several hundred miles away, and no threat. She reminded herself that he was, in fact, her rescue plan, and possibly her last hope. She couldn't afford to make any mistakes now.

"I, uh, just want you to know that I've never done this before," he sort of blurted out after a long pause. "Put an ad in a magazine, I mean. I'm kind of nervous."

"Then that makes us even because I've never answered one before. And I'm...I'm nervous, too."

But Shannon's nervousness had little to do with first-date jitters. Her nerves were taut with months of looking over her shoulders. Jared Markham might very well be the solution to her problems, but she had to be sure. Since her recent past had taught her the best way to deal with difficulty was to meet it head-on, she jumped in with her first question.

"The article didn't mention whether or not you had ever been married. Do you mind if I ask?"

"My...my wife died two years ago."

"Oh. I'm so sorry, Jared."

It was the first time she called him by his name, and for a reason he couldn't explain, the sound of it poured over him like sunshine on the first day of spring. How long had it been since he had heard caring in a woman's voice? And her sympathy was real. That was in her voice, too. If this woman was one tenth what her voice promised, he owed Wynette a big apology for ever doubting her advice.

"Thanks," he said.

"You didn't say anything about it in the ad, so I, uh, take it there were no children."

Jared's breath hit the back of his throat, and his fingers tightened on the receiver. Pain, sharp and familiar, hit him like a fist to his gut. For a moment, her seemingly innocent question tilted his world, spinning him back into painful memories.

"Jared?"

"No," he said finally. "No children."

"But you like them? Kids, I mean."

"Like them?" God, she didn't know what she was asking. He loved kids. He and Amy had planned on having a houseful. "Y-yes."

"Good," she said softly.

Jared was struggling so hard to keep the memories at bay that her response didn't register. "I, uh, I'd really like to meet you," he said, wanting to steer the conversation away from children.

"Yes. I'm anxious to meet you, too."

When Jared hung up a few moments later, he stared at the phone, a little stunned at what had transpired. And how quickly. Once they started making plans to meet, everything just sort of snowballed. She told him that she had some vacation time coming, and before he realized it they had made plans to meet this Sunday afternoon.

He had offered to pay Shannon's airfare from Austin to San Angelo, the nearest airport, but she had declined, saying that she didn't think they should start off owing each other anything but an open mind, and a positive attitude. He thought it strange that she opted to travel by bus, considering her eagerness to arrange an almost immediate meeting, but then he decided that maybe she hated to fly.

It dawned on him that more than anything he had based his opinion of Shannon Kramer on the honesty and credibility he heard in her voice. And his own instincts. It also dawned on him that she had asked most of the questions, ending the conversation with more knowledge of him than he had about her. He hadn't asked if she had ever been married, or what her background was, or...anything. In a matter of minutes he had committed himself to meeting a woman he had never seen, with a possible result of matrimony. He had never done anything so...so spontaneous, or risky, in his life. Suddenly panicked, Jared reached for the phone, intending to call her back and call the whole thing off, but he stopped.

Or rather, remembering the sound of her voice stopped him. She sounded so...warm. And he needed warmth.

No, he cautioned himself. This wasn't about warmth. This was about his need for companionship. He couldn't—wouldn't—allow himself to think about warmth. Even thinking about it felt disloyal to Amy's memory.

He had loved, and been loved, deeply and passionately. Love like that only came along once in a lifetime. Shannon Kramer might be the answer to his loneliness but he didn't expect to love her. Not the way he had loved Amy.

JARED MARKHAM might be the answer to Shannon's prayers, but that didn't make lying to him any easier. In fact, if anything, it made it harder. He sounded so solid, so reliable. And self-confident. Exactly the kind of man she needed.

The twist to this truly bizarre situation was that Jared sounded like the kind of man she'd want to marry. A man she could depend on. A man that was secure enough in himself to give his wife love *and* support. To be a true partner in every sense of the word. For a fleeting moment she allowed herself to fantasize about a real relationship. What would it be like to love Jared? To make love to him?

Oh, this was crazy. She couldn't afford daydreams. And even if Jared turned out to be the man of her dreams, she fell one mark shy of his criteria. Honesty. For there to be even a faint hope of her dreams becoming reality she would have to be totally honest with him. And she couldn't do that.

Sometimes when she thought of everything that had happened and how Hal had driven her to her current state of desperation, she wondered how she could have ever cared about him. But she had, in the beginning anyway.

Growing up as the middle child and only girl in a family of eight, Shannon had learned to stand on her own two feet at an early age. Her independence and self-confidence had been forged in a fire of teasing and torment by her brothers, and she had emerged tempered and flexible, able to take whatever life dealt her. By the time she was in junior high school, she could keep a house, sew and care for her younger brothers every bit as well as her mother. And her skills were put to the test because that was the year her mother became sick. From then until the time Alice Kramer died three years later, for all intents and purposes, Shannon became a mother. Her father did what he could to help, but working two jobs to support his family left him precious little time for parenting. Most of the responsibility fell squarely on Shannon's shoulders.

Dreaming of a better life for herself, she worked nights at the local movie theater to earn her tuition at a community college.

And then came Hal Jackson.

He was good-looking, and treated her as if she were as delicate as English bone china. He made her laugh, and taught her how to have fun. With Hal she felt special and treasured. He offered his protection, and painted a picture of the wonderful life they would have together. For the first time in her life Shannon let someone look after her.

But it didn't take long after they were married for her to realize that Hal's idea of love was one-sided. His side. And his idea of protection was to isolate her from everyone but himself. She had already begun to entertain thoughts of leaving him when she learned she was pregnant. Never one to give up when the going got tough, she stayed, and tried to make the best of her marriage, but when Lily was born Hal got worse, not better. His behavior became obsessive, and the only time he spent away from her was when he went out with his gun-club friends, and an occasional weekend of survival training.

Then the abuse began. Mostly verbal slurs with an occasional slap or shove, but Shannon knew she had to get away from him. Twice she tried, and twice Hal brought her back. Lily was three by the time she was finally able to find sanctuary in a women's shelter, and file for divorce. Fool that she was, she thought that would be the end of it. But it was only the beginning.

Hal's obsessive behavior escalated. He harassed her constantly, causing her to lose first one job then another. Despite a court order, he showed up on her doorstep whenever he chose. Shannon called the police, talked to her lawyer, the judge, anybody who would listen, but to no avail. Later she learned that the judge, district attorney and several police officers were among Hal's gun-club buddies. In this case, camaraderie bred contempt—for her. Soon, it became clear that the deck was stacked against her, and that her only hope was to get as far away from Hal as she could. So, she and Lily had left in the middle of the night with only one suitcase each and the few dollars Shannon had been able to save. But they couldn't keep running forever. She was desperate to throw Hal off their scent.

And desperate women do desperate things. Answering the ad was the biggest risk she'd ever taken, but in hindsight it just might pay off.

Unfortunately, making it to Alpine didn't mean she and Lily were home free. Once she got there, the desperation would require more half truths, and outright lies. And for a woman who prided herself on honesty, deception—no matter how justifiable—was a bitter pill to swallow. But she would swallow it. Of course she would. Because she had to. Because she had run out of options, places to hide, and almost run out of strength. Jared Markham was her last hope.

But she knew from experience that even last hopes should have a backup plan. They would go to Alpine, and pray that Jared accepted her. If he didn't, well… Frankly, Shannon had no idea what she would do next except cut her losses, and move on. She only knew that as hard as it would be, if Jared turned his back on them, she and Lily would survive. Somehow, some way.

"Mama?"

She glanced down into the bright blue eyes of her five-year-old daughter, Lily. Amazingly, Lily had blossomed once free of her father's stinging verbal abuse. Even though she had no permanent home or friends to play with, the once quiet child had come into her own. She laughed freely, and seemed to bear no severe emotional scars.

"Mama, are we gonna move again?"

Shannon bent down until she was at eye level with the one person she loved above all else. The one person she would protect with her life if need be. "Yes, sweetheart," she replied, her husky voice even huskier with emotion. "But maybe this time we can stay for a while."

"Oh, boy." Lily threw her arms around her mother's neck, and gave her a quick hug before drawing back. "I'll cross my fingers, okay, Mama. That'll help, won't it?"

"Sure."

"You, too, Mama."

"Me, too, baby." Shannon held up her right hand, fingers crossed. "Me, too."

2

SHE NEVER SHOULD have come. It was a bad idea from the beginning. Whatever possessed her to think she could look this man in the eyes and lie without him seeing her for the fool she was? She would never have considered it in a million years if she hadn't been so desperate. But absolute desperation hadn't prevented her conscience from eating away at her like acid ever since she had called Jared Markham back to tell him she would be arriving late Sunday afternoon.

And she had almost phoned him a dozen times since then to call off their meeting. But she hadn't. Every time she reached for the phone a mental image of Hal's face, twisted with rage, flashed across her mind.

Now, here she was sitting in a café across from the bus station waiting for him to arrive. Waiting to play out the scene she hoped would eventually win her a hiding place. Her strategy, if you could call it that, was simple, if slightly vague. When she met Jared she would stay as close to the truth as possible without revealing her real reason for answering his ad. Simple, but lying, even by degrees, went against every principle, every moral fiber Shannon possessed.

So she would admit to her lie of omission where Lily was concerned, and that she knew she had probably ruined any chance they might have had. He deserved the truth face-to-face. She owed him that much. With luck, she would come across as exactly what she was— a proud, but poor single mother. That is, if she got the chance, before he stormed out of the café.

"Mama, can I have another Coke?"

"It's not in the budget, sweetie. Besides, too many soft drinks aren't good for your teeth," Shannon told her daughter without taking her gaze from the front window of the café.

Jared had suggested they meet at the Pecos Café in case he got held up, or her bus got in early. The bus had arrived ahead of schedule, and Shannon was grateful for his suggestion because the café window provided her with a view of the street. And she wanted to be sure to see him before he saw her.

"Refills are free for kids under six."

Shannon looked around at the waitress, a thinnish woman with a wide smile. "Thanks, but I'd rather she have water."

"Better for her anyway. Let me top off your glass." The waitress stepped to the counter, picked up a pitcher of ice water, then stepped back, and filled the two glasses on the table. "How'd those grilled cheese sandwiches do you ladies?"

"Fine, thanks." Shannon quickly glanced out the front window again.

"You wanna order somethin' else?"

"No. I, uh...I'm waiting for someone, but..."

"Must be a man."

"What makes you say that?"

"'Cause you've just about mutilated that poor napkin."

Shannon glanced down to discover that she had picked at the paper napkin until almost half of it was in pieces on the table.

"No woman gets that worked up less she's waitin' for a man."

"I didn't realize I'd made such a mess." Shannon quickly brushed the pieces of paper into a pile, then raked them off the table into an extra napkin, and wadded it into a ball.

"Must be some guy."

"I don't know. I've never met him."

The waitress cocked her head. "You mean you're workin' yourself into a lather over a man you've never even seen?"

"And will probably never see again after today," Shannon said, her conscience taking another bite out of her confidence. "Once Jared Markham—"

"Well, I'll be. You must be Shannon Kramer."

Accustomed to denying her own name out of fear, Shannon merely looked at the woman. "I beg your pardon?"

"You are, aren't you? Jared told me you were comin' in today."

"You...you know him?"

"And then some. He's a regular in here. Only decent food he gets if you wanna know the truth. Listen, sugar, I'm the one that pushed him into puttin' that ad in the magazine in the first place. Like pullin' on a sat down mule, but he finally gave in. The name's Wynette

Dickerson." She stuck out her hand, and Shannon shook it. "So, you're the one."

"Yes, I—I guess so."

"And who might this sweet little darlin' be?" Wynette asked, looking at Lily.

"This is my daughter, Lily. Say hello to Mrs. Dickerson."

"Hello," the child said.

"Y'all call me Wynette. Jared never told me nothin' about you havin' a kid."

Shannon glanced away. "He...he doesn't know."

Wynette's hazel eyes widened. "Just an oversight on your part or were you intendin' to surprise him?"

She hadn't planned on having anyone but Jared as an audience, but it couldn't be avoided. Shannon hated this. She hated the way fear now dictated her every action. This woman was an innocent bystander in her flight from cruelty, and didn't deserve to be roped into a circle of lies and a race from the devil, but for now at least, there was no other way.

Unable to look the smiling waitress in the eyes, Shannon glanced away. "I'm ashamed to admit it was deliberate. So ashamed, in fact, that I... I couldn't go through with this. He's probably going to hate me, but I felt the least I could do was tell him in person."

"You may have more guts than you do good sense."

"How mad is he going to be?"

"Hard to tell with Jared. He's not what you'd call real expressive."

"In this case, he's got a right to be rip-roaring mad."

"Like I said, he ain't a rip-roaring kinda guy."

"Well, at least he deserves the truth."

"How come you didn't tell him right off?"

"Uh, sweetheart," Shannon said turning to Lily. "Would you like to go over to the jukebox, and play a song?"

Lily's heart-shaped face lit up. "Can I please? Can I?"

"May I."

"May I, please, please?"

Practically before Shannon got the word *yes* out of her mouth, Lily had wiggled out of her seat, under the table, and come up on the outside of the booth.

Smiling, Shannon gave one of Lily's honey blond braids a tug. "Next time try getting out the conventional way," she said, digging in her purse for change. She handed Lily a quarter. "Pick out a good one, okay?"

"Okay," Lily said over her shoulder, already halfway to the jukebox.

When Shannon knew her daughter was out of earshot, she looked up at Wynette Dickerson. "I didn't tell him because I was afraid he wouldn't want a woman with a child." *Afraid to miss my last chance.*

"And was comin' here so important?" Wynette asked, seeming to forget her two other customers to slide into the side of the booth across from Shannon.

"Yes." That much was certainly the truth.

"Don't seem like a good way to start off, if you ask me."

"You're right, of course, but..."

"But?"

"I was desperate." Shannon looked the waitress in the eyes. "And tired of men thinking I'm easy because I'm alone. Tired of scratching out a living in cramped, dirty cities where people have forgotten what clean air smells like. And tired of living every minute of my life in fear of being mugged or killed, or—God forbid—of something happening to my child. I want more than that for Lily. I know that's no excuse for what I did, but when I saw Jared's ad..." She glanced away. "I just want a chance for us."

"You weren't born a city girl, were you?" the waitress asked. Shannon shook her head. "Figures, or you wouldn't be wantin' fresh air and space." Wynette sighed. "And what about Jared?"

"I thought maybe, just for once in my life, I'd found a trustworthy man. I should have known my luck hadn't changed."

"Had a lot of that, have you?"

"'A lot' doesn't even begin to cover it. Responsibility seems to leave a bad taste in most men's mouths. At least, the ones I've met. They're hardly interested in having children of their own, much less taking care of another man's child. I know I should have told Jared the truth, but—and this may sound corny—your friend sounded like an answer to prayer. Anyway," Shannon said, sighing deeply, "I decided to face the music. Afterward, Lily and I will move on."

"Move on? I thought you lived in San Antonio?"

"We did but...but I lost my job. So," she said, her voice a little too bright, her smile a little too forced, "I thought maybe we'd try California. With all those high-priced restaurants out there, there's bound to be good tips." The truth was, if her meeting with Jared turned out badly, California was as good a place as any to run.

"You wait tables?"

Shannon nodded.

In the eighteen months since her divorce from Hal, she had worked in more eateries than she cared to count. But it was an honest living, and transient, therefore convenient. There was always a diner or a café in the next town that needed another girl. And if she decided to leave on the spur of the moment, no one ever asked why.

The waitress eyed the younger woman for a second, then said, "You know, Alpine ain't exactly on the way to the coast."

"I thought it was important to set the record straight." Shannon shrugged. "Besides, one place is pretty much like the next."

"Got no folks? What about the little girl's daddy?"

"He's dead," Shannon said quickly. God forgive her, but she wished it was true. "Lily, and I are all the family we have."

Wynette frowned. "When were you planning on leavin'?"

"As...as soon as I talk to Jared."

"You mean today? Why, you'll be ridin' that bus all night, and for the next two days before you get to California."

"Well, I..." Shannon ducked her head again, then

looked back at Wynette. "Actually, our ticket runs out in Phoenix."

"What are you gonna do in Phoenix?"

The tickets in her purse *did* show Phoenix as the end of the line. Not that it made much difference where they wound up if she couldn't hide out long enough for their trail to grow cold. Shannon shrugged. "The same thing I've always done. Get a job. Make a living. Keep things together as best I can. Then as soon as I manage to tuck a little cash back, we'll go on to California."

"Lord, love 'ya. You know, even though Jared ain't much of a talker, he's fair. Once he's had a chance to think about it, he may not be too upset. Sure hate to see you just tell him, then light out."

"I doubt I'll have any other choice."

"Uh, well," Wynette said, sliding out of the booth. "You're about to find out."

Shannon looked out the window to see a tall blond man in a tan-and-brown uniform across the street, headed toward the café. "Jared?"

"In the flesh," Wynette replied, then patted the young woman on the shoulder. "Good luck, sugar."

"Th-thanks." After a quick glance at Lily still enthralled with the jukebox, Shannon focused on the man striding across the two-lane street.

Huge was the only word she could think of to describe her first impression of Jared Markham. He was huge. Broad shoulders out to forever, powerful arms, and an athlete's physique. But size was definitely the dominant impression. Size, and the fact that his picture didn't do him justice. Of course, the well-fitted uniform and gun strapped to his hip added an extra dimension to his aura of power.

He looked...substantial. Solid and steady.

And he was handsome in the bargain. Not pretty, but virile and powerful in a way no mere good looks could claim. His blue eyes were sharp, intelligent, and his jaw looked strong enough to withstand a sledgehammer. If the words *ruggedly handsome* ever fit anyone, they fit Jared Markham.

As he stepped on the curb only a couple of yards from the café window, a boy of maybe eight or nine came racing along the sidewalk on a skateboard. Seconds away from the intersection, it was clear he would never be able to stop if he had to. Quick as a striking rattler Markham reached out, and snagged the flying youngster out of the way of possible harm.

Until that moment Shannon hadn't realized she was holding her breath in anticipation of disaster. A disaster neatly avoided by Jared Markham's instantaneous save. She half expected the tall game warden to angrily chastise the child, but to her surprise he went down on one knee, putting himself at the boy's eye level. As he pointed to the intersection then to the skateboard, she didn't have to overhear the conversation to know the finer points of sidewalk safety were being explained to the haphazard youngster. But Jared's expression was calm and concerned, firm, but gentle. Finally, he stood up, and offered his hand. The boy hesitated, obviously surprised at such a grown-up gesture, but shook the game warden's hand, then went on his way. At a much slower pace.

But what riveted Shannon was the smile on Jared Markham's face as he watched the boy move away. She got the feeling that seeing to the kid's safety was more than just a job to Jared. She got the feeling that this was a man who cared.

Swallowing the lump in her throat, Shannon realized she had just been given a glimpse of his personality that she might never have otherwise seen. A very revealing glimpse.

Until this very moment she had thought of him in the abstract, choosing not to think of him as a flesh-and-blood human being. Ashamed of her self-denial, she could no longer escape reality. Jared Markham was a real man with feelings. He was even heroic. And as she very well knew, heroes didn't grow on trees.

If she had serious reservations about how he might be with her child, they had just shrunk to mild concern. But her reservations about what she was doing, about how she was using him had just become major doubts. As much as she needed Jared, he didn't deserve to be used.

She shoved the guilty thought aside by reminding herself that she was doing this for Lily. Lily was all that mattered.

Jared gazed after the boy for several seconds, then turned and entered the café. When he stopped to give Wynette a warm greeting, she pointed to Shannon, and he looked straight at her.

As he walked toward her, Shannon's heart rate

jumped, and a covey of butterflies took flight in the pit of her stomach. And when he stopped at her booth she had to clasp the hands in her lap to keep them from shaking. Torn between the desperate hope of finally being free of Hal, and the reality of what she was doing almost made her sick to her stomach.

Jared couldn't believe his eyes. This woman was beautiful. A little too pale, but maybe that was nerves. She had gorgeous green eyes, the color of the trees as evening settles on the mountainside. Her hair was dark and thick with just a hint of natural curls around her face. Wearing very little, if any, makeup and only a tinted lip gloss, she looked innocent and alluring at the same time. As if she should be sitting in the middle of a field of daisies, her lovely face lifted to the sun.

After having been thoroughly made love to only moments before.

The thought shocked him, but not nearly so much as the image that flashed across his mind. An image of green eyes vibrant with desire. Of dark hair falling over bare shoulders, bare breasts.

He hadn't expected gorgeous, but that's what she was. And he hadn't expected his body to react so strongly.

"Shannon?"

She offered a smile that was weak at best. "Hello."

"Have you, uh, been waiting long?"

He was so tall she had to tilt her head farther back than usual in order to look into his face. "No, not long."

"Good." Then he took the other side of the booth,

but because of his size and build, not easily. In fact, once he was sitting, the booth seemed to shrink.

"How was your trip?"

"Fine." Shannon chanced another quick glance at Lily, and was relieved to see she was still occupied with the jukebox. "Before we go any farther, I have to tell you something."

He smiled, but it didn't quite reach his eyes. "One look at me, and you've changed your mind?"

"No, you're fine. I mean, this is not about you or about wanting to...to get to know you." Shannon took a deep breath, gathering all her courage. She had to tell him the truth. As much as she could. And he would either forgive her, and let her and Lily stay, or he would toss her out on her rear, which, of course, he had every right to do. Shannon wondered if God heard prayers for half truths, even for a good cause.

"I wasn't completely honest when we talked on the phone."

"Oh."

"I, uh, didn't tell you that I'm divorced."

"Actually, you didn't tell me a whole lot about yourself. I take it that wasn't a memory lapse?"

Was he angry? She couldn't tell. If he was, it wasn't any brand of anger she had ever encountered. But then admittedly, she wasn't the best judge of temperaments that were less than raging. "No, it wasn't."

"Well, being divorced isn't the end of the world, nor does it earn you a scarlet letter. So, I assume there's more."

Shannon nodded. "I have a child."

Jared blinked. He wasn't sure what he had expected her to say, but announcing that she had a child was last on his list. Why would she neglect to tell him such an important fact. Unless...

"Is...is there something wrong with your child?"

"There most certainly is not." Her defense was quick, and certain. "She's a beautiful, healthy five-year-old. And very bright, I might add."

"So why keep her a secret?"

"I was going to tell you, but... Well, to be honest—"

"I wish you would."

Shannon looked into his blue eyes, and saw no forgiveness. "I had that coming."

Oh, brother, had she ever blown it.

She could see it in his eyes. Her last hope, and she'd blown it. Right now he probably wouldn't give her the time of day, much less a second chance.

She lifted her chin, refusing to look away from his gaze. All right, if she couldn't convince him to accept her then she could at least exit this disastrous situation with as much of her dignity intact as possible.

"I answered your ad because I want my child to have a real home, security. I want her to be safe and happy. I didn't tell you because I was afraid you wouldn't want a woman with a child. I've had some bad experiences in that area. My hope was that after you got to know us you would want us. Look, the fact of the matter is that I was scared. I've been on my own since Lily was a baby, and I can tell you, firsthand, that men who want what I want are few and far between."

"So, you thought a lonely widower would be an easy mark."

She tried to ignore the caustic remark but it stung. "No. Your ad sounded so...wonderful. The mountains, and a real home. I thought that maybe you were as lonely as I was. I thought that just maybe you needed someone as much as I do." Shannon glanced down at her hands, knotted into fists in her lap, then back up at Jared.

"Is this the part where I forgive you, and ask you to stay anyway?"

"No."

The suspicion in his eyes clearly said he didn't believe her. It was a lost cause anyway.

Shannon squared her narrow shoulders. "I wanted to apologize face-to-face because that was the least I could do after deceiving you. And yes, I *had* hoped we could work something out, but I see now that's not possible."

She had been as honest as she could be under the circumstances. As honest as she dared. From this point on, it was up to Jared Markham.

Before he could say anything, Lily came skipping up to the booth humming the tune to the popular country-and-western song she had just played on the jukebox. "Can I do it—" At her mother's raised eyebrow, she said, "May I do it again, Mama?"

"I'm sorry, baby. That was my last quarter."

The little girl's lower lip jutted out about the same time she noticed the man across from her mother.

"Lily, say hello to Mr. Markham."

The pout was forgotten as her big blue eyes trained on the stranger in the uniform. "Are you a policeman?"

For a second he frowned, and glanced away, almost as if he didn't want to look at the little girl, but it was gone so quickly Shannon wasn't sure. And a moment later he smiled at the child, and there was only kindness in his eyes.

"In a way," he said. "Only I work out in the forest and mountains instead of the city."

"But there's no bad men in the forest, only animals," Lily insisted.

"Sometimes there are bad men in the forest. Then I have to protect the animals."

His statement won instant approval with a wide smile. "I like animals." She turned to Shannon. "Don't I, Mama?" She turned back to Jared. "But I can't have a dog. We can't take a dog with us. 'Cause of all our different houses, and—"

"We've moved around a lot," Shannon interjected, hoping to sidetrack Lily.

"Uh-huh. And no dogs. That's the rule," Lily informed him, punctuating the sentence with a nod of her head. "Do you have a dog?"

"As a matter of fact, I have two."

Lily's eyes went as round as half dollars. "You got two?"

"Have," her mother corrected.

"What's their names?"

"Lily, you're pestering Mr. Markham."

"But, Mama—"

"It's okay," Jared said, gazing at Shannon over the top of Lily's head.

"She can be terribly single-minded when she wants to be. And a real question box."

"How else will she learn?"

There was a wealth of patience in his voice, and Shannon imagined him using the same gentle authoritarian tone of voice with the skateboarder earlier. Jared looked back at Lily. "One's name is Mack, and the other's name is Pit."

Lily wrinkled her nose. "Pit's a funny name for a dog."

"That's because he's a bottomless pit when it comes to food. He eats all the time."

Lily put her hand to her mouth and giggled. A second later Shannon thought she heard low laughter rumble from Jared's broad chest.

It was the first encouraging sign she had seen since he sat down, but it didn't mean he was willing to give her another chance. She touched Lily's shoulder. "Sweetheart, we need to be going."

"But, Mama, I wanna hear about the dogs. And you said we might stay here."

"I know," Shannon said, handing Lily the lightweight jacket she had left in the booth. Then she looked straight into Jared's eyes. "But we can't stay."

He didn't looked away, but he didn't disagree.

Then she picked up the ticket for their lunches, and carefully counted out the change.

"Hey there, sweet pea." From the other end of the counter Wynette waved to Lily and Shannon realized the waitress was probably trying to tempt the child so the adults could continue their conversation. She couldn't know it was a wasted effort. "How 'bout a candy bar for the road?" she asked, glancing over at Shannon for permission.

When Shannon looked dubious, Wynette added, "It's on the house."

"Thank you. Be sure to thank Mrs. Dickerson, Lily." But the child was already halfway to the counter.

Shannon gathered her purse and Lily's backpack, and slipped out of the booth. Again she looked Jared in the eyes. "I'd give anything to go back and start over, but..." She held out her hand. "I'm very sorry for all the trouble I've caused you. I hope you find the woman you're looking for. Goodbye, Jared."

The instant he took her hand, he knew it was a mistake. She had already tapped into his protective instincts, despite the fact that she had lied. But when his wide, rough hand enveloped hers he felt her tremble.

Shannon slipped her hand from his, and walked over to where Wynette waited with Lily.

Conflicting emotions warred inside Jared. Part of him wanted to let her walk out of his life without a backward glance. Part of him wanted her to stay. He couldn't explain it, but he was as attracted to Shannon Kramer's strength, and even her tardy integrity as he was put off by the fact that she had lied in the first place. He hadn't missed the little gesture of pride when she announced they were leaving, her narrow shoulders shifting ever so slightly beneath the faded denim jacket she wore. Proud enough to cut her losses with dignity, yet humble enough to try any avenue if it meant something better for her child.

A complicated woman.

But if his feelings for Shannon were as complicated as the woman herself, his feelings for her daughter were startlingly simple. Lily was a beautiful, charming child. He had no idea where her father was, but the man was a fool to let such a treasure slip through his fingers.

After paying the bill, and saying goodbye to Wynette, Shannon and Lily walked across the street to the service station and garage that doubled as a bus depot. With every step she prayed that the waitress was right—that once Jared had a chance to think it over, he might not be so upset. And maybe, just maybe, he might change his mind. There was some time left. Their bus didn't leave for another forty-five minutes. And if he didn't change his mind...

Well, she thought with a bone-weary sigh, she had been desperate when she arrived, and she would leave the same way. She had managed to escape Hal before, she could do it again. She would do whatever she had to do.

Standing by the register Jared watched them until they went inside the Greyhound station.

"You just gonna stand there, or are you goin' after her?"

He turned to face Wynette. "It didn't work out."

"How would you know? You didn't give it a chance."

"She wasn't honest with—"

"Excuse me?" She propped both hands on her narrow hips. "Since when did you become judge and jury? The woman took a helluva detour just to apologize. And when she damn well couldn't afford it."

"What do you mean?"

"She and that child are down to the bottom of the barrel. She's tryin' to get to California so she can do better for them, but Phoenix is as far as her ticket goes. She'd probably had enough if she hadn't been so all-fired determined to do the right thing by you." She turned, and stomped off toward the kitchen, mumbling, "Hardheaded fool."

Jared glanced across the street just as the door to the bus station closed behind Shannon and Lily Kramer. Suddenly the image of Shannon counting out the exact change for her bill, plus a small tip came to mind. And her telling Lily she had no more quarters. The clothes they wore were clean, but clearly worn.

What if Wynette was right? What if making the effort to apologize had put a dent in their funds? Damn, he felt like a first-class jerk. Maybe he should at least offer to reimburse her for the detour. Recalling the stubborn tilt of her chin, he doubted she would take it, but he would feel better if he offered.

"Mama, my colors are gone."

"What?" Shannon immediately began checking the bench where she had left their suitcases while they had gone into the café. "Where did you put them, sweetheart?"

"Right there." Lily pointed to her Cinderella coloring book.

Sure enough, the new box of sixteen crayons that had been on top of the book was gone. "Maybe they fell on the floor." Shannon and Lily both looked, but came up empty-handed. "Are you positive that's where you left them?"

"Uh-huh."

Continuing to search, Shannon noticed, for the first time since returning to the depot, a boy of approximately nine or ten behind the counter. He was sitting on the manager's desk wolfing down a cupcake and a soft drink.

"Excuse me," she said. "Have you seen a box of crayons? They were laying right here when we left, but they seem to have disappeared."

The boy looked at her as if he could have cared less. "Whatsa matter? Can't your little girl keep up with her toys?" He took a giant bite of his cupcake, devouring almost half of it at one time.

At that moment, the manager of the garage came back inside from waiting on a customer.

"Pardon me." Holding Lily's hand Shannon came to stand in front of the counter. "My little girl put a box of crayons on the bench, and they seemed to have disappeared. I was just asking this boy if he had—"

"Tommy Ray, you know anything about this little girl's crayons, son?" the man asked, wiping his greasy hands on an equally greasy rag.

The kid grinned what could only be described as a

self-satisfied smirk. "Nope. Reckon somebody just musta picked 'em up when I wasn't looking."

"Sorry, ma'am. I been in the garage most of the time, and didn't see anybody come in."

"But they were right here when we left," Shannon insisted.

The station manager gave her a hard look. "Are you sayin' you think my boy took 'em?"

"No, I'm not accusing your son," she said, straightening her shoulders. "But neither am I willing to forget about something I paid good money for and—"

"Maybe your girl misplaced 'em." Then he leaned across the counter, and gazed down at Lily. "I reckon you better learn to take better care of your things, little miss."

"And I suggest you pick on someone your own size," said a voice from behind Shannon.

She spun about to find Jared Markham not three feet away.

The manager straightened. "Hey, Jared," he said a little nervously. "Whatcha up to?"

"Just checking to make sure Ms. Kramer and her daughter are all right."

"Oh, uh, sure. We was just tryin' to find the little girl's crayons." He threw the rag at the boy. "Go help her look, Tommy Ray."

"But, Daddy—"

"Go help her."

"Never mind. They're replaceable. Are these yours?" Jared asked Shannon, pointing to the suitcases.

"Yes. And just who do you think is going to replace them? Do you have any idea—"

He picked up the suitcases he'd indicated, and started for the door.

"Excuse me? What do you think you're doing?" she demanded.

"Taking you home with me."

"But I thought—"

"Changed my mind."

The minute he had walked in and found Tom Garland glaring down at Lily, the decision had been made for him. Shannon and her daughter needed someone to look out for them, and it looked as if he was the best candidate.

"Well, maybe I have, too," Shannon announced.

Jared stopped, turned to face her. "Have what?"

"Changed my mind. Ten minutes ago I did everything but beg to stay, and all I got from you was a stone face. Why the change of heart?" She couldn't believe she was questioning her good fortune, but she wasn't about to go with him until she knew why he had changed his mind. Call it pride, call it lunacy, but it was important to her.

"You look like you need help."

"I do, but I don't need pity, and I—we—don't go where we're not wanted."

Jared took one look at the stubborn tilt of her chin and knew she wouldn't let him off without showing at least as much courage as she had shown by her personal apology.

He shifted his weight from one foot to the other, and said simply, "You're wanted."

3

JARED MARKHAM had a strange way of showing someone they were wanted. He hadn't said more than twenty words since tossing the suitcase into the back of his truck, and helping Shannon and Lily inside, two of those words being the abbreviated question, "Buckled up?" right before they pulled away from the bus station. Not only had he been semisilent, but he had scarcely given her a glance.

Maybe he was already regretting his decision to take her and Lily along? Maybe he was trying to think of an appropriate way to dump them? Or maybe, like her, he just didn't know what to say. In any event, Lily had taken up the slack by talking about their bus trip to Alpine, but even her charm hadn't moved Jared to much more than a few nods, some yeahs and maybes, and one smile. Eventually, mother and daughter both gave up. Lily played with her doll, and Shannon turned her attention to the scenery. The only sounds came from occasional static on the two-way radio that she assumed was on constantly due to his job.

Sitting in the cab of the air-conditioned pickup, for the first time she realized that November in Texas wasn't just warm, it was downright hot. The West Virginia climate she was accustomed to was more temperate, even cold in the mountains, and more often than not, damp. The area around Alpine, Texas, was hot and dry, almost desertlike, at least in the daytime. Now, as the sun slipped low toward evening, the heat began to subside.

As they left the city limits sign behind, and drove east out of the little town, miles of nothingness stretched out before them. Except for mountains off to the south and northeast, which would have been labeled hills where she came from, the area was mostly flat, and covered with sparse grass and occasional clumps of cactus. Shannon had never seen a spot that looked more barren and desolate. From her perspective it looked like the ragged end of nowhere.

"Can I—"

"May I."

"Play with the dogs when we get there, Mama?" Lily asked, breaking the silence.

"Well, sweetheart—"

"Mack and Pit will be around," Jared told her.

Lily smiled, her eyes fairly dancing. "Oh boy, oh boy, oh boy." She turned to her mother. "Both of them, Mama. I get to see both of them. Will we be there soon, Mr. Markham?"

"Lily, don't pester Mr. Markham." Although to be honest, the same question had popped into Shannon's mind.

"Another twenty minutes."

After twenty minutes that passed like two hours, Jared turned the truck onto a gravel road. They rode for maybe a mile before she got her first glimpse of his home, a two-story Victorian farmhouse set back in a grove of trees. Probably built in the early 1900s, it embodied the Victorian love of vanity complete with a turret, ornamented gables, bay windows and a wraparound porch. Shannon's first thought was that the architecture looked oddly out of place in the rugged vastness of the land.

Jared braked the truck to a stop near the back of the house, and from what Shannon could see in the growing dusk, a screened-in porch stretched the entire length of the back of the house. There was a screen door then another door leading to what she thought was probably the kitchen.

"My grandfather built this place for my grandmother in 1910," Jared announced, startling her out of her speculation. "It's old, rambling and in need of some work, but it's paid for."

From the screened-in back porch two dogs barked. "Will they play with me?" Lily wanted to know immediately.

Jared unbuckled the squirming girl, then opened his door and scarcely had time to get out himself before Lily scrambled out, and dashed across the yard.

"Lily, be careful," her mother cautioned.

"Mack! Pit!" Jared commanded, and the dogs quieted instantly. "They sound ferocious but they're really a couple of softies. Besides, the door is latched."

"Oh." Shannon breathed a sigh of relief.

By the time they joined Lily, she and the dogs already had the makings of a fine friendship underway, albeit through a screen. Shannon wasn't sure what breed of dogs to expect, but if the masculinity of their owner and the timbre of their barking were any indication, she anticipated setters or maybe even retrievers. What she got was two...well, the term *mixed breed* didn't even begin to cover their appearance. One had a long, wide body, stubby legs and a tail that curled almost up over his rump. His short, caramel-colored coat was slightly bristly indicating the possibility of terrier lineage, but his large round head and squared muzzle resembled that of a chow. The other dog looked as if it might have started out to be a boxer then changed its mind. With long hair and ears, a chocolate brown coat, and a body that could have belonged to a greyhound, he was the antithesis of the other animal. In fact, they looked like a canine version of Abbott and Costello.

Jared unlatched the screen door, and the dogs shot outside, then immediately returned to display their joy at having their master home. It took several moments before the excitement subsided enough for Jared to introduce Mack and Pit to Lily, and for Shannon to realize they really were indeed a couple of softies. The minute Lily reached out to scratch Mack behind the ears, he rolled over on his back, offering his wide belly for scratching instead. Giggling happily, Lily gladly obliged. Pit stood patiently waiting his turn.

"Okay, guys. Enough." With a hand signal he sent them scampering across the yard. They disappeared into the trees now draped by dusk. "They'll be back when it's time for them to be fed," he promised Lily. Then he unlocked the back door. "Go on in, and I'll get your bags."

Once Shannon was inside the roomy old kitchen with its wonderful ceiling-high glass-front cupboard and cheery blue and white colors, she suffered more pangs of doubt. Jared's first wife had cooked in this kitchen. They probably laughed and talked about how their day had gone. She felt like an intruder coming into another woman's house under false pretenses.

Stop, she cautioned herself. If she kept thinking this way, she wouldn't be any good to Lily or herself. Or Jared. If he was willing to accept her, the least she could do was try to make him happy, if only for a while.

"Can I go find the dogs, Mama?"

"Good heavens, no." Shannon brushed a wisp of too-long bangs from Lily's eyes. "It's already dark outside. Tomorrow," she promised, "you'll have lots of time to get acquainted with Mack and Pit."

"But I wanna—" Lily yawned "—be their friend."

Jared came back in just as the child yawned again. "You need to put her to bed?"

"Well, it has been a long day, and—"

"Down that hall, and upstairs," he nodded, holding their suitcase. "First bedroom on your left. I'll be right behind you."

The bedroom was a lovely surprise, with an antique rosewood canopy bed, cheval mirror, dressing table and armoire. The quilt was a star pattern in shades of blues and lavenders, and the pillow shams were crocheted. Shannon was no connoisseur of antiques, but she had been to too many quilting bees as a child not to recognize genuine craftsmanship when she saw it.

Someone, possibly Jared's grandmother, had hand stitched everything with great care.

"Mama, look." Lily pointed to the crocheted canopy, then turned to Jared. "Did a princess used to sleep here?"

He tilted his head to one side as if giving the question serious consideration. "Nope. Not that I know of. You're not a princess, are you?"

Lily grinned. "No, I'm a girl."

"Well, then you're in luck because this bed is a girl's bed." He turned to Shannon. "I, uh, wasn't expecting two, so I hope you don't mind doubling—"

"It's fine," she said quickly. "It's...lovely. Thank you."

He set their things down beside the armoire. "After you've tucked Lily in, maybe we could talk in the kitchen."

"Of course."

"Sweet dreams, princess," he told Lily, and was rewarded with a giggly good-night as he left the room.

Jared rammed his hands into his pockets, and headed for the kitchen, the question, *now what?* flashing across his brain like a neon sign. The decision that Shannon and Lily needed rescuing had been born out of pure gut instinct, but now logic was demanding a long hard look at the consequences. How would this situation ever work? How could he trust her after she had lied to him?

Her lie. Mentally, he kept tripping over it like the upturned corner of a rug. It was irritating to say the least. Why couldn't she have just been honest? Okay, so a few men had given her a bad time. That didn't give her license to omit something as important as having a child. Logically, he never should have...

What? Brought her home? If he used that basis for logic he probably never should have written the ad in the first place. But nothing about this situation was logical. His instant decision to bring them to his home had proved that. So, she hadn't told him everything for fear of being rejected. Now that he'd had time to think about it, he could understand. But logic and understanding aside, in the final analysis he was a man that relied on his instincts. In his job, intuition often played as big a role as good solid police work. Call it following a hunch, or just a feeling in the gut, it all amounted to the same thing: the small voice inside that whispered you were on the right track. Or off.

Jared's instincts had rarely been wrong, and right now they were telling him to give Shannon Kramer a chance.

When Shannon joined Jared almost a half hour later, the kitchen was filled with the aroma of fresh-brewed coffee. He was at the table, a full mug in his hand, another waiting for her.

"Is she asleep?" he asked.

"Practically before her head touched the pillow. It's been a long day for her." And a nerve-racking one for me, Shannon thought.

He nodded. "I, uh, wasn't sure how you took your coffee."

"A little cream." He pointed toward a creamer already sitting on the table. "Thanks." She doctored her coffee, and waited for him to speak. Again, she wondered if he had changed his mind, and was trying to find some way to let her down gently.

Jared cleared his throat. "Would you, uh, like to take our coffee and go outside to the porch?"

"Sure." She followed him out the back door.

He flipped a light switch beside the door, but nothing happened. "Oh, hell," he muttered. "I'll get a bulb, and be right back."

"We don't need it."

He jerked his head around. "What?"

"There's a full moon, and it's bright as day out here."

"Oh, yeah, it is." Lord, he thought, would they ever get past this awkwardness?

Good grief, she thought, what if she gave him the idea she didn't *want* the light on? What if he thought she was sending him some kind of sexual message? "Of course, if you'd rather have the light on, it's okay."

"No, the moonlight is more than enough." He walked to a small table with two chairs, and pulled one out for her.

"Thanks," she said, clasping the cup in both hands to hide her nervousness.

After a few seconds of silence, he said, "I'm not sure what the proper etiquette is for our situation, so I'm just going to think out loud." She nodded, and he continued. "I thought maybe a trial period would be a good idea. Say four weeks, or six if you need longer."

"Six..." Shannon said a silent prayer of thanks. He hadn't changed his mind! "Six weeks sounds fine to—

to me." It sounded better than fine, it sounded wonderful. If she and Lily could stay hidden for six weeks, surely they could shake Hal off their trail for good.

"That should give us time to get to know each other."

"Yes, I think so."

"And then we'll...sort of see how it goes, if that's all right with you?"

"It's fine."

"Good." He took a deep breath, clearly relieved to have at least that much out of the way. "You, uh, mentioned that Lily is five, so I suppose that means kindergarten. I don't know how you want to handle school, but there's a bus—"

"I home school Lily."

"Oh?"

The note of surprise in his voice almost sounded as if he doubted her capability. Hal had always assumed she didn't have two brain cells to rub together. It was one of the things she disliked most about him. Her defenses went up like the hackles on a hound's back.

"You don't have to be a certified teacher to home school," she snapped.

"I didn't mean..." She had obviously taken his comment the wrong way. "Look," he said. "This situation comes with ready-made stress, and I sure don't want to add to that. If I offended you just now—"

Shannon held up her hand. "No. It wasn't you, it was me. Sometimes I react defensively when it's not necessary. I apologize." She gave him a small smile. "Habit, I guess. And you're right. We've got enough to deal with without looking for trouble. I think the best thing we can do is keep an open mind and a positive attitude."

"Absolutely. There's only one thing I ask of you. It's very important that we be as honest with each other as possible. Otherwise, for me at least, this won't work."

"How many ways can I apologize? I *am* sorry that I didn't tell you about Lily from the beginning."

"And I've accepted your apology. So, we start fresh from here. No more lies. Agreed?"

"Agreed."

Having reached their agreement they both fell silent. Night sounds crowded in around them. Crickets chirped, and she worried the handle of her cup with the pad of her thumb. In the distance a coyote barked, and Jared drummed the fingers of his right hand against the side of his mug.

Finally, Shannon said, "I was wondering..."

He raised the mug to his lips, finishing the coffee in one long swallow. Watching the muscles in his neck, she was again struck by the sheer power of this man who was both stranger and savior.

"Wondering what?"

"What?" she said, realizing she was staring at his neck. "Oh. I was uh, wondering if you would mind if I asked you some questions?"

"What kind of questions?"

"About your job?"

"Ask away."

"Well, I think I have a good idea of what a game warden does, but I'm not sure."

"You think we issue hunting licenses and camping permits, right?"

"Something like that."

"That's part of it, but the bulk of my time is spent dealing with poachers."

"You mean like hunting out of season?"

"And trapping. Everything from deer, fox and bighorn sheep to cactus."

"Cactus?"

He grinned at her shocked expression. "Believe it or not, it's a big business. The yucca and barrel varieties particularly. Some of the large ones can bring anywhere from two to three hundred dollars in landscape areas like California and Florida. And since it's illegal to transport any species of cacti out of the state, that's where I come in. A game warden is a law enforcement officer the same as a sheriff, state trooper, or any policeman. When someone breaks the law, it's my job to apprehend them."

"Do you arrest people...the poachers?"

"Certainly. If we can find them."

"What do you mean?"

"Brewster County has over six thousand square miles, and only two game wardens. It's not unusual for a report of poachers to come in, and by the time I get there, they've disappeared."

"That's a lot of territory to cover for only two men."

"It'd be almost impossible without the complete co-operation of the ranchers around here. They're usually the ones calling in the violation, and more often than not they keep an eye on the perpetrators until a warden arrives. Other times, we happen upon violators while on patrol."

"You mean while the poachers are in the act?"

"Yes."

"That sounds so dangerous."

"It can be."

"Do these people ever have guns?"

"Frequently."

The thought of Jared facing off with some Uzi-toting smuggler suddenly made Shannon's blood run cold. She didn't like thinking of him in danger.

"How, uh, long have you been a game warden?" she asked, wanting to shake the disturbing images in her mind. Images of Jared hurt or worse.

"Over ten years."

"Well, you obviously love your work."

"Obviously?"

"If not, you would be looking for a new profession instead of a new relationship."

He smiled. "Good point. But it has its drawbacks. In fact, my job is the main reason I contacted the magazine in the first place."

"Because of the remoteness of the locale, and the nature of your job."

"Does that bother you?"

"I'm not a bright lights, big city kind of person, and I love the outdoors."

"Well, we've certainly got plenty of the great outdoors."

Shannon smiled. "So I noticed."

"I don't mean to get too personal, but I need to ask

how you feel about spending a lot of time on your own. If I get a call, it could mean I'll be out all night."

Shannon glanced down at the coffee now cold in her cup. "I'm used to taking care of myself, Jared."

"No offense, but there's a lot of difference between taking care of yourself in the city, and out here."

She met his gaze directly. "I'm not a whiner, and I don't have a tendency to panic. I'm a good housekeeper, a decent cook, a lousy laundress, and I can probably fire—with a moderate level of skill—any weapon you own."

"Well, I'm a slob, I'll eat just about anything that isn't charred, I send my uniforms to the cleaners, and I'll keep that in mind in case I ever make you mad."

He delivered the quip with such a straight face that for a moment Shannon didn't realize that it was his attempt to ease the tension. Well, what do you know? she thought. Underneath that strong silent facade is a sense of humor. "I think we just had our first meeting of minds."

"How did we do?"

"On a scale of one to ten, I'd say a six plus."

"I'll take it. Shannon," he said a second or two later.

"Yes."

"I'm...I'm glad I changed my mind."

"So am I," she said softly.

Again they let the night sounds fill a silence that stretched into long minutes.

Sitting in the moonlight with this man she scarcely knew, yet to whom she had committed herself to spending the next few weeks of her life with, Shannon again wondered what it would be like if all this was real. What would it be like to sit in the moonlight with a man who loved her? A man she could depend on without giving up her independence. The idea was delicious, heady...and pure fantasy. She stole a glance at Jared.

But a lovely fantasy, she thought.

"Well," he said finally. "I guess we'd better turn in. By the way, are you an early riser?"

"With a five-year-old you have no option to be anything else," she said as they walked back inside the house.

He nodded. "I have to patrol the area to the south tomorrow, so I'll be leaving around seven, and won't be back until early afternoon."

"Lily and I will be fine."

He took the empty cup from her, and set it on the kitchen counter along with his. "In the morning I'll show you how to operate the radio in case you need to reach me. As smart as you are, you'll pick it up in no time."

Shannon smiled. "Thanks."

"You're welcome," he said, totally unaware of the compliment he had just paid her.

"Well...good night, Jared."

"Good night, Shannon."

He watched her walk down the hall toward the stairs, her hips swaying ever so slightly. She had the kind of figure most women would label too rounded, while most men would consider it a feast for the eyes. She didn't flaunt it, but then she possessed the kind of earthy sensuality that didn't need flaunting. It made its own statement, like the subtle fragrance of a single gardenia in a garden of roses.

That sensuality had been startlingly evident as they sat on the porch. He remembered how the moonlight seemed to caress her face, and thinking that her full mouth looked soft, warm, and made for kissing.

Jared tried to shake himself free of such thoughts, concentrating on making sure the dogs were secure for the night. Success was limited, due to the fact that he kept thinking about Shannon's mouth. How could he think about kissing her when he had only known her a few hours? He hadn't kissed Amy until their second date. But then he was relatively certain, even on such short acquaintance, that Shannon was nothing like Amy. Physically, there were some similarities—a pretty face, long dark hair—otherwise, they were as opposite as daylight and darkness. Amy had a fragile, almost ethereal quality about her that always evoked his protective instincts. On the other hand, while Shannon was definitely soft and womanly, Jared sensed she had a strength that Amy never possessed. The kind of strength required to even contemplate a relationship with a stranger if it meant a better life for her child. A substantive quality his great-grandmother would have called good old-fashioned grit.

Yet despite her strength, she was vulnerable. He'd seen it in her eyes when she reacted so defensively about home schooling Lily. Oh, there had been anger, too. But mixed in with the anger flashing in her eyes, he thought he caught a glimpse of fear. Fear of what?

he wondered. What, or who, had taught her to feel she needed to be on guard? One moment he was a little shocked to realize how little he knew about this woman he had invited into his life. The next moment he admitted there was something...exciting about not knowing, about the prospect of discovering just exactly who Shannon was, what she liked or didn't like. How she felt about politics, religion and the price of tea in China. She intrigued him.

Again, he couldn't help but compare her to Amy. He and Amy had known each other all their lives. They were friends long before they became lovers, and that friendship was one of the strongest parts of their marriage.

Stop measuring one by the other, he told himself. They were two different women in two totally different circumstances. What bothered him was not so much the differences between the two women, but the fact that the memory of Amy's delicate beauty paled next to Shannon's understated, but nonetheless potent sensuality. A sensuality he was finding it difficult to ignore after almost two years of celibacy.

4

"OH!" SHANNON whipped around at the sound of footsteps, her heart hammering in her chest. Automatically, she stepped back, and bumped into the edge of the kitchen counter.

"I didn't mean to scare you," Jared said.

"I...you..." She swallowed hard, clutching the lapels of her thin cotton robe together. "I came down to—"

"Take a deep breath," he advised.

Shannon did, and felt a little calmer. "I heard your shower running, and I thought I would make you some coffee before you went to work. But I couldn't find the coffee, and then you came in—"

"And scared the hell out of you."

She managed a smile. "Something like that."

"Sorry."

"It's...it's all right, or at least it will be as soon as my heart rate slows to a mere gallop."

He smiled back, and she thought again how truly good-looking he was, more so when he smiled.

"Guess I could wear a bell. You know, like a house cat."

Standing there with the early morning sunlight glinting off his badge pinned to one of the broadest chests she had ever seen, the last image he evoked was of a domesticated feline. A tiger maybe, all power and prowl, but definitely not a house cat.

She clutched the robe tighter, suddenly aware that the hemline fell at midthigh, exposing a good deal of her bare legs and feet. For a moment she thought about dashing back upstairs to dress, then decided it would only make the situation more awkward. She might as well just tough it out. "If you'll, uh, show me where you keep everything, I'll brew a pot of coffee."

"Deal. Mine tastes like sludge. One sip, and you'd be headed for the bus stop as fast as you could get there."

"It wasn't that bad last night."

"I guess I was lucky. But usually, it's pretty brutal. Ask Wynette," he suggested, walking straight to where she stood. "She swears it's lethal." He reached over her head, flipped open a cabinet, and retrieved a two-pound can of coffee. "Guess I'll have to do some rearranging. Make sure the things you need are within your reach."

"Or loan me a stepladder." He handed her the coffee. "Thanks."

"You're welcome." He glanced down at her bare feet. "This old linoleum floor can be downright cold in the morning. You might want to remember your slippers."

He was so close.

Her throat went dry, and Shannon had to will her suddenly racing heart to quiet. She hadn't been alone with a man since her divorce, and her first instinct was to flee. Logically, she knew not all men were like her ex-husband, but emotionally she wanted to run like hell. But this man wasn't Hal. And she had made a promise to herself never again to allow anyone, male or female, to treat her as he had. Not that she had turned against men. There had been invitations, which she refused unless they included Lily. But standing here, close enough to smell Jared's after-shave made her realize how much she longed for the kind of intimacy that had only been a dream until now. Someday, when she was sure Hal was out of the picture, she would have it. And with a man like Jared.

"Shannon?"

"What? Oh, yes...slippers. I'll remember," she said, clutching the can of coffee to her chest.

"The pot is in that cupboard."

"Thanks." In less than five minutes the first drops of dark, rich brew began filling the glass carafe. "I'll, uh, be back in a jiffy," Shannon said, and rushed upstairs to dress.

Lily was still asleep so she collected her clothes, and went into the bathroom. Dressing quickly in jeans, a T-shirt and sneakers, she headed back downstairs to fix breakfast. As she walked into the kitchen the sound of a familiar small voice announced the fact that her daughter was not only awake, but jabbering like a magpie, with an audience to boot. Standing over a pan of sizzling bacon, Jared looked as if he were hanging on every word. Even Mack and Pit were listening, their heads cocked attentively.

"Mama, Mama." A tea towel tied over her pajamas as a makeshift apron, a piece of bacon in her hand, Lily danced across the floor to give her mother a hug. "I'm helping Jared fix breakfast. Didya know sometimes Pit and Mack go in the truck, and they smell bad people sometimes so they can..." She glanced over her shoulder at Jared.

"Track," he supplied.

"Yeah. So they can track. They do it with their noses." The child pointed to her own nose. "Jared said so," she proclaimed, clearly proud of herself.

"I hope you don't mind me giving her permission to drop the Mr. Markham. Manners are important, but under the circumstances—"

"No, that's perfectly okay. You're right. Under the circumstances, it was a bit formal."

"Good."

Shannon brushed back a lock of hair that fell over her eyes. She had dressed in such a hurry that she hadn't taken the time to do her usual French braid. "I thought you might expect me to cook."

"Can you?"

"Well, Julia Child doesn't have anything to fear, but I'm a fair hand at a stove."

"Mama cooks cookies the best."

"Bakes cookies," Shannon corrected.

"With chocolate chips?" Jared asked.

"Lots and lots," Lily assured him.

"That's all the reference I need. Be my guest." He handed her the tongs he had been using to turn the bacon. "I'm really tired of my own cooking anyway. Eggs are in that bowl ready to scramble, and the toaster is already loaded with English muffins. All you have to do is push down the lever."

"Do you eat like this every day?" She threw a dollop of butter into the second skillet, and poured in the beaten eggs. Then she started the muffins toasting.

"Nope. Too much fat." He patted his ridiculously flat midsection. "But my pint-size guest made a special request. Of course, I couldn't refuse such a charming young lady."

Shannon looked at Lily. "Little con artist." But Lily only grinned.

"I, uh, hope you don't mind, but I asked Wynette to drop by later this morning to kind of show you the ropes. You know, where everything is, how everything runs." Eager for her not to take offense as she had last night, he quickly added, "Not that you couldn't figure it all out for yourself, but I thought it might save you some time. She cleans for me every week and—"

"If you'd like, I can do that while I'm here." She divided the scrambled eggs between three plates, adding the bacon just about the time the muffins popped up.

"I appreciate the offer, but Wynette and Ellis—that's her husband—fell on hard times last year when he broke his hip. Their daughter and son-in-law moved in to help work the ranch, and Wynette went to work at the café to bring in extra money. Since she and Ellis would starve before they would take anything that even remotely resembled charity, having her clean house doesn't dent her pride, and it lets me help in a small way."

Shannon handed Lily her breakfast, instructing her

to carry it carefully to the table. "I'm sorry. I didn't know."

"How could you?"

"Jared."

"Yes." He took the filled plate she handed him.

"You don't have to qualify everything you say to me. I realize you're probably a little gun-shy after I practically bit your head off last night, but I don't want you to think you need to tiptoe around me. My feelings aren't all that fragile, really."

"All right, no tiptoeing." But he wasn't so sure about the fragile part. No one learned to be so protective without having a few scars to show for their knowledge. He was beginning to wonder if her strength shielded a wounded heart. Another intriguing facet of Shannon Kramer? And how many more were there?

IMMEDIATELY AFTER breakfast Lily had dashed upstairs to dress, then downstairs to play with Mack and Pit on the back porch. Satisfied her child was safe and entertained, Shannon followed Jared into his office so that he could show her how to operate the radio.

"Sit here." He patted the back of an aging leather chair in front of his desk. "Now," he said once she was seated, "this is a transmitter and a receiver. That simply means you can talk to me, and I can talk back. I carry a handheld mobile unit with me whenever I leave the truck."

"All you have to do..." He leaned forward, and for a wild heartbeat or two she fought the familiar urge to bolt from the chair, to get as far away from him as she could. But the feeling passed surprisingly quick.

"I think...I think I've got that."

"Good. Now, there are three repeaters in the county so this unit has no trouble reaching me anywhere, unless I'm in a hole."

"A hole? That doesn't sound good."

"It's not as bad as it sounds. Once in a while when I'm tracking I wind up between two large rock formations or down in a low spot, hence the name. When that happens, the signal cuts out. It's rare, and nothing for you to worry about."

"If you say so."

"I do."

"But how will I be able to hear you on this radio if I'm in the kitchen or out in the backyard?"

"There's an extra mobile unit. Same frequencies. Okay, let's go over it again, only this time you show me."

While she did her best to repeat what he had just taught her, he squatted beside her, balancing himself on the balls of his feet. "Very good," he said when she had finished. "See, I knew you could pick this up in a flash."

"Thanks. I had—" she turned, and found his face barely a foot away from hers "—an excellent teacher."

His size and proximity should have made her nervous. And it did, but not for the reason she expected. Instead of feeling threatened, she basked in the warmth of his compliment. There was something oddly comforting about having this brawny man praise her.

Gracious, but his eyes are blue, she thought. Like a cloudless late summer sky. And his mouth was, well...*beautiful* was the first word that popped into her head. Sculpted like one of those Greek statues. The same could be said of his jaw and chin. Strength in every line, right down to the cleft in his chin.

"You think you've got it now?" Did she know how sweet she looked, he wondered. Her face was free of cosmetics, her hair just the least bit tousled. The package was charming, and more appealing than he was prepared for.

"Yes."

"Don't ever hesitate to call if you need me."

"Okay."

"Even if all you want to do is chat for a while. I'm concerned you may get bored, just you and Lily by yourselves."

"We're used to being by ourselves, but thanks for your concern."

"You're also used to depending on no one but yourself, aren't you?"

"I suppose so."

Their heads were so close he could almost feel her breath on his cheek. Despite the fact that they were still virtually strangers, as he gazed into her green eyes he had a powerful urge to say, Depend on me.

"Shannon." He said her namely so softly it was almost a whisper. "I...I want to tell you—"

"Mama, Mama, we got company," Lily called from the doorway.

The two adults looked up to find Wynette standing beside the child. Normally, Shannon would have corrected her daughter's grammar, but at the moment all rules on tense and diction seemed to have evaporated from her brain. She wasn't sure she liked the idea that Jared could distract her so easily.

"Well, don't you two look cozy," Wynette said, grinning.

Jared stood up. "I was just showing Shannon how to operate the radio."

"Looked like you were doin' a little operatin' yourself," she teased.

Jared wasn't certain but out of the corner of his eye he thought he saw a blush stain Shannon's cheek. As for himself, he decided it was a good thing he wasn't wearing a tie because he would definitely need to loosen it.

"By the way," Wynette said. "Ellis and I figured Shannon would need some wheels while she's here, so Ellis said you could borrow that old Chevy truck of his if you want." She turned to Shannon. "Ain't much to look at. No air-conditioning but it'll get you to Alpine and back for whatever errands you need to run."

"That's very kind of you. I appreciate it."

"Uh, yeah. Tell Ellis I said, thanks. Well, uh, guess I better get moving. You ladies get acquainted, and I'll see you this afternoon."

"Bye-bye." Lily smiled up at him.

He swooped her up into his arms. "So long, princess. You keep Mack and Pit out of trouble, okay."

She nodded enthusiastically.

He set Lily on her feet, paused for a second to glance back at Shannon, then left. Watching his broad shoulders disappear she had an overwhelmingly wifely urge to tell him to be careful.

"Well, that's a load off my mind," Wynette said.

"What?" Shannon had almost forgotten the other woman was there.

"I was gettin' downright worried. Plum scared in fact, that I wasn't ever gonna see that look in his eyes again."

"What look?"

"The me-Tarzan-you-Jane look."

Shannon blushed. "Now, sugar, don't go bashful on me. I'm tickled pink. It's about time he put the past behind him, and started living for himself again."

"Y-you mean because his wife died." Shannon had never been one to pry into anyone else's personal life, but she had to admit that she was curious about Jared's late wife. What had she been like? What had they been like together?

"Took it real hard, that man did. For a while me and Ellis thought he was gonna curl up and die himself. Never seen a man go so silent. I swear, it was almost like if he didn't talk about it, he could pretend it wasn't true. But then, a double blow like that is almost more than a body can stand."

"A double blow?"

"Uh..." Wynette frowned, and quickly glanced

away. "Listen to me jabberin' on. Why don't we go to the kitchen, and I can give you the fifty-cent tour. And you, sweet pea," she said, tweaking Lily's nose, "have got a treat comin'. I've got a brand-new colorin' book and crayons in my bag just for you."

"Yippee." Lily jumped up and down. "New colors."

"Well, then let's go get 'em."

As she followed Wynette out, Shannon wondered what she could have meant by a double blow.

BY NOON SHANNON felt as if she had known Wynette for years. The older woman had an easy way about her, and soon they were talking like old friends. It wasn't difficult to see that she had more or less adopted Jared since his wife's death. And although Wynette didn't ignore his faults, there was no doubt that she considered him to be the son she'd never had. To quote her, "He was the best catch in Brewster County, bar none." As far as Shannon could tell, her new friend was right on the money.

"I'm surprised the women around here haven't been beating down Jared's door," Shannon told Wynette as they were preparing lemonade and tuna sandwiches for their lunch.

"Well, first off, you'd be surprised at how few single women there are around here. But don't think the ones that are didn't pester him."

"Yet he decided to advertise for a woman."

"Wife," Wynette said, snagging slices of bread as they popped out of the toaster. "What Jared needs is someone who'll stick with him, who'll stand beside him on her own two feet. And to answer your question, he doesn't have time to go courtin'. The man gets one day a week off, and it's nearly forty miles to the nearest town. Besides, everybody around here knows everybody else, and he didn't want a woman who had known Amy." She shrugged. "Just didn't feel right about that, I guess."

"Amy?" Shannon put the freshly made pitcher of lemonade in the refrigerator. "Was that his wife's name?"

"Yep. Pretty as a peach blossom, and dainty as a china teacup. She had a big heart, though. Lord, but she loved Jared. They were sweethearts from the time they were in grammar school, and there was never anyone else for either of 'em. Quite a match. The preacher's daughter, and the son of one of the county's oldest families."

Shannon knew she shouldn't be so curious about Jared's life with his late wife, but she couldn't stop herself. "Jared told me his grandfather built this house."

"Oh, sugar, there've been Markhams in this part of Texas since the Civil War. Most of 'em were policemen or politicians. Did Jared tell you his grandfather served two terms in the state legislature?"

"No. Does he have a lot of family?"

"Just a brother, who lives in Wyoming. His mom passed on about ten years ago, and his dad a couple of years later." Wynette shook her head. "That boy's seen a fair amount of grief," she said almost to herself.

"I suppose you knew his wife well?"

"Oh, yeah. She—"

Mack's and Pit's sharp barking cut her off. "That would be Donna Jean," Wynette said, wiping her hands on a tea towel as she headed for the back door.

A moment later she returned with a young woman in tow, carrying a cake. Lily was close behind. "Shannon Kramer, this is my daughter, Donna Jean. And this," Wynette gently patted her daughter's extremely rounded belly, "is my future grandchild."

"Pleased to meetcha." Donna Jean, a lovely blonde in her early twenties smiled warmly.

"Nice to meet you. Both of you."

Donna Jean laughed. "I hope you like chocolate." She held up the cake. "I know it's Jared's favorite."

"I like chocolate a whole bunch," Lily piped up.

"Thanks," Shannon took the cake and set it on the counter. "And as you can see, it certainly won't go to waste. Donna Jean, this is my daughter, Lily."

"Hi there," Donna Jean said, but Lily's attention was focused on the three-layer confection frosted in dark chocolate fudge icing. "If your mama says it's okay, would you like the first piece?"

Lily's eyes lit up like firecrackers in the night sky as she turned to mother. "Only after your lunch," Shannon said.

"Yippee! Chocolate cake."

"You've made her day," Shannon told the young woman. "It was a very neighborly gesture, but from the look of things you should probably be resting, not baking."

"Naw, I get bored doin' nothing. Too much like my mama, I guess."

In response Wynette playfully snapped the tea towel at Donna Jean's backside. "We're just about to eat. You wanna join us for a sandwich?"

"Please." Shannon pulled a chair out from the kitchen table. "And I really would feel better if you sat down."

"Mama, can I take my samich to the porch?" Lily asked.

"Wouldn't recommend it with Pit out there waitin' for the first crumb to drop. Matter of fact," Wynette warned, "you look away once, and he'll take the whole darn thing."

As if to confirm the warning, Pit licked his chops on the other side of the screen.

"Now, don't give me that look," Shannon said at Lily's droopy expression. "After lunch you can go right back out to play. Deal?"

"Deal." Lily agreed, but her acquiescence was hardly overflowing with enthusiasm.

Wynette got the sandwiches and some potato chips while Shannon brought the lemonade from the refrigerator. They were just about to enjoy their meal when Jared came home.

"Well, looks like I didn't arrive a minute too soon," he said from the kitchen doorway. They had been so busy talking none of them had heard him come in. "Got an extra sandwich?

"Of course. There's plenty of tuna. It'll just take a second to make more sandwiches."

"I'll do it, Mama," Donna Jean offered. "I'm not real hungry anyway." With considerable difficulty she began maneuvering herself out of the chair.

"No!"

Shannon and Lily looked up, shocked at the tone in Jared's voice.

"No. Don't you dare get up." For a moment Shannon thought she saw fear in his eyes.

"But it's no trouble—"

"I mean it, Donna Jean. Don't you even think about getting up out of that chair to wait on me or anyone else."

"Oh, Jared. You're worse than Mama."

"Well, this time he's right," Wynette lifted an eyebrow, and wagged a finger at Jared. "And don't let *that* go to your head."

Shannon smiled at the teasing jibe but she couldn't help noticing that Jared's body was as tense as his voice had been. For half a heartbeat he'd seemed ready to rush across the floor and make Donna Jean stay put. Then he relaxed, as if Wynette's snappy retort had broken the tension.

It crossed her mind that perhaps he and Donna Jean had been an item before he married, but then she remembered that Wynette had told her Jared and Amy were sweethearts from grade school. They had never dated anyone else. Then why, she wondered, was he so obviously concerned? Had Donna Jean had a difficult pregnancy? Wynette didn't appear to be overly worried. What was Jared's problem?

"C'mon, Jared. Relax." Donna Jean put a hand on her expanded waist. "And that's an order."

While Lily gobbled her sandwich, Shannon watched Jared, and tried to figure out what was going on.

"Have you given any more thought to my offer?" he asked.

"No. I'm fine. The baby's fine," the new mother-to-be said firmly. "And there's no reason to worry."

"But what if—"

Donna Jean held up her hand. "Jared, Neal and I appreciate everything you've done, but please don't go crazy over this."

Wynette pushed her chair away from the table. "Short trip if you ask me. You finished, sweet pea?" When Lily nodded, her mouth still full, Wynette shooed her outside. That appeared to be the signal to drop the topic because Donna Jean immediately began telling Shannon all about her latest purchase for the nursery while Wynette made Jared a sandwich.

Shannon still wasn't sure what was going on, but she had the strangest feeling that it had to do with some kind of past disaster. Maybe Donna Jean had lost a baby before, and that's where the concern came from. But if that was the case, why did Jared seem to be more concerned than the young woman's own mother?

The rest of the meal passed uneventfully until Donna Jean rose, a bit unsteadily, to leave. In a flash Jared was at her side, assisting her. "You know, I can't even remember what my toes look like or what it's like to get out of a chair under my own steam," she said rubbing the small of her back.

Shannon smiled. "Believe me, none of this discomfort will matter the minute they put that little baby in your arms."

Donna Jean grinned. "Yeah. I can't wait. Three more weeks the doctor says." She waddled over to give her mother a peck on the cheek then said goodbye to Shannon. Jared offered to walk her to her truck, but she declined, and left. For several moments he stood at the back door, watching until Donna Jean drove away.

Shannon felt like such an outsider. As if she had eavesdropped on a conversation she wasn't supposed to hear. Yet, at the same time, she wasn't angry at the exclusion because it hadn't been deliberate. Jared's reaction had been so quick, so spontaneous that it couldn't have been.

"Here you go." Wynette set the plate with Jared's sandwich on the table.

He turned around. "What? Oh, thanks." He glanced at his watch. "Better take it with me. I forgot I promised Dale Thompson I would check out the two mule deer he found shot on his property."

Then he met Shannon's gaze for the first time since he'd walked into the kitchen. "I'm sorry about...about lunch."

She wasn't sure if he was apologizing for what had happened or for excluding her, or both. "It's okay."

He started to speak, then hesitated, and before he could change his mind, Wynette walked up and handed him the sandwich sealed in a plastic bag.

"I, uh, probably won't be home until almost six. If you and Lily get hungry, don't wait on me."

"Lily's appetite is hard to stall, but I'll wait. We can have dinner together."

"I'll look forward to it."

HE WAS EARLY, and carrying flowers. "These are just wildflowers, but I thought you might like to put them on the table."

"They're lovely, Jared. Thank you." She sniffed the bouquet of sunny fragrances all mingled together. "Where's the princess?"

"Upstairs with the new coloring book you so graciously asked Wynette to bring when she came today. That was a very sweet thing to do."

"My pleasure. I'll just say hello, wash up, and be right back. By the way," he said over his shoulder, "whatever you're cooking smells delicious."

"Hope you can still say that after you've tasted it."

A few minutes later she could hear him upstairs with Lily. They were laughing. Shannon couldn't help but smile. She found it hard to believe that two days ago she had never laid eyes on Jared. Now here she was cooking for him, her child was laughing with him, and it all seemed completely normal. As if they had done this every evening for years.

If Jared had expected a quiet dinner for two, Shannon thought, he was disappointed. Not that he looked disappointed as Lily regaled him with practically everything she had seen and done throughout the day. And of course, the dogs played a big part in her monologue. He sat patiently listening while eating his meal, and even managed appropriate responses.

"Wow," he said, when she told him how high she could jump, and "I'll bet that was fun." And his wide-eyed comment, "You got Mack and Pit to fetch a stick. That's amazing!" totally impressed Lily.

Seeing her daughter so enthralled was a bittersweet pain in Shannon's heart. Bitter because it cast a harsh light on how starved Lily was for attention from a gentle man, and the fact that she had certainly never received it from her own father. And sweet because Jared didn't even have to work at being attentive. He simply cared.

He would make a wonderful father. Call it woman's intuition or a mother's instinct, but she knew Jared would be a loving committed parent. And after watching him with Lily, it wasn't much of a leap to imagine the scene was for real. To imagine that she and Lily could have this kind of life—safe and secure, with a husband and father that cared—was the dream she held dear, but one she feared would never be a reality.

And now she saw that dream in her daughter's eyes. A dream. A hope.

To her shame and horror, Shannon suddenly realized she had done her child an unforgivable injustice. Lily was so wrapped up in Jared. How would she feel after living with him—with his kindness and affection—for six weeks? Shannon caught her breath at the adoring look in her daughter's eyes. Lily had bonded with Jared. And the bond was stronger than Shannon could have ever imagined.

What had she done?

How could she not have realized the effect this unorthodox situation would have on Lily?

She had jumped at Jared's ad like a falling mountain climber grabbing for a lifeline. Without any thought to possible damage to her daughter's emotional stability. What kind of mother was she? How could she have ignored the obvious consequences?

The answer, of course, was fear. She had been operating out of fear for so long that it had become the motivation for everything she thought, everything she did. The fear never left her. It was like living with an invisible third person, always present, always out of sight, but never out of mind.

She couldn't let Lily continue to build her hopes around Jared, and then yank her away. They had to leave, and the sooner the better.

"Shannon?"

"What?" She had been so deep into thought that she hadn't realized Lily had left the table.

"Are you all right?"

"Of course," she assured him, forcing a smile. Meanwhile her mind was whirling. How was she going to tell him that they were leaving? She rose from the table, picked up both of their plates, and took them to the sink. As she passed the door, she stuck her head through, and called to Lily, telling her it was almost bath time.

"You're upset about what happened at lunch, aren't you?"

"Oh..." She set the plates down so fast they clattered on the tiled counter top. "No, that's not—"

"I don't blame you. What I did was rude, and unforgivable. Please accept my apology."

"It's not necessary."

"Yes, it is. You see, I'm a little overprotective about Donna Jean and her pregnancy. We grew up together, and she's a good friend. I'd do just about anything to make sure she was okay."

"That's what being a good friend is all about."

He nodded. "But I can't let it go at that. I'm afraid for her."

"I think it's only natural. Babies are born every day, but not to your friend."

"No. You don't understand. I'm afraid something will happen to her and her baby."

For the first time she looked closely at him. He was so tense the muscles in his neck stood out, and there was a line of perspiration along his upper lip. She had been so wrapped up in her own thoughts that she hadn't seen how truly distraught he looked until now.

"Jared?" She put her hand on his arm. He was trembling. "I'm sure Donna Jean's doctor is taking good care—"

"Doesn't matter. It can still happen."

"What can happen?"

"She could die."

"Why would you think—"

"Because Amy died."

Shannon gasped. Oh, no, she thought. His wife had died when she was pregnant.

"Sh-she went into labor, and didn't tell me. Something was wrong. I was out on patrol, and she..." He swallowed hard. "She waited too long, and it was so far to the hospital. I drove...drove as fast as I could but..."

Shannon felt the shudder pass through his body, and into hers, and knew what was coming. She wanted to put her hand on his lips to keep the words from spilling out, but knew she couldn't.

"It was too late," he whispered. "For both of them."

5

EVEN KNOWING what he was going to say before he said it didn't make it any easier to hear. No wonder he had been so protective of Donna Jean. He looked at her and saw his wife all over again.

Sweet heaven, to lose both his wife and child at the same time. The thought of such grief made her sick at heart. How does anyone deal with so much pain? She tried to put herself in his position, to imagine how she would handle anything happening to Lily, but her brain refused to make the connection, refused to even contemplate such a horror. Tears blurred her vision, and she had an overpowering need to put her arms around him.

Instead, she reached for his hand, and held it. "I'm so sorry. So very sorry."

Jared gazed into her eyes, stunned to see not only his pain reflected, but also an understanding that could only come from a kindred spirit. From someone who had survived a soul-deep hurt. She recognized his pain because she had traveled a similar path to torment. For the first time in longer than he cared to remember, he felt truly connected to another human being. Without realizing it, he covered her hand with his, holding it tightly.

"I didn't mean to blurt it out like that." The sigh he released came straight from his soul. "Seeing Donna Jean today, brought back so much...so many memories."

"Of course," Shannon whispered.

"I want to help. To do something for her. But she's as stubborn as Wynette. Ellis can't drive with his bad leg. What if she goes into labor alone? I tried to convince her to go into Alpine, and stay with a girlfriend of hers, but she refused. Said it was too much of an imposition. Hell, I even offered to pay for a motel room if she would go. But she's so sure that it's unnecessary. She's convinced that there won't be any problem, and it just...it just..."

"Terrifies you."

"Yes," he said, the word steeped in desperation.

"That's understandable considering what happened to your wife. But don't you think that for that very reason, she and her husband will be more careful? And Wynette surely will. Because of your experience they all know how quickly something can go wrong. I'm sure they've taken whatever precautions they can."

"Neal did cancel his yearly trip to the agricultural show in Odessa."

"There, you see. A precaution. And I'm sure he's taken others."

Jared looked down at her. "You're right. Neal would lay down his life for Donna Jean and that baby."

"Jared, I've only known you for a couple of days, but I know enough not to tell you to stop worrying. I have a feeling you worry about all of your friends. I also think Donna Jean knows that, and she probably worries about you. We just have to pray that everything will turn out for the best.''

"I guess so. But it's hard."

"Sometimes it helps to talk about our fears. If…if you need to, I'll listen."

"You know about fears, don't you?"

Until that moment Shannon hadn't realized they were still holding hands. Gently, she slipped her hand from his. "What makes you ask that?"

"I saw it in your eyes a few moments ago."

"Everybody's afraid of something." She glanced away.

"I have a hunch it's more than that, but it's not my place to pry. If we knew each other better—when we know each other better—maybe I can return the favor."

"You're a kind man, Jared Markham. Your friends are lucky to have you."

"And I'm lucky you answered my ad. I didn't realize just how lucky until now."

Shannon's heart lurched in her chest. He was making it so hard to tell him she was leaving. Too hard. She couldn't do it now. Not after what had just happened. You don't share such a profound moment with someone then turn, and say goodbye. No, she wouldn't tell him tonight. Tomorrow. She would tell him tomorrow.

"WOULD YOU CONSIDER allowing Wynette to baby-sit Lily?"

In the process of flipping a pancake, Shannon almost tossed it onto the floor. "Baby-sit?"

"Well, you haven't known any of us very long, and as a parent you have every reason to be picky about who takes care of your child. But I think Lily would enjoy seeing a working ranch, and I know Wynette would care for her as if she were her own."

"It's not that..."

"Then what? I always wear a beeper so there wouldn't be any problem reaching—"

"No, why?"

"Why?"

"Why would I need her to watch Lily?"

"Oh. Guess I left that part out. So we could go on a date."

"A what?"

"A date. You know, where we get dressed up. I take you out to dinner or a movie. Promise your folks I won't keep you out late, then pretend to run out of gas so we can neck."

Jared must have noticed the stricken look she couldn't stop from crossing her face. "I'm sorry. Trying to be clever was never my long suit. Should've known better."

Oh, Lord. Here she was trying to get up the nerve to tell him she was leaving, and he asks her out on a date. "No, it's not that... I didn't expect... You're asking me out on a date?"

"Absolutely. We can drive into Marathon and have dinner at the Gage Hotel, or drive into Alpine. You name it, and I'll take you."

"Oh, Jared, that's probably the nicest thing anyone has said to me in a long, long time. And I—"

The beeper, clipped to his holster, cut her off. He depressed the Recall button. "Hold that thought. I'll be right back," he said, already heading for his office.

"Oh, Jared," Shannon whispered to the empty kitchen. "I didn't know they still made men like you."

In less than five minutes he was back. "Shannon."

She was at the sink, her back to him, but the somber tone in his voice alerted her immediately. "What is it?" She turned to find him carrying a heavy jacket and duffel bag. He had the look of a man on a mission, and suddenly she was frightened. "What's wrong?"

"Can I take a rain check on our date?"

"I guess so, but—"

"Good. I'll hold you to that. There's been some trouble. DEA agents cornered a handful of Mexican nationals smuggling a controlled substance, and they need backup. Situations like this rarely last long, but these guys have a good vantage point on one of the peaks close to the park—"

"Park?"

"Big Bend National Park. About sixty miles from here." He handed her a piece of paper.

"What's this?"

"Approximately where I will be for the next eight to ten hours. Now, don't get worried. You can operate the radio like a champ. All the codes and call signs are on a sheet of paper right beside the radio. You know how to reach Wynette if you can't raise her by phone. You'll do great." He reached for his hat hanging from one of the pegs beside the kitchen door. "I hate to leave you like this, but..."

"You have to go." She tried to keep the alarm out of her voice, but was only moderately successful.

"Yes."

"Are there... The smugglers, do they have guns?"

There was no point lying to her. If they were going to make it as a couple, she would have to face the reality of his job.

"Yes. Shannon, I had hoped not to face a call like this until you felt completely comfortable with me, with...everything, but it can't be helped. I've got a job to do."

"I know." And logically she understood. What she hadn't counted on was how she would feel, seeing him headed out the door to face God knew what. She was thankful Lily was still asleep. There was no way she could pretend she wasn't scared. Lily would spot the lie before it was out of her mouth.

"If you need anything, and I mean *anything*, you call Wynette. I'll contact you as soon as I can." He was across the floor in three long strides, and yanked open the door.

"Jared?"

He turned back. This time Shannon didn't hesitate, didn't even attempt to ignore her overwhelming urge to tell him to be careful. "Take care of yourself, okay?"

He smiled. "Always. Kiss the princess for me." And then he was gone. A second later she heard the engine of his truck roar as he tore out of the driveway. And then there was silence.

She poured herself a cup of freshly brewed coffee, and sat down at the table. She needed to calm down, get her act together, she told herself. But when she lifted the mug to her lips, her hands were shaking.

Okay, so she was shaking in her slippers. This might be old hat for Jared, but it was a new experience for her. And scary didn't even begin to describe it. Easy does it, she told herself. This was his job. He probably faced similar situations on a regular basis. He was well-trained, and equipped to handle poachers, smugglers...

Dear Lord, they had guns.

He was going out to face men with guns. For the first time Shannon realized what Jared had meant in the copy of his ad when he stated that his life-style required a special kind of woman. He had told her that he was a law enforcement officer, but until this very minute she didn't fully comprehend what that title meant. As she sat there, images began to flash across her mind. Images of Jared and gunfire and blood.

She had to stop this. Lily would be downstairs shortly and asking for him. Shannon decided that the best thing to tell her was the truth, minus description. As if on cue, Lily padded into the kitchen.

"I'm hungry." She rubbed her eyes. "Where's Jared?"

"Well, sleepyhead, don't I rate a good morning?" Shannon brushed the bangs from her daughter's eyes.

"Good—" she yawned "—morning, Mama. Where's Jared?"

"He, uh, had to go out on a call, sweetheart."

"Can I play with the dogs?"

"May I, and yes after breakfast."

Lily nodded, and Shannon released a sigh of relief. Thank goodness she wouldn't have to lie.

And thank goodness for Mack and Pit, Shannon decided several hours later, grateful that the dogs had occupied Lily from the time her lessons were finished until lunch, then again afterward. She made a mental note to be a little more affectionate toward them as a reward for their unintentional help. Too bad she couldn't find something to occupy her mind so easily. She had tried twice to raise Jared by radio, and got no response. She was tempted to keep trying, but didn't for fear she might be preventing an important transmission. As the day wore on without any word from him, her nerves frayed like an old worn rug.

Late in the afternoon, using the excuse of checking on Donna Jean, Shannon called the Dickerson ranch. But her heart sank when it became clear that Wynette wasn't even aware Jared was gone, much less on an urgent call. By the time she ended the conversation, Shannon was even more worried.

Why hadn't he called?

Every time the question popped into her mind, she got an answer she didn't like. She had read somewhere that there was an extremely high rate of alcoholism among policemen's wives, and a sixty percent divorce rate. No wonder. How did a woman wait like this day in and day out without going a little crazy?

Just look at her. She had practically spent the entire day listening for a message over the radio or by phone.

And here she was again sitting beside the phone, waiting, hoping, praying it would ring, and Jared would be on the other end.

Earlier she had been so worried about Lily bonding with Jared that she hadn't stopped to think about how she might feel if anything happened to him. Now look what had happened. She had done the very thing she knew she shouldn't. She cared about Jared. Maybe too much.

The day crawled by like a tired snake, and as dusk turned to darkness, Shannon was worn down to her last nerve. To her credit, she kept up a reasonable amount of chatter, and enough of a poker face to keep Lily from getting suspicious. And if the child noticed that her mother carried the handheld mobile radio everywhere they went, she didn't mention it.

"I wanna kiss Jared good-night," Lily said as Shannon tucked her in bed.

"Well, sweetheart he's still working."

"When's he gonna be here?"

"I'm sure he'll be back as soon as he can." Shannon kept her voice calm, despite the fact that her insides were jumping like cold water on a hot griddle.

"I can wait 'til he—" Lily yawned twice "—comes home."

"Nice try, slugger, but I don't think you'll make it. How about if I tell Jared to come up and see you, even if you're already asleep?"

"Promise?"

"Promise," Shannon whispered, hoping it was one she wouldn't have to break. When she leaned over to kiss Lily's cheek, two heavy little eyelids were barely open.

"Night, Mama." The last word trailed off and within moments, Lily was sound asleep.

"Good night, my angel."

Two hours later when Shannon peeked in on Lily she envied the way her child slept on, blissfully unaware of what was happening. Not that she actually had any better idea than Lily about what was going on. All that she knew was that Jared was somewhere out there in the mountains. In the dark. With guns. Twelve hours, and still no message on the radio. The phone was deathly quiet.

"Stay busy. Idle minds are the devil's playground, or something like that. Just don't—dwell on—the bad stuff."

Heeding her own advice, she made a grocery list. Then she read a couple of curriculum catalogs for some courses she wanted for Lily. After that she went upstairs and dug out a piece of unfinished cross-stitch she had been dragging around for months, but she couldn't concentrate. Finally, she found a novel on one of Jared's bookshelves that looked interesting. Sitting at the kitchen table so that she would hear him the instant he drove up, she started chapter one. A half hour later, after she had read the first page twice and couldn't remember one word, she gave up.

And all the while the mobile radio sat within easy reach, quiet except for static or the occasional voice of a rancher jumping from channel to channel looking for a chat. Despite the fact that she was unbelievably tired, she kept staring at it as if she could will Jared's voice to interrupt the static with the message "Shannon, I'm coming home. Shannon..."

"Shannon."

Jared was calling her, but from far away. Slowly she lifted her head from the table where she had fallen asleep. "Jared?"

"Shannon, do you copy?" he said over the radio.

She snatched it up, holding it in front of her face as if she could see him. "Jared? Jared, where are you?"

"Shannon." A pause, then, "This is Markham, out."

"No, Jared. Wait!"

Why couldn't he hear her? Oh, she hadn't pushed the damned button to transmit. She was fumbling to hit the right button when she heard the faint sound of an engine. It grew louder, and louder.

He was home!

Shannon plunked the radio down on the table none too gently and jumped up from the chair. She wanted to throw open the door and rush outside to meet him, but thought better of it. Besides, he would probably think she was a hysterical female if he knew how frantic she had been.

The dogs whined and pranced in anticipation as he approached, and Shannon knew exactly how they felt. Her heart was racing like a bullet train.

She heard the door to his truck slam shut, then his footsteps on the porch. He unlocked the back door and stepped inside, duffel bag under one arm, jacket under the other.

He came to a screeching halt when he saw her.

"Shannon? I saw the lights, but I never expected you to be awake."

Dreamed, hoped, he thought, but certainly not expected. She looked like an angel in her white robe and slippers, her hair unbraided and tumbling over her shoulders. He wanted to haul her into his arms and kiss her so bad he ached, but he was afraid she wasn't ready.

His uniform was dusty and dirty. He looked exhausted. And absolutely wonderful. "I...I waited..."

"You didn't have to, but I'm glad you did."

Suddenly Shannon couldn't stand being so far—a whole eight feet—away from him. It was almost as if she had to make sure he was real. She crossed to him. "Are you...are you all right?"

"For the most part."

"You're not hurt? I thought... I was afraid you were..."

"I'm dead tired, starved and filthy, but other than—"

"Thank God," she whispered, her eyes filled with tears. Without thinking about his reaction or the consequences, she put her arms around him, and lay her head on his chest.

The duffel bag and jacket hit the floor with a thump. Jared's arms found much softer cargo. He held her to him, stroking her back, grateful for this much, at least. "It's all right. I'm all right."

"You didn't call. Hours went by, and I was so worried."

He held her tighter. "I'm so sorry, Shannon. Everything happened so fast. We had to track the perps over some rough terrain. When you're in the moment like that, you have to stay focused on the job. And I— Well, it's been so long since I've had someone waiting for me to call."

At that moment being his "someone" sounded like the most wonderful thing in the world, despite its obvious drawbacks. At that moment she couldn't imagine anything more important than being here, in his arms. She wanted him to kiss her. Wanted to kiss him back.

"Crazy as it sounds considering the circumstances, it feels good."

His words snapped her back to reality as nothing else could. She was in his arms, and loving it, and a heartbeat away from kissing him. And then how could she tell him she wouldn't be here the next time he needed someone to be waiting? No, a kiss was too much. Kissing Jared would be too dangerous, too...thrilling. She *had* to distance herself, and that was all there was to it.

"You mean you forgot about us?" she said with a sniff.

"No!" He pulled away to look at her. "Oh, God, no, but—"

"It's all right, Jared." She offered him a tiny smile. "I was only teasing you a little. Besides, I'm so glad you're safe it doesn't really matter." Then with a loosely doubled fist she gave his chest a weak rap. "Where have you been, anyway? Do you have any idea how long it's been since I saw you walk out that door?"

Relief rushed though Jared's body like a spring flood out of the mountains. Enough to enable him to smile back. If she had enough spunk to demand explanations, she was over the worst of her fear. In the hours since leaving her, he had done his fair share of worrying. He didn't know how she would handle the stress his job generated, and the thought that she might not be able to handle it at all terrified him. Thank heaven, she had kept her cool, and found a way to cope. She was as remarkable as she was beautiful.

"Get dish-slinging mad if it will help."

She sniffed again. "Only if I can throw them at you."

"We can probably work something out with paper plates."

Shannon sighed, torn between relief and regret. "No good. Not enough noise."

"Feel better?"

She nodded. "You mentioned starved. How does a meat-loaf sandwich sound to you?"

"Like a gourmet meal. Got enough for two? My belly is rubbing my backbone."

"I think I can swing that."

"Great. I'll go wash up." At the doorway he stopped abruptly, and turned to face her. He stared at her for a long moment. So long Shannon became uncomfortable.

Then he walked straight back, and did what he had been wanting to do since the minute he found her waiting up for him. He took her in his arms and kissed her.

And kissed her.

Later Shannon would question why she didn't flinch when he hauled her into his arms. Later she would question why she hadn't pulled away. For now, the only thought in her brain was, yes, yes, yes.

He fitted his mouth to hers, tasting, but not testing. There was nothing tentative about the way he applied just enough pressure so that her lips parted and warmed. There was no hesitation as he took the kiss deeper. His need was obvious.

What surprised her was her own need. She leaned into him, lifting her hands to the back of his head and gave herself fully to the whirlwind of sensations storming her body. His taste was dark, male, and shot straight to her center like a flash of lightning. When he pulled away, she wanted to pull him back.

"Shannon." Her gaze met his. "I'm sorry I didn't call, but I couldn't. It tore me up knowing you were waiting without any word. It's not fair. It's hard as hell on a woman. But it is my job. It's also part of who I am. I want you to stay." His forehead touched hers. "God, but I want you to stay." Then he drew back.

"But if you can't handle my job—the stress—I'll understand. No one, least of all me, will blame you for leaving."

He was giving her an out.

The very thing she thought she wanted. All she had to do was take it. She and Lily could walk out the door. Move on. Keep running. Eventually, hopefully, she would find a way to shake Hal. They would survive. Jared would survive.

Eventually, she might even be able to convince herself that he wasn't the kindest man she had ever met. Or the gentlest. She might even talk herself into believing that she didn't care. That his kiss had meant nothing.

All she had to do was speak up, and she was out, gone. Free and clear. She could do it. It was what she had planned. And it was probably the best thing for everybody. While her mind agreed, her heart hesitated. She couldn't even use Lily as an excuse anymore.

This wasn't about Lily. It was about her. And Jared. And the truth, whether she liked it or not, was that she wanted to stay. Call it wishful thinking, call it absolute, total insanity, but she wanted to stay. While an insistent voice inside her head urged caution, the stronger voice of her heart whispered, take a chance.

"I—I waited, didn't I?"

Once the words were out of her mouth, Shannon felt as if an enormous weight had been lifted from her shoulders. She had made her decision, and prayed it was the right one for all of them.

"Yes." He cupped her face and kissed her again, this time briefly, then stepped away. "You won't be sorry," he promised. Then he went upstairs, leaving Shannon staring after him.

In the blink of an eye, more specifically with one kiss, everything had changed. She was in serious danger of getting in way over her head with this man, of wanting too much. And far too close to losing her heart.

6

"HOW WOULD YOU two beautiful ladies like to go on a picnic?"

Shannon and Lily glanced up from their reading lesson. "A picnic? Where, where? I wanna go," Lily said excitedly.

"If it's okay with your mother, we can go for a drive along a road called the El Camino del Rio. That's Spanish for The River Road, and it's some of the prettiest country in Texas. It takes most of the day, so we'll have to pack a lunch."

"Don't you have to work today?" Shannon asked.

"Tomorrow is my regular day off, but I traded with Tucker. He was supposed to pick up some paperwork at the state park. Instead, I'll do that, then the rest of the day is ours. I thought you might like to get out of the house."

Three days had passed since their kiss. Three days of wondering if it would happen again, and what she would do if it did. They had gotten to know each other a little better in that time, at least on the surface. They had talked about his job and Lily's schooling. Discussed the weather, and the upcoming Thanksgiving holiday. They had talked about almost everything but the kiss.

And it was driving Shannon crazy. She couldn't think about anything else. An outing might be just the thing to distract her.

She smiled. "We're out of potato chips. How am I going to pack a lunch without potato chips?"

"We'll just have to stop on the way. No self-respecting picnic would be caught dead without potato chips."

"Yippee!" Lily jumped out of her chair, and ran to Jared.

He scooped her up into his arms, and gave one of her braids a playful yank. "Let's see now. I may need someone to help me navigate."

"Me! Me!"

"Can you read a map?"

"I can read *The Spooky Old Tree* all by myself."

"Good enough. I hereby dub you my official navigator." He sat her on her feet.

"Yippee! Mama can help, too."

Jared's gaze met Shannon's. "Of course she can. It wouldn't be any fun without her."

Shannon closed the reader, and stacked it on top of Lily's other books. "Then we better get busy."

Jared watched them walk hand in hand toward the kitchen, and wondered if he hadn't lost what was left of his mind. Three days, and Shannon hadn't uttered one word about the kiss they had shared. Of course, he hadn't exactly been a chatterbox on the subject, either. He wanted to give her time to get used to him, used to thinking of him in more romantic terms. But three days of being with her, listening to her laugh and sing to

Lily, three days of remembering the way she felt in his arms, the way she tasted, was driving him crazy.

Yeah, the picnic was a good idea. He needed the distraction.

Thirty minutes later Jared was loading the cooler filled with sandwiches and soft drinks into the back of the truck when Shannon stuck her head out of the back door and yelled, "Jared, come quick!"

He raced into the house. Shannon was in the kitchen, the telephone receiver in her hand. "What's wrong?"

"It's Ellis. He says Wynette is at the café. Neal is out somewhere on the ranch working with a couple of the hands. And Donna Jean is in labor."

Jared paled. "Oh, God." He took the phone from Shannon. "Yeah, Ellis. I know, but you need to stay calm. Did you get Neal on the CB? Well, how long ago did he check in? Another hour? Damn!" He looked at Shannon. "I'm on my way."

"And we're going with you," she said as soon as he hung up the phone.

"You sure?"

"I didn't find Lily under a cabbage leaf. I might be able to help."

"Okay, get Lily, and I'll meet you at the truck." He headed for the back door, then stopped. "Sorry about our picnic," he said.

"New babies beat picnics hands down."

They were in the truck and racing toward the Dickerson ranch in short order. "Will the new baby be there at Wynette's house?" Lily wanted to know.

Jared and Shannon looked at each other over the top

of Lily's head. "I hope not. No, I don't think so, sweetheart."

"When can I see it?"

"Maybe soon. But you may have to wait. Sometimes babies think they want to be born, but then they change their minds, and wait awhile."

"Did I do that?"

"Nope. You were in a hurry." Shannon prayed Donna Jean's baby didn't come as quickly as Lily had. Hal had barely reached the hospital in time.

It took hardly more than fifteen minutes to reach the Dickerson house. Ellis was standing on the front porch looking terrified and clutching his cane like a life preserver.

Jared made hasty introductions. "Ellis Dickerson, Shannon Kramer, and her daughter, Lily."

"Howdy, ma'am." His eyes were a little wild looking, and she wasn't certain he even saw them.

"Hello," Lily said. "Did the baby hurry?"

Shannon patted Lily's shoulder. "Not now, sweetheart."

"But, Mama—"

"She's in pain," Ellis told Jared. "We've got to do something."

"Did you call Wynette?"

"Told her you were coming, and we'd be there soon as we could. She's gonna meet us at the hospital."

"Okay, I'll put Donna Jean in your station wagon," he told Ellis.

His voice was steady, and he appeared in control,

but Shannon knew he must be tied in knots. "Shannon, can you follow me in my truck with Ellis?"

"Of course."

"What about Neal?" Ellis Dickerson was near panic.

"We'll worry about Neal later." Jared reached for the front door.

Shannon put a hand on his arm. "Jared, why don't you let me go in to check on Donna Jean? We may all be rushing around unnecessarily."

"Oh," he said. "Yeah."

"First bedroom on the right," Ellis told her.

"Lily, wait here with Jared, and I'll be right back."

Ten minutes later Shannon, carrying an overnight case, emerged from the bedroom, her arm around Donna Jean's ample waist.

"You took time to pack!" Jared couldn't believe his eyes.

"Hi." Donna Jean gave him a weak smile.

"I don't believe this—"

"Jared, we need to get to the hospital as quickly as possible, but we don't need to break any speed records. This baby is determined to arrive today, but we do have a little time."

"I'm fine. Really," Donna Jean assured them. "Daddy, will you get Neal—" A contraction cut short her sentence. She clutched her stomach and groaned. Both men blanched.

"We'll find Neal," Shannon promised.

"To hell with Neal." Jared swept Donna Jean into his arms, and headed for the garage.

The entire situation might have been comical if Jared

wasn't scared right down to his toes. But he was in no mood to see any humor in what was happening. Shannon was certainly no expert, but Donna Jean's pains were twenty minutes apart, and the hospital was less than an hour away. They should be able to make it with plenty of time to spare.

If Jared didn't go to pieces first.

In fact, the more Shannon thought about it, the more she was convinced that perhaps she should be the one to drive Donna Jean. She started walking toward the garage, but Jared already had his passenger ensconced in the back seat, and the station wagon backed out.

"Jared." She put her hands on the car, and ducked her head to be able to see his face. "Jared, I think I should go with you."

"But—but, Ellis and Neal—"

"Can come along as soon as Ellis reaches Neal. But I think Donna Jean might be more comfortable if she had another woman along."

"Oh, please." Donna Jean was obviously relieved. "Shannon, I would be so grateful."

"But there's no time—"

She touched Jared's arm. "It will be all right." As quickly as she could, she buckled Lily in the front seat with Jared, praying her presence would be a reminder not to take unnecessary risks. Then Shannon scrambled into the back seat.

She knew Jared wouldn't endanger Donna Jean or her baby, but she also knew he was frantic not to let history repeat itself. She said a quick prayer for all of them—and every other driver on the road between here and the hospital.

They had no sooner pulled out of the gravel driveway and onto the main road leading into Alpine when Donna Jean had another contraction. After it had passed, both women looked at each other, knowing it had barely been fifteen minutes since the last one.

"Is she okay?" Jared asked.

Shannon glanced at her watch. "She's fine. You just concentrate on driving."

Donna Jean clutched her hand. "But—"

"Shh. You're going to be fine, and so is your baby. Now, have you and Neal been to any Lamaze classes?"

"Four times—at the—hospital."

"And you learned how to focus and breathe?"

"Yes."

"That's good. Very good. When you feel a contraction coming I want you to breathe the way they taught you. And focus." Shannon glanced around the back seat of the station wagon in search of something to use as a focal point, and came up empty-handed. "Jared, give me your badge."

"My what?"

"Give me your badge to use as a focal point."

"A focal—"

"Just give me the damned badge," she snapped.

"Mama," Lily's eyes rounded, hearing her mother's profanity. "You're not supposed to—"

"I'm sorry, sweetheart," she said, as Jared all but ripped the emblem of authority from his shirt, and handed it to her.

"Okay." She held up the shiny metal badge. "Here's our focus."

"Maybe you should get her to lie down."

Shannon understood Jared's need to be helpful, but at the moment she could do without it.

"She can't be very comfortable—"

"I'm fine, Jared, really—" Donna Jean groaned, in the grip of another contraction.

"Focus," Shannon ordered. "And breathe." They breathed together until it passed.

The commotion in the back seat sounded too intense not to be urgent. "My God, Shannon. What if we don't make it?" Jared uttered.

She put her hand on his shoulder. "You're doing great." But his white-knuckled grip on the steering wheel testified to the fact that he was scared to death. "We'll get there in time, Jared. This time everything will turn out all right."

Her voice was so calm, her words so caring, they took the edge off his fear. She knew exactly what he needed to hear at that very moment. Jared wanted to reach up and hold her hand, but he didn't dare take a hand off the steering wheel. But when this was over...

"SO, HOW DOES IT FEEL to be a godfather?"

"Is he supposed to be that color?" Jared asked without taking his eyes off the wiggling bundle wrapped in blue on the other side of the nursery window.

Shannon smiled at the intense expression on his face. "Yes."

"You're sure?"

"Absolutely. Lily looked like a little red-faced tomato until she was about two days old."

Jared shot her a disbelieving look. "Really?"

"Cross my heart. In a week young Joshua Jared Hartley will be pink as a rosebud. The only time he'll get red in the face is when he demands to be fed, and doesn't get an immediate response."

"I wish they hadn't stuck him with a name like Joshua *Jared*."

The big, broad-shouldered game warden had actually looked on the verge of tears when Neal came out of the delivery room and announced they had named their baby for Donna Jean's favorite biblical character and her best friend.

"It's a compliment."

"Yeah? He might not think so."

"My guess is that once he gets to know you, he'll be flattered."

They stood gazing at the baby for several moments, content to enjoy the wonder of viewing a miracle.

"Where's Lily?"

"She and Wynette are in the gift shop buying something for the baby."

"But he's only two hours old."

"Spending money on grandchildren is part of a woman's genetic code. I think it's in our DNA or something."

"That reminds me. I need to buy the baby—"

"Joshua."

"I need to buy Joshua a gift. Would you...would you go with me?"

She gazed up at him. "I'd love to. Besides, you'd probably come home with a bicycle or his first pair of boots."

Jared grinned. He liked the sound of the word home on her lips. It felt right. "Not appropriate, huh?"

"In about five years, maybe."

"So, we're talking blankets and diapers." He wrinkled his nose. "Baby stuff?"

"You know, you could do something different."

"Like?"

"A savings bond, or starting a savings account in Joshua's name. If you decide on a savings account, then Wynette and Ellis, or Neal's family could add to it over the years. But then, bonds are—" She glanced up, and found him looking at her strangely. "What? It was just a suggestion. You don't—"

"I haven't thanked you."

"For what? All I did was hold Donna Jean's hand, and remind her to breathe."

"You did much more than that. You were nothing short of a heroine. She should have named the baby after you."

"I hardly think—"

"Seriously. You were great. Calm, steady. Just what she needed."

"I was glad I could help."

"And you were just what I needed." He reached for her hand. "You saved me today, Shannon. I was scared spitless that something bad was going to happen. Just like with Amy. Having you there, knowing you understood was the only thing that got me through it. I'm not much on pretty words, but thank you." He took her face in his hands and kissed her.

She tasted like warm honey and wine, and the taste went straight to his head. The feel of her body against his was a powerful reminder of the hours, days he had thought of nothing else but this. He had intended the kiss to be an expression of his gratitude, but it didn't take long before it became something else entirely. Something hotter. He held her close, his hands molding her to him. Totally lost in the kiss, the sound of an elevator door opening penetrated his consciousness enough to remind him they were in a public place.

Breathless, dazed and definitely aroused, Shannon was grateful to see Lily and Wynette step off the elevator. While her daughter chattered on about every item of baby paraphernalia in the entire gift shop, Shannon kept stealing glances at Jared.

If she wasn't careful she could fall for him in a big way. She was honest enough with herself to admit she wanted him, but it was more than sex. So, where did that leave her? This had started out as a temporary stop on a journey to a new life, but what if this *became* the new life?

Shannon called herself ten times a fool. There was nothing wrong with fantasies, unless they started to take over reality. And she couldn't allow herself the luxury of believing in happy endings. Could she?

"SORRY ABOUT the picnic," Jared said as they drove home. "And that drive down south along the El Camino del Rio."

"You're off the hook so long as I get a rain check."

"Promise."

"Okay, I'll hold you to it." Lily was asleep, her head in Shannon's lap. She brushed a lock of hair from her daughter's forehead. "You must admit, the day was exciting."

"No question about that."

"And exhausting."

"You tired?"

"Funny, I wouldn't have said so until the last few minutes, but yes. Particularly since I know what the first question out of my daughter's mouth will be bright and early tomorrow morning."

"When can she go see little Joshua?"

"Bingo. She wanted to bring him home with us."

Jared laughed. "I'm sure she'll be welcome at the Dickerson ranch as often as she wants to go. That reminds me. You owe me a date."

"What?"

"A date, remember? We talked about it right before I got the call for the DEA assist."

"Oh, yeah."

"Unless you've changed your mind."

She was surprised at how quickly the denial sprang from her lips. "No."

"About the date, or about staying."

"What makes you say that?"

"You know, when you waited and worried about me the other night, I was thrilled. It made me feel...well, closer to you. But I realize that we've never really discussed how my job might affect you and Lily.

For instance, I've noticed that you don't seem the least bit uncomfortable with the fact that I wear a gun all the time. Even when I'm off duty."

"I...no. I grew up around guns. All of my brothers learned to shoot while they were still in grade school."

"How many brothers have you got?"

"Seven."

"Seven? None of them live close by with shotguns, I hope."

Shannon laughed. "They're all back in West Virginia."

"That's where you're from, I take it."

For a second the questions pushed her panic button, and she had to remind herself this was Jared asking. He had no ulterior motives. Still, months of evading such questions were hard to forget. "Originally. But I haven't lived there in a long time."

"Your family still there?"

"Scattered. One in the Navy. A couple married. One in college in Charleston. One working in Pittsburgh. The rest, God knows where." Talking about her brothers was a bittersweet reminder of all she had given up. All Hal had cost her. But, if not seeing her brothers for years meant keeping Lily out of Hal's reach, it was worth it.

"So, you're not close to them?"

"No, not since my divorce." The words were hardly out of her mouth before she realized it was an opening to a subject she didn't want to talk about. Of course, Jared had no way of knowing that.

"Is your ex-husband still in West Virginia?"

"He...he died not too long after we were divorced."

"Oh, I'm sorry."

"I'm not."

At the coldness in her voice Jared shot her a quick look. "Did he hurt you or Lily?"

Shannon almost laughed out loud. He couldn't know, must never know how close he had come to the truth. "He wasn't one tenth the man you are. Not as a friend or a father."

"Shannon—"

"Oh, good," she said hoping to distract him. "We're home."

Jared parked the truck, and carried Lily into the house, then upstairs to bed. He was on the front porch in a bench swing when Shannon joined him.

She sat down beside him, wrapping her arms around herself.

"Cold?"

Gazing at the sky, she shook her head. "Goose bumps. Look at those stars. You never see them like this in the city."

"Too many artificial lights."

"The city's loss. It's wonderful," she whispered.

"Hmm."

They swung silently for a while, content to savor the soft star-filled night. Shannon found herself leaning toward him until finally her head was on his shoulder. Jared held her close.

"Do you realize that you and Lily have been here a whole week?" he said finally.

"Seems longer."

"Is that good or bad?"

"Good. Comfortable."

"Yeah, for me, too."

After a long silence, Jared said, "You know, you were right about me from the beginning. I am lonely. Or I was until you came along. Shannon, I..." He leaned forward to look into her eyes but they were closed. Her chest rose and fell with the even rhythm of sleep.

Gently, ever so gently, he lifted her until she was cradled in his lap like a child. Then he rose, his well-muscled body barely straining under her slight weight, and carried her inside, upstairs, and placed her beside Lily on the bed. He covered her with a quilt.

And then he simply watched the two of them sleep.

The two princesses that had come into his life. Lily had already won his heart, and now he realized her mother had, too.

He hadn't intended to fall in love. Until today he had felt guilty merely thinking about loving someone other than Amy. His guilt about not being there when Amy needed him, and his fear that it might happen again were all tangled up together, and had a choke hold on his emotions, on his life. The instant Shannon had put her hand on his shoulder and said, "This time everything will turn out all right," he had felt that it truly would.

Watching Shannon's quiet strength had made him see that he had never confronted his fear, and had allowed it to isolate him from living life as it should be. He would always have a place in his heart for Amy, and he would always grieve his unborn son, but that didn't mean he couldn't make a place in his heart for someone else. For these two females who'd come along and changed him.

And the thought that he had almost walked away from them made him tremble.

Fate, he thought, sure had a strange way of bringing people together. A week ago, he had felt sorry for Shannon Kramer, and her freckle-faced little girl, and now...

Now he was in love with both of them.

The only obstacle he could see was Shannon herself. Or, more appropriately, whatever she was afraid of. From the beginning, he had sensed that trusting someone didn't come easy to her. After the way she had changed the subject tonight, he had a good idea where her fear might have originated. Her ex-husband. Had he abused Shannon? Maybe Lily as well?

The thought made him sick to his stomach. He broke out in a cold sweat. It was a good thing the man was dead, because if he had hurt them and was still alive, Jared would have been tempted to go after the bastard himself.

Softly, he walked to Shannon's side of the bed, and bent down until his face was close to hers. He would teach her to trust him. To trust what they could have together. He already knew she was a passionate woman. All she needed was the freedom to express her passion with a man she trusted. Jared intended to be that man.

7

GAZING OUT the kitchen window at a field of wild flowers on the edge of Jared's property with the mountains
in the background, Shannon found it hard to believe
that she had ever thought of this country as barren or
desolate. It was majestic with an unadorned grandeur
that could take your breath away at times. Last night's
sunset was one of those times.

Lily and the dogs had been playing in the backyard
while Jared grilled hamburgers. She had brought them
both a soft drink, and stayed to watch the sun gasp its
last breath of the day, expiring in a blaze of golden
glory. And Jared had kissed her.

Come to think of it, there had been a lot of that going
on lately. Ever since the night Joshua was born. In fact,
she had begun to think he was waging an all-out, one-
man war on her senses. Not a day went by that he
didn't find an opportunity to touch her. And it was
more than a casual peck on the cheek as he left in the
morning, or an occasional arm draped companionably
about her shoulders.

There was nothing casual or companionable about
the hundreds of very creative ways he found to be near
her, to touch her.

For instance, the other day, he'd been playfully teasing Lily by pretending to whisper a secret in Shannon's ear. And while he whispered nonsense his lips skimmed along the rim of her ear, and sent sensual currents shooting through her nerves like live wire in an electrical storm. He was short-circuiting her will-power, and he knew it.

Then, the night afterward, when they had all been cleaning up the kitchen, some 40's big band era music started playing on the radio. Jared had asked Lily to dance. With her little stocking feet on top of his massive boots, they had waltzed around the floor, the five-year-old alternating between giggling and gazing adoringly at Jared. Then in one quick, smooth move, he changed partners. He overrode Shannon's weak protests, and before she knew it, they were swaying to Glen Miller's "Moonlight Serenade." Quickly forgoing the traditional hold he lifted her arms to encircle his neck. His hands went to the small of her back, then slipped slightly lower to the curve of her hips. He pressed her to him ever so gently.

Shannon almost gasped at the contact. Every nerve, every cell in her body responded in the most elemental way. When his hand coasted up her back and pressed again, she could feel her nipples harden against his chest. Her throat went desert dry, and she almost stumbled. By the end of the dance she was tingling from head to toe.

And then, there was the time he had caught her massaging the muscles in her neck, and insisted on taking over the task, his big hands gently kneading. Then he made her lie down on her stomach on the sofa so—according to him—he could do it properly. What began as an effort to relax her backfired. Big time.

Jared worked the tendons across her shoulder blades, down her spine to her waist. His fingers kneaded the muscles from the small of her back, around to her rib cage. And each time his hands lightly brushed the sides of her breasts. The first time she hadn't been able to prevent a betraying hitch in her breath. The second time she had clamped her teeth together, but by the fourth and fifth strokes, a soft moan slipped from between her lips. She lay beneath his powerful hands, her body languid from the massage and aroused from his "accidental" touches.

But the final straw, the pièce de résistance of his sensual assault had been the ice cream. Plain old vanilla ice cream.

One afternoon after dusting off Jared's electric ice cream freezer, and searching through the cookbooks at her disposal, Shannon had succeeded in preparing a gallon and a half of rich vanilla frozen custard. She was just removing the dasher as Jared came inside after stacking some firewood in a rack alongside the house. He was wearing jeans and a T-shirt and she was impressed all over again by his size and build.

Naturally, he asked for a taste.

She spooned some of the cream into his mouth. Watching him lick his lips, her stomach did a couple of somersaults. Then he had returned the favor by offering her a spoonful of the cool confection. Thinking back, she was certain that he had deliberately left a drop or two on her lips so that he could kiss it off. And, oh, but he had done a wonderful job.

First his tongue coasted slowly over her lower lip. Once, twice as he collected the dot of sweet vanilla. He drew back just far enough to look into her eyes as he licked his lips again. Those faultless blue eyes sparked with desire as he watched her. Long seconds. Enough time for her to turn away. When she didn't, he fitted his mouth to hers and kissed her deeply. The lingering sweetness of the ice cream mingled with desire was like ambrosia, and went to her head like too much wine. If Wynette hadn't picked that moment to stop by with a share of the harvest from her garden, Shannon wasn't sure where all that heat would have taken them. No, that wasn't true. She knew.

Shannon shivered with the memory. She sighed. Even now gazing out at the wildflowers, she could still hear her own voice, husky with need as she called his name. But as well as she remembered the heat they generated, she also remembered that on each occasion he had never pressed her to go any further than she wanted to go. Each time—during the dance, the massage and the ice cream tasting—he had given her plenty of opportunities to walk away or to tell him to stop. He let her call the shots. And instinctively Shannon knew that, had she protested at all, he would have stopped. He had given her that power. The fact that she had repeatedly chosen not to exercise it was more a testimony to his patience than her willpower.

And his campaign was still going on. It was almost as if once he had discovered how to turn her on, he couldn't resist doing it. Every day, in every way, he made certain she was aware that he wanted her. More important he made certain she was aware that she wanted him. She couldn't even escape him in her dreams. Night after night she had the most erotic dreams. Several times she had awakened in the dark to find she was clutching the sheets, her skin damp with perspiration. She wasn't sure how much more she could take.

The torture was sweet.

It was hot.

And it was driving her crazy.

Maybe it was a good thing Jared was going to be out in the hills most of the night. Even though she worried, it gave her a much needed opportunity to do some serious thinking. And to ask herself some very important questions.

Like, how was she going to tell a man that placed a premium on honesty that she had lied to him? And in the next breath tell him that she was falling in love with him?

THE QUESTIONS were still unanswered as Shannon and Lily drove to the Dickerson ranch to visit Donna Jean and the baby. Disappointed to find the baby asleep when they arrived, Lily had gladly accepted Ellis's offer of a pony ride as a consolation prize. Shannon, Donna Jean and Wynette sipped iced tea, and talked about what each was preparing for the Thanksgiving dinner they would be sharing, as well as how best to schedule dinner around the trillions of football games the men always wanted to watch.

Shannon kept peeking into the cradle, checking to see if Josh was awake. She peeked so often that she finally woke him herself.

"He's awake," she announced with a sly grin. "Can I pick him up?"

"Might as well," Wynette said. "You been working on it for the last fifteen minutes."

Laughing, Shannon scooped little Josh into her arms. "Look at this. Not even a whimper. He's such a good baby."

"For the most part." Wynette had cut back on her hours at the café, and the reason was clear. She couldn't stop smiling around her grandson. "Might argue that point around three in the mornin' when his belly gets empty."

Donna Jean rolled her eyes. "As if he cried for more than two seconds with you around. I'll bet you didn't jump and run every time I made a peep."

"Hey, that's one of the perks of bein' a grandmother. You get to pick'em up any time you want to, then when they start to cry you get to hand'em back to their mama."

Shannon held the baby high in her arms. "You don't cry, do you Joshua? No, sir. Why, you're an angel, aren't you? And such a handsome boy," she cooed. Gazing at the sweet face of this beautiful child, her heart turned over. For half a second, just a heartbeat, she thought about holding a child of her own—hers and Jared's. "Oh, sweet baby," she whispered. "What a lovely dream you are."

Donna Jean and Wynette exchanged glances.

"Don't you think Shannon looks real natural with a baby in her arms, Mama?"

"No doubt about it," Wynette concurred.

"And a little brother for Lily would be nice to kinda round things out, don't you think?"

"No argument there. You know, I bet if she put her mind to it, among other things, I figure she could be holdin' her own baby in say, ten or eleven months from now."

Shannon nuzzled Josh's baby-powder-scented cheek. "You two are not exactly subtle." The baby began to root at her breast. "You either." She kissed the top of his downy head.

"We were hopin' you'd get the message." Donna Jean relieved her of Josh who had now began to fuss. "And I'm about to get a loud message from my son."

While Donna Jean took the baby into the nursery to change and feed him, Wynette fetched more iced tea. Lily arrived, ecstatic to learn Josh was awake, and dashed inside to the nursery. Shannon smiled at the excitement in her daughter's voice.

"She's pretty crazy about that baby," Wynette said.

"If she had her way, we'd be over here every day."

"Wouldn't bother us. You're family."

Shannon looked over at her friend. "That's nice. Thanks."

"You know, Donna Jean and I were serious a while ago. You do make a pretty picture holdin' a baby. And unless I miss my guess, you got a man dyin' to make that picture a reality." Wynette set her glass of tea aside, and leaned forward. "He's gone on you. Gone as gone can get."

"I...I don't know what to say."

"Don't have to say a thing. The way you looked at little Josh just about says it all. Admit it, Shannon. You were lookin' at Josh, but you were thinkin' about holdin' Jared's baby."

Shannon opened her mouth to protest, then closed it.

"Just what I thought. Does Jared know you're as crazy about him as he is about you?"

"Did...did he tell you that he was in love with me?"

"Didn't have to. It's there for any fool to see every time he looks at you. What I want to know, is what you're going to do about it."

"I—I'm not sure," Shannon answered honestly.

"Listen, sugar, I know you had good reasons for buyin' a pig in a poke, so to speak. And I always got the impression there was somethin' in your past you'd just as soon not talk about."

"What makes you say that?"

"Call it a hunch. The point is, no matter how this thing between you and Jared got started, or what you left behind, I'm tellin' you straight out that now you got yourself a good man, an honest man. He'll love and cherish you and that darlin' Lily 'til the end of your days, if you'll give him the chance."

Wynette had just described Shannon's dream of a lifetime. If she only knew, Shannon thought. If she only knew....

At that moment Donna Jean and Lily came back into the room. "One baby, full, burped and dry. Thanks to my assistant."

Lily beamed. "Mama, can we get a baby like Josh?"

Wynette's gaze met Shannon's. "Out of the mouths of babes."

"I can take good care of him. Donna Jean says so. Can we, Mama?"

"May we, and we'll talk about it later. Now, it's time we headed for home."

"Y'all don't need to run off," Donna Jean said. "Why don't you stay for supper?"

"Thanks, but we should—"

"You ask your Mama about the calf?" Ellis asked, joining them.

Lily jumped out of her chair. "I forgot. Mama, Ellis said I could see the baby calf when it gets borned." She turned pleading eyes to her mother. "Please?"

"What calf?"

"Got a cow that's due to calf any minute," Ellis explained. "And I told Lily she could stay and see the newborn if it was all right with you."

Being raised in West Virginia, Shannon had seen more farm animals give birth than she could count, and knew that most turned out fine. But occasionally a delivery might go bad, and she didn't want Lily witnessing a stillbirth. "After the birth, right?"

"Oh, sure," Ellis said.

Wynette grinned. "Seems like babies are poppin' up all over the place."

Shannon cut her a glance, then redirected her attention to Lily. "I suppose we could— Oh, no. I forgot that I've got two loaves of bread rising. I'm sorry, sweetheart, but we have to go home."

"Neal can bring her home after supper," Ellis offered. "Be no trouble."

"I got a better idea," Wynette said, still grinning. "Why don't you let Lily stay over?"

"Oh, I couldn't—"

"Sure you could. She'll be fine."

"But what about pajamas?"

"She can use one of Neal's T-shirts for a gown, and she can sleep on the sofa bed," Donna Jean suggested. "It would give you some time to yourself."

"Jared's gonna be out most of the night. Take a bubble bath. Do your nails. Read a book."

Shannon sighed. "Sounds like heaven."

Ellis frowned. "Not afraid to stay by yourself, are you?"

"No, not at all. But I hate to impose—"

"Impose, nothing," Wynette insisted. "This little darlin' is a joy, and no trouble at all. Now, scoot. Go home, and relax. We'll bring her back safe and sound right after breakfast tomorrow morning."

Shannon hesitated, but the offer was too good to pass up. She couldn't remember when she'd had time to herself, just for herself. "On one condition," she said to Donna Jean.

"Name it."

"That you let me keep Josh one night so you and Neal, *and* you and Ellis can have an evening out."

"You got a deal."

After strict instructions to Lily on minding her manners, Shannon kissed her daughter, said her goodbyes, and headed home in the old truck Ellis had loaned them.

On the short drive home, Wynette's words, *an honest man*, kept playing in her head like an old phonograph album with the needle stuck. The first night she had come into his house she had agreed there would be no more lies between them.

But she hadn't known what a loving, generous man he was then. She hadn't known what life with Jared could be like. Not that her lack of knowing excused the fact that she had lied. It didn't.

But she hadn't loved him then. And she did now.

Wynette had come close to being physic today, Shannon thought. She *had* gazed down at little Josh, and thought about holding Jared's baby. The realization of how much she longed to hold his child in her arms was like a fist to her gut.

She loved Jared. Loved him so much it hurt.

She wanted their life together to be real. She was living her dream, and she didn't want to give it up. But would her dream turn into a nightmare when Jared found out that she had come to him under false pretenses? Of course there were no more pretenses, and what she felt for Jared was definitely not false. But would that make a difference to him?

Thanksgiving was only two days away, and never in Shannon's life—with the possible exception of the day Lily was born—did she have so much to be thankful for. And so much to lose.

THE POP AND CRACKLE that proceeded a transmission woke her up. "Shannon."

She picked up the handheld radio and depressed the talk button. "Jared? Where are you?" The digital clock read 4:14 in the morning.

"Go to channel two."

She did, but suddenly her stomach knotted with anxiety. Channel two was their private channel. "Are you all right?"

"I'm fine."

"You're not bleeding anywhere, are you?"

He laughed. "Over a couple of guys trying for a trophy kill? Not a chance."

"That's a relief," she sighed.

"You shouldn't worry so much."

"Too bad, Game Warden Markham. I worry every time you leave the house."

"Must mean you care."

Shannon yawned. "Or I'm crazy."

There was a long stretch of dead air before he asked, "If you had to pick one right now, which would it be?"

She went very still. "I care," she said softly.

She wasn't sure but she thought she heard him sigh in relief. "I'll be home in ten minutes," was all he said.

"I'll be waiting," she promised, knowing she was promising much more.

Shannon threw back the covers, and slipped out of bed. Going to the closet, she pulled out a pair of jeans and a blouse, then stopped. If she greeted him fully dressed he might get the message that although she cared, she wasn't ready to take their relationship to the next level. Namely, intimacy. But greeting him in her gown and robe could be sending a too blatant message....

"Oh, to hell with it," Shannon whispered to the darkness as she put on her robe, and tied the sash around her waist. She had just told the man she cared about him. Neither one of them was foolish enough to think that meant she wanted to go steady.

She dashed to the bathroom. As she frantically ran a brush through her hair in hopes of looking even moderately appealing, she heard him brake the truck to a stop in the driveway. As usual, his speed amazed her. By the time she closed the bedroom door, and raced to the landing, his hand was on the newel post, one foot on the bottom stair. She flew down the steps, hesitated for a second when she got to the bottom, then went straight into his arms.

His uniform was cool and damp from his time in the hills, but she didn't care. This was what she wanted. This was the only reality that mattered.

"Shannon, Shannon," he murmured against her mouth.

He had kissed her before, but this was different. This time there was no teasing, no restraints. He was kissing her for real. Her head spun, her knees went weak, and she could have sworn she heard her own blood racing, heating in her veins. Never in her life had she felt so sane and delirious, so powerful and fragile, all at the same time. His mouth, warm and demanding, drank from hers. His hands, strong and confident, moved over her. And she simply let the sensation take her wherever he led.

She had kissed him back before, but this, too, was different. This time she held nothing back. This was a fire-meets-fire kiss. An unmistakable, you-want-what-I-want kiss. Jared had to caution himself not to devour her mouth. Not to devour her. Oh, but he wanted to. She was so hot, and he was so needy.

He could have gone on tasting her mouth forever. Silky, smooth and warm. He took the kiss deeper, and was rewarded with a throaty moan, the soft sounds almost shoving him over the edge of control. With his mouth still on hers, he pulled her with him into the living room only a few feet from the stairs until they were in front of the sofa. Then he proceeded to seduce her mouth, slowly, deliberately, as his hands freed the sash of her robe. He opened the garment, and pushed it off her shoulders. If he had expected the gown beneath to be plain cotton, he was in for a shock. It was red, silk and short. Middle-of-her-thighs short. And it clung to her breasts and narrow hips like a lover's caress. Jared's hand trembled as he reached out and gently stroked her small, firm breast through the thin silk.

She quivered, her breath catching in her throat as he continued to stroke her, pet her, until her nipples were hard. When he cupped her fully, she sighed his name.

"You're beautiful," he whispered, kissing her mouth, her throat, the enticing curve of her breasts.

Any concerns of modesty quickly vanished under the heat of his gaze. "I—I— You make me feel beautiful."

With a moan of pleasure, she wrapped her arms around his neck, and her body melted into his. She wanted to be close to him, so close her skin felt like his, and vice versa. When he lifted her off her feet then lay her on the sofa she reached for him, her eyes intense with desire. "Jared, please..."

Seeing her lying there, hearing her call for him was ecstasy...and agony.

She was his. His alone.

But he couldn't take her. Whatever part of his brain that still produced rational thought told him to get himself under control. Told him this was Shannon, a woman to be treasured, respected. Loved. And as much as he wanted her, he reminded himself that they were not alone. What if Lily woke up, and came looking for her mother?

"I—we can't do this."

Shannon couldn't believe what he was saying. Could there be any question in his mind that she was willing? Surely not. "Jared, I want you. Can't you see how much I want you?"

"Yes," he whispered, a bit dazed that he had called a halt to something they both wanted so badly. But he had to.

Beginning to feel embarrassed, she sat up, reaching for her robe. "I thought..." She gazed up at him, confused, hurt. "Don't you...don't you want me?"

Jared scrubbed his hands over his face. "So bad it hurts."

"Then I don't understand. Did I do something wrong?" She had only been with one man, and it suddenly crossed her mind that perhaps her experience was too limited for him. "Something you didn't like?"

"No. You were—are—perfect. Shannon..."

"Jared you're scaring me. Tell me, please. What's wrong?"

He all but collapsed beside her on the sofa. "Lily."

"What about Lily?"

"I couldn't bear to hurt her."

"Of course not. What does it have to do with—"

"What if she came looking for you, and found us...you know? She might be frightened or angry or—"

"She won't come looking for me."

"How can you be so sure? If she wakes and you're not in bed with her—"

"She's not here."

"What?"

"She's spending the night at Wynette and Ellis's house."

"The night? You mean...that means we're—"

"Alone."

He gazed into her eyes for several seconds, then stood up and held out his hand. Without a word, she took it and they went upstairs. At the landing, he hesitated. At first Shannon didn't understand why, then she realized he was once again putting control in her hands. He was giving her the opportunity to choose. His bedroom, or hers. Try as she might, Shannon didn't feel right making love to him in the bed that he had shared with another woman.

"Come with me." She pulled him toward her room.

When he closed the door behind them, it took every ounce of self-control he held not to toss her on the bed and devour her. Gently, he reminded himself, without much success. Amy had always needed tenderness, and out of love for his wife he had learned to temper the beast in himself. Now, the wildness in him clawed its way toward freedom, and the tether on his control was weak at best.

"Shannon—"

"Just kiss me."

His mouth was fire on hers, burning, blazing. She welcomed the heat, courted it, even as she felt him try to control the flame. His lack of control didn't scare her. This was Jared. He was not to be compared to anyone before. She trusted him with her life. And her heart. She didn't need gentleness, and she tried to tell him so, but her lips were too busy for speaking. Instead, she let her body tell him. She wrapped her arms around him, her own greed more than evident in the way she met him hunger for hunger.

"I need you," she whispered.

His own need was beyond verbalization as he pulled her into his arms, kissing her harder, deeper. Her mouth was so hot and wet, he thought he might just die from the pure pleasure of her taste. He feasted on her mouth, and still wasn't satisfied. It was as if he had waited all his life to kiss this woman, just this way. If he had expected her to be willing and pliant, he was in for a shock, or a treat, depending on the point of view. What he got was willing, no doubt about it. But he also got wild. And hungry. And hot.

He slipped the straps of her nightgown off her shoulders leaving her bare to the waist. He crushed her to him, running his hands over her back, down to her hips, then under her gown. She wore nothing beneath the silk. No panties. Just Shannon. Soft, smooth, wonderful Shannon. He thought his body might snap in two from the tension, but he couldn't bring himself to stop touching her.

"Take it off," she demanded, but when he reached for her gown she was way ahead of him. In one swift movement a slash of red silk flew across the room. It landed on the rocking chair. "No, I mean you."

Her words snapped the lease on the beast. "Sweet heaven. You're driving me crazy."

"Yeah?" Frantically, she worked at the buttons on his shirt. "Just as long as we go together."

"That's a given." He reached down to unbuckle his holster, and discovered his fingers were almost useless, until...

She yanked the shirt free of his pants, shoved it away and put her mouth—her wicked, wicked mouth—on his bare skin.

"Hurry."

"Sh-Shannon," he whispered, rocked to the core. His fingers went from fumbling to frenzied, and in seconds he was as naked as she was.

They tumbled onto the bed. Jared had just enough restraint left to taste her, to worship the satin softness of her breasts, her belly. But she wouldn't let him linger, as she writhed under his touch. Maddened by her response, he brought his mouth to hers again, crushing her lips as he filled her.

Gasping with pleasure, she arched her back, forcing him deeper, straining for more as her body tightened, climbing that ever-spiraling staircase to release.

And Jared was with her heat for heat, stroke for stroke. Together they flew over the moon. She cried out his name, sounding very close to a sob. Her name exploded from his lips on an oath, or a benediction. It didn't matter. The only thing that was important was that their souls joined.

THE SUN WAS SHINING when Shannon opened her eyes. She smiled, gazing at the landscape of Jared's broad and deliciously naked back. So delicious, in fact, that she couldn't resist a taste. She raised up on her elbow, and kissed him ever so lightly on the shoulder.

"Hmm," he murmured into his pillow. "That feels good."

"Tastes better."

He rolled over to face her. "Careful." He lifted a wave of dark hair from her bare shoulder, his fingers skimming her neck. "I might bite back."

"I'll risk it, if you will." Her eyes darkened, sparked with desire.

Jared pulled her into his arms. "Good morning."

"Morning."

"For a minute I thought I was still dreaming."

"Still?"

"Last night must have been a dream because it was like nothing I've ever experienced in real life. It was..."

"Wild?" She had done and felt things with him she hadn't even known she was capable of. It scared her. And excited her. Maybe she had been too wild.

"Incredible. You were incredible. We were incredible together."

"I thought so."

"We were. It's never been like that. So free, so..."

"Wild."

He grinned. "Oh, yeah."

"You liked it."

"Let me think." He rubbed his hand over his jaw, seemingly lost in concentration. "You know, for the sake of being fair and honest, maybe we should try it again. Just so I can be sure."

"A comparison test?"

"Something like that." Shannon gasped as he lifted her on top of him. "Something like this."

"Oh, oh-h. Jared? Jared!" She gasped again as he slid into her.

With his hands on her fanny he moved slowly, deliberately. "You may not have much to say, but I like the way you say it."

"But we can't—oh, oh, oh-h-h-h. I..." Her bones were melting. She was sure of it. "I guess we can." And they did.

AFTERWARD, THEIR arms and legs entwined, their sweat-slick bodies recovering from the passion, Jared stroked her hair.

Free. Never in his life had he felt so free or peaceful. Shannon had liberated him from a prison he hadn't even known he was holding himself in until she came along. She was his springtime, sweet, fresh and exhilarating, and he loved her totally, completely.

But how did she feel about him?

Oh, he knew she cared about him. Last night was proof positive that she cared deeply, but that wasn't the same thing as love. Not the kind of love he wanted from her. The kind of love that would last them a lifetime. That's what he wanted. To be with her until they were both old and gray, to love her, to help her raise Lily. And, he realized, he had wanted that practically from the first day she arrived. From where he stood, the future was as sure and true as his love for Shannon.

But where did Shannon stand? What would her answer be if he asked her to marry him?

While a part of him wanted to get down on bended knee and propose, another part cautioned that he might be pressuring her for a decision she wasn't ready to make. And he didn't want to rush her. But he didn't want to lose her. He couldn't lose her. Instinctively, Jared pulled her closer.

Shannon snuggled into his embrace, reveling in the absolute joy of loving Jared. Their night together had been perfect. No, beyond perfect. For the first time in her life she realized how it could be, should be, between a man and a woman. For the first time she understood the difference between sex and making love. As clichéd as it sounded, the difference was that simple, overused, media-exploited, four-letter word. *Love.*

While an inner voice warned her that Jared was not the kind of man to play house for long without wanting to take the next logical step in their relationship, Shannon simply wanted to enjoy the moment without thinking too far ahead. She just wanted to stay here in his arms and leave the rest of the world outside.

At that moment Jared's stomach growled. "I think my stomach is reminding me that I was in such a hurry to get home to you last night that I forgot to eat dinner."

"You know," Shannon said, yawning, "I don't think we even locked the back door last night."

"Don't worry. I know the law in these parts. Besides, I have reliable neighbors."

"Neighbors! Oh, my stars." She sat up in bed. "Jared, Wynette and Ellis are bringing Lily home this morning right after breakfast."

"What time is it?"

The sound of two hoots from the horn of Ellis's pickup truck made a clock unnecessary.

They scrambled out of bed, Jared looking for his clothes, Shannon grabbing a sheet.

"I'll go down and stall them while you get dressed," she said, trying to run to her closet and hold the sheet around her. She reached inside, snatched a pair of jeans and stepped into them.

"Okay."

She yanked open a drawer, pulled out a bra, then T-shirt. Faster, and with more expertise than any man had accomplished in the reverse, she had both on and was stuffing the T-shirt into her jeans, at the same time looking for her shoes. "I'll tell them I let you sleep late."

"Fine, but—"

She shooed him out of the room. "Just hurry up before they start asking questions I can't answer fast enough."

After Wynette's comments the afternoon before, Shannon decided it wouldn't take much for her friend to put two and two together, and come up with an "I told you so." As soon as Jared was on his way back to his room, she washed her face, ran a brush through her hair, and raced down the stairs. The threesome was stepping onto the back porch just as she entered the kitchen.

"Hi." She smiled. And prayed she could—they could—pull this off. "Did you have a good time, Lily?"

Thirty minutes later as they watched Ellis's truck jolting down the driveway, Shannon turned to Jared. "You think they suspect anything?"

"Like the fact that we were making mad passionate love about two minutes before they arrived? Or maybe that you looked like you had just tumbled out of bed—"

"I had."

"—and I looked like a cat who'd just devoured a bowl of cream. Naw." He put his arm around her. "They didn't suspect a thing."

Shannon had a good idea that at least part of her Thanksgiving holiday would include the third degree from Wynette. But that was tomorrow, she thought. And for now, she wanted to savor every moment with Jared. Just once, she wanted to pretend that there was going to be a happily ever after.

8

ALL THROUGH THE DAY, Shannon pretended. It was easy to do—she was gloriously happy.

Because of the long and late hours Jared had been putting in, plus the fact that he had worked on most of the holidays for the last two years, he had today *and* Thanksgiving Day off. He decided an all day trip into Alpine for some shopping was in order, along with a visit to the Woodward Agate Ranch. So, after a quick breakfast, they all piled into Jared's truck, and headed for Alpine.

The first stop was at the feed store, to buy fertilizer for a garden Jared planned to start. Then, they stopped at a toy store to buy Lily a doll which Shannon insisted Lily didn't need, but he purchased anyway. The third stop was for lunch. As they walked through the door of the café, Wynette greeted them with a big smile.

"Well now, don't y'all look like a happy bunch."

"I get to hunt—" Lily turned her smiling face up to Jared. "What's that thing?"

"Agates."

"Uh-huh. Ag-its and Optals. Jared said a princess has to have jewels." She beamed proudly. "And I'm a princess."

"That you are, sweet pea." Wynette grinned at Lily,

then said to Jared, "Must be goin' over to Woodward's."

He nodded and looked down at Lily. "So, princess," he said as he fished a quarter out of his pocket, "how about helping me play some music?"

"Yes, yes." She jumped up and down.

"Looks like Jared has fallen head over heels in love," Wynette said, leading Shannon to a booth while Lily led Jared off by the hand.

Shannon's head snapped around. "What?"

"With your daughter."

"Oh...yes." She slid into a booth not far from the jukebox. "Believe me, the feeling is mutual."

"Yeah. I could tell that this morning."

Shannon didn't dare make eye contact with Wynette unless she was prepared to deal with a barrage of questions. Some of which she didn't have the answers for.

"So...what time do you think y'all will be over tomorrow?"

"T-tomorrow," she stuttered, grateful Wynette had decided not to question her. "Uh, didn't you say the turkey would be done around eleven?"

Wynette plopped two menus onto the table. "Close enough. Bet you never thought you'd be eating a holiday dinner with Jared that first day you walked in here."

"No, I sure didn't.'

"I can tell you now that even though I prodded him into that ad, I wasn't holdin' my breath. I figured if he even got a date out of it, he'd be lucky. And look what he got."

"I don't know how lucky he is—"

"Hey, you're the best thing that's happened to that big yahoo in a long time. Take my word for it. Why, just a few days ago I was braggin' about the two of you."

"Bragging?"

"There was a couple of hunters in here, and I was tell-in' them about how romantic it was, you and Jared findin' each other kinda sight unseen as it were."

"Hunters?" Alarm bells went off in Shannon's head.

"Well, sorta. You know, all dressed up in army clothes."

Shannon's mouth went dry. "From around here?"

"Naw. There's usually a dozen or so come out here once or twice a year to play those phony war games. Lord knows we got enough space."

Survivalists. Hal's kind of people. With her heart pounding in her ears, Shannon had to struggle to keep her voice from betraying the sheer terror that had gripped her like talons. "These, uh, hunters you were talking to. I'll bet they thought the story was mushy."

"Nope. They were real interested. We weren't very busy that day, and you know me, I love to visit. But it was kinda nice to see that a couple of real macho guys could appreciate a happy ending."

"Happy ending?"

"You, Lily and Jared. A nice little family." She winked at Shannon. "And don't tell me I'm imagin' things. I saw how you two were tryin' not to look at each other this morning."

Thankfully she didn't have to comment on Wynette's observation because at that moment, Jared and Lily approached the booth. "We're starved," Jared announced.

"Can I have a cheese sandwich, please, Wynette?" Lily asked, crawling in beside her mother.

"You sure can, sweet pea. With extra pickles and chips."

"I'll take a burger, double meat, French fries and a vanilla malt." Jared looked over at Shannon, a decidedly wicked gleam in his eyes. "I've developed a taste for vanilla ice cream lately."

Shannon smiled, praying her eyes didn't betray the panic screaming through her mind. The last time Hal found them was with the help of a fellow gun collector that had seen them, and called the gun club he belonged to. Hal had also circulated a flyer, with a picture of her and Lily on it, amongst his gun-toting, Saturday morning soldier friends. What if these men related Wynette's story to some of their comrades in arms, then those men told it to others, and so on? Was it possible Hal could pick up such a slight lead, and track them down?

Anything was possible, she reminded herself. And she had learned the hard way not to underestimate her ex-husband's blind determination. It would be bad enough if he found them, but if he found her with another man... She didn't even want to think about what he might do to Jared.

"Shannon?"

"What?"

"I asked if you were ready to order."

"Oh, uh...I'm not as hungry as I thought I was. You and Lily go ahead."

"Are you sure?"

She nodded. "I'll get something later."

Until this moment she hadn't fully considered what might happen to Jared if he and Hal should ever cross paths. Jared was sworn to uphold the law, and technically *she* was a lawbreaker. Even though she had custody of Lily, the court had granted Hal visitation rights. Not that he had ever used them, but she had taken his daughter out of the state without permission. Dear Lord, what if Hal showed up with some kind of court order, and Jared was forced to turn her over to the authorities?

Or worse. What if Hal decided to include Jared in his thirst for revenge? If anything happened to Jared because of her, she wouldn't be able to live with herself.

Shannon made it through lunch without looking over her shoulder every time someone came into the café, and finally her panic receded. But it wasn't until they were out of Alpine headed for their rock hunt that she began to feel more at ease. She told herself she was overreacting. Hal couldn't possibly know where they were. Almost four weeks had gone by without so much as a glimpse of him. But how many times had she been into town in that time? Twice. Three times, at the most. He could easily have missed seeing her—

Stop it. Stop it right now, she warned herself, knowing the more she worried, the bigger the worry became. No, Hal was in West Virginia. She and Lily were

safe. And she was making a mountain out of a mole-
hill. Besides, Jared knew how to handle men like Hal.

But then that was part of the problem now, wasn't it?
Unintentionally, she had involved the one person
other than Lily whom she wanted to protect.

For the rest of the day Shannon forced herself not to
think about the hunters. Instead, every time a worri-
some thought popped into her head, she glanced at Jared. One look at this man who had made her happier in
a few short weeks than she could ever remember, and
the dark thoughts were pushed aside.

They drove to the Woodward Ranch, and were able
to join a group of tourists ready to hunt. Shannon focused her attention on the guide as he explained that
the ranch was known for the red plume agate, called
dendritic agate, which was formed in gas pockets of
lava. He told them that the beauty came from iron crys-
tals trapped in the rock, and that Woodward agate was
so well-known because it formed a feather or tree de-
sign.

The day was sunny with a light breeze, and the outing proved to be not only great fun, put productive. To
Lily's delight, she found two quality agates, quickly labeled "her treasure." And to Shannon's joy and
amazement, she too, found several exceptional stones.
But nothing compared to the small opals that Jared discovered.

"Thank you for a wonderful day," Shannon told him
later that evening as they sat in the front porch swing.
Lily had just gone to bed. Dusk was creeping up on the
night, and the stars were warming up to twinkle.

"My pleasure. I think we may have quite a little rock hound on our hands. Lily was a natural."

"She was, wasn't she? But you were the big winner. Those opals were small, but so lovely."

He smiled. "They don't even compare to your eyes, or your skin." He nuzzled her neck.

"Hmm, flattery. Continue."

"Let's see, now. How about, incredibly sexy?"

"Sexy is good."

He lifted her dark hair from her neck and kissed her earlobes. "You can say that again."

Shannon sighed, fully relaxing for the first time today. "Sexy is good."

"Think you're cute, don't you?"

"Don't you? I think you're awfully cute."

"Men aren't cute. They're handsome or distinguished or—"

"Sexy?"

"I'll take what I can get." He pulled her to him and kissed her long and hard. "Shannon," he said against her temple.

"Hmm."

"I—I need to tell you something."

She could feel his body tense. "It must be serious."

"Yeah, serious. But I need to say it, so bear with me."

"All right."

"That first day, when you and Lily came home with me, I had some preconceived notions about how things would be if you stayed. I thought all I wanted, all I needed was for us to be friends. Figured that was the best I could hope for. But I was wrong. I don't want to be your friend. I want to be your best friend. But I also want to be the one who makes your eyes sparkle with desire. I want to be the one who touches you, holds you. I love you, Shannon. I think I've loved you since the minute I walked in, and found you waiting up for me that first time."

Stunned and thrilled, she couldn't form a thought, much less a coherent sentence.

When she didn't answer, Jared's courage deflated like a punctured balloon. His heart felt as if it had suddenly been ripped in two. With a groan, he sat forward on the swing and put his head in his hands. "You weren't expecting this. I rushed you. I'm sorry. Things happened so quickly. Last night... I wanted you. It was wonderful. Beyond anything I had ever dreamed. But... Oh, hell, I'm babbling like an idiot. What I'm trying to say—" He looked up, and saw the tears on her lashes, and his heart sank. "You're crying. Oh, God, I've made a mess of this."

"Jared."

"Now you're hurt, and crying—"

"Jared."

"I never meant to hurt you—"

"Jared." She took his face in her hands. The action accomplished what her words couldn't. He stopped talking. "I'm not crying because you hurt me."

"You're not?"

What lucky star had she been born under to finally stumble across this marvelous man? she wondered. Maybe he was her reward for what she had been through. Maybe it was just fate. What difference did it make? He loved her. He loved her!

"I'm crying because you love me, and it's so wonderful."

"It is?" His hands covered hers, then he pulled them to his lips. "It is. And before you say anything else, I want you to know I don't expect you to say you love me back. I know—at least I think I know—that you have feelings for me, but they may not be love. And that's okay. But I love you and Lily, and I want you both in my life."

This all sounded suspiciously like a proposal.

She should have known after last night. Jared wasn't the kind of man who took making love to a woman lightly. She should have seen this coming. What a fool she had been. She had created this nice little fantasy for herself, and now reality was knocking at the door. He would be hurt when he learned she had lied to him. He would be hurt, and ashamed to learn he had asked a liar to marry him. Near panic, she had to stop him before he made, and asked for a commitment she couldn't give, no matter how desperately she wanted to. "Shannon—"

"We're in your life."

"Yes, and—"

"Can't we let that be enough for now?"

"No." He put a hand under her chin and tilted her head so that he could look into her eyes. "We can't. I want more."

"Jared—"

"Much more."

Please don't, she prayed. Don't ask. "Jared, don't—"

"I want to marry you. Live with you, love you forever. I want to be a father to Lily, and someday watch you hold our child in your arms."

Oh, he was killing her. "Aren't we...rushing things?"

"Are we? You've known from the moment you read my ad in that damned magazine that marriage was my ultimate goal. This isn't a news flash."

He was angry, and he had every right to be. "Of course not, but I thought we agreed—"

"You and I made love last night, or did I dream that?"

"No, but—"

"Then help me understand what's going on here. What had you planned on doing if our arrangement worked out to your satisfaction? Live in sin?"

"No, of course not."

"Then what?"

"I don't know. I...I wasn't expecting this. You said it yourself. Everything has happened so quickly."

"But last night—"

"Was the most beautiful night of my life. You're a wonderful lover. A wonderful man. Any woman would be lucky to have you. I—I just want to be sure. Can you understand that?"

She knew it was a lame excuse. It was as weak as she had been.

"All I understand is that if you're not sure after what happened between us last night, then maybe you're not the woman I thought you were."

Without a backward glance, he went inside, leaving her alone.

THANKSGIVING MORNING dawned cool and crisp. Inside the Markham homestead as well as outside. Breakfast was a rather somber affair with poor Lily totally confused about why her two favorite people in the world didn't look happy. By the time they all got dressed, packed up the food they were taking, loaded everything, including the dogs into the truck, then drove to the Dickerson ranch, the tension was as thick as cold gravy. Shannon was relieved when Jared disappeared into the den to join the other men in front of the television. Lily too, made herself scarce, going outside to play with Mack and Pit.

"What put a burr under his saddle?" Wynette asked immediately.

"Me, I'm afraid."

"Wanna talk about it?"

Shannon shook her head.

"Let me know if you change your mind."

The Thanksgiving meal with all the traditional trimmings, plus a few Texas additions such as salsa and tortillas, was served shortly after noon. When everyone was finally seated around the long dining table, Ellis asked that everybody hold hands while he said grace. Jared was sitting next to her, and for a moment Shannon thought he might refuse to take her hand. But he entwined his fingers with hers, and for a split second after the amen she thought he squeezed her hand. After everyone was stuffed and relaxed, the men once again drifted back to the football games, and the women began cleaning up.

The children of one of the ranch hands came to the back door, asking if Lily could play, and Shannon gave her permission. Why shouldn't at least one of them have a nice day? she thought.

Shannon, Wynette and Donna Jean had just finished washing the dishes, and had started on the pots and pans when they heard Lily scream. Shannon dropped the skillet she had been drying, and headed for the door, but before she could open it, one of the other children came bursting into the kitchen.

"Ms. Dickerson, come quick! The fire ants got Lily!"

Shannon nearly knocked the child down in her haste to get through the door. Behind her she heard Jared's heavy step.

Jared got to Lily before she did. Frantically, he swatted at Lily's legs, with almost no effect. To Shannon's horror her daughter's legs were literally covered in ants almost up to her knees. Parts of her hands, arms and neck were also dotted with ants. Screaming hysterically, Lily swatted at herself, and tried to reach out for Shannon at the same time.

"Oh, baby—"

"Don't touch her. They'll be all over you," Jared yelled, his own hands already dotted with ants.

"My God, Jared—"

"They're inside her clothes. Get 'em off," someone hollered out.

But Jared was way ahead of them. He yanked Lily up into his arms, and raced to the side of the house where a garden hose was connected to a faucet. In five seconds he had Lily stripped to her bare feet and panties, and was hosing the vicious insects off her trembling body.

Practically hysterical herself, Shannon stood two feet away, sobbing, waiting to snatch her traumatized child into her arms.

"Neal, get a towel outta the bathroom right quick to dry her off," Wynette ordered. "Poor little thing. She musta been standing in an ant bed to get so many on her so quick."

"We were playin' hide and seek," one of the kids said. "She was countin' with her eyes closed."

"Here you go." Neal came running out of the house with a towel, and handed it to Shannon just about the time Jared was satisfied Lily had been washed clean.

Choking back a sob, Shannon flung the towel around Lily, and hugged her to her. "Shh, shh, baby. It's okay." Lily's little body shook violently. "Everything is going to be all right." Shannon was none too steady herself.

"Gimme that hose." Ellis said, taking it from Jared. "You got'em all over you." He proceeded to hose off Jared's hands and arms, soaking his shirt and jeans in the process.

"Wynette, I need a blanket to wrap her in so she doesn't get chilled before we get to the hospital," Jared stated.

Shannon's head snapped up. "Hospital?" Insect bites weren't trivial, but Lily had no insect allergies.

She didn't understand why Jared thought a hospital was necessary.

"Ellis, will you call ahead and let them know we're coming?"

But Neal was already headed toward the house. "I'm on it."

"Jared—"

"No, Neal. Let Ellis do that." He pitched his set of keys to Neal. "Equipment box in the bed of my truck. First aid kit. Will you put it up front?"

"Done," Neal said as he dashed off.

"Jared?" Shannon swallowed another rising tide of panic.

"We don't have much time," he told her calmly. "Fire ant bites are like bee stings. Highly toxic. Lily needs to see a doctor. Now."

Holding her sobbing child close, her brain on overload, she still didn't understand what he was trying to tell her. Then Jared reached down, and flipped back one corner of the towel. Shannon's eyes widened in shock.

Both Lily's legs were red, and already swollen.

"Oh, my God," Shannon whispered, her terrified gaze meeting Jared's even as he was reaching for Lily.

Everybody moved at once, and miraculously, by the time they reached the truck the blanket was there, the first aid kit was on the front seat, and the motor was running. Jared helped Shannon in, set Lily in her lap, threw the blanket over them, jumped behind the wheel, and they were off in a spray of gravel.

Shannon had no idea how much time had actually

passed, but it felt like hours. Long, terrifying hours. In her arms, Lily whimpered, her body feverish. And just when they drove into Alpine and Shannon thought everything would be okay, Lily's breathing became labored. She was almost gasping for air.

"Do you know CPR?" Jared asked.

Shannon's heart leapt into her throat. Wide-eyed, she shook her head. Jared's grim expression and white-knuckled grip on the steering wheel testified to the fact that the situation was getting worse, not better. Minutes later he whipped the truck into the parking lot of the Alpine hospital, killed the engine, ran to the passenger side, and practically yanked the door off its hinges. A second later Shannon found herself in the middle of the tiny emergency room in another frenzy of people.

And Jared was like the center ring of a wheel, holding all the spokes together while the hospital staff did their job. His voice was calm as he related where and when the ant attack had taken place, and as she listened it was easy to believe that nothing bad could happen to her child as long as Jared was there. As long as she had his calm, steady presence beside her.

Lily was immediately put on oxygen, and after establishing that she had no allergies, she was given an injection of antihistamines, and a topical cream to aid in reducing the swelling, and to prevent her from scratching the bites. The emergency-room doctor explained that most children responded to the treatment within a half hour, but to be on the safe side he had also phoned a pediatrician to take a look at Lily. Sure enough, within twenty minutes Shannon began to see a change for the better. Lily's breathing became easier, and she seemed more comfortable. If Jared's strong arm hadn't been around her, Shannon thought she might have collapsed from relief. A short time later a nurse came in and requested forms be filled out and questions answered concerning Lily's general health.

"I don't want to leave her," Shannon said when the nurse insisted.

"Go fill out the forms. I won't leave her side until you get back," Jared promised.

Shannon went, reluctantly. As she was completing the last of the tedious forms the doctor came out.

"Ms. Kramer, I think your little girl is going to be just fine. If you had waited another ten or fifteen minutes, it might have been a different story. Those ant bites are bad enough for adults, but they can be lethal for kids. But she's responding to treatment very well." He pulled a prescription pad from his pocket, and began writing. "This is for more antihistamines. A little stronger than what you can buy over the counter, so you can expect her to sleep a lot. Let her. The more she sleeps, the less she will scratch the bites, and the less chance there is of infection setting in."

"Thank you, doctor. Thank you for everything."

"You're welcome. Now, I'm going to let you take her home in about an hour. If you've got any Epsom salts you might try putting some in her bath water to ease the itching. And I'd like you to call me tomorrow and let me know how she's doing."

"Thank you, again." Shannon couldn't help it, she started crying all over again. "I'm just so grateful—"

"Now don't you worry. A week from now you'll be scolding her for leaving her toys out, and all of this will be just a memory. I saw her give her daddy a great big smile not two minutes ago, so she's on the mend."

"Oh, but he's—" Before she could finish her protest a nurse called the doctor to the phone. He excused himself and took the call. Shannon went in to see Lily.

IT WAS DARK by the time they got home. Again wrapped in the blanket Wynette had loaned them, Jared carried a sleeping Lily upstairs.

Knowing everyone at the Dickersons would be anxious for news, they had called before leaving the hospital to assure them Lily would be fine.

At the top of the stairs, Jared turned to Shannon. "Why don't you go to the kitchen and get a glass of water in case she wakes up and needs more of that stuff the doctor prescribed?" he asked. "I'll put her to bed. You can dress her later."

"All right," she whispered.

Returning with the water, she heard Jared talking. "Oh, princess. You scared me to death today."

Shannon stopped outside the room.

"Do you know how precious you've become to me? I would die rather than let anything happen to you. But today I felt so helpless. Lily, sweet Lily. Thank God, you're all right."

Shannon heard his voice break, and her heart shattered into a million pieces.

It seemed like years ago that she had come up with the perfect way to start a new life for her and her child. She should have known when she saw Jared rescue that young skateboarder that she was doomed to love him. Real-life heroes don't grow on trees, and she had stumbled across one by pure accident.

And she would be a fool to turn her back and walk away from him.

She realized that she had lived with fear for so long that she couldn't see past it to what a normal existence could be. Until now. Here was what she had been looking for all along. He was the man she needed forever. He was the answer to her prayers.

"Jared." She stepped inside the door.

He had been kneeling beside the bed, and stood up when she entered. "That stuff really knocked her out," he said, keeping his voice low.

"I know."

"You think she'll sleep through the night?"

"I think so."

"If she wakes up—" he looked at Shannon "—will you call me?"

"Yes. I promise."

He nodded, and left the room. Shannon took one of Lily's gowns out of the drawer, and put it on her. Lily never stirred, but slept on peacefully.

But Shannon knew peace would elude her until she faced Jared with the truth.

He was on the back porch, the dogs at his feet. The light from the low-wattage yellow bug light cast the area in pale outlines and gray shadows.

"I think Mack and Pit know that she's sick," Jared said when she took the chair across from him. "Animals have a sense about the humans they bond with." As if on cue, Pit went to the door, whined, then came back, lay down and put his head on his paws.

"Jared, I want you to know how grateful—"

"Don't." He held up a hand. "I don't deserve gratitude."

"Of course you do. You saved my daughter's life today."

"No, I didn't."

"Jared, I'm not going to sit here and argue the point. If you hadn't thought of using that garden hose, I shudder to think what might have happened to Lily. So, whether you want to hear it or not, thank you. You're the bravest man I've ever known."

"How can you say that?" The words almost exploded out of him. "You know that I couldn't even save my wife. My own child."

She reached out and held his hand. "Being brave doesn't mean you always succeed. Being brave means you try, and you keep on trying. And letting someone look into your heart in the place you're most afraid of is the purist form of bravery. You did that the night little Joshua was born. And again...just a few moments ago when you were talking to Lily."

"She's so... If anything had happened..."

Shannon went to him, and kneeled beside his chair. "It didn't, thanks to you." She stroked his cheek. "I was a fool to think that I could ever walk away from you. I love you, Jared."

"What did you just—"

"I love you."

"Is this your idea of gratitude? You've already said thanks."

"But I haven't told you the truth. I haven't said what's in my heart. Look at me." When he turned to her, she looked straight into his eyes. "I love you, Jared Markham, with all my heart, all my soul."

He stared at her, letting her words sink in. Then he leaned forward, picked her up and put her on his lap, cradling her, holding her. "Oh, Shannon. I love you so."

"I'm sorry I hurt you last night. I didn't mean to."

"It's forgotten."

"No, Jared. I have to explain why—"

"It doesn't make any difference. Whatever your concerns, we can work them out together. Say it again."

"I love you. I—" The rest was smothered by his kiss.

His lips were warm, tempting and she wanted to give in to the kiss, wanted it to go on forever. But she still had another truth to tell, and she knew if she let herself melt into the kiss, she would never be able to tell him everything.

"Jared, wait. I have to tell you—"

"Doesn't matter." He pulled her to him again.

"Yes it does." She slipped out of his arms, and returned to her own chair. "It matters a great deal. And you have to hear this, or...or we..." She was painfully aware that there might not be a *we* when she continued, "...don't have a chance."

"All right," he said, seeing her determination.

She gathered her courage, held on tight, knowing she would need every ounce. "I...I answered your ad under false pretenses. When I came here, I never intended to stay."

"You had reservations. I knew that, but—"

"No, Jared. I lied to you."

9

HE WAS GOING INSANE. That had to be the answer. He'd just been through one of the most horrific days of his life, and she was telling him that she had lied to him? Used him? No, he was experiencing the normal confusion and fatigue after the kind of sustained adrenaline rush that comes with life-and-death situations. He was ready to drop in his tracks. He simply must have heard her wrong.

"I never meant to hurt you. And I would give anything if I didn't have to hurt you now, but I have to tell you the truth."

"The truth?"

"Yes."

"That you used me," he said, his eyes still glazed with confusion.

"To begin with, my ex-husband isn't dead. He's alive. And...and I'm what you might call a fugitive. There's probably a warrant out for my arrest in the state of West Virginia."

"You're wanted?"

"Jared, please...if you can just listen until I finish, all your questions will be answered. At least I hope they will," she said, wondering if he would ever again ask the one question she wanted to hear. "Promise me, you'll listen before you ask any more questions?"

He nodded.

"My ex-husband, Hal Jackson, didn't want the divorce, but I was determined." She clasped her hands together to keep them from shaking. "Hal was always a physical man. At first it was just an occasional shove then..."

She swallowed hard, her eyes stinging with unshed tears. She would not cry! She wanted Jared's understanding, and most of all she wanted his love. She didn't want sympathy.

"You're so secure in your masculinity, but Hal... wasn't. He thought we belonged to him, and his ego had been wounded. After the divorce he started harassing me. I did everything by the book. Called the police, got a peace bond, went back to court to get his visitations restricted. I did everything I was supposed to do only... Only Hal had *friends*."

The venom in her voice finally cleared the fog from his brain as if a veil had been lifted. She was so rigid she look as if she might snap in two. For the first time since she told him she had lied, the pain in her voice got through to him.

"They were his gun-club friends, and his weekend survival training comrades. All macho maniacs. Lawyers, cops, even a couple of judges. Funny how that worked. I took Hal to court and one of his gun-club buddies turned out to be the judge. Guess who got her hand slapped? Guess who was told she didn't have any choice but to let her unbalanced, raging ex-husband spend time with her four-year-old daughter? When that asinine excuse for a family court judge said, 'A child needs a father,' I wanted to scream. Hal was never a father to Lily."

At this point Shannon got up and gazed out at the peaceful night. "I tried to get away from him. Changed jobs, moved to another town. He always found us. The last time..." She shuddered with the memory, then turned to look at Jared. "He said would kill me. Or worse, he would just take Lily and I would never see her again. I believed him. So, we ran, and ran..." She took a deep breath, exhaling slowly. "Then one afternoon in a bus station I picked up the magazine and saw your ad. Your home was so remote. I thought that if I could keep Hal off our trail for a few weeks, we could start a new life. It was all so simple. After a time I intended to tell you that I had made a mistake, that it wasn't working for me, then Lily and I would leave. But I hadn't counted on falling in love with you.

"And I know that doesn't mean anything to you now, but it's true. I don't think I knew what real love was until I met you."

For a long time the only sound was the wind whistling through the trees, the occasional distant howl of a coyote or the call of a night bird.

Shannon waited for the questions. And the anger. Lord knew he was entitled

"The last time?"

"What?"

"What happened the last time he found you?"

The question was so unexpected that for a moment

she just stared at him. "I— He tried to strangle me. My landlord showed up or he would have succeeded."

"And Lily?"

Now the tears came. "Sh-she saw it all."

Jared's blistering oath made the dogs jump. "Tell me," he said between clenched teeth. "Tell me he didn't hurt her. If he took out his rage on a helpless child—"

"No. He never touched Lily. In fact, under the circumstances, she's amazingly well-adjusted."

"If the son of a bitch ever crosses my path, that'll probably be the only thing that keeps me from killing him." His gaze met hers. "He's damned close for what he did to you."

Shannon had never seen this side of Jared. This steely-eyed malice toward another human being. Undoubtedly, this was the man poachers and smugglers faced, the man who not only wore a badge but was prepared to back it up. All of that controlled rage, dark and furious, in a man of his size was intimidating. Given her history with Hal, she should have been terrified, but she wasn't. As awesome as she knew his anger to be, it *was* controlled. But there was more to it. Instinctively, maybe even from the first moment they had met, she had trusted him. At least her heart had. It had just taken her head a little longer.

But just because he wasn't aiming his rage at her didn't mean he was willing to forgive her. That was too much to hope for.

"I would give anything if I could go back to that first day, and start over, but I can't."

"You said almost those very words the day we met."

"Did I? That much hasn't changed."

"But we have—I have. I fought loving you, Shannon. You were so different from Amy, and I was convinced I could never love again."

"Jared—"

He held up a hand to silence her. "I can't trivialize lying by saying it doesn't matter, but I understand why you didn't tell me the truth. It's not like you've had a long list of trustworthy people in your life. In a way, it boils down to the self-preservation for you and your child. I can't—won't blame you for that."

"I—I'm not sure I understand what you're saying," she said, daring to hope.

"The first day we met, you told me that you wanted a real home, security. For Lily to be safe and happy. Was that part of the lie?"

"No. Never."

The thrill of her words shot through him, then settled soft and glowing around his heart. "You also told me that you hoped I would find the woman I was looking for."

"I r-remember."

"I found her."

Shannon was afraid to move, to even breathe for fear that this was all a dream. Was he saying what she thought he was saying? Could she be that lucky?

He came to her, lifted a wisp of dark hair then tucked the escapee from her French braid back into place. "We found each other, Shannon. Call it fate, or whatever name you choose. The road we took wasn't exactly

conventional, but *we found each other*. The rest of this—"
he waved his hand as if in dismissal "—we can deal
with. You don't have to run anymore. The question still
stands. Will you marry me?"

She was thunderstruck. Marry Jared? Live and love
with him for the rest of her life?

Jared tried to read an answer in her eyes, but all he
found was a shimmering, stunned expression. He had
poured his heart out at her feet, and she would either
take it or... Without realizing it, he took a step back. If
she didn't want him...

Shannon did the only thing she could do. She
stopped him. Her hand shot out, and grabbed the front
of his shirt.

"What are you doing?"

"Giving you my answer," she said, pulling him into
her arms, right where he belonged.

"WELL, AT LEAST there's not a warrant out for your arrest."

"Are you sure?" Shannon asked. Jared had been in
his office since he finished breakfast making calls on
her behalf, and talking to Niles Winston, the lawyer he
had asked to handle everything for her. It was now almost noon.

"Winston says you're clean as a whistle."

"I'm surprised."

"Me, too, after what you told me." Jared didn't add
that he thought the reason her ex-husband hadn't
turned her in was that he wanted to get to her before
the law could. Weekend warrior types like Hal Jackson

often considered themselves justified in taking the law into their own hands. The thought didn't make him feel any easier, but there was no point in giving Shannon more to worry about.

"Winston is making some inquiries, and trying to keep it discreet, but sooner or later we'll accumulate a paper trail that your ex-husband will be able to track. That means he'll know where you are."

She took a deep breath. "I know."

"And since you did take Lily out of state without the court's permission, eventually you will have to return to West Virginia to clear this mess up once and for all."

"I know that, too." She yanked the sheets from the bed in order to put on fresh linens. "But Jared, what if he shows up here? What if he causes trouble for you?"

"I can take care of myself. As for him showing up here, I have to admit there's a part of me that hopes he does so I can have the pleasure of beating him senseless before I arrest him. He might have some pull in West Virginia, but if he breaks the law in Texas, his buddies can't do him any good."

"Well, I'm not thrilled about the prospect of going back, but I understand that's what has to happen."

"And you know that this time will be different. They won't take advantage of you like they did before. I'll see to it because I'll be coming with you."

"That's so sweet of you, but—"

"No buts. Do you honestly think I would let you face that creep alone?"

"I can't ask you to drop everything and go with me. The lawyer you hired has already recommended a colleague in West Virginia. It may take days or even weeks. I may have to—"

"We may have to."

"Jared." She straightened from smoothing out the clean sheets. " You can't just take off from your job, and go flying halfway across the country."

"Even game wardens get vacations. I'm going with you, and that's final."

Shannon gave the pillows an extra fluff, and put them on the bed. "At least when I go, I'll be Mrs. Jared Markham."

"I like the sound of that." The sight of her leaning over the bed was just too tempting. He came up behind her, grabbed her by the waist, and spun her around and up against him a split second before they fell onto the bed. "And the feel of you."

"Hey, no fair," she teased, laughing and breathless.

"You know what they say, 'All's fair in love and war.'" He nuzzled her neck.

This sort of sexual play was new to her, but she was rapidly getting used to it. It was flirtatious, and fun. She liked it. Even now, knowing they didn't have the time to play, she hated to be the one to call it to a halt.

"Uh, need I remind you that Lily is playing in the new sandbox you made for her right outside the window?"

"She's downstairs, we're up." He nibbled on her earlobe while his hands slid possessively over her hip.

"Sound, ohh, uh...travels."

"So be quiet," he whispered against her lips. His mouth lingered, then gently deepened the kiss.

"Hmm." She barely managed to extricate herself from the kiss. "As much as I'm enjoying this—" he reached for her again, but she wiggled away "—we can't."

Jared rolled onto his back, and threw his arm across his eyes. "Oh, the rejection."

"I'll show you rejection if you mess up my freshly made bed."

He lifted his arm, and she caught the wicked little glint in his eyes. "We could mess it up together."

"No, we couldn't."

When he got off the bed and came toward her, she started backing up. "Now, Jared, you know what we decided—"

"Changed my mind."

"It's only one more day. We're getting married tomorrow and—"

He stalked her. "You're too tempting. I'll never make it another hour, much less another day."

She kept backing up. "Oh, yes you can. Jared. Jared, stop right there. Don't you come any—"

At that moment Wynette's rattletrap old station wagon came bouncing into the driveway, horn honking.

Shannon grinned. "Saved by the horn," she said, sidestepping him for a clean getaway.

By the time he came downstairs, Shannon and Wynette were already deep into a discussion about where to place the flowers that had been ordered to decorate the living room where the ceremony was to take place. In planning the wedding, they had gone from just the three of them before a justice of the peace, to a simple home affair with a handful of friends to witness their vows. Only it seemed everyone in Brewster County called Jared a friend.

"With the fireplace, there's really not a lot of wall space," Shannon said.

"Yeah, and you got all those windows on one side and that big old armoire on the other."

"Even with the sofa pushed against the windows, I'm not sure how much room we'll have. What's the count so far?"

"With Tucker and his family, plus a couple of Jared's friends from Marathon, we're up to thirty-five."

Shannon sighed. "Guess everyone will just have to stand."

"Well, if too many show up, we'll just have to stick 'em out on the front porch."

Shannon's eyes lit up. "That's a wonderful idea."

"Leavin' folks on the porch? I was only—"

"What do you think, Jared?"

"Oh, no," he said, in the process of polishing off the sandwich Shannon had made for lunch. "This wedding stuff is strictly off-limits as far as I'm concerned. You ladies do it the way you want. All I have to do is show up with a best man and a ring."

"No, really. What do you think about having the ceremony outside?"

"On the porch?"

"No, silly. In the backyard by the big redbud trees."

"You know," Wynette propped a hand on her hip. "For an idea, that ain't half-bad."

Jared looked down into Shannon's face, flushed with happiness and excitement. She had never looked more beautiful.

"If that's want you want, then go for it."

She squealed, and threw her arms around his neck, pecking kisses all over his face. His arms closed around her. "I'll give you fifteen minutes to stop that."

"Oh, Jared, it'll be wonderful."

With her still in his arms, he dipped his head and kissed her. "You're wonderful. I don't care if we say our 'I do's' in the middle of town, just so long as you're mine by sunset tomorrow."

"Hmm," she said against his mouth.

Wynette cleared her throat. "I hate to break this up, but if you two are gettin' hitched outdoors, we've got some changin' and rearrangin' to do."

"Killjoy," Jared said without malice. "All right." His hands on her waist, he set Shannon away from him. "I can see from this point on, I'll just be in the way. Besides, I've got to be in court in Fort Stockton to testify in a smuggling case at two o'clock." He gave her a quick kiss, and headed out the door.

"Be careful," she called after him.

"We got things to do, and places to go," Wynette announced.

"Where?"

"Alpine. We gotta talk to the florist, go by the hardware store—"

"The hardware store?"

"Sugar, you can't serve food outdoors without some of those bucket candle things to keep the bugs away."

Shannon laughed at her practical, wonderful friend. "Then we'd better get a move on."

"I'll go get Lily cleaned up while you change clothes," Wynette said.

As she climbed the stairs Shannon heard Wynette bribing Lily with the promise of an ice cream cone if she would hurry, and thought that her life just couldn't get any better.

Two hours later, their errands completed, it was time for Wynette to pay up.

"A promise is a promise, and I'm a woman of my word," she told Lily as the three of them exited the hardware store.

"Can I have two dips?" The child looked at her mother, her big eyes soft and pleading.

"You little hustler. Okay. I'm in a generous mood."

"Yippee!" Lily jumped up and down.

They set off toward the ice cream parlor. As they passed a fabric store, Shannon suddenly stopped. "Oh, I need to pick up some ribbon to match the dress Lily is wearing tomorrow."

"Why don't you go ahead? Lily and I will walk on up to the ice cream parlor, and you can catch us after you get your ribbon."

"All right. Save some rocky road for me." Wynette and Lily went ahead, and Shannon went inside. After making her purchase, she set off toward the ice cream store. She stopped at a crosswalk to wait for the light to turn green, and casually glanced across the street.

And her heart almost stopped beating.

There was a man standing outside one of the stores, and he looked exactly like...

She blinked, looked again, but the light had changed, and cars were zipping through the intersection, obscuring her view. When she could see the spot clearly again, the man was gone.

It couldn't have been Hal. It couldn't have been.

But her pounding heart wasn't listening. What if he had found them? What if he knew where they lived?

"No," Shannon said out loud, and a passerby gave her a strange look. She was letting her imagination run away with her, that's all. So there was a man with dark curly hair on a street in Alpine, Texas. There were probably hundreds of people matching that description in this town. No reason to go ballistic. She had to get a grip on herself before she joined Wynette and Lily.

Stay calm, she told herself. But she was only moderately successful. In fact, her apprehensiveness increased as she walked on. Once, just before she reached the ice cream store the hair on the back of her neck stood up on edge, and she had the feeling she was being watched. But when she looked around, she saw no one she recognized. Nothing out of the ordinary.

She reminded herself that Hal wasn't a subtle person. He favored the direct bulldozer approach, rather than relying on stealth. In the past when he had discovered their whereabouts, he had simply waited where they lived, and snagged them when they came home. Not once had he ever shown up during the daytime. Shannon breathed a sigh of relief. See there, it couldn't have been Hal. She had just caught sight of a man who looked like him, and panicked for a second. It was just too many months of running. Yes, that was it. A normal response after living in fear for so long. Shannon managed to settle her jangled nerves, and put on a smile as she joined Lily and Wynette, but the incident had left her shaken. And uneasy.

So uneasy, in fact, that even locked safely inside the house, with Jared sleeping only two rooms away, she found herself listening to the night sounds, trying to decipher them. Was that rustling a man sneaking around the yard, or an armadillo rooting for food? Was that twig snapped by a four-legged varmint or a two-legged one?

She was losing it. Tomorrow she was marrying the most loving, sexy man on the planet—in the galaxy—and here she was lying in bed conjuring up bogeymen. All because she looked up and saw a man that she *thought* looked like her ex-husband. What was wrong with her? She didn't have anything to be afraid of anymore. Not while she had Jared.

Oh, maybe this was all just prewedding jitters. After all, it wasn't every day a girl wound up with her heart's desire, and a prince charming to boot.

Shannon closed her eyes, and took a deep breath. Tomorrow was the beginning of more happiness than any woman had a right to dream of. She would not think about the past. Tomorrow was her future.

JARED LOOKED AROUND his backyard at the activity— Ellis setting up tables, Neal and a couple of his hands stringing lanterns in the trees. He shook his head. "We should have eloped."

"Too late," Shannon said, setting the box containing the new shoes she had bought to go with her dress on the front seat of his truck. The dress, in its clear plastic bag, was hanging from a hook over the passenger window. "Besides, Wynette has worked her heart out on this wedding. She would never forgive us."

"I don't see why you have to go to the Dickerson's to get dressed. I promise I won't peek."

She raised herself up on her toes and kissed him. "Humor me. I want to knock your socks off the first time you see me."

"Why stop at my socks?"

"After the reception, after everyone has gone home, then we'll discuss socks...and various other unnecessary articles of clothing."

He rolled his eyes. "You're killing me." Then on a more serious note, he asked, "Is Lily okay spending the night at the Dickerson's?"

"Are you kidding? She's already volunteered to get up and feed Josh his breakfast. And speaking of that, I better get over there before she drives Donna Jean nuts." She reached over to open the door of the truck, but he stopped her.

"Do you realize that the next time I kiss you, I'll be your husband?"

"I know," she whispered, her eyes misting. "Do you realize that this is the happiest day of my life?" She put a hand to his cheek and stroked it. "I love you so much, Jared."

"And I love you."

"Hey, Jared," Neal called out. "Just kiss her, and get your butt over here, or you're gonna be saying 'I do' in the dark."

"Keep your shirt on." He turned back for one more kiss, but she was already in the truck.

"See you in—" she checked her watch "—exactly three hours and twenty-two minutes," she promised, then blew him a kiss, and drove off.

LILY CAME RUNNING out of the Dickerson house the minute she saw the truck pull up. "Mama, Mama, you gotta come see the new kittens. Ellie said I could have one. Can I, Mama? Can I, please?"

"Whoa," Shannon said. "One major event at a time, sweetheart. Today, we marry Jared. Tomorrow we'll talk about cats."

"She's a single-minded little thing when she wants to be." Donna Jean stepped onto the porch, holding three-week-old Joshua in her arms.

"Tell me something I don't know." Shannon carried her dress and shoes, along with a small bag containing her makeup into the house.

Growing up with brothers, Shannon had never realized what a difference women friends could make in her life. Oh, she'd had school friends, but no one close. She had married Hal her first year in college, and the wives of his buddies formed her circle of friends. But she had never related to them the way she did to Wynette and Donna Jean. Most of those women had marriages similar to her own, and looking back, they were more like fellow victims than real friends. It was pure pleasure to share the hours before her wedding with true friends.

Wynette, Ellis and Neal had arrived, cleaned up and dressed up, and now they, along with Lily and Donna Jean, were ready to drive to Jared's place. Neal was chauffeuring today, and in charge of coming back for Shannon.

"Sure you don't mind being here by yourself while Neal takes us over?" Wynette asked. "I could stay, and ride with you."

"No, really. It would be kind of nice to have a few minutes alone."

"All right then, we better get goin'. Neal will be back in a jiffy."

Shannon kissed Lily goodbye, then waved them off, and went back into the bedroom where she had dressed. Standing in front of a full-length mirror, she admired her wedding dress.

True, it wasn't the fancy white gown every girl dreamed of, but then she wasn't a girl anymore. She was a woman, with a woman's dreams. The dress she had selected, with Donna Jean's help, was simple, elegant and made the most of her figure. It buttoned down the front all the way to the hemline which almost reached her ankles. A princess style made of shimmering beige silk with a scalloped neckline and long, fitted sleeves, the dress flowed around her with each step. It was understated, and maybe even a bit old-fashioned, but the moment Shannon spotted it in a shop in Fort Stockton, she knew it was the one. She'd decided to forgo a veil, and had done her hair swept up and captured at her crown, then strategically placed some fresh flowers among the curls.

She smiled back at her reflection. If she did say so herself, Jared's socks were definitely about to be knocked off. The sound of tires crunching on the gravel driveway told her Neal was back to collect her. With one last glance in the mirror she went into the living room.

"You were gone so long I thought you had forgotten about me," Shannon said, her back to the front door as she lifted the florist box containing her delicate bridal bouquet of roses and baby's breath. She turned, expecting to find a smiling friend...and froze. The box tumbled from her nerveless fingers and hit the floor.

"Hello, darlin'," said the dark, curly-haired man standing in the doorway. "Long time no see."

10

SHANNON SHOOK her head in disbelief even as she spoke his name. "H-Hal."

"In the flesh. You're looking good, Shannon. Real good, in fact." He glanced around. "Where's the kid?"

"G-gone. She's...she's not here," she said, numb with shock.

He shrugged. "We can always get her when we're ready to leave."

"Leave?"

"Sure. I've come all this way to bring you back to West Virginia where you belong."

Shannon stared at him as if he had lost his mind, then realized that he had. At least on some level, because in his twisted brain he had never gotten past thinking of her as his wife, his property. She realized with chilling certainty that he never would.

If she had any hope of reasoning with him, it went right out the window. Her only hope was escape, and in order to escape she had to come up with a plan. But for any plan to work, Shannon knew she had to keep Hal from raging. No matter what it took.

"Shannon? Did you hear me?"

"Y-yes." Now that the initial shock of seeing him had worn off, her mind whirled, calculating a method of escape. She was no match for his brute strength, but if she could get away from him, she could hide until Neal arrived. She looked around the room for something she could use as a weapon to defend herself, and spied a lamp base on an end table about ten feet away. It looked substantial enough for her purposes, and she began backing toward it.

"Shannon—"

The sound of Neal's truck on the gravel driveway cut him off. "Don't you open your mouth, you hear me?"

She was a split second away from screaming Neal's name when Hal reached around behind him, and pulled out a gun.

In that instant everything changed. Hal had never carried a weapon before. The fact that he had one now was a sign that he was more unbalanced than ever, and it turned Shannon's blood to ice. Neal would be coming through the door any second, and she had to warn him.

Hal positioned himself so that when the door opened he would be behind it.

Dear Lord, no, she thought. The front door flung open.

"Hey, Shannon, who does that car—"

"Neal!"

In a blur of motion, Hal stepped out, raised the gun, and struck Neal on the back of his head. Neal crumpled to the floor.

"Oh, my God." Shannon rushed over to him. There

was a bloody gash on the side of his head, but he was alive.

"Get away from him," Hal ordered, pointing the gun at Neal's bleeding head.

"But he's hurt."

"Get away from him. You didn't really think I was going to let you marry him, did you?"

"Mar— I'm not marrying him. This is Neal Hartly."

"You're lying. Look at him, all dressed up for your wedding."

"Hal, he's not the one. Look." She picked up Neal's left hand, and pointed to the plain gold band on his ring finger. "I'm telling you the truth."

"Hartly? Not, Markham?"

"No." She scrambled over to the sofa table, and snatched a handful of tissues. Think, think, she ordered her frenzied brain. She had to escape and she couldn't do it without a plan. One thing was in her favor. Hal might know Jared's name, but he obviously didn't know his face.

"Where is he?"

"Who?" she asked, feigning ignorance. Gently she dabbed at the blood around the gash in Neal's head.

"Don't play dumb with me, Shannon. Where is Markham?"

"He's..." If Hal knew Jared was only minutes away there was no telling what he might do. "He's waiting at the church."

As soon as the words were out of her mouth, Shannon knew she had her plan. It wasn't dynamic or even original, but if she was convincing enough, it would work. At least it would keep Hal away from Lily. And give Jared time to find her.

"Yeah? Well, he can wait 'til Hell freezes over."

"I doubt he'll wait that long, but it doesn't matter." Neal was out cold, and probably had a concussion, but she had managed to stop the bleeding.

"What do you mean, it doesn't matter?"

Shannon got to her feet. "I mean, that I had already decided not to marry Jared before you ever showed up. I couldn't go through with it."

Obviously, he hadn't expected this turn of events, and for a moment he just watched her. "Why not?" he finally asked.

She sighed. "Because I realized it was no good. It wouldn't work. I thought I could start a new life without you, but I was stupid—" she had to grit her teeth to get around the word "—to think you wouldn't find me. You always do."

"And you always run."

"Not anymore. I'm tired of running, Hal." She sat down in a nearby rocking chair. "And I never would have admitted it before, but trying to stay on the run with a child is enough to wear even the strongest woman down."

"But you were set to marry this Markham fella."

"I told you, I couldn't go through with it. Neal, the man you knocked out, was coming back to get me, and...and take me to Alpine. The, uh, couple that's taking care of Lily—this is their ranch—went to the church to...to tell Jared I wasn't coming. I was supposed to meet them later at the café."

"Then what?"

"They were going to drive us to the bus station."

"Where were you going?"

She shrugged. "One place is as good as the next. Sooner or later you would have found us."

"Damn straight I would have."

"I'm just so tired of being alone. Back home I had my brothers, my friends. But now... I had no idea how hard it would be."

"Big bad world out there, isn't it?"

Oh, he was gloating, loving every minute of her groveling. "Yes, but it's more than that, Hal." She lifted her eyes to his. It was go for broke time. "I realized I...I still had feelings for you."

He narrowed his gaze at her. "If you're trying to sweet-talk me, forget it."

"No, it's the truth. You were my first love, and I'll always feel something for you." *Contempt* was the word that came to mind. "Besides, I've finally come to understand that the only time we had trouble was when I disobeyed you. I'm so sorry." Shannon thought she might throw up from the bitter taste of her words.

"If you're so all-fired sorry, why didn't you just call and come home?"

"I was ashamed of the way I treated you. For all I knew, you had the cops looking for me."

"I should have."

"I'm grateful that you didn't. I wouldn't blame you if you didn't want anything to do with me."

Shannon sat quietly, submissively...praying as she had never prayed before. She watched the expression on his face and could tell he was trying to decide if he believed her or not.

"You're willing to go back with me? Just like that?"

"Just like that."

"I don't believe you."

"Would you believe me if I said I would marry you again?"

Shock flickered across his face for a moment. "How do I know you're not just stringing me along until you can run away?"

Shannon licked her lips, knowing this was her last roll of the dice. He would either believe her, or...

"The Mexican border is only sixty or seventy miles south of here."

"So?"

"So, there's no waiting period. We could get married today." Her stomach roiled at the thought, but she would even go through with it, if it would keep Lily and Jared safe from this demented man.

Then she played her trump card.

"And I'll leave Lily here. My friends—the ones that were going to drive me to the bus station—are crazy about her. I'm sure they wouldn't mind letting her stay with them for a few days. We could pick her up on our way home. I could call them—" She reached for the phone.

"Don't touch it!"

Meekly, Shannon folded her hands in her lap. "All right. Whatever you say."

"If this is some kind of trick, you'll be sorry, Shannon."

"I know." She held her breath, waiting.

Hal paced back and forth in front of her, stopped, studied her, then started pacing again. The whole time Shannon was trying to think of how she could leave some kind of sign or message so that Jared would know which direction they traveled.

"You'd go with me, and leave the kid behind?"

She looked him straight in the eyes. "For a few days." *Please, God,* she thought, *let Jared find me in a few hours.*

"Right now?"

"I won't even bother to change clothes."

Hal's gaze drilled her, searching for any sign of betrayal. Heaven must have heard her prayers because he put the safety back on the gun, and stuck it into the waistband of his jeans. Relief flooded Shannon's entire body.

"Let's go," he ordered.

"I've got to call my friends—"

"Dammit, I told you not to touch the damn phone!"

Shannon shrank back from the familiar prelude to rage. "I have—have to contact my friends."

"No."

"What if they think something has happened to me and call the police?"

He thought about that for a moment, then said, "Leave them a note, but make it short, and don't tell them where we're going. Say you'll call later."

Thank Heaven, she thought. She had no doubt Hal would read whatever she wrote, so it would have to be subtle. She tore a page from a notepad Wynette kept by the phone and wrote:

Dear Mack and Pit,

My ex-husband has come for me, and we've decided to try again. I would appreciate it if you could watch Lily for a couple of days. Maybe now she can go on that picnic Jay promised her. I'll call you tomorrow.

Thanks for everything,
Shannon

Hal snatched the paper from her the instant she finished writing.

"Mack and Pit? What kind of game are you—"

"It's no game. Honest, the husband's name is Mack, and his wife's name is Petunia. Everyone calls her Pit."

"What is this about a picnic?"

"One of their ranch hands promised to take Lily on a picnic with his kids, that's all."

He read the note again, then handed it back to her. "Put it where they'll see it, and let's get the hell out of here."

A half hour later Jared, followed by Ellis and Tucker Weiss, came through the door just as Neal was trying to get to his feet. Jared caught him under the arms when he staggered.

"Where's Shannon?" Jared wanted to know immediately.

"What happened?" Ellis asked.

"Somebody..." Neal touched the gash on his head "...came in the door...hit me from behind."

"Neal?" Jared was almost shaking the already dazed man. "Where is Shannon?"

Neal looked around, trying to focus. "Don't... know."

"She left a note."

Jared's head snapped up. Tucker was standing a few feet away, holding a note. "You better take a look at this. It doesn't make any sense to me but—"

Jared all but jerked the note from Tucker's grasp. "Dear, God," he whispered when he finished reading. "He's got her."

"Who?"

"Jackson. Shannon's ex-husband. He's been hounding her ever since their divorce."

"Then why would she go with him?"

"She wouldn't. And she would never leave Lily unless she was forced to. The main reason she answered my ad in that magazine was to get away from Jackson."

"Why would she address a note to a couple of dogs?" Tucker asked.

For the first time since realizing something was very wrong when Shannon was late to her own wedding, Jared smiled. "Because she knows that occasionally Mack and Pit help me track perpetrators. She's trying to tell us to track her."

"Okay, I'm with you so far. But what's this business about a picnic, and who the hell is Jay?"

Jared read the note again, then again before he realized what the cryptic message meant. "Not long ago I had to cancel a picnic, and I promised I would make it up to her. I'm Jay, and they're headed south."

"How can you be sure?"

"Because the canceled picnic was supposed to be along the El Camino del Rio. She wants us to know they've gone south."

"Toward the border," Tucker reminded him.

"You call it in," Jared said, peeling out of his suit jacket, discarding his tie. Tucker headed for the phone.

Jared went over to where Neal was nursing his injured head. Ellis had brought him some ice wrapped in a tea towel. "Neal, did you see the guy that hit you?"

"Nope. I stepped through the door, and the lights went out."

"Can you remember anything about what happened? Anything Shannon might have said, or anything you heard?"

"It all happened so fast, Jared. I wish I could be more help, but..."

"What?"

"There was a car here when I drove up. I remember thinking it was one I'd never seen before."

"What color?"

"Light blue, I think. No, gray. Yeah, gray."

"Can you remember a make or model?"

Neal made the mistake of shaking his head, and groaned. "Not sure. Ford, maybe. A sedan."

"Thanks," Jared said.

Tucker was already on the phone with the authorities, and relayed the information Neal had provided.

"Got an APB out on the vehicle with a description of Shannon. If they're going south the first obstacle will be getting into the park. Rangers have been alerted. They'll contact us the minute there is a sighting."

"If you think I'm going to wait around for someone to spot them, you're crazy." Jared was already out the door.

"Hold on," Tucker called. "You okay here?" he asked Ellis and Neal. When Ellis assured him they were fine, Tucker took off after Jared, who already had his truck in reverse.

Tucker yanked open the door, and jumped in. "Take it easy, we'll get this guy. And Shannon's smart. She left that message, didn't she?"

Jared put the truck into gear and it roared out in a spray of gravel. "You don't understand, Tuck. This guy messed her up the last time he caught her. He's a rager, an abuser. If he goes off the deep end, she won't be able to defend herself."

Tucker strapped himself in. "He's not going to get past us and the park rangers. And he's not stupid enough to go cross-country."

Jared shot him a hard look. "The guy is one of those macho types. Into guns, and survival training. He probably fancies himself more than a match for the law."

Tucker began removing his tie. "Then I suggest you step on it. We need to get your dogs, and our weapons."

IT WAS NEARLY DUSK when Hal approached the entrance to Big Bend National Park. He handed Shannon a map.

"How much farther to the border?"

"Maybe another twenty miles to Boquillas," she lied.

"I hope to hell they've got a decent motel."

Shannon cringed. "I'm sure they will."

They were fifth in a line of cars waiting to enter the park.

"What's taking so long?" Hal put down his window, and stuck his head out. "Those aren't just rangers up there. They've got cops, too. They're making everybody get out, like they were..." He pulled his head back inside the truck. "Like they were looking for somebody." The glance he gave her was pure hatred, raw, primal. "You wrote something in that note, didn't you?"

Her eyes wide with fear, she shook her head,

"Yes, you did. It was all a setup."

Shannon knew what was coming but she wasn't quick enough to steel herself.

"You lying bitch," Hal yelled as his fist struck her jaw. Shannon saw stars, then nothing but blackness.

When she came to, her head felt as if it had been used as a kettle drum, her bottom lip was cut and bleeding, and her body was being whipped back and forth as the car bounced violently. She blinked, realizing they were no longer on a road, but headed cross-country. In the dark!

Behind the wheel, his mouth set in a hard line, Hal was punctuating each dip, roll and pitch of the car with an obscenity. They hit a hole or low spot, throwing

Shannon hard against the door. Her head hit the window, and she groaned.

"Shut up," he growled.

She deliberately let her head loll to one side as if she were still unconscious, but opened her eyes slightly. If she could get a fix on a few landmarks, then she could find her way back when she found a chance to escape. *If* she found a chance to escape.

No, she couldn't afford that kind of thinking. Jared would find her. He would read the note, and know what she was trying to tell him. He would find her.

Suddenly the car jerked to a stop. Hal shoved the gearshift into park, killed the motor and pulled the keys out of the ignition. Still feigning unconsciousness, Shannon's head dropped back on the headrest, and she let her body go limp. Outside all she could see was the outline of a stand of trees some twenty or thirty yards away.

Hal popped the trunk lid, and got out of the car. Then she heard noises that sounded as if he were unloading something from the back. If she could get out of the car, and run into the trees... Before she could finish the thought her car door was flung open. Hal reached over, unbuckled her seat belt, and yanked her out of the car. He threw her to the ground.

"I ought to kill you right here and now. I would if I didn't think I might need you as a hostage to get out of this godforsaken country."

He kicked her in the ribs. "Get up. You've been playing possum for the last ten minutes."

Shannon groaned, the pain in her rib cage making

her gasp for breath. He raised his foot to kick her again, and she opened her eyes.

"That's more like it. Now, I said, get up."

Slowly, she rolled on her side, and got to her knees. But it wasn't fast enough for him. He reached down, grabbed the cluster of curls atop her head, some still dotted with flowers and pulled her up by her hair.

"Don't give me more reason to kill you, Shannon. You're hanging by a thread as it is." He shoved her up against the car where he could keep an eye on her.

Now she saw what he had hauled out of the trunk. Equipment. Lots of it. A camouflage jacket, which he already had on. Night goggles. Two rifles, one with a scope, probably infrared. And plenty of ammunition.

"Where are we going?" she asked, holding the right side of her rib cage. Merciful heavens, but it hurt to breathe.

"Into those hills."

"In the dark? You're insane."

In a move so quick she didn't even see it coming, he reached up and captured her face in one hand, squeezing her jaw until she thought he might break it. "I won't tell you again to shut up."

When he released his hold, the rush of blood back into her face was almost painful. He was insane if he planned on trekking into the mountains at night. She had no idea where they were, but she surmised that he had panicked when he saw the police at the park entrance. For all she knew, they could be a mile from the road they had been on or ten miles from the border.

Busy stuffing equipment into a backpack, Hal straightened, listening.

Shannon's heart leapt. Was that the sound of a helicopter somewhere off to the right? Oh, please let it be.

"Put this on." Hal threw a plastic camouflage-colored poncho at her. "And start walking toward those trees," he ordered, slipping on the backpack. When she didn't move fast enough to suit him, he grabbed her arm and practically dragged her along with him. In seconds they were in the trees. Hal pushed her to the ground then hunkered down beside her. Overhead the *whop-whop-whop* of the helicopter became louder.

From their position Shannon could see the chopper had spotted the car. Hovering, it shined its intensely bright searchlights on the vehicle and surrounding area. Beams of light swept the stand of trees that provided their cover, then moved on. Finally, the helicopter moved away to search another area. They stayed where they were for several more minutes, then Hal yanked her to her feet.

"Move. Ahead of me." He fitted the night goggles to his face, and shouldered a rifle. "And don't even think about running. I'd catch you before you got twenty feet. And you wouldn't be happy when I caught you, Shannon. I promise."

"I can't see where I'm going."

"I can. Keep walking straight ahead."

Only once did she glance back, but she was almost certain she saw lights in the distance. Headlights, she wondered? Could that be Jared and other officers coming to rescue her? It was only a glimpse, but it was enough to bolster her sagging hopes.

Using the night goggles to direct her, Hal continued their forced march into the hills. The lower half of Shannon's once beautiful dress became shredded as the undergrowth clawed at the fabric like demons trying to hitch a ride. By the time they made it up into the rocky hills she was cold, dirty and exhausted. She had no idea how much time had passed. It felt like days.

Hal marched them up to the crest of a peak that was more rock formation than mountain. Even though he wasn't familiar with the lay of the land, he knew the kind of high place needed to provide a vantage point. From his position atop the plateau he could easily see anyone that approached.

He shoved her down between two huge boulders. "Stay there." Then he moved six or eight feet away, almost to the edge of the peak. He put his rifle down, pulled a small tripod out of his backpack, set it up, and snapped a night scope into place.

"Wh-what are you g-going to do?" Shannon asked, trying to keep her teeth from chattering.

"Wait for daylight, then get the hell out of here."

"You can't get away."

"Sure I can. I could live in these mountains for a week, and they would never find me."

"Then why don't you just go? Leave me here. You could be in Mexico in no time. I promise I won't tell—"

His harsh laughter cut her off. "You think I'll fall for that a second time? Oh, no, darlin'. We're going with your original plan. You and me, and a justice of the peace. Then I'm going to take you back."

She couldn't believe she heard him right. He couldn't mean he actually intended to marry her. "I won't..." She heard something. Another helicopter? She stood up. "I won't do it." This way, Shannon prayed. Come this way.

"Sure you will." Now, Hal had heard the sound. It was definitely a helicopter. "Get down."

"No." She whipped off the poncho as the sound of the helicopter blades became a roar. In the light of a waning moon what was left of her beige silk dress shone like a bright beacon. "You might as well kill me because I'm not going anywhere with you. Not now. Not ever."

As he turned to reach for his rifle, Shannon saw her chance, and ran for her life.

"Bitch!" he yelled, his voice almost drowned out as the helicopter came roaring over the tops of the trees, searchlights crisscrossing the face of the mountain.

Shannon heard the gunfire, and knew Hal must be shooting at the helicopter, but she didn't look back. Now that he had been spotted, she knew it was only a matter of time—perhaps even minutes—before officers would arrive. Picking her way in the dark through rocks and shrubs she stumbled, falling hard on her left knee. Sobbing with pain, she got up, took several steps, then stopped.

"Oh, God, no," she cried. She had run right to the edge of the plateau. Right to the edge of a sheer drop-off.

Then she heard someone running behind her. Hal! She had to hide.

Jared and a handful of other officers had worked their way up the back of the mountain, and around to the plateau. They came out of the trees just as Jackson started firing on the helicopter. Before they could return fire, Hal started running.

With his heart in his throat, Jared prayed Shannon was all right. But he didn't see her. What if Jackson had already... No, he couldn't, wouldn't think like that. With Tucker right behind him, he took off after Jackson.

But the chase was short-lived. In minutes Jared and the others had Jackson cornered with them in front of him, and an eighty-foot drop-off behind him. Not surprisingly, in the face of an armed helicopter and almost a dozen law enforcement officers, Jackson threw down his rifle.

"This one's mine," Jared said.

Tucker didn't argue. Jared moved in, his gun aimed at Jackson. "Spread your feet. Put your hands behind your head."

"Where is Shannon?" he demanded as Jackson assumed the position. Standing directly in front of Hal Jackson with less than three feet separating them, Jared fought the urge to smash the man's face in. "Where is—"

"Jared!"

From over Jackson's shoulder, Jared saw Shannon stand up from behind a rock. He only took his eyes off

Hal for a split second, but it was enough. Jackson dropped and lunged all at the same time.

Shannon screamed as Hal knocked Jared to the ground, and jumped on top of him, fists swinging. The other officers converged on the scuffle, but before they could separate them, Jared and Hal rolled toward the ledge.

"Hey," one officer yelled. "They're going over."

But Tucker Weiss already had a hand on Jared's shirt, pulling him back. Hal wasn't so lucky. He slid off the edge of the plateau, falling only a few feet before grabbing hold of a tree growing between two rocks.

"Help me," Hal called frantically, his feet dangling some sixty-plus feet from the bottom of the mountain.

With an officer holding on to Tucker, and Tucker holding tight to him, Jared stretched out a hand. Hal grasped it with one hand, then with both. The officer pulled him up to solid ground.

Jared had barely let Jackson go and got to his feet before Shannon came flying into his arms. Holding on to each other tightly, it would have been difficult to say who was smothering whom with the most kisses.

Epilogue

"I NOW PRONOUNCE YOU man and wife. What God has joined together, let no man put asunder." The minister smiled and gave the groom a nod. "You may kiss the bride."

Jared Markham was way ahead of him. Scooping his soon-to-be-adopted daughter up with one arm, he embraced his wife with the other, and kissed her deeply. The entire gathering of their friends applauded.

"Yippee!" Lily said, her little arms around Jared's neck. "Now we get to stay here forever and ever, don't we, Mama?"

"Forever and ever," Shannon repeated, smiling up at her new husband.

"'Bout time y'all got around to havin' a proper weddin'." Wynette gave Shannon a big hug while Ellis pumped Jared's hand.

"Now, Mama," Donna Jean said, holding three-month-old Josh propped on her hip. "You know, they wanted to be done with their trip to West Virginia and all that legal stuff before throwing this party. Besides, it's not like they've been living in sin for the last three months."

"Oh, it's absolutely, one hundred percent legal." Jared sat Lily down, then slipped his arms around his wife.

Wynette put a hand on her hip. "Goin' off to a justice

of the peace in the middle of the night. That's the kinda stuff teenagers do."

"I wasn't taking any chances." Jared kissed Shannon's temple. "I came too close to losing her. The minute we got down off that mountain, I found a justice of the peace and made it legal."

Shannon leaned back in her husband's arms, and gazed up at him. "As if I would want it any other way."

"I'm going to hold you to that for say, the next fifty or sixty years."

"I had more like forever in mind."

"Even better," Jared said as he kissed her again.

Realizing when three-plus was definitely a crowd, Wynette nudged Ellis. Donna Jean nodded, taking Lily's hand to lead her over to the refreshments. "Don't get so carried away you forget to cut the cake," Neal called over his shoulder.

Jared waved him on. "I suppose we will have to join our guests."

"Hmm. I suppose," she said, luxuriating in the feel of his arms around her.

"The sooner they eat, the sooner they'll all go home," he reminded her.

"And the sooner we'll be alone."

"Works for me."

She smiled. "Then we can start our second honeymoon."

"We never really had a first." Jared turned her to face him. "I'm sorry about that. I wish we could have gone—"

Her fingers against his lips stopped him. "I don't need a honeymoon. I don't need anything but you and

Lily and our life together." She lifted her hand, admiring the ring guards that had been added a few moments ago to the plain gold band Jared had given her at their first ceremony. He had taken the agates and opals they had found that day at the Woodward Ranch, and had the ring guards custom-made. They were stunning, and special. Like her life.

"You know, I still can't figure out how I got so lucky." Smiling, he shook his head. "That silly ad. The odds were at least a million to one against me. Yet here you are."

"Never call that ad silly. And if anyone is lucky, it's me. I don't know what might have happened if you hadn't understood my note, and come after me that night. It makes my blood run cold just to think about it."

"All of that is in the past now. Jackson is going to be a guest of the Texas Department of Corrections for a lot of years. And after Texas is done with him, he's got some charges to face in West Virginia." He held her tighter. "You're safe and so is Lily. No more running. No more secrets."

"No more secrets," she whispered against his lips.

Well, maybe one more. A sweet, tiny secret she would share with him tonight when they lay in each other's arms. And they would dream about a son. And one day she would tell their son as she now told their daughter, the story of how the little princess and her mother had gone looking for a hero and found love, and a family. And happily ever after.

Cowboy's Kiss
Victoria Pade

Prologue

Elk Creek, Wyoming
Population: 1804

The sign was the first thing Ally Brooks saw when she stepped off the train onto the platform. She stood in front of a one-room station house that could have come straight out of an old Western movie—whitewashed, with its gingerbread trim painted a deep hunter green. It was nothing at all like the stately gray stone of Union Station in downtown Denver, where she'd boarded.

And also, unlike Union Station, with its array of porters, clerks and other travelers, there wasn't a soul in sight. Nor was the station even open—the ticket window was shut tight behind iron bars and a sign that said so.

"Is this it?"

Ally glanced at her eight-year-old daughter, who had just joined her on the platform beside their suitcases. She pointed out the sign. "This is it. Elk Creek."

Meggie's hazel eyes were so wide she looked like a scared kitten, and, seeing it, Ally had a flash of doubt—maybe they shouldn't have come.

But she tried to ignore that inner voice and instead wrapped an arm around her daughter. "It's okay. Remember we talked about how a small town would be different from living in Denver? Well, one of the ways is that places in a small town close early. Although actually it isn't early. It's after ten—we sat nearly three hours while they fixed that problem with the rails or we would have been here a long time ago."

"But if everything is shut, what are we going to do?"

Ally tightened her arm and hugged her daughter to her side, aching at the sound of worry beyond her years in the little girl's voice. "Not *everything* is closed for the night. Look across the street," she urged, nodding to what appeared to be a huge refurbished barn. There were probably two hundred cars and trucks parked around it; people and music spilled out the open doors and a banner proclaimed the grand opening of The Buckin' Bronco.

"That looks like The Grizzly Rose—that place Shag took Grandma to country-dance on Saturday nights. We'll just go over and find out how we can get to the Heller ranch from there."

Meggie didn't look reassured. But then, in the past

three years not much of what Ally had said or done had seemed to help. It was incredibly difficult to convince a child that the worst was not always going to happen when it had happened again and again already.

But Ally had to keep trying.

"Come on, kiddo," she said with another squeeze. "We'll leave our suitcases here in the shadows where no one can see them, and before you know it we'll be back for them and on our way to our new home—that great big ranch house Shag showed us pictures of—with all the horses and cows and chickens, and the swimming pool...it's going to be so great and so much fun!"

Meggie nodded but Ally could see that she was just humoring her. There was no enthusiasm in her expression.

Still, she pretended not to notice. She dropped her arm from around Meggie and took her daughter's hand instead. "It's just going to be great," she repeated with too much zest as she headed for the honky-tonk, praying along the way that it really would be.

"Hee-yaw! We've kicked this place off with a bang!" Linc Heller shouted.

Jackson Heller laughed at his younger brother's high spirits as Linc brought drinks to their table and did a rebel yell of celebration. No sooner had Linc set the tray down than he planted a huge kiss on his wife, Kansas, until she squealed for air. Then he moved around the table to shake their brother-in-law Ash Blackwolf's hand as if it were a water pump, and rub their sister Beth's extremely pregnant belly as if she were Buddha. He followed up with a quick peck on her cheek.

Then he came around to Jackson.

"Kiss me and you won't live to enjoy this place," Jackson warned with a grin.

Linc ignored it, yanked him out of his chair and bear hugged him.

Jackson hugged him back but, as if he hadn't, Linc said to the rest, "We gotta loosen this boy up!"

"You're loose enough for the both of us," Jackson joked when his brother had let him sit back down again.

"No, no, there's somethin' missin' here." Linc continued talking as he served each person a drink. "I have my beautiful bride, Kansas. And Beth and Ash have each other and that baby that's 'bout to pop out any day now. But look at you, sittin' there all by your lonesome."

Jackson spoke to everyone else. "He's three sheets to the wind."

"Linc is right, though," Beth chimed in. "It's about time you found someone nice and started a family of your own to fill that big house. Linc and Danny are all moved in with Kansas now, and Ash and I are in the remodeled bunkhouse—"

"And I can finally get back to normal," Jackson finished before she could, taking a gulp of fresh beer after saluting them all with the glass.

"He needs a woman," Linc decreed.

"He doesn't want one from around here, though," Beth informed knowledgeably, as if Jackson weren't right there listening. "He says there's nothing but the same old faces he's been looking at his whole life and that would be like marrying me.''

Jackson laughed at the sound of his own words repeated by his sister. Not that they weren't true. He'd meant it when he'd told her he just couldn't be romantically attracted to the single women Elk Creek had to offer. Hell, he'd grown up with them. He knew all their secrets. There weren't any surprises left, not to mention any chemistry.

"Let's see." Linc's voice broke into his thoughts. "With all the folks here tonight there must be somebody we could fix him up with."

Jackson shook his head and laughed at his brother's obvious deafness to what Beth had said. "You *invited* everybody here tonight—there isn't a soul we don't know inside and out."

"Oh, yeah?" Linc said just then, victory in his voice as he pointed a long index finger in the direction of the front entrance.

Everyone at the table adjusted themselves to see who he was picking out of the crowd.

Everyone except Jackson, who took another swallow of his beer and just shook his head again. He felt sure that even if his brother had spotted someone Linc didn't know, he'd recognize whoever it was. After all, Linc had missed a lot of years in Elk Creek, but Jackson had spent barely a few weeks away his whole life.

"Who is she?" Kansas asked.

Jackson's sister-in-law sounded genuinely curious. And if anybody knew everyone there was to know the way he did, it was Kansas. So Jackson finally glanced up.

At the same time, Linc said, *"That's a new face for you."*

A pretty one, was Jackson's initial, answering thought when he spotted the woman standing in the great open doors of what had once been an auctioning barn. She looked to be about thirty, holding the hand of a seven- or eight-year-old little girl.

And Linc was right, Jackson didn't know who they were.

He couldn't help watching as she stepped inside the honky-tonk and looked around with eyes that seemed to sparkle so brightly he could see it even at a distance.

She was a wisp of a woman—probably not more than five feet three inches, with just enough flesh on her bones to make her unmistakably female. She had curly, curly copper-colored hair that fluffed all around her head and well past her shoulders, framing a face with skin so fair it looked as if the sun had never touched it. Her nose was thin, her cheekbones high and round, and her mouth was so full and pink that if it had been a peach, Jackson would have thought it was ripe for the picking.

"You all really don't know her?" Ash marveled as the group watched her stop a waiter and apparently ask him something.

"Nope," Linc said. And then a moment later, he added, "But it looks like we're about to meet her. She's headed this way."

She was, too.

Hanging on tight to the little girl, the woman wove her way through the crowd, her gaze locked on them.

And as she came, Jackson still couldn't seem to tear his eyes away.

But wanting to cover it up, he hooked his thumbs into his pockets, tipped his chair back onto two legs and watched from down his nose as if he were much less interested than he was.

"Excuse me. I'm sorry to barge in," she began when she reached the table.

Her voice ran over his nerve endings like warm honey even through the noise in the place.

"Are you the Hellers? Shag Heller's family?"

"The whole lot of us," Linc answered.

She smiled then, but just slightly, tentatively, as if she were unsure of herself. Or of them. And yet even that appearance of uncertainty had Jackson riveted.

Close up she was more than just pretty. She was beautiful. And when she smiled, those sparkling eyes of hers—as green as the sea—seemed to come to life with the most unwitting sensuality he'd ever seen.

"And who might you be?" Linc asked with a wink in his voice.

"My name is Ally Brooks. I don't know if your father told you anything about me, or if my inheriting part of his estate came as much a surprise to you as it did to me, but…well, here I am." She nodded toward the little girl. "Here *we* are—Meggie and I. We've come to live at the ranch."

The two upraised legs of Jackson's chair hit the floor with a loud thud and he raised his fists to the table. "You're Shag's lady friend?" he nearly shouted.

It was Kansas who smoothed the edges of that by

saying, "So you're the Ally Brooks we've all been wondering about."

Suddenly Linc let out a hoot and holler loud enough to be heard in every corner of the honky-tonk, ending in an uproarious laugh as he slapped Jackson on the back and said to her, "This is the man you want to see, right here."

But Jackson didn't find anything amusing in the revelation of who this woman was and why she'd come.

In fact, it made him all-fired, spitting mad.

Chapter One

Ally pulled down the covers on the bed in one of the guest rooms at the Heller ranch house an hour later. She and Meggie were there alone, and since her daughter had just gone into the bathroom to change into her pajamas and brush her teeth, Ally let herself fall back over the bed like a newly cut tree to wait for her.

As she did, the full impact of where she was struck her. Not only where she was logistically—in Wyoming, on a ranch, of all things; away from the city she'd grown up in; away from all her friends and family—but also where she was in her life.

Divorced, a single parent, struggling miserably for the past three years, and now a part owner of a ranch, a house, other buildings, land, cattle, horses, oil and mineral rights to wells and mines that were apparently high producers. Not to mention the share of cash, stocks and bonds Shag had left her.

None of it was what she'd ever envisioned for herself—not that anyone grew up with a desire to fail at marriage and be left struggling to raise a child alone. But equally shocking was the good turn things had taken. That part was like winning the lottery, just when she'd needed to.

Only there had had to be a death for it to happen, which tarnished the good. And on the other end were three people who shouldn't have had to share with a perfect stranger a full and equal portion of what their father had bequeathed them—that fact didn't polish it up bright and beautiful, either.

Although Linc and Beth hadn't seemed to care, she reminded herself as she heard the water go on in the bathroom.

Linc had found something about Ally and Meggie being there very funny and he'd welcomed them like long-lost family.

Beth had been warm, friendly, gracious. Shortly after Ally had introduced herself and Meggie, she'd claimed to be tired and ready for the evening to end—something Ally didn't doubt, seeing how far along in her pregnancy Beth was. She'd offered to bring Ally and Meggie home, show them around and get them settled for the night, and through all of it, Shag's daughter hadn't shown so much as a hint of hard feelings.

But Jackson Heller? He was another story.

Cornflower blue eyes had bored into her as if she were the devil incarnate.

Two of the most beautiful cornflower blue eyes she'd ever seen...

Not that the color of his eyes made any difference. What did matter was that he'd either hated her at first sight or hated that she'd inherited a full quarter of what rightfully belonged to him, his brother and sister.

The second possibility seemed the most likely.

And Ally understood it. She'd been astounded herself to learn what was in Shag's will. And whether or not he'd warned Linc or Beth or Jackson of what he was going to do, they had every right to resent it. To resent her. No matter that the inheritance had saved her and Meggie from financial doom.

Maybe we shouldn't have come, Ally thought for the hundredth time since setting foot in Elk Creek.

But just then Meggie opened the bathroom door.

Ally sat up in a hurry and hid her own doubts behind a smile.

Dressed in a summer nightgown, her daughter looked thin. Too thin. Too sad.

One look at the little girl reminded her why she'd moved here.

Since Meggie's father had left, she'd watched Meggie go from being a gregarious, happy, energetic child to one so depressed over their broken family and Doug's complete neglect of her that Ally had had to take her for counseling.

And even that hadn't helped.

But something had to. It just *had* to. And Ally would do absolutely anything to find what it was. To bring back her sweet, smiling child.

So here we are.

It was for Meggie's sake they'd come. For Meggie's sake that Ally had turned down the offer Jackson Heller had made to buy out her share of the actual property in Wyoming.

Small-town life. Open countryside. Fresh air. Animals. Ally was counting on it all to heal her daughter's broken heart.

And maybe her own in the process.

Whether Jackson Heller liked it or not.

"Do you think this will be my room?" Meggie asked as she climbed into bed and arranged a dozen dolls and stuffed animals all around her body like a cushion from shoulders to ankles—a practice she'd taken up since the divorce.

"I don't know. Would you like this to be your room?" Ally pulled the sheet up and tucked it in around Meggie and the menagerie and then sat on the edge of the mattress, being careful not to disturb anything.

"It'd be nice to have my very own bathroom."

"From what I saw when Shag's daughter gave us the grand tour, all the bedrooms have their own bathrooms."

"Will Daddy be able to find us here?" Meggie changed the subject without a segue as only an eight-year-old could.

The sound of longing and hurt in her daughter's

voice was yet another wrench of Ally's heart. "Sure. Grandma knows where we are and the post office will forward all of our mail. But you know—"

"I know." Meggie cut her off and recited the words Ally had had to say too often. "Don't get my hopes up, just go on about my business and try not to think about Daddy maybe coming back to see me."

Or phoning or sending so much as a birthday or Christmas card or acknowledging he's a father in any way at all, Ally added silently.

More than the money Doug Brooks had withheld from Meggie—the money that had earned him a place on Colorado's list of child-support evaders—what Ally could have strangled him for were the love, affection, attention and interest he had also deprived his daughter of. Instead, his efforts all seemed to go into skipping from state to state, not even practicing medicine after all those years of school and training, to avoid being made to meet any responsibilities whatsoever.

It was awful enough to have made a rotten choice in a husband for herself, but it was absolute agony to watch her child suffer for that same rotten choice in a father. Luckily, the inheritance from Shag freed her from the financial disaster divorce and no child support had wreaked, and left her able to concentrate on making it up to Meggie. And hopefully finding a way to help her daughter forget about Doug the way he'd clearly forgotten about her.

It was Ally's turn to change the subject. "Hey, do

you believe this place? It's even bigger than Shag let on.''

"If Daddy moved back to Denver, could we, too? So I could see him?" Meggie asked as if Ally hadn't said a word.

"That's one of those things we'd talk about if it ever happened."

"That means you don't think it will."

"I don't think you ought to think about it. I think you ought to be thinking about this terrific house and the big-screen television downstairs and having horses and all the fun we'll have making our new beginning."

"That man with the mustache didn't like us," Meggie informed flatly, as if it might have escaped her mother's notice.

"Jackson—that's Shag's oldest son. And he'll get used to us." *I hope.*

"He looked mean."

"Nooo, not mean. He's probably just a little gruff, like Shag was. It'll be fine."

"Shag said we should move up here, that it'd be good for me. Is that why he leaved you part of his will?"

"*Left.* And he didn't leave me part of his will, he left me part of everything he owned—the will was just the paper that said it. And yes, he did it because it was good for us both."

"So it's okay that we're here? Even though that mustache man might not want us in his house?"

"Yes, it's okay that we're here, because this isn't

only *his* house, it also belongs to us now. But if we don't like living with the mustache man, we'll build our own house.''

"But not where Daddy can't find us.''

"No, not where your daddy can't find you,'' Ally assured, sighing to herself and wondering if anything would ever get Meggie's mind off her absent father.

She stood and smoothed away her daughter's burnished curls to kiss her forehead. "It's late. You need to go to sleep. You know where my room is, right?"

"Across the hall.''

"If you need anything, just holler or come in there.'' Ally tapped the tip of her daughter's small, turned-up nose. "I love you. Sleep tight.''

"Mom?'' Meggie stopped her from leaving. "What are you gonna do here?''

Ally smiled. "I'm not sure. Maybe I'll open a restaurant or a catering business. Or maybe I'll just be a mom—Shag left us enough money to live even if I don't work.''

"I'd like you to just be a mom,'' Meggie said.

"Well, we'll see. But for right now, let's concentrate on getting settled in.''

Meggie wiggled to a comfortable spot amongst her bumper pad of dolls and stuffed animals, and finally closed her eyes. "See you in the morning.''

"See you in the morning.''

Ally slipped out the door, closing it behind her. But she didn't go straight across the hall to the room Beth had suggested she use. Her throat felt full of travel dust and the late August heat seemed to still be with her in spite of the coolness of the house. Something cold to drink was too appealing a thought to resist.

Well, she might have resisted it if Jackson Heller had been there. But since he wasn't, she decided to take Beth's advice to make herself at home.

The nearly silent hum of the air conditioner was the only sound in the whole place as she padded down the stairs and across a huge entryway, and stepped into the sunken living room with its three couches in a U around a square coffee table and the biggest television she'd ever seen.

Through the living room, she went into a connecting dining room and around a table large enough to seat a whole summit conference.

Then she pushed open the swinging door that led to the kitchen and stopped short.

Jackson Heller was standing at the refrigerator, one long arm draped over the open door, the other lying across the top as he peered inside. Clearly he hadn't heard her entrance, because he didn't budge.

Until that moment Ally hadn't realized how big a man he was. Six foot three if he was an inch, divided perfectly between long, jean-encased legs and a torso that grew like a symphony from a narrow waist to shoulders a mile wide, filling out a Western-style shirt better than the designer of it would ever have believed possible.

Ally considered sneaking out before he realized she was there, but just as the thought occurred to her, he must have sensed her presence, because he turned his head in her direction and caught her with those blue eyes.

Lord, but he was good-looking! Somehow, even though she'd noticed his eyes in the honky-tonk, she hadn't realized just how good-looking the rest of his face was. But it wasn't only his eyes that were strikingly gorgeous. This guy was drop-dead handsome.

He had thick hair the color of espresso, cropped short on the sides and longer on top. His brow was straight and square, his nose slightly long, slightly narrow, slightly pointed—what the romance novels she read called aquiline.

The mustache Meggie had noticed was full and well-groomed, not so much hiding his exquisitely shaped mouth as making it seem all the more intriguing. His cheeks dipped into hollows hammocked between chiseled cheekbones and a jawline sharp enough to slice bread, giving his face a rough-hewn ruggedness. And he had the same cleft in his chin that his father had had, the same one she'd noticed in his brother, only on Jackson Heller it was so sexy that every macho movie star in the world would have killed for it.

But handsome or not, he was no happier to see Ally in his kitchen than he had been to see her in the honky-tonk.

He slammed the refrigerator door closed without having taken anything from inside and faced her.

Showdown at the O.K. Corral Kitchen.

Salad shooters at the ready.

Oh, Lord, it must be late, Ally thought, *I'm getting goofy.*

She stood as tall as she could and met him eye to eye. "I came down for something to drink."

He just went on staring at her, his eyes boring into her like spears. "You sure as hell aren't what we expected," he finally said. "Never knew old Shag to dabble with a younger one."

"Excuse me?"

"I just want to know one thing." He poked his chin toward the ceiling. "Is that little girl up there our half sister?"

"Your half sister?" Ally repeated as what he was alluding to began to dawn on her. "You think Shag and I—"

"You were the mysterious lady friend he hightailed it to Denver to be with these last ten years."

Lady friend—he'd referred to her as that earlier, too, but only now did the meaning of it sink in. "No, I wasn't."

His eyes narrowed at her. "Don't play coy with me. I'm no ignorant country bumpkin. You slept your way into a quarter share of this ranch and I don't appreciate it. I don't give a damn about anything else that old man left you a part of—spending ten years cozied up with him earned it for you. But Linc and Beth and I paid our dues on this place being worked like dogs by that contrary cuss of a man, and if you think you can sashay in here as if it's some kind of resort where you can lie around the pool all day long while somebody waits on you, you have another think coming.''

"Now hold on," Ally said, her voice louder than she'd intended it to be, and just as stern and angry as his. "In the first place, Meggie is not your half sister and I didn't sleep my way into anything. Your father's *lady friend* was my mother and for the last ten years the relationship they shared was nothing as sleazy as you'd like to make it."

Jackson Heller merely went on goring her with his cornflower blue eyes.

Ally wanted to hit him. But instead she just continued. "As for Shag leaving me an equal share of his estate—I concede that you and your brother and sister have every right not to be thrilled by it. I was hoping you all wouldn't resent it and I'm sorry to find that even one of you does. But Shag's including me in his will was the kindest, most generous thing anyone has ever done for me and it just happens to have come at a time when I couldn't have needed it more, so if you think you're going to scare me into refusing anything, it's *you* who can think again."

"I told you, the only thing I give a damn about is the ranch. You're welcome to the rest. Hell, you're even welcome to stay in town if that's what you want to do—"

"Oh, thank you so much for your permission!"

"But you're not welcome on my ranch!"

"It's *our* ranch and I don't have to be welcome to be here."

They'd both been shouting and now he stopped.

But the quiet, barely suppressed rage in his voice was somehow worse. "I made an offer to buy you out through all those lawyers a few months back. I'll up it by five thousand dollars right now."

"I'll make you the same offer and you can go," she bluffed.

He saw it. "Don't make me think you're a fool."

No, for some reason she didn't want this man, of all men, to think of her that way. Though she didn't understand why it should matter. It did, however, change her tone to one more reasonable. "Look, I came here to live for a reason that doesn't have anything to do with money. I'm not leaving."

"Ten thousand more."

"A hundred thousand more, a million more—it wouldn't matter. Meggie and I are staying."

Oh, what an ugly look he gave her!

"Let me guess," he said with a sneer. "You have some damn television idea of what it's like to live on a ranch and you thought you'd come up here and have a little Western adventure. Or you've had a falling out with some desk jockey in Denver and you thought you'd show him, you'd just pack up and move. Or—"

"Don't make me think *you're* a fool to believe drivel like that," she countered.

Again their eyes locked in a stare-down.

"Fifteen thousand."

"I'm not going anywhere."

Unless of course he picked her up bodily and threw her out, which at that moment Ally thought was a possibility from the look of utter contempt he had on that incredible face of his. But incredible face—and body—or not, he was still the most disagreeable man she'd ever encountered and she didn't like him any better than he liked her.

Then, through clenched teeth, he said, "Why would you stay somewhere you're not wanted?"

"I have my reasons," she answered just as dourly, having no intention of confiding any more than that.

"There are no free rides with me," he threatened. "If you live here, you work here."

"I wouldn't have it any other way," she claimed, hoping she wasn't biting off more than she could chew. "And before you go around smearing verbal mud on my mother's good name again, you also had better know that *she* didn't *sleep* her way into my inheritance, either. Originally Shag had wanted her to be left the quarter share, because he genuinely loved her and wanted to provide for her should he die before she did. But she wouldn't hear of him leaving her anything at all. She didn't know until after his death, when the lawyer contacted me about the will, that he'd honored her wishes about herself and given it to me instead."

"And you're going to earn it," he said, the threat in his voice again. "Tomorrow I have to take some oilmen out to the wells on the farthest end of the ranch and I'll be gone until suppertime, so you have until the next day to rest up. And then—if you don't get smart and leave—you're mine."

Okay, so he did manage to send a shiver up her spine.

Still, Ally toughed it out, raising her chin to him as if accepting any challenge he could toss her way. "Fine," she said. "But there's one stipulation I have, too."

This time he lifted his chin at her, daring her to venture it.

"No matter what your feelings about me or my being here or your father's will, my daughter is not to be burdened by it. I was hoping to find that you were like Shag—kind, patient—"

"Shag, kind and patient? You must be out of your mind."

Ally had no intention of arguing that with him, too, though she was curious as to why he seemed to dislike his father so much. She went on as if he hadn't interrupted her. "My daughter has been through a lot in the last few years and I won't have any more inflicted on her. So I'm telling you here and now that you'd better watch your step around her."

"Who the hell do you think you're talkin' to, lady?" he shouted again.

"You," she shouted back. "Just keep your bad attitude clear of my daughter."

He let out a sound that was equal parts disgusted sigh, mirthless laugh, and disbelief at her audacity. But Ally wasn't going to let it bother her. Too much. Instead she turned and hit the swinging door she'd come through and left the kitchen in what she hoped was a blaze of righteous indignation, feeling those blue eyes on her the whole way.

Jerk! she thought. *Insufferable, rude, insulting, hot-headed jerk!* No wonder Shag had kept his connection with her mother and her and Meggie so completely separate from his life and family in Wyoming. He'd probably been embarrassed to let anyone know he was related to a person like that!

Yet Ally remembered Shag suggesting that she and Meggie might benefit from some time up here, so he couldn't have been hiding his oldest son. And in spite of him, he must have thought the good outweighed the bad.

Which was what Ally had to hope for. Because now that she had Meggie here, now that she'd talked herself blue in the face about how great this new beginning was for them, she couldn't just turn tail and run before giving it a chance. Regardless of Jackson Heller the Jerk.

She'd just have to comply with whatever he wanted her to do to *earn* their right to be here and hope he steered clear of Meggie.

No, she wouldn't *hope* he'd steer clear of Meggie. He'd *better* steer clear of her. Because if he so much as looked cross-eyed at her daughter, he might find himself with a rolling pin stuck up that romance-novel nose of his.

Ally climbed the steps and stormed into the room across the hall from where Meggie was, wondering what she'd gotten them into, praying that it wasn't yet another wrong turn she was taking with both their lives.

But even as she worried about it and cursed Jackson Heller for making this as difficult as he possibly could, she also wondered why it was that her recalcitrant mind kept flashing a mental picture of the to-die-for handsome face of that very same man.

With whom she now shared a home.

Chapter Two

Jackson was in no better temper when he got up the next morning just before dawn than he had been when he had gone to bed the night before. In fact, after spending more hours mentally rehashing his argument with Ally Brooks than sleeping, he was madder still as he stood in the spray of a steamy shower.

He had half a mind to post Lady, Go Home signs all through the house. *His* house. And Linc's and Beth's if they ever wanted to come back to live in it. But not some damn Denver woman's house.

About two in the morning he had conceded a couple of things. He believed she hadn't been Shag's lady friend, because his father just wasn't the type to play footsy with a woman young enough to be his daughter.

Which led to Jackson's second concession—that he might have been out of line to accuse Ally Brooks—or anyone else—of sleeping their way into the old man's will. Jackson of all people knew that Shag Heller had never in his life done a single thing he hadn't wanted to do, regardless of what anyone else tried to maneuver or finagle, and no matter what the relationship.

But it did sound like Shag to try to provide for the woman he'd been involved with for ten years, a woman he'd clearly had feelings for. And barring that, to leave what he had been determined to give her to her daughter.

Jackson turned off the water, yanked his towel from where it was slung over the shower door and dried off with punishingly angry strokes, too aggravated to feel any pain. Then he threw his towel into the hamper with a vengeance and went into his pitch-dark bedroom, turning on the light near the closet that held his clean shirts.

He hadn't been lying when he'd told Ally Brooks he didn't care that she'd inherited what she had—excluding the ranch. What Shag owned was Shag's to do with as he pleased, and not Jackson, Linc or Beth had been financially hurt by that fourth piece of the pie being served outside of the family.

But the ranch, that was something else again.

It was Jackson's whole life.

Linc and Beth had grown to hate the place, probably because of old Shag's harsh methods when it came to chores. To say he'd been a taskmaster was to soft-soap the reality of it. He'd worked all three of his children twice as hard as any of the ranch hands he was paying for the job, and often in the form of some pretty unreasonable punishments.

But for some reason Jackson didn't quite understand, the more he'd worked the place, the more he'd loved it.

Linc said he had mile-deep roots here and his brother was right. Deeper roots even than old Shag had had.

Their father had tired of the life. By the time he got Beth off to college, he'd been ready to wheel and deal and concentrate on the business end of things, so he'd turned the place over to Jackson.

Jackson had been twenty-two then and more than willing to take the reins. And for the past fifteen years there hadn't been a day he'd regretted it. Not a day he'd been sorry to rise with the sun, work in the heat or the cold, dirty his hands or break his back.

Beth thought he loved the ranch like a man loved a woman, but he thought it was more the way a man loved his only child. He fed it. He groomed it. He tended to its every need. He put his blood and sweat into it. He sacrificed for it. And never once had he resented it.

Not even when that sacrifice had nearly ripped his heart out....

He pulled on his boots, pushing away old memories as he did.

The point was, this place belonged to him and he belonged to it.

And no damn woman from Denver had any business walking in and claiming any part of it.

He was dressed by then and turned off the light to leave. As he did he was tempted to slam the bedroom door closed after himself, just for the sake of disturbing Ally Brooks. She'd disturbed him enough to have it coming, that was for damn sure.

A man needed a decent night's sleep when his day started before sunrise. He didn't need to be all riled up, tossing and turning, telling off a blasted woman in his mind. Plotting how the hell he was going to get rid of her. Devising jobs for her that were bad enough to match the worst old Shag had ever come up with.

Wondering if those crazy wild curls of her hair were as soft as they looked....

Damn, but she'd made him mad. First at her. Then at himself for thinking ridiculous things like that.

But he closed the door quietly rather than slamming it. Unlike his father, he wasn't usually given to fits of rage and he didn't like the way it felt. Didn't like giving in to it, and that's what slamming the door would have been.

Still, though, as he passed by Ally's room he muttered, "Take the money and get out of here," wishing she'd do just that.

His offer to buy her share of the ranch had been more than fair. That, on top of the rest of what she'd inherited could keep her in a Denver penthouse—or wherever else she wanted to be—for the rest of her life without her ever lifting a finger. So what was she doing here?

No doubt she had a fantasy of the place as some sort of dude ranch. Jackson could just imagine the brochure—*Life on the range. Horseback riding. Swimming. Napping in the shade of an old oak tree. Barbecuing under the stars of a Wyoming sky....*

Ha!

He supposed he'd given her credit for better sense than to think the ranch was like that. But why else would she have come here? Surely if she had had any idea of the reality of it, it would have been the last place on earth she'd have ever shown up.

And that's what he'd been counting on. Not in a million years had he thought the mystery woman in the will would actually take that part of the inheritance seriously enough to move here.

He'd figured on buying her out and never having to set eyes on her. Even when she'd turned down his offer through the lawyers, he'd thought it was just a ploy to raise the price—the way he'd done the night before, trying to get her out.

But no, here she was, moved in as if she belonged.

And giving orders!

Jackson was in the kitchen by then and he poured water into the coffeemaker with such disgust at that very thought that he splashed more on the counter than he got in the reservoir.

Damn woman had a lot of nerve to get on his back about how he was to treat her daughter. Where did

she come off jumping on him about being mean to
that child before he'd so much as spoken to the girl?

And she thought he had a bad attitude, did she?
Well, by God, he had a right to his attitude. How
would she like some stranger prancing into her life,
her house? Uninvited. Unwanted. Just showing up
and announcing she was there to live. And not only
her, but her and *a child*. Lock, stock and barrel.

And fiery hair. And sparkling Irish eyes. And one
of the sweetest little behinds...

Jackson shook himself out of *that* bit of mind wandering, wondering what was getting into him. It had
been happening ever since she'd walked into the
honky-tonk. Right in the middle of a full head of
steam his crazy brain would flash a picture of her. A
picture that was all too vivid and in more detail than
he had any business having noticed. Or remembering.

Damn her all to hell.

Well, he'd meant what he'd said about there not
being any free rides around here. He'd give her a taste
of what old Shag had dished out so heartily. Shag
nice? Shag had been as ornery as a grizzly bear. By
the time he'd finished with Linc, Beth and Jackson,
any one of them could run the ranch single-handedly.
And if this blasted woman wanted to live here, she
was going to learn what it was all about, too. From
the ground up.

As Jackson watched coffee as black as coal tar drip
into the pot, he realized that the more he thought
about putting that mouthy little woman to work, the
more the idea appealed to him. Dirt and grime and

dust. Manure and chicken droppings. Sweat and blisters and backaches to beat the band.

Oh, she was in for it. If he had to have her here, he was going to have some fun with it.

"We'll just see how long you want to stay when you find out it's no picnic."

No sirree. Sweet little behind or no sweet little behind, he was going to work it right off and relish every minute of it.

Every single, solitary minute of it.

And in the meantime, he'd just have to find a way to get the image of that particular backside out of his mind....

After traveling, getting in late, arguing with Jackson Heller and then stewing about it until the wee hours of the morning, Ally slept late. Luckily, so did Meggie, who slipped into her bedroom at eleven and finally woke her.

"I don't hear anybody else in the house," the little girl whispered as she climbed onto Ally's bed.

"Jackson had to go somewhere," Ally told her in a normal voice. "We'll have the place to ourselves for the day. I thought we could explore, get to know our way around, and then maybe swim after a while."

"Did you ask if it was okay?"

"Of course it's okay. We aren't going to do anything but look around and swim," Ally answered with a laugh, although she was beginning to wonder if being here at all was okay. Still, she couldn't show that concern to her daughter. "Go get dressed. I need to call your grandmother and give her the phone number up here. Then we'll see about something to eat.''

''Remind Grandma to give the number to Daddy if he calls.''

''I will,'' Ally assured, biting back the urge to warn her daughter not to get her hopes up. Again. Instead she said, ''Make your bed,'' and sent Meggie back across the hall.

Twenty minutes later Ally had left the message on her mother's answering machine, dressed in her swimming suit, a pair of tennis shorts and a big shirt that covered it all, and had made her own bed.

Breakfast was just cereal and milk, and while Meggie dawdled over hers, Ally checked out the kitchen.

Like every room in the house, it was huge, open, airy and more functional than fashionable.

Navy blue tile made up the countertops and back splashes. White cupboards lined three of the four walls; the matching appliances were all commercial size, though not industrial looking. Only the eight-burner stove and two ovens were stainless steel, but the mammoth cooking center was recessed in a cove all its own and was hardly unsightly.

In the center of the room was a butcher block large enough to hold a side of beef, and off to one end was a breakfast nook that would easily seat twelve.

To Ally's chef's eye, the place was a dream. Until she opened the cupboards and discovered only rudimentary pots, pans and utensils, and nary a Cuisinart to be found.

If she stayed she'd have to send for hers.

GET 2 BOOKS FREE!

®

To get your 2 free books, affix this peel-off sticker to the reply card and mail it today!

MIRA® Books, The Brightest Stars in Fiction, presents

The *Best* of the *Best*™

Superb collector's editions of the very best novels by some of today's best-known authors!

★ **FREE BOOKS!** To introduce you to "The Best of the Best" we'll send you 2 books ABSOLUTELY FREE!

★ **FREE GIFT!** Get an exciting mystery gift FREE!

★ **BEST BOOKS!** "The Best of the Best" brings you the best books by some of today's most popular authors!

GET 2

HOW TO GET YOUR
2 FREE BOOKS AND FREE GIFT!

1. Peel off the MIRA sticker on the front cover. Place it in the space provided at right. This automatically entitles you to receive two free books and an exciting mystery gift.

2. Send back this card and you'll get 2 "The Best of the Best™" novels. These books have a combined cover price of $11.00 or more in the U.S. and $13.00 or more in Canada, but they are yours to keep absolutely FREE!

3. There's <u>no</u> catch. You're under <u>no</u> obligation to buy anything. We charge nothing – ZERO – for your first shipment. And you don't have to make any minimum number of purchases – not even one!

4. We call this line "The Best of the Best" because each month you'll receive the best books by some of today's hottest authors. These authors show up time and time again on all the major bestseller lists and their books sell out as soon as they hit the stores. You'll like the convenience of getting them delivered to your home at our special discount prices . . . and you'll love your *Heart to Heart* subscriber newsletter featuring author news, horoscopes, recipes, book reviews and much more!

5. We hope that after receiving your free books you'll want to remain a subscriber. But the choice is yours – to continue or cancel, anytime at all! So why not take us up on our invitation, with no risk of any kind. You'll be glad you did!

6. And remember…we'll send you a mystery gift ABSOLUTELY FREE just for giving "The Best of the Best" a try.

SPECIAL FREE GIFT!

We'll send you a fabulous surprise gift, absolutely FREE, simply for accepting our no-risk offer!

Visit us online at
www.mirabooks.com

® and TM are trademarks of Harlequin Enterprises Limited.

BOOKS FREE!

Hurry!

Return this card
promptly to
**GET 2 FREE
BOOKS &
A FREE GIFT!**

▼ DETACH AND MAIL CARD TODAY! ▼

Affix
peel-off
MIRA
sticker here

YES! Please send me the
2 FREE "The Best of the Best"
novels and FREE gift for which
I qualify. I understand that
I am under no obligation to
purchase anything further, as
explained on the opposite page.

(P-BB3-01)

385 MDL C6PQ   **185 MDL C6PP**

NAME   (PLEASE PRINT CLEARLY)

ADDRESS

APT.#   CITY

STATE/PROV.   ZIP/POSTAL CODE

Offer limited to one per household and not valid to current subscribers of "The Best of the Best." All orders subject to approval. Books received may vary.
©1995 MIRA BOOKS

The Best of the Best™ — Here's How it Works:

Accepting your 2 free books and gift places you under no obligation to buy anything. You may keep the books and gift and return the shipping statement marked "cancel." If you do not cancel, about a month later we will send you 4 additional novels and bill you just $4.24 each in the U.S., or $4.74 each in Canada, plus 25¢ shipping & handling per book and applicable taxes if any.* That's the complete price and — compared to cover prices of $5.50 or more each in the U.S. and $6.50 or more each in Canada — it's quite a bargain! You may cancel at any time, but if you choose to continue, every month we'll send you 4 more books, which you may either purchase at the discount price or return to us and cancel your subscription.

*Terms and prices subject to change without notice. Sales tax applicable in N.Y. Canadian residents will be charged applicable provincial taxes and GST.

If offer card is missing write to: The Best of the Best, 3010 Walden Ave., P.O. Box 1867, Buffalo, NY 14240-1867

BUSINESS REPLY MAIL

FIRST-CLASS MAIL   PERMIT NO. 717   BUFFALO, NY

POSTAGE WILL BE PAID BY ADDRESSEE

THE BEST OF THE BEST
3010 WALDEN AVE
PO BOX 1867
BUFFALO NY 14240-9952

NO POSTAGE
NECESSARY
IF MAILED
IN THE
UNITED STATES

If?

That thought surprised her, for it was the first time she'd seriously doubted that she would make her home here. She'd considered this move permanent. The new beginning she'd promised Meggie and herself. She'd thought it only a matter of time and seeing what she needed and didn't need up here before she definitely sent for her things.

The fact that she was hedging now made her realize just how intimidated she'd actually been by Jackson Heller. This was not something she was happy to acknowledge even to herself. And certainly not something she'd give in to.

"Let's take a look outside," she suggested to Meggie then, as if familiarizing themselves with the place would remind her that she'd come here intent on making this more than just a lark she could be scared away from.

The house itself was a two-story H-shaped structure built like a mountain cabin of split logs and mortar. Within the rear arms of that H began what yawned into four hundred square feet of brick-paved patio with enough tables, lawn chairs and loungers to service a large garden party.

There was also a net hammock to one side and an enormous bricked-in barbecue with a pit next to it that Ally warned Meggie to stay away from when she suffered a mother's paranoid vision of her child falling into it.

Beyond the patio was the pool, predictably as large as any public one around. To the east was the former bunkhouse Beth had pointed out the night before from the sliding doors off the kitchen. She'd explained that after some quick and extensive remodeling, it had been turned into the home she and her Native American husband had moved into only in the past few days.

Beside that was a much smaller house Ally imagined was a guest cottage, and—at some distance farther out—there was a barn, a pigsty, an extensive chicken coop, several paddocks where a number of horses grazed peacefully, and a windmill that turned eagerly against the hot breeze that was blowing as Ally and Meggie headed in that direction.

The main house, the cottage, the patio and pool and even the renovated bunkhouse could have been on any highbrow estate playing at being rustic without actually accomplishing it. But the barn and everything around it, though well tended, left no doubt that this was a working ranch. And in the temperatures of that late August day, the smells that greeted them let them know it for sure.

"P-yew," Meggie said as they approached the barn, its great doors open wide.

"Animals and the scents that go with them on a sweltering summer day," Ally informed.

"Camp wasn't like this."

The camp her daughter referred to was one they'd just spent two months at before coming here—another of Ally's attempts to raise Meggie's spirits. Ally had accepted a job as the camp cook in order for Meggie to be able to go while Shag's will was in probate.

"We were in the mountains where it was a whole lot cooler and we never really got near the stables. The horses were always brought to us, remember?"

But before they headed into the barn where a long center separated a dozen stalls on either side, Meggie spotted a filly in the adjoining paddock and veered off in that direction, apparently forgetting her complaint about nature's odors.

They spent nearly two hours on that area of the property, going from horses to cows to pigs to chickens to goats, as if they were at the zoo. When they finally did check out the barn, they even happened upon a box in one corner where a mother cat and four kittens had residence.

By that time Meggie had brightened somewhat and stopped shooting furtive glances around as if they were thieves in the night who might be caught at any moment, even though they never saw anyone at all.

And when her daughter dropped to her knees to play with the kittens, for just a moment Ally had a brief glimpse of the little girl Meggie had been before the divorce. It reminded her why they'd come here and gave her a renewed sense of determination not to let Jackson or his threats frighten her off.

Back at the house Ally made sandwiches while Meggie fretted over their eating Jackson's food. Ally assured her that, as soon as Shag's son got home, she would discuss with him providing for her and Meggie's share of things like that.

Then Ally filled two glasses with ice and tea, and

took it all outside onto the patio, where they passed what was left of the afternoon.

Only as it neared five o'clock did Ally begin to consider that Jackson could be back anytime, and since she didn't want to be caught lounging next to the pool as if this were some kind of resort, she herded Meggie inside for a shower and a change of clothes for them both.

Ally was just getting dressed in a pair of khaki shorts and a yellow T-shirt after her shower when she heard the sound of a helicopter very nearby. Having lived her life until then in the suburbs, the first thing she thought was that it was a hospital flight-for-life. She rushed to the window just as it landed on a square of tarmac to the west of the house, a patch she'd noticed earlier and somehow thought might be the beginnings of a tennis court.

But the tarmac was a landing pad and the helicopter was not medical. It was private.

And as she took a closer look, she realized Jackson was the pilot.

She didn't know why she kept on standing there, watching as he flipped switches and turned knobs on the panel control in front of him, but she did. She didn't move when he climbed out of the aircraft, either.

Tall and terrifically handsome, there was something very commanding about him. He wore sunglasses that lent a dashing, dangerous air to his appearance, and a white dress shirt that almost made him seem more like an executive than a cowboy—except that the sleeves were rolled to his elbows, the collar button was open rakishly, and no self-respecting executive would have been caught dead on the job in his tight jeans and roach-killer boots.

Of course, Ally had never seen an executive who could do for a pair of jeans what Jackson Heller could. His legs were long and so thickly muscled they bulged against the denim. His hips were narrow but not so narrow that they were slight. And the outward curve of his zipper stirred up things inside of her that hadn't been stirred up in a long time.

Ally wondered at that fact. At herself for being stuck to the window like glue, studying the way he walked—smooth, graceful, confident, and with just a hint of swagger to the slightly bowlegged gait.

She ordered herself to move away, to stop gawking like a hormonal teenager who'd never seen a man with quite that much raw masculinity and just plain sensuality oozing out of his every pore.

But there she stayed, anyway.

It was just curiosity, she reasoned. Purely academic. It wasn't as if she were really interested. Or mesmerized. She was only appreciating the sight the way any red-blooded woman would have.

It didn't mean anything. Good-looking or not, Jackson Heller was too unpleasant and difficult for her to enjoy anything *but* the sight of him. And Lord knows, she would not have been in the market for a relationship even if Jackson had been different. Her hands were full trying to get Meggie through the divorce residual, trying to get both their lives back on course.

The last thing Ally needed, wanted or would even entertain thoughts of was any kind of involvement with a man, even a man who *wasn't* as cantankerous as Jackson Heller.

No, she told herself as she watched him step around the barbecue pit, this was just a bit of voyeurism. She was still human, after all, and cantankerous or not, he was a gorgeous hunk of manhood. She just didn't want anything more than the sight. At a safe distance. When he didn't know she was looking.

And when she was out of the range of his temper.

The bedroom door opened just then and Ally spun away from the window as if she'd been caught doing something she shouldn't be. She expected to find Meggie, but instead a tiny little boy stood there solemn faced, reminding her suddenly of the very person she'd been spying on.

"'Lo," he said in a serious voice.

"Hi," Ally answered with a note of question to it.

"I'm Danny. We comed for supper and there's a girl in my room and this one was my dad's 'fore we went to live at Kansas's," he informed, sounding almost as put out as Jackson about Meggie and Ally having trespassed on territory he considered his own.

Meggie came up behind the smaller child just then and said in a hushed aside aimed at Ally, "He just walked in!"

Ally nodded to her daughter and smiled at Danny. "Your dad is Linc, isn't he?"

Danny nodded in return, slowly, stoically. "Who're you guys?"

Ally introduced herself and Meggie, and as if that made it all right for them to be there, Danny took an arrowhead out of his pocket and held it for them to see. "This makes me strong. My uncle Ash gave it to me and he's downstairs, too, wis my aunt Beth and uncle Jackson and my Kansas and they're all wonderin' where you are."

With the exception of Jackson, the rest of the Hellers must have arrived while Ally was in the shower, because she hadn't heard anything. It had been bad enough to think of having another confrontation with Jackson alone, but now she wondered if they'd formed some sort of joint force with which to face her.

Maybe Jackson had managed to win them over to his side and they were all waiting downstairs to tell her she'd better accept his offer and leave, or face the wrath of the whole family circle.

Ally's stomach lurched at the prospect, but she forced another smile for Shag's grandson and said, "Then I guess we'd better go downstairs so they can stop wondering."

Whether for her own reasons or because she sensed her mother's uneasiness, Meggie had suddenly lost the blush of color the day had put into her cheeks, and her hazel eyes were wide. Wanting to spare her daughter any scene that might be about to unfold, she suggested Meggie and Danny go out the front door and around to the barn to see the kittens.

Meggie hesitated, clearly wanting to escape but worried about leaving Ally alone, so Ally turned her by the shoulders and gave her a little push. "Everything will be fine," she assured in a tone that sounded as if she were convinced of it.

Then she followed the two kids down the stairs and watched them go outside before she headed for the kitchen where the sounds of Heller voices drifted out.

As she approached the swinging door, she overheard Linc say something about Jackson yawning, teasing him over not sleeping well the night before. All she could make out of Jackson's reply was something about "that damn woman."

Ally took a deep breath, squared her shoulders and went in—*that damn woman* trying to look as if she were ready, willing and able to take them all on.

But when everyone looked at her from various spots around the kitchen, four of the five expressions were just as warm and friendly as they'd been the night before, dispelling her fear of what she was about to face.

Only Jackson scowled at her.

But somehow that had more effect than the rest combined.

"There you are!" Beth said. "I was just going upstairs to get you. We thought we'd throw together a little supper while we got to know each other."

"Great," Ally said, hating the tentative tone in her voice and amending it. "I just met Danny."

"Is that where he got off to?" Linc mused. "What'd he do, go tell you to get yourself down here?"

"Something like that." Ally answered Linc's smile

with one of her own to assure him she hadn't taken offense. "Is he always so sober and serious?" she asked, her gaze skirting over to Jackson as if the question were about him. Which it actually could have been.

Still, she was trying to pretend he wasn't there and that those blue eyes of his weren't boring into her as if he wanted to boot her out of his kitchen, his house, his life. Literally.

Linc slapped his brother on the back much the way he had the night before. "Danny and Jackson here— the old and the young version of sober and serious— that's them, all right."

Jackson turned his scowl on Linc for a moment, then went to the refrigerator to get himself a beer.

Ally noticed he didn't offer her anything to drink as courtesy might have dictated.

Kansas must have noticed, too, because she jumped in and did.

Since everyone except Beth was drinking beer, too, Ally accepted one of those before peering at the foodstuffs that were on the butcher block now that several grocery sacks had been emptied and everyone had gathered around it.

"What can I do?"

"Know how to make guacamole?" Beth asked.

Ally smiled. "A pretty good one, actually."

"Then you can have the job."

Ash piped in. "We're having burritos with Jackson's green chili. It isn't for sissies," he warned as if he'd had a previous surprise with that dish himself.

On cue, Jackson took a container out of the freezer and put it into the microwave, waiting there as it thawed rather than joining the group.

Ally tried to ignore him and the fact that she could feel that fierce stare on her again from off her right shoulder, and instead searched for a subject on which to make conversation as she peeled ripe avocados.

She knew a lot about Shag's children. At least about their lives up until his death. He'd talked freely about Beth being married to an Indian who owned and oversaw a charitable foundation for Native Americans. About Linc riding rodeo and having lost his wife, Virgie, to a car accident just weeks after Danny was born.

She even knew Jackson had been married young and very briefly, then divorced—though she didn't know any of the details. What Shag hadn't said was how unpleasant Jackson was and she wondered if the divorce was what had made him such a hard case. Or maybe his being such a hard case had driven his wife away....

But rather than address that part of her curiosity, she decided to update herself on the other changes that had apparently taken place in the Heller clan since their father's death.

She started with Beth and the most obvious question. "When is your baby due?"

"We aren't sure," Beth answered with a laugh.

Ash chuckled from beside his wife as he chopped onions. "Approximately nine months from just before we got divorced."

"Or about three months from when we got remarried," Beth added as the two of them seemed to share a private joke.

"What that translates to," Kansas added, "is that the baby is probably due in about a month. As close as anyone can tell."

"Shag said you lived on the Wind River Reservation, so I didn't expect to find you here," Ally said to Beth and Ash again, wondering suddenly if the reason they'd remodeled the bunkhouse was because Jackson had been so difficult to live with when they'd made the move.

"I came back right after the divorce," Beth told her. "Ash followed three weeks later and when we worked things out between us, we decided to stay."

"But not here in the house..." It was a leading statement, though Ally carefully didn't glance at the still-staring man who was uppermost in her mind even when she was among these other people and he was keeping himself removed from them all.

"We wanted our own place," Ash said, giving no clue as to whether or not his surly brother-in-law was the reason.

Linc asked what she needed for the guacamole and brought the spices, lemons, limes, sour cream, tomatoes and Tabasco sauce for her.

"And how about you and Kansas? You guys can't have been married long," Ally said then, beginning to feel as if she were catching up on old acquaintances.

"Since the Fourth of July," Kansas answered, standing on tiptoe to kiss her husband's cheek.

"Kansas owns the general store, so anything you need she either has or can get for you," Beth informed.

"And Linc rides in rodeos," Ally added what she knew.

Or what she thought she knew until Linc said, "Not anymore. Now I'm running that honky-tonk you walked into last night. Which, by the way, you also own a share of, since the building was part of what we all inherited."

He dipped a chip into her guacamole just as she finished it and went into rapture—eyes rolling, face scrunched up blissfully, moaning like a lovesick cow. "That's incredible!"

Ally laughed. "*That's* what *I* do."

"Make avocado dip?" This from Ash.

"Cook. Actually, I'm a chef," she said with exaggerated flair to let them know she didn't take herself as seriously as the formal title might have seemed.

"Hear that, Jackson?" Linc called as if his brother were a mile away rather than a few feet. "A genuine chef right under your own roof. I'll tell you, the honky-tonk could use somebody who can make guacamole like this. Jackson? You with us?" he asked when the other man didn't respond.

Then, in the silence that followed, the slow purposeful sound of Jackson's heels on the tile floor warned of his approach. He came to stand directly across the butcher block from Ally, bracing both hands on the table and leaning toward her as if he'd have pressed his nose to hers if he'd been able to, just to be more menacing.

Showdown II.

He glared at her as he answered his brother. "I think that's a fine idea. She can get a place in town, cook for The Buckin' Bronco and live real well on what I'll pay to buy out her share of the ranch."

Ally stared back at him, meeting him eye to eye, stubbornness to stubbornness, and also spoke to Linc without breaking the standoff. "I'd love to cook for the honky-tonk. But I came to live at the ranch and I'd still live here even if I did. I wouldn't think of moving into town *or* selling out," she said pointedly, firmly.

"Live here, work here," Jackson warned.

"And I'll bet you have all kinds of plans for that, don't you?" she heard herself say with more courage than she felt and too much challenge to be smart.

He didn't answer her, leaving another tense silence to hang there between them. Around them.

Ally wondered how it was possible that under those circumstances she could be noticing every rugged plane of that handsome face and feeling some of the same stirrings she'd felt watching him from her bedroom window earlier.

Then that great face, which looked as if nature itself had carved it, slowly eased into a small smile.

Not a nice smile. But one that sent shivers up her spine.

He looked at her as if she were a rabbit in a cage and she had the distinct impression that he was going to enjoy meting out the rough time he had in store for her.

Ally reminded herself that she'd come here for Meggie's sake. That already—in just this one day—she'd glimpsed a little of what she hoped this place would accomplish in giving her daughter back her childhood. And for the second time since she'd arrived she told herself she could handle anything in order to do that.

Finally it was Linc who broke the silence and some of the tension in the room by laughing at Jackson, slapping him on the back yet again and saying to Ally, "Don't let him buffalo you. If you knew Shag and could put up with him, you can put up with old Jackson here."

But *old Jackson* just went right on staring at her, smiling that smile.

And Ally got the message loud and clear: *Don't be too sure.*

The evening turned out to be pretty pleasant once Ally managed to get used to Jackson's ever-present glare. He kept to himself otherwise, and Linc, Kansas, Beth and Ash were all good company.

By the time they left, around nine, Ally felt as if she'd known them forever and could count them as friends.

Meggie had spent most of the time watching an animated movie with Danny, but once everyone had said good-night and gone, Ally told her to go upstairs and get ready for bed.

"Not yet," Jackson vetoed from behind, having followed her in from the front door after seeing Linc, Kansas and Danny off.

"What?" she asked, glancing over her shoulder at him.

"There are some people the two of you have to meet and then I'll show Meggie the chores she'll need to do tomorrow while we're off working."

It took a moment for all of that to register and for Ally to choose which to take issue with first. "Whatever work I do, Meggie will need to be with me."

"No, ma'am, she won't. The people you're about to meet are Hans and Marta. Marta does the housekeeping here and Hans takes care of the grounds and the handiwork close to home. They'll look after the girl while we're gone, make sure she's doing what she's supposed to."

Issue number two.

Ally turned to face him. "I'll do what you feel is necessary to *earn our keep*, as you put it, but Meggie—"

"It's okay, Mom," Meggie interrupted, suddenly at Ally's side, sounding worried and as if she were feeling responsible for smoothing the waters. "I can do chores. I fed Grandma's cat before, remember?"

Ally put her arm around her daughter's shoulders and hugged her close, besting Jackson with a glare fiercer than he'd given her all night. She didn't say anything else. Not then, with Meggie there. But Jackson Heller had not heard the end of this. Not by a long shot.

He ignored what her expression conveyed and turned toward the kitchen, saying as he went, ''Hans and Marta went into Cheyenne today but I saw them coming back as Beth and Ash left. We'd best get over there before they turn in for the night.''

Apparently that meant Ally and Meggie were to follow him, which Meggie was quicker to do than Ally. Ally might have just stood there staring daggers at his broad back except that her daughter took her hand and dragged her along.

The small cottage Ally had thought was a guest house was where the two caretakers lived. Marta and Hans were well into retirement years and seemed more like resident grandparents than employees.

Hans was thin, wiry and bald on top; he slipped his dentures in as Marta welcomed them into their home. She was as wide as she was tall—but agile in spite of it—with rosy red cheeks, white hair cut like an inverted bowl, and kind, jolly eyes.

There was an underlying tone of joyousness to her high voice as she asked Meggie what kind of things she liked to eat for lunches when Jackson informed her she was to look after the little girl during the days while he and Ally worked.

The older woman seemed to view the news as a gift that delighted her and Meggie responded to that, warming up to her, and to Hans's teasing, too.

Ally only hoped her daughter wasn't just putting a

good face on things to keep the tension with Jackson down to a minimum.

They didn't stay but a few minutes before leaving Hans and Marta to go to bed. From there Jackson led the way to the chicken coop while explaining to Meggie that one of her daily chores would be to feed the chickens, gather eggs and bring them to Marta.

"Meggie is just a little girl," Ally warned from behind the two of them, trying again to make it clear she didn't want her daughter to have to do this.

"On a ranch even little girls work," Jackson informed in a tone of voice more even and equable than Ally's had been.

Meggie shot her a look that begged her not to make waves, and again Ally put off further argument as Jackson showed her daughter what to do.

Ally watched like a hawk, staying close to Meggie, ready to swoop should Jackson take one step out of bounds.

But, to her surprise, what she witnessed was patient tutelage that even she couldn't find fault with.

In spite of that, she was still bristling when they left the chicken coop. "Are you finished?" she demanded of him.

"For tonight. There'll be more she'll need to do tomorrow and along the way. Plus whatever Hans and Marta need help with."

Ally turned to Meggie. "Go on up to the house, honey, and get ready for bed. I'll be there to tuck you in in just a few minutes."

Meggie glanced from Ally to Jackson and back

again, but in the end she left them without another word.

Ally watched her go, waiting until her daughter had slipped through the sliding doors into the kitchen before turning to Jackson in the white glow of moonlight.

He was having his turn at watching her again, his weight more on one hip than the other, his arms crossed over his chest, his expression daring her to come at him with all she had.

"Meggie is not your slave and you are not to order her around."

One bushy eyebrow arched. "Doing chores doesn't make anybody a slave."

"I didn't bring her up here to work. What I do will have to count for us both."

"No, ma'am, it won't. I don't give a damn what any piece of paper says about your owning this place. I run it and if you want to live on it, you—and your daughter—will do what I say in regards to it. Gathering eggs and feeding chickens and anything I set that child to do, she'll do. Just the same as you'll do what I tell you to do or neither of you will stay. Understood?"

"I understand that you'd better not—for a single second—forget that Meggie is my daughter and that our living here does not give you any authority over her."

"As far as the ranch goes, I have full authority. I'll set her to doing chores and I'll speak up about anything else I need to speak up about when it comes to that. But beyond what she does for her keep is your business.''

If Ally hadn't seen his patience with her daughter a moment earlier she might have thought that he intended to mistreat Meggie to drive them off. But there hadn't been anything abusive in his actions. And since her daughter had seemed willing to comply, and gathering a few eggs and feeding some chickens was not a huge, hard job, she supposed it was possible she might be jumping the gun slightly to be so angry over it all.

She decided to reserve judgment on what he might be up to. Temporarily. But she would still keep close tabs on what he required of Meggie and how he acted toward her.

First, though, another warning.

''Bear in mind that you can push this only so far. I'm cooperating because I realize we've come into your domain. But legally I don't really have to. We can be here, on our share of this place, doing anything we please, whether you like it or not.''

Wow! She'd surprised herself. She sounded every bit as tough as he did.

At least to her own ears.

Apparently it hadn't had quite the same potency to his, because there was that smile again—the one he'd shown her at the beginning of the evening. The one that said she was really in for it and that if she thought she could avoid anything she was mistaken.

''Five o'clock tomorrow morning,'' he said. ''Be ready to move cattle. I have a herd needs to get to a pasture with more grass on it. You can ride a horse, can't you?''

"As a matter of fact, I can." Though she didn't tell him that she'd learned just a few weeks ago at camp and that she had ridden only on timid ponies that never went faster than a sightseer's walk.

He looked dubious but only eyed her up and down with a slow, steady gaze that seemed to take in every inch of her. "You'll need to dress in something different than what you're wearing. Jeans. No shorts. No sandals. Wear socks."

She considered snapping to attention and saluting him but thought better of it. She had enough to deal with, just fighting the unwelcome and wholly surprising rush of her blood through her veins, the sense that she could actually feel heat from the gaze he'd rolled over her.

"And you'd better do somethin' else with all this," he added, reaching to catch a long, curly strand of her hair between his fingers. "Tie it up off your neck or you'll die of the heat."

Had his voice grown slower, thicker, huskier? Or was it just that Ally heard it that way through some very confusing emotions that suddenly popped up inside of her at even that small contact?

Let go! she ordered. But only in her mind. Somehow the words didn't go beyond that, and instead she found herself looking up into the shadow of his eyes, too aware of the way the moonlight kissed the hollows of his cheeks, christened the sharp rise of his cheekbones and dusted his mustache. The mustache that made his mouth so intriguing....

Ally pulled back, realizing only as she did that they'd somehow moved closer together, that she was suddenly not too far away from that mustached mouth.

Oh, Lord.

"I've been dressing myself for some time now, and I think I can figure out what to do with my own hair," she snapped, though it lacked the bite she'd meant for it to have.

He'd lost the smile she was coming to think of as sinister and seemed as taken aback as she was by the currents that had passed between them.

After her comment, his smile slid into place again.

He shrugged a broad, powerful shoulder to let her know he'd only been offering a suggestion, that he didn't really care whether she took it or not, or what consequences she might suffer if she didn't.

"At 5:00 a.m. Sharp. And that doesn't mean that's what time you get yourself out of bed. That means you're downstairs, dressed and ready to go then."

"I'll be there." She sneered back at him, turning around and following the same path her daughter had to the house as he stayed right where he was.

The whole way she could feel Jackson's gaze on her as surely as she'd watched Meggie. Well, if he was looking for some sign that he'd cowed or frightened her, he was going to be disappointed. She kept her back straight as a board and her walk confident.

But internally she was a mass of jelly, though not

over the prospect of being ready to work at five in the morning or of wondering what that work might entail.

What had left her quivering inside was that moment when he'd held her hair and she'd been drawn to him.

That same moment when she must have lost her mind.

Because for just a split second she'd actually had a flash of curiosity about what it might have felt like to melt into his arms....

Chapter Three

Ally was not a morning person and when she left her bedroom at 5:00 a.m. on the dot the next day, her doubts about being at the ranch were at an all-time high.

A small house in Elk Creek without a resident tyrant who ordered her up before the sun, cooking at the honky-tonk—all seemed vastly more appealing.

But that wouldn't have been too different from what she'd left behind, and then Meggie wouldn't be around the animals she loved and have the advantages of the ranch, which was why they'd come in the first place, so Ally discarded the notion of calling ranch life quits before it had even begun.

Besides, she thought on her way downstairs, wouldn't Jackson have a heyday over her being shooed away by something as minor as one crack-of-dawn day!

And she was not about to give him the satisfaction.

He was already in the kitchen when she got there. Dressed in worn jeans and a chambray shirt with the sleeves rolled up above his elbows, he looked ready for work and ruggedly terrific.

Ally forced herself to think about something else. Like the ground coffee beans he was pouring straight from the can without measuring.

"Are you making mud?" she asked, her grumpiness echoing in her voice.

He glanced at her from the corner of his eye, slowly, steadily, clearly accustomed to the hour and unperturbed by her mood.

And in that instant she had a flood of realization about him—the satisfaction she'd thought to deny him had been, instead, accomplished when she'd shown her temper. It told him he was getting to her and he liked that.

So, of course, she decided on the spot that he'd seen the last of it.

"Why don't you let me make the coffee?" she suggested, if not bright and cheery, at least almost congenial.

"That's right, you're a *chef.* Guess you ought to be doing all the cooking." He stepped away from the coffeemaker and swept a hand toward it as an invitation to have at it.

Ally dumped all the ground beans back into the can and started over, measuring them this time and then adding vanilla to them before starting the machine.

As she did she suffered Jackson's unrelenting stare that seemed to assess her jeans, T-shirt, and hair piled atop her head and held there by an elastic ruffle.

Apparently he couldn't find fault with anything because after a while he went to the butcher block and swung a leg over one of the stools there.

"Change of plans," he said then. "On my way in from the chicken coop last night Ash came out and asked if I'd help him move some furniture this morning. So we won't be heading out for the cattle until I'm done with that."

Ally took a quick glance through the window above the sink and found that Beth's place was still dark. Which meant that Ally was up this early for no good reason, and that Jackson had known last night that she didn't need to be and could have let her sleep awhile longer.

She fought the urge to vent her aggravation at that fact and demand to know what she was supposed to do until he needed her. Instead she said, "I think I'll go back to bed, then."

He shook his head and chuckled as if she were out of her mind. "Not when you have my breakfast to fix and lunch to pack for us all."

"Us all?"

"There'll be four ranch hands working with us. Figure three sandwiches a man. Plus whatever else *chefs* rustle up for midday meals."

He was trying to get her goat every time he said

chef, because he made it sound like a joke. And while Ally had slightly mocked the title herself the night before, she hadn't done it disparagingly. Which was the way he did it.

Still, she was not going to let him see that he was succeeding in goading her.

"And for breakfast?" she asked as if she were the waitress and he the customer.

"Bacon, eggs, hash browns, toast. The bacon and potatoes both crisp. Eggs over easy. Toast light, plenty of butter. Tabasco on the side for the eggs," he answered as if he were, indeed, in a restaurant.

"Will I be needing to go out and slice the bacon off the hoof, coax the chickens to lay the eggs, pick the potatoes, and bake the bread first?"

Apparently she'd actually amused him with that bit of facetiousness, because a genuine smile came very near to slipping out before he checked it.

Still, Ally had seen enough to know that a smile made the corners of his eyes crease and tilted one side of his mouth more than the other.

It also had the oddest ability to warm her from the inside out....

"You should find everything in the fridge. This time," he answered as if those things she'd only been joking about were possibilities for the future.

But then it occurred to her that anything was possible for the future, since she didn't have the foggiest idea what living and working here would really entail.

"Does every day start this early?" she asked conversationally as she took what she needed from the refrigerator and began making breakfast.

"I sleep in until six now and then," he answered matter-of-factly enough for her to believe he was being honest and not just trying to paint a worse picture for her benefit.

Then, as if he couldn't sit still anymore, he got up, put place settings on the butcher block, and made the toast while she cooked everything else at once on a huge griddle.

"You don't want to be out working in the worst heat of the day if you can help it," he informed her as he did. "It's better to get going in the coolest hours. Plus, there's always so much to do on a spread like this one, there's no time to waste lying in bed."

"And what about weekends? Holidays?"

"There are still chores. Animals need food and water and lookin' after no matter what day it is."

"Is that what I'll be doing—looking after animals?" she ventured cautiously, hoping to avoid more of his you'll-do-anything-I-tell-you-to-do bluster.

Maybe it was the early hour or the quiet intimacy of the kitchen, but he answered her civilly, straightforwardly. "You'll be doing everything I do, or would do if I didn't have your help."

"Which involves?"

"Too many things to talk about. You'll see as we go along."

"But it won't be nice," she guessed.

He shrugged and poured two cups of coffee while

Ally filled their plates, and they both sat on stools at the butcher block and began to eat.

"Guess that all depends on what you consider *nice*," he answered. "Along with the everyday chores and upkeep and care of the animals, there's heat and wind and fires and dust galore in the summertime. Harvesting, canning, drying a winter's supply of what comes out of the gardens in the autumn. Blizzards in the winter that'll keep everybody from reaching town. Planting, rounding up the stock, calving in the spring—"

"But it *is* all work and no play—is that what you're saying?"

Again the shrug while he ate the eggs he'd smothered in Tabasco sauce without so much as a flinch. "The nearest neighbor is five miles away and doing the same kind of work."

"Which means they're too busy to socialize, too?"

"Yep."

"So all we have to look forward to here is sweat and toil and days that start before dawn," Ally summarized, realizing that while what he said might be true, he was still putting a worse spin to it than could possibly be the case or no one in his right mind would live the life he did.

She raised her chin to him and said with conviction, "I'm not afraid of hard work and long hours. I've done it before."

"Done much ranchin', have you?"

"Ranching isn't the only thing that takes hard work and long hours."

"And you're up for it?"

"Bright and early."

He watched her with more curiosity in his expression than had been there before. "Why?" He repeated the question he'd asked the first night she'd been here. "Why do this when you could live in the lap of luxury somewhere, pick and choose what you do, set your own schedule?"

But despite his almost amiable tone, she was no more inclined to tell her problems to him now than she had been then. So she merely met his stare evenly and said once again, "I'm not afraid of hard work and long hours."

He chuckled a little at her reticence to confide in him, then nodded, slowly, as if he knew something she didn't—like just how hard that work was going to be and how long the hours. "I guess we'll see, won't we?"

Ally knew *he'd* see, all right, because she didn't have a doubt that he'd be watching her every move just the way he was watching her right then.

With those blue eyes that she could get lost in if she wasn't careful.

Good thing she was.

A quick glance at his wristwatch when Jackson finished helping Ash move furniture told him the morning was headed for nine o'clock and he was getting a late start on his own day's work.

Still, he made sure he wasn't needed any longer before he headed out of the remodeled bunkhouse.

"Wait for me," Beth said, catching up with him as he did. "I want to talk to Ally for a few minutes before you take her away."

Jackson didn't comment, he merely held the door open for his sister and then followed her out into the bright August sunshine.

But a few steps away from the bunkhouse, Jackson spotted Meggie at the chicken coop and sent Beth to tell Ally to get a move on while he veered in that other direction.

"How you doin', Miss Meggie?" he asked as he approached.

The little girl smiled a shy, tentative smile up at him. "Good," she answered, sounding unsure of it. "I did just like you said—I threw the chickens' food around first so they'd go eat while I took the eggs. And it *worked*," she finished as if it were magic.

"'Course it worked. Think I'd steer you wrong?" He plucked an egg and added it to her basket. "Got another job for you to do today while your mother and I are gone."

Her expression turned pensive, almost fearful, and Jackson wondered if it was just him she thought such an ogre or if something else was the cause.

If it was him, he was sorry for that. He might be damned unhappy about having these two city girls on his hands, but scaring children was not something he did under any circumstances. He liked kids. And just in case he'd frightened this one, he wanted to show her there was no cause.

"See that big ol' doghouse over there?" he asked

in a friendly enough tone, pointing out what he was talking about. "How'd you like to give it a coat of paint for me? Spruce it up some?"

"I never saw a dog here," she answered.

"Name's Mutt—because that's what he is. A big black-and-white hound with a long tail and ears that hang way down. He's around somewheres—or he will be. He likes to wander but he always finds his way home again. Let's give him a nice clean house to come back to."

"Think I can do it?"

"Don't know why not. I'll show you how soon as we're through here, and Hans will be around if you need help."

"Can I paint flowers on it?"

"I only have a can of barn red for now. But maybe we'll get some other colors later on and you can add them."

The little girl's smile turned more pleased than wary, making him feel as if they'd gotten off on a better foot. Hoping to keep that going, he pitched in to help her gather the eggs.

They did it in companionable silence, with Meggie glancing up at him every few minutes to give him a smile that seemed to offer friendship now.

She was the spitting image of Ally. Her curly coppery hair was the same color, though it was a short cap around her head rather than long like her mother's. Her skin was just as pale and flawless, her lips as pink, and her ears as small and perfect. Only her eyes were different—plain hazel instead of her mother's striking green.

The one thing he couldn't judge the similarity of was their smiles, because he'd never seen Ally's.

Not that he cared.

But somehow he couldn't help wondering.

Any more than he could help thinking about her every minute since she'd walked into the honky-tonk...

Lord help him, it scared the hell out of him.

Not that he'd admit that to a single living soul.

But there'd only been once before in his whole life that this same thing had happened to him, one other woman he couldn't pass on by and forget about.

Sherry.

And that had been a disaster.

A disaster he *wouldn't* repeat. Ever.

"I think that's all of them." The little girl's voice interrupted his musings.

Jackson took a look at the nests he'd been emptying by rote, without really watching what he was doing, and found she was right—the eggs were all gathered.

"Good job," he praised, not only for what she'd done with the eggs but for pulling him out of thoughts he didn't want to be lost in. "Remember what I told you to do with them?"

"Take the basket to Marta," she repeated.

"Right. And while you do that I'll get the paint things together."

He watched the child as she did as she was told,

telling himself that there wasn't any connection whatsoever between the fact that he couldn't get Ally out of his mind and that he hadn't been able to get Sherry out of his thoughts all those years ago.

The only reason he couldn't stop thinking about Meggie's mother was because she'd gotten his back up. The *only* reason.

It didn't have anything to do with any kind of attraction to her. No sir. She was just a vexation. A thorn in his side that couldn't be ignored until he could get rid of it. Get rid of her.

And that was all there was to it.

Marta must have seen Meggie coming, because the older woman came out of her house and met the child halfway, sending Meggie on a return run at full speed once she'd accepted the egg basket.

"Whoa there, slow down. There's no hurry—I haven't headed for the shed to get your gear yet," he told her when she reached him, ruffling up her hair.

But the feel of those silky locks flashed him back to the night before, and it wasn't the child's hair he was focused on so much as the memory of fingering the long strand of Ally's curls. And somehow what shot through him at that moment, purely in response to the mother, was the same thing that had washed over him when he'd had Ally before him.

But it didn't seem to fit with just being riled by the woman.

No, if he'd had no other reason to want Ally Brooks off his ranch before, he had an all-fired powerful one right then.

He'd be damned if he'd let anything start up with another woman who didn't belong here.

No matter what.

Ally was in the kitchen packing the saddlebags Jackson had brought her when Beth came in through one of the sliding doors from the patio.

"'Morning," the pregnant woman greeted as she did.

"'Morning," Ally answered, though she'd been up so long by then it seemed as though it ought to be afternoon.

"What's all that?" Beth asked with a nod at the food Ally was carefully putting into the heavy leather satchels.

"Lunch."

"Ah. Better bring a lot to drink, too, it's a hot one out there today." She stole a cucumber-and-dilled-cream-cheese pinwheel before Ally wrapped them. "We just finished up at my place. Jackson was headed here with me but he stopped to see how Meggie was doing with the eggs. He told me to tell you it was time to leave and send you out."

Jackson with Meggie?

Trying not to be too obvious, Ally went to the kitchen sink and rinsed her hands while taking a quick glance outside.

She couldn't see the chicken coop from there, but she imagined she could hear the harsh criticisms and rebukes that poor, defenseless Meggie was no doubt suffering at that very moment from the man who didn't want them around.

"Relax," Beth said from where she sat on a stool at the butcher block. "Jackson is great with kids. He should have a dozen of his own."

Only if they didn't show up without warning to trespass on his precious ranch, Ally thought, tempted to rush out of the kitchen to her child.

But she knew that wasn't a good idea, that what she was imagining was probably not happening and that charging in, in her overprotective-mother mode, would only make Meggie think there was something to be afraid of from Jackson. Ally had to hope that wasn't the case. Certainly if what she'd seen of his treatment of her daughter the night before was any indication, there was nothing to worry about.

So why was she worrying?

"How about you?" Beth asked, interrupting her thoughts. "Do you want more kids?"

Standing at the window wasn't doing her any good, so Ally decided a better course of action would be to finish packing the lunch so she'd have an excuse to get outside to Meggie.

Somewhat belatedly she answered Beth's question as she went back to the butcher block. "I'd like to have more kids, yes." But mostly she'd just like to save the one she had now. She no longer carefully set food in among the cold packs, but stuffed everything in in a hurry.

"I know that in this mood Jackson seems pretty daunting, but he really isn't as fierce as you may think," Beth said again as if she could tell what was going through Ally's mind. "You have to understand what this ranch means to him."

"He made the analogy that it was like his child."

"It's true. Just the way Meggie is your child. And think how you'd feel if someone showed up one day to claim part of her. But he'll get used to the idea if you just give him a little time. And then you'll see that underneath that stern, tough exterior is a pretty tender heart."

Ally thought that she'd have to see it to believe it. But the lunch was all stowed in the saddlebags by then and she didn't want to waste time debating the subject.

Instead she hoisted the satchel to her shoulder, surprised by the weight and leaning low on that side because of it. "I'd better let him know I'm ready to go," she said by way of an exit line.

Beth followed her out. "I came over to tell you that I'll be around all day—along with Hans and Marta—to look after Meggie, so you don't need to be concerned about her. Not that you'd need to be even if it was just Hans and Marta. They've been friends of the family for years and years. Hans used to run the lumber mill, then he retired, but the two of them were getting on each other's nerves, so Jackson offered them light work here. It helps him out and them, too."

Ally didn't think it prudent to tell Beth that it wasn't Hans and Marta she was worried about.

Beth went on as they headed for the barnyard.

"Hans and Marta just got back from an extended vacation to Sweden to visit relatives they haven't seen since they came to this country as newlyweds. The trip was Jackson's gift to them for their fiftieth wedding anniversary this past May. They've been gone almost all summer."

Ally assumed this sudden wealth of information was meant to illustrate just what a good guy Jackson really was. But at the moment it didn't help ease her mind.

And then the two of them turned a corner of the paddock fence and came upon Jackson and Meggie not too far in the distance.

Ally's steps slowed as she drew near and finally stopped just short of reaching them, shocked to the core by what she was seeing and hearing.

Jackson was teaching her daughter to paint a doghouse. He was actually smiling and so was Meggie as the deep sound of his voice carried to Ally.

There were certainly no harsh criticisms or rebukes coming from him, though he also wasn't fawning over the child or talking down to her, either, the way some people who didn't have any experience with kids did. Instead he was treating her with the same respect he would have an adult. And something about the way he took for granted that Meggie could do the job once he'd shown her how seemed to make Meggie respond with a new self-confidence.

"See?" Beth said from beside her. "Nothing to worry about. Kids and animals—Jackson is great with them."

He caught sight of Ally and his sister just then, took a sweat-stained Stetson from the doghouse's roof to put on his head, patted Meggie on the back, and crossed to them. As he did, his expression changed completely—sobering first, then turning fierce.

"It's about time," he growled.

Beth let out a laugh, turned and left as Jackson reached Ally to stand accusingly before her, his legs apart, his hands on his hips, his head slightly forward on his neck as if he were a drill sergeant berating a miscreant private.

"How long does it take to make a few sandwiches?"

Ally just stared at him for a moment, amazed by the transformation between what she'd witnessed of him with Meggie and what faced her now. Jekyll and Hyde, alive and living in Wyoming.

Still, she was grateful that Meggie was seeing the Dr. Jekyll side.

But she didn't answer his question. Instead she set the saddlebags on the ground at his booted feet and stepped around him to go to Meggie to kiss her good-bye. Then she came back.

"What are you waiting for?" she asked as brusquely as he had.

His cornflower blue eyes narrowed at her as if the look alone could put her in her place. Then he blew out a derisive snort of a breath and headed for the barn. "Saddle up," he ordered.

Saddle up? Did he mean find a horse and mount it or did she actually need to put a saddle on one?

She had to jog to catch up with him, because after having given the command he hadn't waited for her to fall into step, and his long legs carried him away fast, even with the heavy leather bags slung over one broad shoulder as if they were no more than a towel he'd used to dry himself after a shower.

As she followed, Ally wondered whether to tell him that all the horses she'd ridden had come already saddled or to try bluffing her way through the task if he'd meant she needed to do it herself.

How difficult could it be? A bunch of straps and buckles. Like a pair of shoes. Just match up the right strap with the right buckle and that was that.

Wasn't it?

Maybe.

Or maybe not.

But the one thing she was sure of was that if she told Jackson she'd only ridden the presaddled kind and didn't know how to go about doing it from scratch, he'd bite her head off. So she decided to go with the how-hard-could-it-be theory.

Still, she was not at all disappointed to find "saddle up" had been an order to get on an already saddled horse.

She breathed a sigh of relief as they headed for two that were tied to the paddock fence waiting for them.

"The men are already out rounding up the herd," he informed her as if she'd asked, swinging easily up onto the taller of the animals after he'd attached the saddlebags.

So much for gallantry or helping a lady mount.

Ally was left standing beside a gray mare, her eyes barely level with the curve of the saddle seat.

Somehow the camp horses had seemed shorter than these ranch horses. Plus there had always been a stable boy to offer a boot up. Or a tennis shoe up as it were, because Ally didn't own any cowboy boots.

But here she was on her own.

"Whoa, girl," she murmured, though the animal was only standing docilely in place, staring at the white rail in front of it.

Hoping the horse was as calm as it looked, Ally pulled her knee nearly to her chin to get her foot into the stirrup.

She missed.

It was higher than she'd thought.

She took a step backward and tried again.

"Oh, for crying out loud," Jackson barked when she missed a second time. "Move 'er beside the fence and climb on from there if you have to," he ordered disgustedly.

Wishing she'd thought of that herself, Ally took his advice, finally making it into the saddle. She felt good about it until she realized she couldn't reach the reins to untie them.

Jackson realized it, too, at about the same time.

"Damned woman," he muttered under his breath. And with that, he reached over to yank the reins free and handed them to her.

Then he nudged his own mount and headed away from the barn, leaving Ally to play catch-up again.

"Oh, this is going to be loads of fun," she grumbled to herself so softly she didn't think he could possibly hear her.

She was wrong.

"We aren't out here to have fun. We're here to work," he barked at her.

And though she knew it was childish, she couldn't help sticking out her tongue at his back.

His broad, straight back...

She hated herself for noticing that. For admiring the magnificence of the man in the saddle. For appreciating the graceful way he rode, flowing with the rhythm of the animal so smoothly horse and rider could have been floating on air.

And it didn't help matters at all that her wayward gaze slid to the jeans pockets that so snugly hugged his great derriere, then slipped right on down the thick, hard thighs that finessed the horse with subtle pressure to do his bidding.

Ally suffered a sudden horribly delicious image of those same thighs on either side of her, nudging, guiding, riding....

Her mouth went dry, her heart raced, and beads of perspiration erupted on her upper lip.

Could she be suffering heatstroke already?

But she knew better.

Hunk stroke was more like it.

And it would never do. She had to fight it. To keep her thoughts—and her eyes—off him.

It helped that about then they reached the section of the range where the ranch hands were.

It *didn't* help that Ally couldn't keep herself from

comparing the other men to Jackson or that they came up short as he did a cursory, first-names-only introduction.

Then he solved the problem of distraction for her.

"You'll take up the rear," he told her. "That means you keep an eye out for any of the herd that try to stray, and don't let them."

At that, one of the cowboys grimaced and exchanged a glance with the man beside him.

Ally wondered why but didn't say anything as she waited for Jackson to explain how she was supposed to keep a cow with wanderlust from roaming.

But further instructions never came. Instead he shouted, "Let's move 'em out of here," to the ranch hands and they all took off.

For a moment Ally just sat there, watching them go and feeling like an idiot for not knowing what to do. Then she realized the only way she was going to learn was by trial and error, because Jackson was not likely to fill her in. So she set her horse to a canter and followed along, taking up a place behind the herd as the cowboys hee-yawed them into motion.

It didn't take long for Ally to understand the reason she'd been given the rear position, or the cowboys' reaction to her being relegated to it. Driving cattle on a dry, ninety-five-degree day was dirty, dusty work. And Ally got the worst of it as she rode straight into the clouds the cattle and horses stirred up.

By the time they stopped near a stream for lunch, she felt as if she'd personally experienced the dust bowl. She was covered with grit from head to toe. It crunched beneath her teeth, clogged her nose and scratched her eyes. Every fold of her clothes carried enough soil to pot houseplants; it had settled into the creases of her skin and sifted through her hair to her scalp. Even her ears were full of it.

Off their horses the men all went to the stream to wash their hands and splash water on their faces.

Ally joined them and then—though she hated having to do it and turned away from them when she did—she had to use some of the canteen water to swish in her mouth and spit out, and blow her nose on the tissue she'd luckily stuffed into her pocket before they'd left.

And still she was dirtier than she'd ever been in her life. Which was no doubt exactly what Jackson had had in mind.

"What the hell is all this?" he demanded as he started to unload the saddlebags of the food she'd packed.

Ally hiked from the stream to the shade of a huge tree where they were sitting to eat. "I believe those are the sandwiches you told me to make," she answered him evenly rather than allowing a hint of how awful she felt.

"With the crusts cut off?" he asked incredulously.

"Trimmed, yes."

Jackson rolled his eyes. "Froufrou food, boys. She's packed us froufrou food."

"Oh, stuff it, hard case," she heard herself shout back before she even realized she was going to. "If you don't like it, don't eat it."

That brought a few smiles and at least one laugh disguised as a cough from the other men, who accepted their sandwiches without comment.

Ally took over from there, explaining what everything was as she opened each container.

Besides the cucumber pinwheels there were marinated green beans, chick peas and carrot curls; crackers she'd seasoned and toasted, and a vegetable pâté to go with them; and a flour tortilla torte layered with refried beans, onions, olives, peppers, tomatoes, spicy sour cream and cheese, and cut into triangles that sent Jackson into another muttering of "froufrou."

But everyone—including Jackson—ate heartily. The ranch hands were effusive in their praise of the picnic, wanting to know what the special flavor on the ham and turkey club sandwiches was, and arguing over who got the last of each dish as it disappeared.

Jackson, on the other hand, grumbled between mouthfuls about the ridiculousness of having food like that on a cattle drive, as if she'd ruined some centuries-old tradition.

Once they'd all finished eating and drinking, it was back to work.

The ranch hands headed for the horses where they grazed near the stream, but Jackson held back, handing Ally a handkerchief scarf. "Tie it around your nose and mouth. It'll block out some of the dust," he advised as if he were doing it against his will.

"Thanks," she said, accepting it and wondering if froufrou food had won her the concession or if his conscience was just getting the better of him. But either way, she'd take what help she could get.

"Come on, let's get going," he ordered then.

The afternoon was more punishing than the morning, mainly because the temperature climbed and, besides the heat and dust, Ally's backside began to protest the abuse of the saddle. Half-hour joyrides at camp had not prepared her posterior for the kind of prolonged punishment it was getting.

Of course, none of the men seemed disturbed, but then clearly they were all accustomed to it. For Ally, as the hours passed, that saddle became a private torture all its own.

And then the call of nature struck, too.

For a while she tried to ignore it, but she'd had more to drink than to eat at lunch and ignoring it became less and less possible until she finally accepted the fact that she was going to have to slip away from her dusty position at the back of the herd and find a discreet bush. Fast.

No one would miss her, she thought, since the cows were a cooperative lot and, besides having to urge on a few laggers periodically, she really didn't do much.

So when she spotted a likely clump of bushes amid a stand of trees, she steered her horse off in that direction.

By then she was so stiff and sore that getting out of the saddle was more a fall than a dismount. Not that she cared at that point. She was less concerned with gracefulness than with just hitting the ground and running for the foliage.

It was hardly a luxurious accommodation but she got the job done and then hurried back out of the bush as quickly as she could.

Getting into the saddle again was not an easy proposition, however.

Lifting her leg high enough to reach the stirrup just couldn't be done with muscles that were crying out for mercy. Fleetingly she considered walking rather than riding, wondering if she could keep up, but of course she knew that wasn't really an option, just wishful thinking when *anything* seemed preferable to sitting in that saddle again. If she could even get there.

She searched for something to use to boost herself up, spotting a tree stump on the outskirts of the small clump of bushes she'd just availed herself of.

She took her horse to that spot; though she still could have used a bigger lift, with a moan of misery, she managed it.

For a moment she closed her eyes, swallowed hard and waited for the pain to pass. Barring that, she at least waited for it to ease up.

Then she opened her eyes, pulled up the scarf that was tied around her neck to cover her nose and mouth and went around the trees and bushes to return to work.

There was only one problem.

There wasn't a cow or horse or cowboy or so much as a cloud of dust anywhere to be seen.

Thinking that maybe she'd just lost her bearings and was facing the wrong direction, Ally made a full circle of the stand of trees and bushes, searching the distance for signs of the herd.

But there weren't any.

In fact, there wasn't anything but wide-open countryside. Quiet. Beautiful. Empty. And she had most definitely lost her bearings, because she didn't have any idea which direction she'd come from or where to go to get back.

"Oh, boy," she said as reality sank in. Then, as loud as she could, she called, "Hey, is anybody out there?"

No answer. Not even her own voice echoed back to her.

"You don't think we're lost, do you?" she said to her horse, the only living thing within earshot.

It didn't answer.

It didn't need to. They were in trouble and Ally knew it.

Still, she had to try to get out of this. Keeping her fingers crossed, she took a guess and ventured as far as she could without losing sight of the trees.

Nothing.

Back she went, trying another direction. And then another and another, always keeping the trees as home base. But still there was no sign of the herd. It was as if they'd disappeared into thin air.

Which left her with the camp rule applying to lost hikers—stay in one place. So for the last time she went back to the trees and bushes, thinking that when Jackson realized she wasn't bringing up the rear, he'd backtrack and find her.

Wouldn't he?

A sinking feeling washed through her with the doubt.

Maybe he wouldn't. Maybe he'd figure it served her right and she was on her own. That she could find her way home or die trying.

The vast expanse of the open countryside seemed to stretch out even farther than before, all around her. And she had an overwhelming sense of how completely vulnerable she actually was.

"Thank God, Meggie didn't come with me," she murmured when that thought occurred to her, her own voice sounding loud in the silence.

But then she realized she was being silly. Surely Jackson wouldn't just leave her. Or even if he would, someone else would come looking for her.

She just needed to wait awhile.

But she didn't need to do it sitting on the back of that horse.

"Unless, of course, you know your way home. Any chance of that?" she asked, bending over the animal's mane to speak into its ear.

The horse snorted and shook its head as if to rid itself of a fly.

No help there.

"Okay for you," she said. "No horsey treats when we *do* get back."

She slid to the ground again, groaning the whole way and longing to be anywhere but where she was— preferably in a bath full of bubbles. At home in Denver where there wasn't so much dust and dirt and grime. In the middle of the nice, familiar suburbs where a person couldn't get lost if she tried...

But since that was nothing more than a pipe dream, she led the horse to the shade of the tree farthest away from the others so she could be seen from nearly any direction and slipped down the trunk to sit on the prairie grass. She didn't really feel afraid. At least not of being alone in the countryside. Or even of spending the night out there, if it came to that.

But the thought of Jackson Heller when he did find her, now that was something else again....

"Ally? Ally? Are you all right?"

Oooh, nice voice. Ally thought she was dreaming it. Deep, rich, resonant, masculine. It rolled over her like warm syrup, seeped into her pores and made her moan.

"Ally! Are you okay?"

The voice was louder this time.

But it wasn't a dream, she realized as she drifted awake. It was real.

And she wasn't in bed asleep. She was on the ground with a tree root for a pillow and waning sunshine for a blanket.

And the voice belonged to Jackson.

Her eyes flew open and there he was, standing over her, tall, gorgeous, and, surprisingly, not glaring at her. Instead he'd taken off his hat and held it down next to his knee, leaving his eyebrows bare so she could see that they were pulled together, almost as if he were worried about something.

"Are you hurt?" he asked. *Asked,* not demanded.

It was very nice. Why couldn't he always be this way?

"No," she finally answered, sitting up, though not without flinching when she landed on her sore seat. "I'm okay. I just left the herd so I could use the bushes and when I came out you guys were gone. Completely. And I couldn't figure out what direction to go to find you again, so—"

"What about your horse? Where's the mare?"

She didn't realize until he'd said that that the horse was gone. She glanced around to confirm it. "I asked it if it knew the way home. Guess it did. All I know is that I sat down to wait for someone to come back for me and I guess I dozed off. The horse was standing right here before that. It must have wandered away while I slept."

"You didn't tie it to something or at least leave the reins hanging forward from the bit so it would think it was tied?" His tone was growing more impatient.

"It didn't occur to me to tie it to something. And I didn't know that if I left the reins hanging forward it would think it was. Is that true?"

He didn't answer her. Instead she saw the sharp edge of his jawline tense. "The horse didn't throw you?" He was back to demanding.

"No."

"And you aren't hurt?"

She didn't suppose a sore rear end counted. "No."

"Damn fool woman," he muttered, angry again.

Then through clenched teeth, he said, "I ought to let you walk back."

Ally made it to her feet with a wince she hoped he didn't see. "I'm sorry. I guess it was probably dumb to just slip away, but I didn't know what else to do and I never thought you could disappear so quickly."

He stared daggers at her. Then he jammed his hat onto his head and spun away from her, swinging up onto his own horse as if he really were just going to ride off. In a hurry.

But he didn't. Instead he looked at her over his shoulder and said, "Come on."

"Come on?"

"You'll have to ride with me. Get over here and I'll lift you up."

Oh, dear. "Isn't there another way?"

"You can walk," he said flatly, as if the choice were hers.

Walking did not sound like such a good idea. Not only was she miles from the ranch house, but while she'd slept, her muscles and abused parts had tightened up considerably.

But sitting on a horse again, up close and personal to Jackson, was not a great alternative.

"Make up your mind," he ordered when she hesitated.

Her mind was made up. She just didn't like what it was made up to.

Trying not to flinch, she went to stand beside horse and rider.

Jackson had left the stirrup free. "Put your foot there and give me your arm."

He didn't know what he was asking of her.

Remembering the tree stump she'd used earlier, she pointed to it and said, "Can we do this over there?"

He sighed but moved to that spot and waited for her.

Even climbing the eighteen or so inches onto the stump was painful, but she managed to do it without showing just how much it hurt. Then she did as she'd been told before, and Jackson hoisted her to sit just behind the saddle.

A slight squeak escaped her throat when her rump met the bony one of the animal, but she squelched it in a hurry.

"Hang on," Jackson barked.

"To what?"

"Me."

Ally swallowed hard and did that, too.

No sooner were her arms around his waist than he nudged the horse into a trot as if he were very anxious to get this over with.

But regardless of how anxious he might be, he couldn't have been as anxious as Ally was, because she didn't know which was worse—the agony of pain that shot through her body with every jarring bounce of that horse, or the unwelcome pleasure of having her arms around what she'd only admired from a distance until now...

Jackson Heller. Of all people.

* * *

"Mom!" Meggie ran from Hans and Marta's house when Ally and Jackson rode up. "Where've you been for so long? Hans was thinking maybe he should go look for you 'cuz he thought you were lost or hurt 'cuz your horse came back without you."

The little girl's worry flooded out and the moment Ally was on the ground Meggie wrapped her arms around her waist and hung on tight.

"I'm fine. But I did do something silly and got a little lost," she soft-pedaled as Jackson led the horse to the barn.

"Are you okay?" Meggie asked.

"I'm absolutely fine," Ally said, slowly enunciating each word to convince her daughter.

Meggie let go and studied her from head to toe. "You *look* okay."

"I *am* okay. I had a nap until Jackson found me and here we are. No big deal."

"Then does that mean you can come see how I painted the doghouse?" Meggie asked, apparently reassured since she switched willy-nilly to a new subject.

"Sure," Ally said with a laugh.

She followed behind Meggie as the little girl excitedly led the way, hopping and skipping and urging her mother to hurry.

This was a new twist, Ally realized, because usually once Meggie entered her worried mode, it was very difficult to get her out of it. And yet it hadn't taken much at all just then.

"Can't you walk any faster than that?" Meggie asked, jumping up and down beside the doghouse.

Ally had never seen her so proud of anything. She had done a great job, Ally realized when she finally got there. But more than her painting skills, what impressed Ally was the fact that Meggie was so pleased with herself. There wasn't a trace of the depression that had caused the school counselor to recommend a psychiatric evaluation. Not even an inkling of the depression that had been ever present, underlying even happy events, since the divorce.

And when Jackson joined them belatedly and praised her on top of it, Meggie beamed.

Ally could hardly believe what she was seeing. Not that she thought there had been an instant cure to her daughter's woes, but even an interruption in them was a first.

Suddenly, being sore and dirty and lost seemed like a small price to pay for what was happening right before her eyes.

Jackson began to talk to Meggie about painting the paddock fence, showing her what he had in mind as if she were a great artist he was commissioning for the job after being so impressed with what he'd seen of her work.

"If you two don't mind, I'm going in for a bath," Ally announced when it seemed that neither of them even remembered she was standing there.

It barely distracted them, so she added, "See you in a few minutes," and went to the house.

Unfortunately the bath didn't feel as good as she

expected it to. When she sank into the water, she realized just how raw her backside was and added a brutal stinging pain to her other complaints.

Descending the stairs again after that was no mean feat, either, and when she got to the kitchen and learned Marta had left a casserole for their dinner she silently blessed the woman for sparing her the chore of cooking.

Instead, there was Jackson—freshly showered in the time she'd left him outside with Meggie, his hair still damp, his face clean-shaven but for his mustache. He was dressed in a pair of jeans and a crisp white T-shirt.

Meggie was setting food, dishes and silverware on the butcher block for an informal supper and the two of them were laughing over something.

Ally offered up a second silent thanks for being spared the slide around the breakfast nook's bench seat and the opportunity to stand to eat her meal without making it too obvious just how much pain she was in.

Over dinner Meggie was full of questions for Jackson about the workings of the ranch and the animals, quoting Hans in what seemed like a sudden case of hero worship and bragging about Marta's making the best chocolate-chip cookies in the world and having shared them with Beth for an afternoon snack on the patio.

Clearly Meggie's day had been better than Ally's and Ally was grateful for it.

When they were all finished eating, Ally sent her

daughter up to get ready for bed and Ally and Jackson began to clear the dishes.

"I owe you a thanks and an apology," Ally said to him as they did.

He hadn't actually spoken to her since pulling her up behind him on his horse when he'd rescued her earlier, and he didn't now. He only raised an eyebrow at her as if he didn't have a clue about what she meant.

"I appreciate your coming back for me today," she began.

"What did you expect me to do? Leave you out there?"

"Or make me find my own way home."

"More likely you'd have found your way farther out on the range," he said, but he wasn't growling or grumbling or being irascible about any of it. For once they were merely exchanging conversation and Ally was grateful for that, too. Though she thought the enthusiastic charm of her daughter had had more to do with softening him up than anything.

"And I'd like to apologize for getting mad at you for giving Meggie chores to do. After all the pampering and spoiling I've done to try helping her, I'd never have guessed that putting her to work would do the trick."

"Helping her?" he repeated. "What's wrong with her?"

This time Ally felt as if his treatment of her daughter had bought him the explanation she'd avoided until then. "She's had trouble adjusting to the divorce.

I never knew kids could get clinically depressed, but that's what happened.''

"She doesn't seem depressed to me."

Ally felt so good about the change she'd witnessed in Meggie in the past few hours that she laughed as if she hadn't taken it seriously, either. "No, not tonight, that's for sure. But she has been. Shag kept saying it would be good for her—for us both—to come up here. I thought he meant as sort of a retreat—fresh air, a calmer life-style, being around animals—things like that. But giving Meggie chores has done a lot more to boost her confidence and self-esteem than what I had in mind."

"So old Shag tried to get you up here even before he died?"

"He felt bad for what Meggie and I were going through," Ally said somewhat ambiguously, because she still didn't want to go into all the details.

Then she remembered Jackson's suspicions about her being his father's lady friend and wondered if he was still thinking along those lines. "Shag wasn't considering bringing us here himself or anything like that. He'd have stayed in Denver with my mother. He just suggested Meggie and I come. That's all there was to it."

"It's all right," Jackson said with a small chuckle that seemed to brighten the kitchen considerably. "I gave up thinking it was you the old man was keeping company with."

Ally was glad to hear that, but she didn't say anything. She merely went on loading the dishwasher.

Jackson reached around her to wet the sponge to wash off the butcher block, giving her a whiff of clean-smelling after-shave that she caught herself enjoying much too much.

"We never knew anything about the woman he was with in Denver," Jackson volunteered then. "So it was just the logical conclusion that the Ally Brooks he put in his will was who he was sweet on."

"You didn't even know my mother's name?"

"Nope. We had his lawyer's name, address and phone number—if we needed to contact Shag, we did it through him—but that was it."

"Why?"

"That's just how he was. He didn't think it was right for us—Linc, Beth or me—to see him with a woman who wasn't our mother, even after we were grown. For years, probably up until he met your mother, he kept company with Margie Wilson in town here, but only as a backdoor romance. He never so much as danced with her at a town celebration."

"Wow. I knew he was old-fashioned, but that's pretty incredible."

"He was close to your mother?" Jackson asked hesitantly.

"It was as if they were married. Though she did think it was strange that he never brought her up here or would have you or Beth or Linc there, even for holidays. She tried to talk him into getting everyone together, but he just wouldn't hear of it."

Jackson blew a derisive sigh. "That was Shag—stubborn as a mule."

"Why does it sound as if you didn't like him much?"

"Wasn't much to like. Mean and ornery. There wasn't a soft spot in him after my mother died. Leastwise not one we ever saw. He was easier on his horses than he was on us. Seemed to like them better, too."

The kitchen was back in order by then and Ally gingerly leaned against the counter's edge as Jackson settled a hip on one of the butcher-block stools.

"That doesn't sound like the man we knew," Ally said, surprised by Jackson's description of his father.

"Maybe he mellowed with age and he just wasn't around us enough for us to see it."

"Maybe."

Talking the way the two of them were made Ally feel as if the wall between her and Jackson might be breaking down. A little, anyway.

Wanting to keep it going—as well as wanting him to know his father really had loved him and his brother and sister—she said, "He spoke highly of you all. You in particular. He said you ran this place better than he ever had. That that was part of the reason he had turned it over to you. He thought he ought to just get out of your way so you could have a free rein."

"He said that?"

"More than once."

"I'll be damned."

Jackson stared off into space, thoughtful for a moment. Then he raised those incredible blue eyes to her again, backtracking through their conversation. "Is Meggie the reason you came here instead of just selling your share of this place? Because the old man suggested it for her mental health?''

If she said yes, would his treatment of her daughter change to drive them off? Ally wondered in a flash of her earlier concerns. Somehow she doubted it now, but still she was afraid to risk it, so the answer she gave touched on the other aspect of their moving to the ranch.

''We both needed a fresh start. A new beginning.''

''Lots of easier ways to do that,'' he observed, though not in the same way he'd said similar things before about the wisdom in their being here. This was just a statement. It didn't hold any threat or warning.

And though Ally waited for it to be followed up with another offer to buy her out, it never came.

Instead he let the conversation end there, pushed off the stool and said, ''Come on, I'll get you some liniment that'll help that sore backside of yours.''

So much for thinking she hadn't been obvious in favoring it. Still, at that point, she wasn't about to turn down something that might ease her misery. ''Thanks,'' was all she said.

He headed out of the kitchen, turning off the lights as he passed the switch.

Ally followed, amazed by how much tighter and sorer everything was getting as the evening wore on. She tried not to distract herself from it with the appealing sight of Jackson's great derriere in front of her. But it wasn't easy.

He went through the dining room, the living room, the foyer, and headed up the stairs.

That was as far as Ally got—one foot on the bottom step. The pain was so great it took her breath away in a gasp and her hand shot to the railing as if it were a lifeline.

There was no way she could climb those stairs. At least not without pulling herself up by the banister and allowing a slow enough pace to accommodate the pain. Not something she had any intention of doing with Jackson watching.

"You know, on second thought," she said as if there weren't a thing in the world wrong, "why don't you just leave the liniment in my room? I think I'll stay down here and watch some television before bed."

Jackson had reached the top landing by then. He turned around from there and frowned down at her. "Television?"

"Sure. I had that nap this afternoon and I'm not really tired," she lied through her teeth.

He just stared at her for a moment and then he came back down the stairs. "You nearly fell asleep over your supper."

She was hoping he hadn't seen that. "Well, you know, I guess I got a second wind."

His handsome face eased into a lazy, knowing grin. "Yeah, I just heard it a minute ago when you took this first step here. Wouldn't be that you can't make it upstairs, would it?"

"No, I'm okay in that department."

"Sure you are."

Before she realized what he was doing, he grabbed

her by one arm, bent over and hoisted her unceremoniously over his shoulder.

"You need a good night's sleep so I can get a decent day's work out of you tomorrow," he said as he climbed the stairs again.

He carried her all the way into her room and for a fleeting moment Ally thought he was taking her to the bed. Images of scenes like that from her romance novels shot through her head and wicked excitement danced down her spine.

Then he stopped short, as if the bed might have been where he was headed until he remembered himself or thought better of it, and he set her on her feet on the floor.

But it was too late. The contact and the stray fantasy had awakened a whole world of things inside Ally that left her standing there dumbly while he went to his room and came back with the liniment tube.

She could only hope what she was feeling right then didn't show in her expression the way her misery had.

"Here, use it liberally," he said in a voice that was surprisingly quiet, making her wonder if he was feeling some of what she was.

"Thanks." She accepted the tube, barely glancing up at him. But somehow, once that glance reached his face it got stuck there.

Beautiful eyes. Ruggedly gorgeous facial bones. Lips parted just slightly beneath his mustache....

He was nearer than she'd thought he was. Or had he just moved?

He had, because he was moving still, so slowly it was almost imperceptible....

Was he going to kiss her?

Curiosity tipped her chin.

Or was it something else that did it? Was she inviting him to press that oh-so-supple mouth against hers?

Even though she told herself to back off, to break the spell that seemed to be wrapping around them, she couldn't do it. Because if she was honest with herself, at that moment, she was dying to know what it would be like if he *did* kiss her....

Then he snapped out of the spell himself and he was the one to step away from her, heading for the door again.

"Get some sleep. You'll need to be downstairs at five sharp tomorrow morning," he ordered in the same harsh tone he'd used so much since she'd met him.

Yet, even with that harsh tone lingering in the air after him, Ally couldn't help feeling the oddest sense of disappointment.

Why? she wondered as she crossed the hall to peek in on her sleeping daughter. Was it disappointment that he'd gone? Or disappointment that he hadn't kissed her?

It didn't matter, either way it was bad, she told herself as she retraced her steps to her own room.

And what was even worse was that she suddenly found in herself an eagerness for 5:00 a.m. to come around again.

As impossible as that seemed....

Chapter Four

The second day of ranch work was harder than the first.

Ally spent the morning cutting weeds out of a gully with a scythe, raking them and hauling them where they could be safely burned.

After a lunch she'd again packed for herself, Jackson, and only two ranch hands today, Jackson sent the ranch hands off to check on stock somewhere apparently far away. He and Ally set out to dig postholes and repair fence.

The good part of it was that beyond riding in Jackson's pickup truck, none of the chores required much sitting on her abused rear end.

The bad part...

Well, it was all bad.

Hot and dirty, backbreaking, muscle-wrenching, punishing hard work.

But the worst was that despite wearing gloves, her hands went from sore to raw to blistered.

And even though she kept reminding herself it was all worth it by picturing Meggie's improved spirits the evening before, as the afternoon wore on she couldn't help thinking that this was not the life she'd planned for herself.

Not by a long shot.

Once her former husband's schooling and training were over and his career was on track, she was supposed to have been able to quit work. To have more kids and stay at home to raise them.

Maybe it was old-fashioned, but having a family and family life, being a stay-at-home wife and mother—this was all she'd ever really wanted. She had even been looking forward to downsizing her cooking to accommodate only the people she loved rather than a restaurant full of strangers.

Yet here she was, sweaty and grimy, fighting biting horseflies, with her back, shoulders and arms aching. Her hands hurt so bad she could cry, her fanny was sorer than if she had just delivered quadruplets, and she was fixing fence in the middle of a Wyoming prairie with a man she hardly knew, who seemed to want to work her to death.

Okay, so he was working right alongside her, every bit as hard.

But still…

What she wouldn't give to be in that kitchen she'd

dreamed of for so many years, listening to the sounds of tiny voices playing in the backyard while she made hot-cross buns.

Instead it was Jackson's buns her gaze strayed to. Tight and just round enough, easing into long legs as thick and hard as tree trunks....

Ally sighed, surprising herself with the wistful sound of it.

Not that she was wistful over Jackson. Of course not. It must have just been a belated wistfulness for what she'd been thinking about before, because there was no way it could have anything to do with Shag's eldest son.

No way at all.

"Get that roll of barbed wire off the truck," he ordered just then, not so much as glancing at her as he hammered nails into a post they'd set earlier.

Nope, nothing about that to inspire wistfulness.

Ally did as she was told, bringing the fencing material to him.

Jackson didn't thank her or even acknowledge her help. He went right on as if she were some handmaiden doing his bidding as she was obliged to.

Not that Ally expected anything different by then. She was actually getting used to his brusqueness.

Still, feeling a little ornery herself, she said, "You're welcome," as sweetly as if he'd expressed his gratitude effusively.

Then she got back to her current job of yanking off the old, rusty wire they were replacing, once again forcing herself to picture Meggie as she had been the evening before: so proud of her handiwork with that freshly painted doghouse, chattering over dinner....

And into that mental image sneaked a memory of Jackson from last night, too.

They'd had a nice meal. A pleasant conversation as they'd shared cleanup duty. In fact, that whole time had been surprisingly enjoyable.

Ally's gaze wandered to him on its own again as if to confirm that this man and the one from the evening before were the same.

He wore a gray T-shirt that clung to his broad back like a second skin, leaving nothing to the imagination.

Although she couldn't have imagined anything better even if she'd tried.

His shoulders were a mile wide and his spine was so straight that between the two he looked as if he could bear the weight of a whole house.

He had the short sleeves of the T-shirt rolled up above his biceps—not out of vanity, as she might have suspected of another man, but because his arms were so big the sleeves would be binding if they were any lower. And what they bared was the swell of work-honed muscles, hard and strong and glistening in the blaze of the sunshine.

Something else about the evening before flashed through her mind as she watched him just then—the moment when he'd handed her the liniment, when she'd thought he might be about to kiss her.

Or had that all just been in her mind?

She didn't think so. She distinctly remembered him

easing nearer to her, almost as if he were drawn to her.

Unwillingly. Or else he wouldn't have snapped back as if he'd been on the precipice of a deadly fall.

So why had he almost kissed her at all? At the worst he seemed to despise her. At the best, he barely tolerated her. Those were not inspirations for kissing a person.

But then she couldn't say she was fond of him, either. Not really. And yet when he'd been easing toward her, she'd done her share of moving his way, too.

Which was the craziest part of the whole business.

But crazy or not, it was true. If he'd have kissed her, she'd probably have kissed him back.

Right on those lips that hid beneath his mustache.

She'd never kissed a man with a mustache before....

She imagined that it would have tickled.

But she didn't want to imagine that it would have tickled in a pleasant way, so she decided kissing Jackson would probably have been awful. Like kissing somebody with a hairbrush attached to his upper lip.

And his mouth would probably have been as hard and cold and closed off as he was. As stiff and unyielding.

And he'd have probably given her orders—just how to wrap her arms around him, where to put her hands, when to close her eyes, when to part her lips, which side to angle her head....

She'd have probably hated it. The whole thing.

From start to finish. She'd probably never want him to do it again. Once would have completely cured her....

Cured her of what?

Of wondering about it?

Yes, all right, so she was wondering what it might have been like if he'd actually done it.

Cured her of wanting it?

Oh, Lord.

Okay, maybe deep down—really deep down— she'd wanted him to kiss her.

There just wasn't any other explanation for why she'd been on the verge of meeting him halfway.

Or any other explanation for why she'd lain awake in bed thinking about what it would have been like to be held in those powerful arms, against that rock-solid man's body. No other explanation for why she'd relived again and again what it had actually felt like to have him pick her up and carry her over one of those broad shoulders....

But still, she couldn't let herself believe any of those things would be good. That any of them might be so good that they would make her knees weak.

She had to convince herself that everything to do with Jackson was as horrible as the work he had her doing made her feel.

Because the man in the kitchen the night before, the man who'd carried her up the stairs, the man who'd nearly kissed her, was the same man who tortured her by day because he didn't want her around.

And that was something she needed not to forget.

* * *

Jackson had Ally stretching barbed wire while he went behind her and did the finish-up work—tightening the wire around the nails, pounding the nails against the loop, shoveling dirt in around the cement that held the posts in place.

Like everything he'd set her to do, she was inept at it. Slow, weak and not tremendously coordinated. A greenhorn through and through.

But he had to give her credit. She worked without complaint under the toughest conditions, doing her best—no matter how inadequate that was—at the most unpleasant jobs he could throw at her.

He respected that.

And he felt a little guilty for subjecting her to so much.

But it was for her own good, he told himself.

Besides the fact that he didn't want her here, that she was nothing but trouble and extra work for him, women like Ally didn't belong in a place like this. They came with romantic fantasies and television-fed images of what life on a ranch was like. They didn't know what they were getting into and they were a danger to themselves because they weren't as serious about it as they needed to be. They didn't take precautions.

Getting herself lost the day before was a prime example. Just wandering off in the middle of wide-open range she wasn't familiar with. Without any food or water on a mercilessly hot day. Letting her horse get away from her...

Where the hell was her common sense?

But he knew the answer to that. It was back in Denver. That was part of the problem—women like Ally might have city sense, or suburb sense. But they didn't have country sense.

They just didn't belong here.

"Keep it tight," he told her, barking at her as if slack in the wire were a felony.

She didn't say anything. She just put an extra effort into pulling the heavy coil more taut, trying not to show how much her hands were hurting as she did. Just the way she'd tried not to let him know how saddle sore she'd been last night and still was today.

He admired that, too.

Damn her.

Damn her for everything she was stirring up inside of him. Like the worry that had made him nearly frantic when he'd discovered he'd lost her yesterday and thought the worst—that maybe she'd been thrown, that she might have broken her neck.

That if she had, or even if something else had happened to her out there alone, it would have been his fault....

Well, damn it all to hell, what was he supposed to do? Just let her move in here as if it were some resort? This was a working ranch and if she wanted to live on it, she'd better know it, she'd better do her share of pulling the load, and she'd better learn how to do that without risking her neck.

Except that he didn't want her living here. Underfoot, getting in his way, causing him problems. Making him mad at himself for working her the way Shag had worked him and Linc and Beth. Making him mad for being worried when he'd lost her, for being relieved and grateful when he'd found her. Making him maddest of all for wanting to wrap his arms around her and hold on to her to convince himself she really was okay....

No, he didn't need this. Not any of it.

And he sure as hell didn't need her right there in front of him every minute where he had to look at that wild, curly copper hair, and those eyes that made him think of the ocean, and that rear end that wasn't much more than a couple of handfuls...

So he was pouring the work on pretty thick. Ignoring every inclination to ease up on her. To accommodate her.

To kiss her....

Not that he'd actually ignored *that* inclination. He'd damned near given in to it. Only at the very last second had he stopped himself.

She didn't belong here—that's what he'd reminded himself to keep from making a huge mistake. And that's what he said yet again to himself now.

He needed her to get the hell out before it was too late.

Too late for him.

Before he got used to having her around. Before he started to like it. To count on it.

Because about the time he did, he knew what would happen. The reality of life here would hit her. It would get to be too much for her.

And that would be when she'd leave.

So no matter how much he hated himself for what he was doing to her, he'd go on making things rough, trying to speed up the process of her getting her fill of this place before he got in too deep.

And if there was a part of him that almost hoped it wouldn't work?

He was fighting it. Hard.

Much, much harder than he was working her.

It was nearly seven when Ally and Jackson finished for the day. By then the fence they'd fixed stretched behind them for more than a mile. But when they got into the truck, Jackson didn't head back the way they'd come to return to the ranch.

"We aren't going home?" Ally asked, wondering if he actually had more work for them to do today. And how she could possibly do it being as tired as she was.

"First I have to pick up a randy stallion that went courtin' a neighbor's mare last night," he answered, going on in an unusual bit of talkativeness. "I swear the horse has radar. Every time this particular mare comes into season he seems to know it and he gets to her. I think if he was on the East Coast and she was on the West, he'd still catch the scent and make a beeline."

Ally tried not to be uncomfortable with the subject. "Maybe it's love."

Jackson gave her a sideways glance that said how silly he thought that idea was, but didn't comment on it. Instead he said, "Didn't you wonder why I had the horse trailer hitched up?"

"Not really. This is my first time in the truck. I thought maybe it was just always there."

That won her a second of those looks from the corner of his eye, but there was no time for more than that as they reached a small yellow ranch house. A boy of about fourteen sat on the porch doing what looked like exercises with his left arm—which was missing a hand and the forearm nearly up to the elbow.

Without preamble or an invitation to come along, Jackson hopped out of the truck.

"Jackson!" the boy greeted as if he were thrilled to see him.

"'Evenin', Josh," Jackson answered as Ally did a quick debate with herself about whether to just wait or join them.

She finally decided that if she was going to live around here, she needed to know her neighbors and not be considered unfriendly, so she made the effort to move her weary body and got out, too.

She followed Jackson to where he stood with one booted foot on the lowest of the six steps that led to the porch. When she got there, he nodded in her direction and said, "This is Ally Brooks, Josh. You've probably heard all about her by now. Ally, this is Josh Mercer."

"Hi," Ally said, wondering about the curious introduction. Why had this boy probably heard all about her, and from whom?

"Nice to meetcha," Josh answered, looking down at his feet rather than at her.

But his teenage shyness didn't extend to Jackson when he switched his attention back again. "You still gonna fly me into the hospital next time in the helicopter?" he asked eagerly.

"Sure. Said I would, didn't I?"

"They're gonna fit up a hook then. I'll be glad to get it."

"Looks like you're doin' good, though. Last time I saw you, you weren't movin' much yet."

"Pretty good, yeah." The boy came down the steps then. "Mom's in the barn. I'll go tell her you're here and we'll bring up ol' Buck."

Jackson gave just one nod at that, turned around and hitched a hip on the stair railing to wait.

Ally watched Josh go and, when he was out of earshot, she said, "What happened to him?"

"He was fixing a thresher—that's a piece of farm equipment," Jackson added in case she couldn't figure it out.

Ally ignored the condescension. "His hand couldn't be saved?"

"Nope."

"But he's just a boy. What was he even doing near a dangerous machine, let alone trying to fix it?"

For the third time Jackson's expression showed disbelief. "Josh and his mom run this place themselves. His father was mule-kicked in the head and died of a brain hemorrhage about five years back. Josh's been doin' more than his fair share ever since. He's a good boy. But accidents happen," Jackson added. "And out here there's the chance of a lot of them."

She knew he was seizing the opportunity to point that out and scare her. And, truthfully, she was picturing Meggie in Josh Mercer's shoes. But rather than giving in to the fear Jackson was trying to encourage, she reasoned that she'd make absolutely sure her daughter was never in a position to repair farm machinery and vowed to give the little girl some new warnings of things to be wary of.

"Hello, you handsome devil, you."

That drew Ally out of her thoughts. She looked up to find the owner of a very sultry voice headed their way, with Josh bringing up the rear, leading the horse.

The woman, who had to be Josh's mom, had on a pair of the tightest blue jeans Ally had ever seen and a V-neck T-shirt that looked as if it had been spray-painted on so that every lush, well-endowed curve of hers was shouting to be noticed.

Although she'd have been noticed even had what she worn whispered. She was tall, thin, tan and very attractive, with sun-shot blond hair pulled back into a French braid that hung past her shoulders—something Ally's own unruly curls wouldn't allow her to do.

The gleaming golden hair framed a lean, high-cheekboned face that would have turned heads anywhere in the world. Her features were perfect, that rare female countenance that was no doubt pretty in her girlhood, but had changed to beauty with a few years and a little maturity added.

And she had eyes only for Jackson—big, round nearly coal black eyes.

Suddenly Ally was very aware of her own appearance in comparison to Ms. Mercer. Short, freckled, frizzy haired, dirty and grimy was her own self-conscious, self-demeaning assessment. She was certainly no competition for this woman who could have been every man's dream of a farmer's daughter.

And suddenly Ally wished herself back into that truck.

But it was too late now and all she could do was tough it out.

"How come it takes a mare in heat to get you over here for a visit?" the sultry voice kidded Jackson as she reached them.

He laughed, but Ally couldn't tell if there was a sensual undertone to it or if she was just imagining it.

"Hello, Marilyn. How's it going?" was all he said in answer.

"Goin' good. Goin' real good," she said in a slow bedroom drawl that somehow appraised, approved and devoured him, leaving no doubt things hadn't been nearly as good before his arrival.

"This is Ally Brooks. Ally, this is Marilyn Mercer." He finally introduced them.

Marilyn Mercer's gaze hung on Jackson for a long moment before it swung away to take Ally in. "Ally Brooks—the whole town's talkin' about you," she said with a friendly enough smile, as if she didn't consider her any threat at all.

"What did I do to be so interesting?"

"The mystery woman Shag Heller left part of his holdings to, finally showing her face? Why, that's fresh fodder. And small towns live for gossip," she informed. "We'll all be discussin' you until somethin' juicier comes along." Then her eyes slid back to Jackson and her voice turned even sultrier. "Won't we?" she added as if the subject might come up as pillow talk between them.

And that was apparently the extent to which Marilyn Mercer was going to be distracted from him, because she acted as if the two of them were suddenly completely alone, and proceeded to flirt outrageously.

So outrageously that it was embarrassing to watch. Without saying anything—though she didn't think either Jackson or Marilyn would mind or even notice that she'd left—Ally went to the horse trailer to watch Josh instead.

But the horse was fairly cooperative, the teenager surprisingly adept using only one arm, and Ally didn't really have any interest in the process. Which made it difficult for her to keep her gaze from wandering back to the scene at the foot of the porch steps again and again.

Were Jackson and Marilyn Mercer more than just neighbors?

Certainly the overtures the blonde was making were not merely friendly. She was in shameless pursuit. Nearly predatory.

But what about Jackson? Was he encouraging it? It was hard to tell. He didn't seem to be trying to escape. And that crooked smile on his face wasn't from pain. But did he look enamored?

Maybe.

Maybe not....

He lifted his hat then, finger-combed his hair and put it back again. At a more rakish angle.

That added a few points to the enamored column. He might not be as obvious as Marilyn Mercer, but he was flirting back, all right. With that hat of his.

Except that he also took a step away from her at the same time.

Hmm. Mixed messages? Maybe he was enjoying the strokes to his ego even though they embarrassed him a little.

Or maybe something really was going on between them and he just didn't want it going on with Ally watching. Maybe it was something too personal and intimate to be paraded out here for her or Josh to see.

Then Ally watched him snatch a quick eyeful of the cleavage that peeked out of that V neckline, and she took it as confirmation of the latter of those possibilities.

"I think I'll wait in the truck," she told Josh as he closed the rear of the trailer when he had the horse settled inside. Not that she needed to explain to the boy, who went about his business in bashful silence as if she weren't there and headed for the barn again.

Ally barely noticed the pain that shot all the way up her arm from her abused palm when she grabbed the handle to the passenger door. Or the sting of landing heavily on her rear end on the seat inside. Or the loud sound she made as she slammed the door after herself.

She just wondered how long she was going to have to sit in that hot truck after a long day of taking that man's orders and putting up with him when she'd earned the right to go home to her daughter and a cool shower and some food to fill the ache in her stomach.

Maybe she'd honk the horn to remind Jackson Heller that he and his *neighbor* weren't the only two people in the world and that he needed to get those buns of his over here, take her home and save this little tête-à-tête for a time when he could do it without an audience!

But just as her hand snaked across the cab to the wheel, she caught sight of him touching his hat brim with a two-fingered goodbye and stepping around Marilyn to come to the truck.

When he climbed in a moment later, she bit back an it's-about-time.

What she couldn't seem to keep herself from saying as he pulled away from the front of the property was, "So, is that a backdoor romance like you said Shag had, or a front-door one?"

Very slowly, Jackson turned his head until he was staring straight at her. "Excuse me?"

She wanted to stop herself from the course she'd tripped onto, but she seemed to have lost the ability. Instead she nodded over her shoulder at the house they were leaving behind. "Your involvement with your neighbor "

"With Marilyn? I'm not involved with Marilyn. Though she'd like it if I was," he added with a slight chuckle that said he was flattered if not interested. "What's it matter to you, anyway?"

Matter? What did he mean *matter*? Of course it didn't matter to her.

But that question was like a bucket of water that brought her back to her senses enough to manage an elaborate shrug and some forced calmness into her voice. "It doesn't *matter*. I was just wondering if she was the woman in your life."

He went back to watching the dirt road they were on. "No, she's not."

"Who is, then?"

This time he shot her one of those sidelong glances. "Well, let's see. Women in my life...there's Beth, of course. And Kansas. And I guess now I'd have to say you and Meggie—for the time being, anyway— wouldn't I?"

He was teasing her. He knew exactly what she'd been asking him and he'd purposely skirted it.

But this calm, better-natured side of him was such a nice change from what she'd been dealing with all day that she didn't mind a little teasing. In fact, it actually helped ease some of what was itching at her from the inside and let her tease back.

"What does that mean? That you're a monk or something?"

In profile she saw his eyebrows shoot up and disappear under his hat. "A monk?" he repeated in mock affront at the very idea.

"Well, if you don't have a lady friend..." She let that trail off into a challenge.

"Not having a particular lady friend doesn't make me a monk."

"So there isn't any one particular lady friend?"

Again the glance from the corner of his eye. "Is there a reason you're fishin' in this pond?"

"Just curious. Back there I didn't know whether to rescue you or give you some privacy."

"What did you decide?" He actually grinned at her and suddenly Ally had a vivid image of what she hadn't even noticed in her behavior before—huffing into the truck, slamming the door, nearly honking at him...

And she knew that while she may not have been conscious of what she was doing at the time, he had been.

"I...I just didn't know what to do," she hedged, embarrassed. And inexplicably warmed by that wide, white-toothed grin of his, too.

Once more he went back to watching his driving, but his tone turned ruminative. "There are times when I feel the need to be rescued from man-hungry females around here, all right. I like Marilyn well enough, but she can be one of the worst. Trouble is, it'll take a whole lot more than a little door slammin' to save my neck from her noose."

Ally was beginning to realize that he dropped the gs at the end of his words only when he chose to. And he seemed to choose to either in anger or at moments like this when he was very nearly charming.

Even if he was still goading her. "I didn't slam the door. It slipped," she lied.

He laughed. And unlike the laugh she'd heard from him in response to Marilyn, this sounded more genuinely amused.

Ally liked it. Although she would have liked it better if it had also had that sensuous ring she'd thought the earlier one had had.

"I guess it would go a whole lot further in protecting me from the Marilyns of Elk Creek if I just hooked myself up with a particular lady friend, wouldn't it?" he said reflectively.

"If you could find one who would have you," Ally countered.

Her reward was that laugh again.

"Think that'd be hard to do, do you?"

"As mean and ornery and cantankerous as you are?" she answered, tempering the words with more of a teasing tone.

"Mean and ornery and cantankerous, am I?"

"On your *good* days."

"Guess you better hope you never see a bad one."

"With all my heart—you can bet on that."

He chuckled at her then, a low rumbling from his chest that seemed to mingle devilish delight and enough sensuality to let her know what the real thing sounded like—not what she'd heard before with Marilyn Mercer.

That knowledge went a long way in making her feel better. In fact, it sent sparks skittering up her spine.

"Scarin' you, am I?" he asked, clearly enjoying this.

But then, so was she. "I'm terrified," she said with enough facetiousness to disabuse him of the notion.

"Want to take my offer to buy you out and save yourself?" he challenged, for the first time almost making it sound as if he didn't really want her to accept it.

"I'm not *that* terrified."

He laughed once more, filling the cab of his truck with a rich masculine noise that swirled around her, found its way into her pores and sluiced through her veins to make those sparks dance everywhere this time.

They'd made it home by then, and as Jackson pulled around the ranch house to the garage, Meggie came running from Hans and Marta's place to greet her.

When he stopped the truck, Ally got out to meet her daughter without another word to Jackson.

But even as she focused on the little girl, she took with her a secret pleasure at what she'd just learned about Jackson Heller.

He could be charming.

He could be pleasant.

He could even be funny in his way.

And he didn't have any one special *lady friend* that he was involved with....

"...and Mutt came home all muddy and smelly, so me 'n' Hans gave him a hose bath and Mutt stayed real still while I got him soaped up good and then all of a sudden he shaked and shaked and suds went everywhere on me and Hans, and Hans looked so funny and…''

While Ally stood in the spray of the shower a few minutes later, Meggie sat on the clothes hamper and regaled her with tales of her day.

Every muscle in Ally's body ached. Her hands were a mess of raw flesh and angry blisters. And she was so exhausted she was leaning against the wall, letting the water rain over her and trying not to fall asleep standing up.

But every bit of it was worth it to her to hear her daughter chattering the way she was. Meggie was turning back into a little girl, and no amount of work or misery or fatigue was too high a price for Ally to pay for that.

''I have to wash my hair now, honey,'' Ally called through the shower curtain, forcing herself to straighten away from that wall. ''I won't be able to hear you with my head under the water, so hold on a minute.''

''That's okay. I better go downstairs and set the table for dinner anyhow.''

Ally heard the bathroom door open and close as she reached for the shampoo. The image of her daughter scurrying off to do a chore made her smile.

In the past three years Ally had jumped through hoops trying to bring Meggie out of her divorce depression. She'd gone into debt for a vacation to Disneyland and for every toy her daughter had seemed even remotely interested in. She'd taken her bike riding, camping, hiking, to every kids' movie, museum, amusement park or entertainment that had come along. She'd gone after the job as camp cook and slopped more oatmeal and boiled more hot dogs than she hoped to see the whole rest of her life. She'd done anything and everything imaginable to brighten Meggie's spirits.

Except given her chores to do.

Who'd have thought that would have done more good than anything?

Or that Jackson Heller, of all people—whip cracker, taskmaster and sometime nice guy—would have been the one to accomplish it?

It was still Meggie's voice that Ally heard as she approached the kitchen half an hour later when she'd finished her shower, dressed in a pair of cutoff jean shorts and a T-shirt, and dried her hair. Only her daughter's audience now was Jackson.

Rather than revitalizing Ally, getting cleaned up had sapped what little was left of her energy and for a moment she paused outside the door, closed her eyes and reveled in her daughter's voice while she tried to summon the stamina to get through the evening.

What she heard surprised her.

The conversation that was going on on the other side of the door could have been one between herself and Meggie. Not only was her daughter telling the same stories, but with as much warmth and spirit and lack of inhibitions—as if she felt almost as relaxed with Jackson as she did with Ally.

And for his part, Jackson laughed in all the right places and asked just enough questions to show he was interested, to encourage her, to pave the way for Meggie to open up even more.

Gratitude to him for all of that made Ally forgive him a lot at that moment. It also made it occur to her that maybe, like his father, beneath the gruff exterior he had a pretty soft interior.

Just then she heard her daughter say in a conspiratorial voice, "Let's set it all up before Mom comes down so she can't say no."

And with that Ally decided it was time to join them in the kitchen.

"Can't say no to what?"

Meggie made the face of someone caught in the act. "Me and Jackson want to eat on the coffee table, in front of the TV tonight," the little girl said as if the idea were already doomed.

"I can't see the harm." Jackson added his support.

"I usually like for us to have dinner together, at the table."

"Oh, ple-eease," Meggie begged. "Just this once?"

Indulging Meggie always came easier than sticking to the rules, and tonight Ally was too tired not to take the easy way out. Plus, with Jackson throwing in his encouragement, she didn't want to be the bad guy. "I suppose it would be okay just this once."

Marta had left them food again—meat loaf, potatoes, peas and bread—and they all took what they could carry and headed back the way Ally had just come, putting it on the square coffee table in the center of the three sofas that formed a U around the big-screen television.

It was the call of those overstuffed couches that did Ally in.

When Jackson and Meggie went for drinks, Ally eased her exhausted bones and sore posterior onto the downy cushions of one of them.

Just a little rest, she told herself. She could lay her head on the sofa back and close her eyes for only a minute while Jackson and Meggie were out of the room and then she'd feel so much better....

Ally was sure not more than a few seconds had passed when she felt her right hand being lifted gingerly from her lap.

Meggie, she thought. Meggie was probably going to pull her arm around those narrow shoulders and cuddle up to her side the way she did sometimes when they were watching television.

That would be nice. In fact it made Ally smile. But only with her eyes closed. Her lids were too heavy to raise, so she granted herself a moment's more rest and stayed where she was, waiting to feel that tiny body against hers before she'd tell Meggie to go ahead and eat, that she'd join her and they could snuggle later.

But no tiny body curled up under her arm.

Instead a big, callused hand cradled the back of hers and four long, thick fingers began to rub something cool and smooth over her palm.

This was not Meggie.

And the realization of that fact forced Ally to drag herself from a deeper sleep than she'd thought she was in.

When she finally managed to open her eyes, it was to find Jackson sitting crossways on the couch beside her, holding her hand while he rubbed some sort of ointment on her blisters.

Without moving, Ally glanced around the room. Meggie was nowhere in sight, the coffee table that had been laden with dishes and food was now clear of everything, and she sensed that the hour was much, much later than when she'd sat down.

But she was still so weary, so weighted with the deep sleep she'd just come out of, that she couldn't make herself do more than stay the way she was.

Of course, helping to persuade her was the fact that Jackson was concentrating on what he was doing and didn't seem to know she was awake. And his ministrations felt so good she couldn't resist letting them go on.

Carefully. Very carefully, he dabbed the ointment and then smoothed it around with a gentleness that amazed her.

As she basked in the slow, steady strokes, she watched him.

The man was almost too good-looking to be real there in the dim glow of a single lamp that dusted the hollows of his cheeks with shadows and gilded the chiseled crests in gold.

His features were relaxed—a state she hadn't seen

them in much since she'd arrived—and the lack of furrows in his brow only enhanced his handsomeness.

His hair was combed in a careless way that said it had seen more action from his fingers than from a comb; his mustache was neatly trimmed, and he smelled pretty terrific, too.

But more than with the way he looked, he was enrapturing her with his touch. Warm, tender, almost loving—though of course, that was a silly thought.

Finished with her right hand, he set it on her lap and picked up the other.

Ally was just tired enough to remain sleep-limp without effort, so still he wasn't alerted to the fact that she was awake.

And yet if he had been, he might have glanced up and given her a view of those incredible blue eyes of his—something she suddenly craved.

"That's nice," she said, hoping he wouldn't stop but willing to risk it to satisfy that need.

Up went his brows and, with them, his lids as he finally looked at her, still holding her hand but not applying the cream just then. "You missed supper," he said in a quiet, husky voice that only informed without criticism.

But even if he had criticized, it would have been worth it for the sight of those eyes.

"What time is it?" she asked.

"Almost eleven."

"And Meggie—"

"Upstairs asleep." He dipped his fingertips into the jar of ointment and went back to her blisters.

"This is the second night I've missed tucking her in."

"I did it tonight," he said, his gaze on what he was doing again. "She asked to take Mutt with her and when I brought him up to her I got her all settled in."

"Mutt the dog?"

"Mmm. He's sleeping at her feet." Jackson let a split second of silence pass before he said, "I've never seen anyone brace themselves with all those dolls and things the way she does. What's that about?"

His tone held more than curiosity, it actually rang with some concern and compassion, too. And something about that melted her insides even more than the soft touch of his hands. "Insecurity, I guess. She started doing the bumper pad of toys after the divorce and she hasn't been able to sleep any other way since."

He nodded as if she'd only confirmed what he'd suspected.

He had finished with her left hand by then and let it go. Ally immediately regretted losing his touch, but at least he didn't move away. He stayed where he was, so close beside her that the shin of the leg he had up on the couch ran the length of her thigh.

He leaned an arm along the back of the sofa where her head still rested and stared at her, studying her, but in a thoughtful way now, unlike the other times when his eyes had bored through her.

"What about you?" he asked. "Do you have insecurities from your divorce?"

"I don't know. One or two, I suppose. Comes with the territory." Territory she didn't want to talk about. She held up her hands, palms first. "Thanks for this."

He only nodded and changed the subject yet again. "With that red hair and those green eyes, I keep wondering if you're Irish. Are you?" he asked out of the blue.

"On my mother's side."

Again he nodded. "Irish eyes—that's what I thought."

Those sparks he'd raised in her at the end of the day came back to play along her nerve endings with the dark whiskey tone of his voice just then and the words that let her know she wasn't the only one noticing things she shouldn't be noticing.

"You should sell out to me and go away, Ally," he told her then, not an order, more a suggestion, unlike even the warnings he'd delivered in the past. This was quiet, heartfelt, as if he were wishing she'd do it before whatever it was that was wrapping around them both at that moment got any stronger or pulled them any closer.

But even as he said it, he kept on studying her face, searching her eyes, and she didn't seem able to do more than shake her head in denial as she lost herself in the sight of his face, too.

For a moment time seemed to stand still as the intimacy of the room, of being so close together on that couch, of the touch they'd just shared, wiped away all the harsh words that had been said since they'd met, all the harsh treatment. Suddenly they were not two people at odds. They were two people attracted to each other.

Intensely attracted...

Very slowly, Jackson came nearer, pausing—hesitating—with his mouth poised a scant breath from hers. But only for a heartbeat before closing that last distance and kissing her.

Had she really thought he might not be good at it? She'd been wrong. He was better than good at it. He was great. His lips felt as supple as they looked. Just slightly moist, just slightly parted, just...wonderful. His mustache was soft, almost silky and the little bit it tickled was tantalizing. Titillating. Very sexy...

He kissed the way he did many things—expertly, firmly but gently, with knowledge and experience. And with a quiet passion that took her breath away.

She shouldn't be doing this and she knew it. She knew she should put a stop to it right then.

But it felt so terrific to be cocooned in the soft cushions of the couch with Jackson's big, powerful body looming over her, his hand tenderly cupping the side of her face, his mouth on hers. She just couldn't do it.

Then all at once, Jackson did, pulling away so abruptly it was as if someone else had yanked him back.

He shook his head in a strong denial, and his expression seemed to be full of self-disgust. ''Damn it all to hell,'' he muttered.

Then he shoved himself off the couch and stood there, tall, gorgeous, angry again. ''Are you going to make it up the stairs under your own steam tonight or do I have to carry you?'' he demanded as brusquely as ever and as if the end of the previous night had irked him, too.

"I can make it on my own just fine, thanks," she answered with a fair share of coldness to mask her confusion and embarrassment—though what she had to be embarrassed about she wasn't quite sure.

"Good, then do it," he ordered. And with that, he headed for the foyer with one last bark. "We start at 6:00 a.m. tomorrow."

Ally watched him go, wanting to throw something at that broad, straight back; wondering why the sound of his boots on each step that took him to the second level echoed in her pulse; and wishing—wishing hard—that she'd pushed him away the moment her eyes had opened and she'd found her hand in his.

Hearing his bedroom door close, she got to her feet and moved stiffly in the same direction, all the while telling Jackson off in her head, calling him names, letting him know in no uncertain terms just how much she didn't like him.

And she *didn't* like him.

Yet after she'd looked in on Meggie and finally eased out of her clothes with the agony of the sore, tired muscles and raw flesh that *he'd* caused, the memory of those scant few minutes when things had been so different between them got into bed with her.

As angry as she was at Jackson for stirring things up and then pulling the rug out from under her, she was more angry with herself for remembering too vividly that warm, sweet kiss.

And worse than that, longing for another one…

340

Chapter Five

Jackson never set an alarm to get himself up in the mornings. He didn't need to. Waking early just came naturally.

But four o'clock was *too* early. Especially when he hadn't fallen asleep until after one.

Oh, he'd gone to bed long before that. Nearly two hours before, in fact. But he'd tossed and turned, fighting off thinking about that kiss. Wanting to kick himself for having done it.

Wanting to do it again.

When he'd finally managed to get to sleep, it hadn't been restful. He'd had so many dreams that he might as well not have slept at all.

He'd dreamed Ally was in danger and he was stuck where he couldn't get to her. He'd dreamed that Ally was in the shower and no matter how hard he tried, he couldn't see through the curtain. He'd dreamed Ally was in his bed and he was locked in a glass box from which he could see but not touch. He'd dreamed of Ally in someone else's arms....

A shot of adrenaline had finally jolted him out of that torture.

And now here he was, all churned up inside, staring at a pitch-black ceiling before the sun had so much as thought about rising.

Churned up over Ally.

Over those dreams.

Over that kiss the night before.

Hell, even over Meggie.

The trouble was, he was getting to like some things he shouldn't be liking. Too many things. Too much.

Meggie, for instance.

He really enjoyed her. Enjoyed her shyness, her quiet humor, her sweetness and innocence. The sight of her welcoming her mother when they got back to the ranch at the end of the day warmed and delighted him, just as her saying that first hello to him did.

He liked finding her in the kitchen when he got there after his shower. It was nice to hear her talk as they set out supper together while Ally took longer than he did washing off the work grime. Nice to have someone to talk to.

But then, suppertime was a weak spot for him.

That was when he felt the loneliest here. It always seemed like the whole damn world went home to people around the dinner table while all that waited for him was a silent, solitary meal. So of course he was susceptible to having company then.

But getting to like that family atmosphere of sharing supper with a chatty child wasn't good. Not at all. Not when he knew that family atmosphere was only a temporary thing.

Because when it ended, when Ally and Meggie were gone, facing this big old empty house after a day's work would only be worse. He knew that from experience. Adjusting to that emptiness wasn't something he ever wanted to go through again. Consistent loneliness was better than that.

Safer.

His mind went on wandering as he lay there, back to the night before, to Ally sleeping on the couch.

The memory of how she'd looked haunted him. So soft. So beautiful. Long eyelashes resting against her high cheekbones, her lips parted just enough to look inviting...

Oh, yeah, he'd liked that, too....

Too damn much, he thought, trying to force the image out of his mind.

He didn't want to be thinking about her all the time the way he was. He didn't want to be dreaming about her. He didn't want to be having feelings for her. Wanting her...

His emotions were running amok and it was driving him crazy.

He was a man who knew how to live with external things being out of his control. The crops. The cattle when they had a mind to stampede. The blizzards, the torrential spring rains and floods, the drops in beef prices and rises in the cost of feed.

But the interior things being out of his control, that was something else again. Thunder and lightning and gale-force winds inside of himself over this woman, or even the feeling of internal sunshine that had come as he'd watched her sleep on that couch, were a damn sight tougher to tolerate.

In fact they scared the living hell out of him.

Why couldn't he be attracted to a woman who understood what a rancher's life involved? A woman who wouldn't be done in by it? Scared off by it?

That would solve the loneliness around here without so much of the risk that things wouldn't work and he'd find himself lonely again.

So why wasn't he attracted to a woman like Marilyn Mercer?

His neighbor was pretty enough. Sexy enough. Willing enough, that was for sure.

She'd grown up on that place next door, helped her father run it, helped her husband run it after him, run it herself for the past five years. She'd never be daunted or overcome by everything around here. She'd even be a good partner. They could join the properties, work side by side. Have a real future together. One he could count on. He'd never have to waste a single minute worrying that she'd light out of here because the going got too tough for her to take.

But thoughts of Marilyn Mercer didn't get a rise out of him. Even Marilyn Mercer herself—all trussed up in clothes tight enough to strangle her and hangin' out the top—hadn't stirred him up the way Ally did in loose-fitting, work-grimy duds.

Standing there with his neighbor flaunting everything she had to offer, he'd only wanted to get the hell away from her and back to the truck and Ally.

Go figure.

A gorgeous, sexy woman had been throwing herself at him and he'd been more alert to the forlorn, dejected look that had eased across Ally's features when she'd first set eyes on Marilyn. He'd wanted to bend over and whisper in her ear that if she was feeling less a woman next to his neighbor, she should stop. That she was every bit as beautiful, as desirable...*more* because it wasn't Marilyn he'd been itching for, it was Ally.

Even when Ally had walked off and left him stranded with his neighbor and Marilyn's suggestions had turned to outright propositions, he'd barely heard her. Instead he'd been more aware of Ally's tight little behind as she'd walked away from him. Of how she'd kept looking over at them. Of the jealousy that had cropped up in her features and caused her to beat an angry path back to the truck.

He'd liked that, too. If she was jealous it must mean she was having the same stirrings he was.

But he didn't want to like it. He didn't want to care. Didn't want to be so attracted to her he ached to kiss her again, to get his hands on her...

Why the hell couldn't he feel that way about Marilyn Mercer or any of the other women around these parts? he demanded of himself yet again. Women he was more suited to. Women who were more suited to him.

But he didn't know why.

He only knew he wasn't. They just didn't appeal to him.

And Ally Brooks did.

Before going downstairs every morning, Ally poked her head into Meggie's room just to have a look at her daughter. Even if she hadn't ordinarily done it, she would have this morning, because as she left her own room she could hear a soft, intermittent whine coming from there.

Not a human whine, though. A dog's.

Mutt, Ally remembered, had spent the night and most likely wanted out.

She eased the door open and went into the shadows that were barely lightened by the dawning sunshine sifting through the curtains.

The sight that greeted her was unusual. Since Meggie had begun the practice of surrounding herself with toys to sleep, she'd not once woken up having disturbed any of them. But today the dolls and stuffed animals were all scattered—half on the bed, half off— and Meggie was at the foot of the mattress, sleeping against the big dog's back as if discarding the makeshift bumper pad hadn't mattered.

Mutt didn't move even as Ally approached. He only stared at her with eyes that begged for help.

She patted his head and carefully lifted Meggie's arm from over the top of him.

That and the dog's escape woke her daughter.

"Iss a-right," Meggie said in a sleepy stupor. "Jackson said Mutt could sleep with me."

"I know, but it's morning and Mutt was whining. He probably needs to go outside."

Meggie rolled onto her back and rubbed her eyes. "I been hungry for pancakes. If I get up now, would you make some?"

Marta had been coming over in the mornings to wait for Meggie to get up and to fix her breakfast. Ally had missed that time with her daughter and so rather than encouraging Meggie to get the extra couple of hours of sleep she could, she said, "Sure. I think I can squeeze in a quick batch before I have to do whatever Jackson has planned today. I'll go and start them and let Mutt out. You get dressed and then come down."

Twenty minutes later Ally was beating egg whites when Meggie joined her.

She climbed up onto one of the tall stools at the butcher block where her mother was working. "Is Jackson still asleep?" the little girl asked, glancing around as if he might be somewhere she hadn't noticed.

Ally nodded at the coffeemaker. "Looks like he was up a long time ago—he's already had half a pot of coffee. But I don't know where he is." The affection in her daughter's voice when she'd asked intrigued Ally. "You like him, don't you?"

"He's nice to me now. Not like when we first got here and he was mad."

"So it was okay that he tucked you in last night?"

"Sure. He bringed Mutt up."

"He *brought* Mutt up," Ally corrected. "I'm sorry I fell asleep the way I did."

"You must'a been real tuckered out. We couldn't even get you to wake up to eat. But it was okay. Me 'n' Jackson took everything back in here so's we didn't bother you. And then he played the Candy Land game with me, and checkers and chest—"

"Chest?"

"It's like checkers 'cept there's all these different-shaped things—like a horse head and a queen and a king and fawns and stuff."

"Pawns," Ally amended again, smiling at her daughter's mispronunciations. "And the game is called *chess* not *chest*."

"Okay. Anyway, then we had cookies and milk outside on the patio and talked about stars, and then it was time for bed so I went up and got ready while he rounded up ol' Mutt."

Ally couldn't help a second smile at the jargon and mode of speech her daughter was picking up. And at the image of Jackson talking to the little girl about stars while the two of them shared cookies and milk. "Sounds like you had quite an evening without me." One that Ally was sorry to have missed, though she didn't want to admit it even to herself.

"I did."

Ally took the bowl of batter to the stove where the griddle had been heating, and Meggie went to one of the sliding doors that led out back.

"Should I go look for Jackson? We wouldn't want him to miss your pancakes."

"Maybe he already ate," Ally hedged because she wasn't anxious to see him this morning. Not after that kiss she'd liked much too much and relived a million times in bed before she'd been able to fall asleep again. And certainly not after Jackson's swift about-face when he'd ended it.

"Uh-oh…"

Ally glanced over her shoulder at her daughter. "What's the matter?"

"Jordy must be sneakin' a smoke back of the chicken coop again—that's what he calls it. But Hans'll get mad if he catches him like he did yesterday."

Jordy was one of the ranch hands. A very young one with a cocksure attitude and what seemed to be an ever-present sneer in his expression.

Meggie went on talking. "Jordy's not s'pose to be smokin' out there on accounta Hans says all the grasses are real dry this time of year. Jordy said a bad word at him and called him a old man, and Hans said that's right he was a old man, old 'nuff to know one hot match was all it took to start a fire that'd burn down this whole place. Hans hollered at Jordy and everything."

It occurred to Ally belatedly to wonder how Meggie could spot a wisp of cigarette smoke from behind the chicken coop at this distance. She flipped her pancakes and went to see for herself.

But the smoke coming from that direction was not a wisp. It was a big black cloud.

"Oh, Lord, Meggie, that *is* a fire! Find Jackson and tell him!'

Meggie looked stunned for a moment but then dashed out the door. Ally followed her a few steps, remembered the pancakes and the hot griddle, ran back to turn it off and then made a beeline for the chicken coop, where the sounds of wildly cackling birds called to her.

Jordy was the culprit all right, because he was the only one back there, trying to stomp out flames that were moving faster than his feet.

"Is there a hose or some way to get water back here?" Ally asked without preamble.

"Nothin' reaches," he shouted at her. "Git help!"

It arrived just then in the form of Jackson at a full run, carrying an armload of empty burlap feed sacks. He dropped them onto the ground, tossed one to Jordy, one to Ally, and took one himself. Then he ordered Ally to the other side of the blaze while he filled in the space between her and the young ranch hand, and they all began beating at the fire.

It was still getting the best of them when Hans and Marta came running with Meggie close behind. Ally assumed Jackson had sent her daughter to get them, but even with two more people the blaze was hot and high. All of Ally's attention was focused on the fight, and slapping at those licking tongues of flames that spat sparks to further their reach.

And then suddenly she heard Marta's voice call out, "Meggie's caught!"

Meggie's caught? Ally didn't know what the other woman was talking about but her head shot up in time to see her tiny daughter clumsily trying to help swat out the flames with a sack that was bigger than she was and standing much too close to the conflagration. So close that the ruffled hem of the T-shirt she wore had caught fire.

"Oh, my God!" Ally shouted, dropping her own sack and running for her child.

But Jackson was quicker.

He tackled the little girl and rolled with her on the ground away from the inferno. Over and over they went as if they were tumbling down a steep hill.

"Oh, my God! Oh, my God! Oh, my God!" Ally chanted with each furl, her heart in her throat.

Finally Jackson stopped, checked to make sure the little girl's clothing was no longer burning before he stood her up in a hurry and pulled the shirt off with one quick swipe.

Ally reached them at that moment, just in time to hear Meggie say, "I just wanted to help so everything didn't burn down like Hans said it would."

"Are you hurt?" Ally asked, frantically joining Jackson in the search of her daughter's body for signs of it.

"I think it was just my shirt. I'm okay."

And she was, too. Luckily her shorts had been between the T-shirt and her body and Jackson's fast action had kept the fire from getting past that barrier.

"We aren't going to let anything burn down, Meggie. It's better if you don't help. Just stay back away from it," Jackson said then, firmly but without anger before he ran for the grass fire again.

But Ally didn't rush back with him. She couldn't. Instead she knelt down in front of her daughter and took a second, closer look to make sure Meggie really was all right. Then she wrapped her arms around the little girl and held on tight as her heartbeat raced and she fought back the terror that had surged through her.

"Damn it, Ally, get over here. We need help!" Jackson shouted.

If he hadn't been the person who had just saved Meggie from harm, Ally might have ignored him. She might have followed her own instinct at that moment, picked up her daughter and gotten them both as far away from that fire as she could.

But that wasn't what she did.

Shaken to the core, she nevertheless let go of her hold on Meggie and turned her toward the house. "I don't want you anywhere near here. You wait inside," she said, giving her a slight push and making sure the little girl was on her way before she turned back to the fire that was finally coming under control.

Ally was still on edge even after the fire was out, water was thrown on the singed ground from buckets everyone hauled, and Jackson had said only a curt "You're out of here, Jordy," to the ranch hand.

Back at the house she checked on Meggie, had her undress completely, and let her put on clean clothes only when she was once again satisfied that the little girl hadn't been burned anywhere.

Then she went back to the kitchen, made a new batch of pancake batter and scorched the first few in her preoccupation.

But Jackson had the cure for lingering tension over the near-miss accident.

Work.

And lots of it.

Ally was just grateful that it was all close to home so she could keep her daughter within sight and reassure herself Meggie was really okay every time a shiver of fear at what might have happened ran up her spine.

Shoveling horse manure out of the barn was the first order of business when they finally got going. Twenty-four stalls had to be mucked out and then hosed down.

The horseflies were worse around the manure than they had been out in the wide-open spaces the day before and they seemed to feast on Ally, who had to stop every other minute to brush one away.

And the smell really got to her. She had missed dinner the night before and, after the fire fright, hadn't had an appetite for breakfast, so the pungent odor of fresh manure in the hot space turned her empty stomach. Plus the shovel handle ate into her blistered palms and turned them to welts that increased the agony of each hour.

But, outside, her daughter sang silly songs with

Hans as the two of them painted the paddock fence and Ally tried hard to ignore her own agony.

It was also nice to have lunch with Meggie. Nothing fancy, just sandwiches and macaroni salad Marta had made for them all, but everyone gathered around the picnic tables on the patio, the conversation was lively, and most of the attention revolved around Meggie, who delighted in it.

What the afternoon made up for in odor it lost as a backbreaker. Jackson, Hans and Ally stacked forty-pound hay bales in a lean-to behind the barn. The hay itself was sweet smelling, but the work was hard as Ally handed each bale to Hans, who handed it to Jackson where he stood halfway up a stair step of the things.

Even when Ally was ready to drop and eyeing the swimming pool with longing in her heart, Jackson sent her to dig potatoes. On her hands and knees. In the late-day sun.

How long was this slave driving going to keep up? she wondered, feeling irritable.

Did Jackson mean for her to work like this every day for the rest of her life? Because she wasn't going to do it.

Sure she wanted to contribute, to do her share, but this was ridiculous. Housecleaning, cooking, even doing his laundry, seemed reasonable enough. Some gardening, some small chores close to home, maybe. Canning, preserving, drying food for winter. But she was doing the work of a full-time, hard-core ranch hand and it was killing her. And she didn't believe that was what Shag had intended when he'd urged her to come here and bequeathed a portion of this place to her.

So what was she going to do about it? she asked herself.

She could confront Jackson head-on. Refuse to co-operate in any more of this gamut he was having her run. Tell him straight out that there was no stipulation that she owed him this kind of work in order to accept her part of the inheritance.

And she knew just what his reaction would be.

He'd goad her. He'd say she wanted to lounge around while he worked his fingers to the bone as if he owed it to her. He'd say if she couldn't earn her keep, she had no business being here. That she'd better sell and get out.

He'd sneer. He'd snarl. He'd say he knew she wouldn't be able to handle it. And then he'd be miserable to live with.

And she'd have to face him every day knowing she'd given in. That he'd beaten her. That he'd won, that even if she didn't let him buy her out he would have proven that she really didn't belong here, that she was a freeloader.

Blisters, welts, sore muscles, abused flesh, horsefly bites and stench were better than that, she decided.

At least for a little while longer.

For a little while longer she'd go along with this, work like a dog and keep her mouth shut.

Maybe eventually he'd see that this tactic wasn't going to drive her away—which she had no doubt was his intention. And then maybe he'd ease up. Maybe he'd accept that she and Meggie were here permanently and he'd get used to it.

Then, maybe they could come to a more reasonable division of labor.

One that would keep Ally removed from Jackson.

And maybe, if they didn't spend so much time together, she wouldn't be so aware of every bulge of every muscle. Of every flex of every magnificent sinew. Or every nuance in that deep, rich voice.

Then maybe, too, things like that kiss the night before wouldn't happen....

A soft rattling sound distracted her from her thoughts just then. Like a baby's rattle, only more subtle. More efficient.

Ally sat back on her heels and looked around her. But she was the only person within fifty feet. Jackson and Hans were discussing something over near the barn and Meggie had gone with Marta to a pond somewhere on the property to pick cattails.

When the sound came again—closer than before— she shifted her gaze to the ground just in time to see a snake slither down one of the holes left by a potato she'd dug and then up the one next to it.

Without considering the wisdom of quick movement, she jumped to her feet and ran like crazy for the two men.

"Who lit dynamite under you?" Jackson asked before she could get her throat to work.

"Snake!" was all she could manage to say when she did. *"Rattlesnake!"*

Both men eyed her as if she'd lost her mind and took a placid glance in the direction of the garden.

"You want this one or shall I take it?" Hans asked.

"Go ahead," Jackson answered.

"It's a *rattlesnake*," Ally reiterated as if they might not have understood.

But still neither man seemed concerned.

Hans pushed off the paddock fence he'd been leaning against and sauntered carelessly in the direction from which she'd just come as Jackson said, "Prairie rattler. They're all over." Then he nodded at the garden patch. "Hans has 'im."

Ally couldn't help turning around and looking just as the older man yanked up on the thing then snapped it against the ground, literally knocking its head off.

"Oooh," she moaned in a revolted grimace, squinting her eyes against the sight and backing up far enough to make her bump right into Jackson.

His big hands came to her shoulders to steady her as his laugh sent the heat of his breath into her hair. But whether he was laughing at her or what Hans had just done, she didn't know, because he called, "Good one," to the older man as if he'd enjoyed the spectacle.

Then, to make matters worse, Hans took out his pocketknife, cut off the rattle and, after tossing the body and head into the trash bag Ally had been putting plant debris into, he brought it to them.

"Bet Meggie would like to have this."

"Wouldn't every girl?" Ally muttered under her

breath, wondering if Jackson's scorn might be a whole lot more palatable than that snake rattle.

But she didn't have much time to actually consider it, because just then Ash came running toward them, looking as panicked as Ally imagined she had moments earlier fleeing from the snake.

"We're in trouble!" he shouted even before he reached them.

Jackson's hands were still on Ally's shoulders and they tightened reflexively. But he still didn't let go of her and, deep down, Ally experienced an unwanted pleasure at his touch.

"The baby's coming!" Ash announced as he stopped in front of them, going on to a flood of words. "And I mean it's coming right *now!* Beth's been having what we thought were those practice contractions but I guess they weren't just practice, because she's already having trouble keeping herself from pushing and the damn doctor went fishing way out at Snow Lake and even though his office got hold of him on his cellular phone he can't make it back for at least half an hour and Beth says it isn't going to take that long and please tell me somebody around here knows something about delivering more than a calf or a foal!"

"I do."

Hans looked at Ally curiously. From behind her, sounding incredulous, Jackson said, "*You* do? What are you talking about?"

"I can deliver a baby," she told them all. "Believe it or not, it's something I know a lot about."

"Ally—"

"I'm serious," she said forcefully, glancing over her shoulder at him.

"Just because you're a woman and you've had a child yourself—"

"That is not the reason I can do it. And if Ash is right and the baby is that close to being born, we don't have time to argue about it."

Jackson turned her around to face him and frowned at her as if to shame her into telling the truth.

She answered that frown in no uncertain terms. "I may be lousy at ranch work and think snakes are not a whole lot of fun, but that doesn't mean I can't do anything else in life. And delivering a baby just happens to be one of the things I *can* do," she said, enjoying turning the tables for once.

"We're desperate, Jackson," Ash said, sounding it.

Jackson stared at her another moment and then finally released her from his grip. He didn't say anything, but his expression nearly shouted that he still wasn't convinced.

Ally didn't wait around to reassure him. She said, "Let's go," and headed for the renovated bunkhouse, leaving Hans behind and paying little attention to Jackson and Ash, who followed her like ducklings after their mother.

At the bunkhouse Ally sent Ash to be with Beth and put Jackson to work finding a bottle of alcohol, some clean sheets and towels, and sterilizing scissors. While he was at it, she thoroughly scrubbed her hands and forearms and then had him pour the alcohol over them.

It seemed strange that she was now in charge and giving the orders for a change. Jackson watched her as if he couldn't believe what he was seeing, but she ignored his doubts and simply said, "Looks like when excitement happens around here it comes in threes."

He didn't comment on that. Instead he said, "The doctor's office will have alerted the hospital to send their helicopter. Do what you can to wait for them."

Just then, as if in answer, a moan came from upstairs.

"Doesn't sound like there's going to be any waiting going on," she said, holding her hands in the air like a surgeon to let them dry.

But still he wasn't confident in her. "I've helped in the birthing of the animals around here. If you aren't damn sure you know what you're doing, you better let me see to this."

She looked him straight in the eye and said, "I'm damn sure I know what I'm doing."

Then she led the way to the bedroom upstairs where Beth was laboring.

Ash met them at the door, taking from Jackson all Ally had had him accumulate, and then she and Ash left him standing in the hallway.

"I'll be right out here if you need me," he called after them.

But Ally ignored him. For one of the few times since she'd arrived here, she was in an element that was more nearly her own.

"It's coming!" Beth announced in greeting the moment Ally was in the room.

Ally asked Ash to bring a chair for her to sit on at the foot of the bed and then sent him to hold his wife's hand.

"Not only is this baby arriving a few weeks early, it's not even going to wait for the doctor, is it?" Ally joked to lighten the tension in the room.

But Beth was in no condition for it. "I have to push!"

Ally took a quick look and said, "You're right, you do. It's already crowning with a full head of Dad's black hair." And then she got down to business. "Now here's what we need to do...."

Both Ash and Beth did everything she told them to, Ash helping his wife sit forward when she pushed, and coaching her through her breathing when Ally told her to stop.

The baby was definitely in a hurry, because after no more than six or seven pushes, a healthy pink girl announced herself to the world with a lusty wail that competed with the noise of a helicopter landing just outside.

Ally ignored the commotion going on beyond the room and instead set the infant on Beth's stomach and said, "Ten fingers. Ten toes. Great lungs. Congratulations, you guys have a daughter."

And then all of a sudden the door opened and in rushed the doctor and two air ambulance attendants. They had Beth and the baby bundled onto a portable gurney in no time and, with Ash fast behind them, they whisked mother and child out.

In the aftermath of the moment the impact of the birth settled in on Ally and the power of it brought instant tears to her eyes.

A baby!

Lord, how she longed to have another one of her own....

Then into the doorway stepped Jackson.

His eyes locked on to hers, held them with a new respect, a new depth. He nodded slowly, relaying his approval of what she'd done for Beth, his appreciation.

And something more.

For in his eyes there was a hint of a change.

Ally couldn't quite put her finger on what that change was, maybe an acceptance of her that hadn't been there before, maybe even a bond, a new closeness...

But whatever it was, she had the sense that a barrier had just been lowered from between her and Jackson.

And that somehow, at that moment, their relationship had turned a corner.

Two hours later, when all the bustle had died down and Ally had had her shower, she went downstairs and found the dining room table set.

It looked very festive, with flowers from Marta's garden in the center of three place settings of fine bone china.

Ally assumed she, Meggie and Jackson were cel-

ebrating the birth of Beth and Ash's baby, but it surprised her a little that Jackson felt the inclination.

Not that he wasn't a proud uncle, because he was.
He'd congratulated his brother-in-law with gusto.
He'd kissed his sister and held her hand all the way
to the helicopter that whisked the small family to the
hospital. And he'd been the one to tell the story of it
all to Marta and Meggie when they'd come running
back to the ranch to see what had happened.

But Ally hadn't expected him to celebrate with dinner in the dining room, complete with linen napkins
and candles.

Meggie came through the swinging door from the
kitchen as Ally was surveying the scene; she stopped
short at the unexpected sight of her mother.

"I was just comin' to get you!" the little girl said.
"You're bein' late for your own party."

"Party?"

"Well, not really a party, just you and me and
Jackson. But Jackson says it's like a party 'cuz it's in
your honor for helpin' the baby get borned. Whatever
in your honor means."

"Oh," Ally said, more surprised to hear that than
she had been to think Jackson was just celebrating.

"Marta pinched Jackson's cheek when he asked
her for some flowers and said what a nice man he was
and brought us some cake and ice cream for dessert,
too."

"Marta's right, this is a nice thing to do."

"I told 'em Dad used to help babies get borned all
the time so it was no big deal, but they all think it is

anyway, and we get cake and ice cream like it really was a party, so it's okay.''

''I guess we better go into the kitchen and see what we can do to help, then,'' Ally said, wanting to avoid the subject of Meggie's father.

However, she noticed that Meggie hadn't gotten the dejected look on her face she usually got when she mentioned him. In fact, the reminder of her father didn't seem to disturb the little girl at all tonight.

''No, you can't go in the kitchen,'' Meggie was saying as Ally studied her for signs of depression. ''I'm s'pose to make you sit in the big chair and you have to just wait for us to serve you like waitresses.''

Happiness was all Ally spotted in her daughter and after all the excitement of the day, it was a private joy of her own to see it. ''The big chair, huh?'' she asked as she played along.

''Yep. I'll tell Jackson he can take the tornados off the grill.''

''Tornados?'' Ally repeated as Meggie ran back the way she'd come. ''Could she mean tournedos?''

Meggie returned a few minutes later, carefully carrying a salad while Jackson followed her in with a tray that held a breadbasket, three fruit cups, baked potatoes, and a platter of bacon-wrapped fillets that were, indeed, tournedos, not tornados.

''Wow,'' Ally breathed as he set the tray down.

Jackson cleared his throat and grinned a little sheepishly at her. ''Thought you'd earned a nice supper playin' midwife today.''

Ah, so that was what it took to get appreciated

around here! Killing herself to meet his demands didn't mean anything, but doing an emergency delivery of the latest Heller offspring made her in like Flynn, she thought. But she didn't say it aloud. Instead she answered his smile with one of her own and said, "It looks great."

Meggie went around the table to Ally's left and Jackson served the three of them from her right. Then he lighted the candles and poured full glasses of wine for Ally and himself, and a splash for Meggie so she could join the toast he stayed standing to make.

"To you, for saving the day."

"And to the new baby, who really didn't need all that much help from me," Ally demurred.

They did a round of clicking glasses and sipping a dry red wine that Meggie made a face at and clearly had no intention of finishing. Then Jackson sat down and they all began to eat.

"Ash called a few minutes ago," he told them as they did. "The baby is five pounds, one ounce—not bad for being early, the doctors said. She's healthy and Beth's doing fine, and everyone seems to agree that no one could have done a better delivery than you managed." He looked directly into Ally's eyes with those gorgeous blue ones of his. "I know I couldn't have done as fine a job."

"I'm glad I could help."

For a moment he held her gaze with his, frowning slightly, as if he were taking a much closer look at what he'd been trying not to see since she'd gotten here.

That gaze, much like the one they'd shared just after the birth this afternoon, warmed her from the inside out and Ally couldn't help wondering if her delivering his niece had somehow even altered his feelings about sharing his precious ranch.

Well, whatever that heated gaze and pampering meant, she wasn't going to question it. Or anything else that might have caused a change in his attitude. She was just going to sit back and enjoy it, for the moment at least. Because today she'd earned it.

Jackson refused to let Ally so much as remove a dish from the table when they were finished and instead sent her to the living room with a glass of wine while he and Meggie cleaned up.

When they'd finished, it was Meggie's bedtime.

"Please can Mutt sleep with me again tonight?" she begged as Ally tried to herd her upstairs.

Ally looked to Jackson to see if he minded and he answered her daughter.

"It's all right with me if it's all right with your mom."

"Ple-eease?"

"Sure, I don't see why not."

"I'll go find him and be up in a few minutes," Jackson promised.

While Meggie put on her pajamas and brushed her teeth, Ally turned down the bed and gathered the toys her daughter used as a bumper pad. Then she waited as the little girl climbed in and bolstered herself. But tonight she only used about half of them.

"I don't need so many. Last night they got in my

way," Meggie informed her as if it were strange for Ally not to have known.

Instead the little girl chose only her favorite dolls and discarded the stuffed animals to the floor.

Ally stared in amazement, unsure whether to congratulate her daughter or praise her or question her or act as if it were no big deal that for the first time in three years Meggie wasn't surrounding herself with over a dozen toys to sleep.

But the moment to say anything at all passed just then when Jackson knocked on the door.

Meggie called for him to come in and with him arrived Mutt to jump onto the bed, lick Meggie's face and curl up at the bottom of the mattress as if he'd been doing it all his life.

"How'd you girls like to spend tomorrow in town?" Jackson asked then.

"Instead of working?" Ally said, her shock shooting the words out before she even realized they were coming.

"We'll do a few chores in the morning and then take the rest of the day off for a little holiday. Seems like it's about time you had the grand tour of Elk Creek, for what it's worth."

He really was in a good mood tonight, Ally thought, jumping on the offer before he could rescind it. "That would be great. Wouldn't it, Meggie?"

"Mmm-hmm," Meggie agreed, already half-asleep.

Ally chuckled at her daughter and joked to Jackson, "Meggie thinks it would be great, too."

He stood by as she kissed the little girl good-night and moved the pile of discarded toys closer to the side of the bed just in case Meggie should change her mind and need them during the night. Then Jackson followed her out into the hallway.

"It's only eight-thirty and there's still half a bottle of wine downstairs. What do you say we finish it?" he asked then.

Ally hadn't planned to go to bed just yet, but the invitation was another surprise in a day full of them.

Was this really Jackson Heller, chivalrously suggesting they spend the end of a quiet evening alone together with a bottle of wine?

And was she out of her mind to accept?

Whether or not she was, she heard herself say, "That sounds nice."

And before she knew it, there they were, back downstairs, both of them on one couch as Ally sat straight forward in the center and Jackson angled toward her from the corner, much the way they'd been positioned when she'd awakened to find him treating her blisters the night before.

Tonight, though, his shin wasn't pressed against her thigh—there was an inch or so separating them— and he wasn't concentrating on her palms, he was studying her face.

But differences aside, there were still enough similarities to give Ally a vivid memory of the kiss they'd shared, and it both unnerved her and washed heat through her at once.

"How is it you know about deliverin' babies?" he

asked when he'd refilled their glasses and handed her hers.

So that was what this was all about—he just wanted his curiosity soothed.

Ally knew a moment's disappointment before she buried it. What had she thought? That there had been something romantic behind his invitation? And why on earth should it bother her that there wasn't? Better that it had just been a friendly gesture to go with his good mood tonight.

A mood she didn't want to sour by not answering his question, even if it did mean getting into the subject she'd been avoiding up until now.

She sipped her wine, sank a little lower in the cushions and rested her head against the sofa back, trying to think of them as any two people who were just getting to know each other. "My ex-husband was an obstetrician," she began.

"Meggie's father?"

"Right. I spent more hours than I could count quizzing him on the how-to's of birthing babies as he studied. Then I watched him perform several deliveries, and actually got to do it myself—basically— when my sister had her son. She had a home delivery and the midwife was a friend, so she sort of oversaw my doing the deed, while Doug was in the other room just in case there was a problem. Today was the first time I flew solo, though. Lucky for us all it was an easy, uncomplicated birth."

"You seemed so calm and confident I thought maybe you were an old hand."

"'The patient's needs come first. A physician must ignore his own feelings and think only of the good of that patient,'" she recited. "That was a quote from one of my ex's instructors. But the truth is, it all happened so fast today I didn't have time to be nervous or doubt myself. I just did what needed to be done."

"The same way you look at the chores I give you."

She only shrugged and took another sip of wine.

"If you were that involved in your husband's studies and work, the two of you must have been pretty close."

"I thought we were."

"Then what happened?" he asked bluntly, clearly not considering his probing question out of line. But then, that was Jackson. There was no beating around the bush with him. And suddenly Ally decided to give that practice a rest herself. In this instance, anyway.

"I wish I could tell you an original story, but the truth is that about the time Doug finished his residency and could have set up practice so all the schooling and training finally paid off, he decided he wanted a different life. With different people in it. In particular, a very young woman he'd met a few months before. No sooner was the ink dry on the divorce than he married the model and disappeared. My guess is to play vagabond through Europe—something he'd talked about before. All I know for sure is that when the fourth child-support check didn't show up and I called him, his phone had been disconnected. And when I went to his house, someone else was moving into it and no one knew—or would tell me—where he'd gone. That was three years ago and we haven't heard from him since.''

Jackson's eyebrows dropped into a dark frown. ''The way Meggie refers to him—''

''I know. As if he's away on vacation and will be back any minute. I guess that's what she needs to pretend in order to deal with it. She was upset when he moved out, of course, but when he turned his back on her completely and then vanished, she went over the edge into that depression I told you about before.''

''So you brought her up here.''

The calm, quiet tone of Jackson's voice made Ally realize how shrill her own had become. There had been a time—a long time—when she'd wanted and needed to talk about her divorce, her ex's misdeeds. But that time had passed; it wasn't cathartic anymore. Dredging it all up just aggravated her.

''So I brought her here,'' she answered, taking a deep breath and sighing it out. Then she drank more wine, letting it relax her again. ''I'm sorry for that little tirade. I've worked through my own feelings about the divorce and being deserted, but seeing your child in pain and not being able to do anything to fix it—you never get over that.''

He was watching her very intently, those striking eyes of his studying her. He reached an arm across the sofa back to finger a strand of her hair. ''So you're trying to compensate for what you can't fix.''

''Sure.''

''Men like your ex should be horsewhipped.''

''That's what your father said.''

"No wonder he left you part of everything to help get you and Meggie through. I'd have done the same thing."

Those words meant a lot to Ally. She hadn't actually realized how uncomfortable she'd been with having received a portion of what rightfully belonged to him and Linc and Beth, or how that uneasiness had hinged on Jackson's feelings, until he revealed his acceptance. Suddenly a great relief washed over her.

To thank him for it, she opened up to him even more. "Your father was there to see just how tough things were for Meggie and me. I'd been the only one working—and just as an assistant chef—while Doug went through school. I didn't make terrific money, so there were huge debts by the time he finished. The kind of debts with payments that were deferred until he was through. But that was when he disappeared and since I'd been silly enough to cosign the loans, everything fell to me. I was actually in worse shape financially than when I'd been supporting him, even though I'd been promoted to chef by then. Meggie and I had to move in with my mother—and Shag when he was with her. Which was how we got to know him so well."

Jackson shook his head in disgust, his stoic expression turned stern. "Horsewhipping is too good for somebody who would do all that to you."

Or to anyone else, Ally thought. And yet, that small qualification from him sent a surge of feelings through her that added to her gratitude to him. Jackson cared. She could see it as plainly as the long, thin, chiseled nose on his face. He was angry on her behalf. Outraged. Protective.

And it was nice. It was comforting. It was sexy.

"What's worse than what Doug did to me," she went on in a hurry to escape that wandering of her mind, "is what he's done to Meggie. She adored him and he just threw her away, like a toy he'd tired of or a pet that was too much trouble—something he just couldn't be bothered with anymore. How do you explain that to anyone, let alone to a little child?"

And where had the tears that suddenly flooded her eyes come from?

Ally blinked furiously, but one escaped to roll down her cheek.

Before she could brush it away, Jackson caught it with the backs of his fingers, smoothing her skin at the same time in a soothing gesture.

"You don't explain it," he said quietly. "You let her come to it herself, in her own good time."

The tears were gone as quickly as they'd come, chased away by the sparks that came to life at his touch. But fighting those was not nearly as easy as fighting not to break down in front of him.

"You're right," she said, again using the subject to help keep scarier emotions at bay. "There's nothing I can do but let her figure this out for herself. And I know she will. I'll just have to be there to pick up the pieces when it happens."

"Oh, I don't know. She may surprise you and not fall apart at all," he said with such confidence that Ally hung on to it as if it were an ironclad guarantee.

She smiled at him, thinking that there seemed to be more to him than she'd given him credit for before. More compassion. More caring. More kindness.

And Lord, but the man was great looking. Especially when he smiled at her in a way that seemed to wrap around her like silk and make her feel as if she were floating on a cloud.

It occurred to her then that maybe she'd had a little more wine than she should have, on top of yet another day of marathon hard work and a whole variety of excitements. It all left her very vulnerable to this calm after the storm. To the comfort of nearly lying back on that overstuffed couch with her feet up on the coffee table. To Jackson and the warmth that his cornflower blue gaze bathed her in, making her feel as if they were the only two people in the world....

He leaned forward and put his wineglass on the coffee table. Then he took hers and set it there, too.

But when he straightened, he was suddenly just above Ally. So near she breathed in the scent of his after-shave.

"You're quite a woman, Ally Brooks," he said very softly and maybe with a hint of reluctance, his eyes delving into hers almost as if he wished he weren't seeing what he was.

Then his big, callused hands slipped up her neck into her hair and lifted her head just slightly, at the same moment his mouth lowered to hers in a kiss that began slowly, softly...

It didn't stay that way for long.

Instead his lips parted; he deepened the kiss and it quickly grew hungry and insistent.

Not that he needed to insist on anything, because even before he'd reached for her, Ally had been hoping—deep down—that he was going to kiss her again. And when he did, she met him willingly, every bit as hungry as he seemed to be for more of what they'd only toyed with the previous night.

Her own lips parted in answer to his and she gave in to an urge she thought she'd had since she'd first set eyes on him—raising her hands to the bulging muscles of his biceps.

They were as hard as they looked, as magnificent. And so were his shoulders, she found, when she slid her hands up to them. And his back, when she reached her arms around him...

And oh, but the man could kiss!

Whether he'd had plenty of practice with willing women like Marilyn Mercer, or whether it just came naturally to him, Ally didn't know. Or care. His supple lips possessed hers; his tongue came teasing, courting, exploring.

Like a match set to a gas jet, he ignited passion in her that she thought might have died three years ago. But instead it seemed to burn hotter, brighter now.

For him...

And suddenly that scared her. More than being lost in the open countryside. More even than Meggie's shirt catching fire. More than the rattlesnake....

She trailed her hands from his back in a suspender's path to pectorals that were too firm not to notice and linger on for a split second before she forced herself to push against them.

"I don't think this is any better an idea tonight than it was last night," she said in a breathy voice that exposed just how deeply she'd lost herself to it.

He frowned at her for a moment, as if he, too, had been so involved in what was happening between them that her words didn't at first register.

Then he seemed to remember himself.

He closed his eyes and she saw his sharp jawline tense, deepening the hollows of his cheeks. He looked almost as if he were enduring torture to have this cut short.

"You're right," he said finally, when he opened his eyes to her again.

And even though she knew she was, it still disappointed her to hear him agree.

To hide it, she stood, very straight, very stiffly. Very formally she said, "Thanks for the special dinner tonight. You didn't have to do it, but it was really thoughtful of you."

For a moment he still stared at the spot on the couch she'd just left.

Then, slowly, he angled his head up in her direction. "You're welcome," was all he said, putting a final seal on their silent pact to go back to the way they'd been with each other before.

Although not all the way back to his anger and goading of her.

"You can sleep in till seven tomorrow," he told her then.

"That'll be nice," she answered, fighting the urge to return to where she'd been moments before, on the sofa beneath him, his hands holding her head, his hot mouth over hers....

"Good night," she blurted out in a hurry.

"'Night," he answered much more slowly.

And that was that. All she needed to do was go upstairs to the solitary sanctuary of her room.

So what was she waiting for? Why was she still standing there, staring at him, wishing he'd pull her down to the couch with him again?

"Good night," she repeated, forcing herself to take that first step away from him. And then a second. And a third...

But even as she finally left the room and crossed the foyer to the stairs, she could feel him following her with his eyes.

And much too big a part of her wished much too much that the rest of him had followed her as well....

Chapter Six

Ally had not noticed much about Elk Creek itself when she'd first arrived from Denver. It had been late at night, dark, and she'd been more intent on the Hellers and their reaction to her and Meggie.

But driving into town the next day in Jackson's truck, she was eager to take in the sights and sounds of this place she'd chosen as her and her daughter's new home.

On the way they passed Heller-owned cornfields that gave way to a lumber mill Jackson explained was also part of their holdings and the beginning of the north end of the town proper.

Next came a three-story school—one floor each for the levels of education it provided, elementary on the bottom, middle school on the second, and high school on the third.

Sitting between Ally and Jackson on the truck's bench seat, Meggie was impressed with the playground equipment that Jackson informed them was all new.

His mood was light today, friendly, as he played tour guide and host. And though Ally knew she should resist the appeal of it, of him, she couldn't help relaxing, sitting back and enjoying it.

Elk Creek was divided right down the middle by Center Street, which, at the north end, blossomed into a circular drive around the park square with its Victorian streetlamps and benches, tall oak trees, and a huge gazebo where a sign announced dancing every Saturday night.

Across from the park was the fire station; an imposing courthouse with a tall clock tower; an old red-brick Georgian mansion that had been turned into a medical facility; and a steepled church that took turns being all denominations, Jackson said.

He had the radio on low, but when he stopped at the red light at the neck of the straightaway of Center Street, he turned it up slightly. Then he pointed a long finger in the direction of a glass-fronted building. The brass sign above the door proclaimed it a mining company, founded in 1888, but much bigger lettering on the windowpane below updated the place to WECW radio station.

And with that, the disc jockey who faced the street waved at them and said over the airwaves, ''Well, I'll be hog-tied, folks, if I didn't just look up and see what I thought was a family of three I didn't recognize stopped at the corner light. But only two of the faces are new and it isn't a family at all. It's Jackson Heller finally bringing in our newest citizens—Ms. Ally Brooks and her daughter Meggie. 'Bout time, Jackson.''

Jackson just grinned over at the man.

"Mom, he said our names on the radio!" Meggie exclaimed delightedly, perking up to peer around Jackson.

"That's Bucky Dennehy—he's Kansas's brother-in-law," Jackson informed them as the DJ went on.

"And yes, the rumors you all've been hearin' are true. Ally—hope you don't mind my usin' your first name but we're pretty informal 'round these parts—Ally was the one delivered Beth and Ash Blackwolf's baby girl yesterday. Guess we all know who to call when the stork's comin' and the doc's gone fishin'. Now don't be keepin' those two pretty women to yourself, Jackson. Everybody's anxious to meet 'em. And let me be the first to say a big howdy and welcome to Elk Creek, ladies.''

The light turned green just then and Jackson tapped the brim of the cowboy hat he wore with one finger and aimed it at the disc jockey in part wave, part salute as he headed into the business district.

Or what passed for a business district, which was nothing like the skyscrapers of Denver. Elk Creek's center of operations consisted of stately old buildings—some stone, some brick, some weathered wood—lining either side of Center Street, an avenue wide enough for two lanes of traffic and cars to park nose first in front of the offices and shops the buildings housed.

Ally drank in the quaint, charactered charm of one-, two- and three-storied structures, some fancied up with shutters bordering paned windows, some mimicking country cottages, others looking like buildings out of an old Western movie, but all clearly well cared for and showing pride in what they had to offer.

What they had to offer, as far as Ally could tell, was a little of everything. Insurance. Hardware. Maternity clothes and baby things. Real estate.

There was an attorney. A baker. A butcher. A jeweler. A veterinarian. A small boutique and a much larger Western-wear store. Two restaurants. A movie theater. A bingo palace. An appliance store. A Laundromat and dry cleaners. An ice-cream parlor.

And, of course, Kansas's general store, which was where Jackson finally pulled over to the curb and parked.

"Here we are," he announced as he turned off the engine and swung out of the cab.

Ally and Meggie had gotten into the truck without Jackson's assistance at the ranch while he'd answered a question from Hans before they left. Certainly the last thing Ally expected now was for Jackson to come around to the passenger side and open the door for her.

But that's what he did, and in a hurry, too, before she could do it herself.

Then he offered her a hand in climbing down.

Ally looked at it, stunned.

She'd gotten in and out of the truck a number of times working on the ranch and not once had he helped. So why now?

Was it because she was wearing a dress? It was a loose-fitting flowered concoction with a flowing skirt—not anything binding that would make the descent hazardous.

Or was he offering gentlemanly aid because they were in town now? Where friends and neighbors could see?

That hadn't mattered before, in front of the ranch hands, or his sister and Ash, or the Mercers.

Or maybe it was just part of his pampering from the previous night. A payback for delivering his niece.

But no matter what the reason for that extended hand, she suddenly remembered too vividly what the callused palm and long, thick fingers had felt like against her cheek when he'd kissed her at the end of the last evening. And she knew if she accepted it at that moment, even out in public, the contact would make the same sensations erupt inside of her. Sensations she should avoid having aroused at all.

Yet there he was, being chivalrous again, and if she were to refuse him, it would set a sour tone for the whole rest of the day they were about to spend together. A day that had begun very pleasantly.

So what else could she do? She took a deep, steeling breath and set her hand in his, trying to ignore the instant melted honey that sluiced up her arm.

"Thanks," she said when her feet hit the pavement. But her voice was softer than she'd have liked it to be, and much breathier.

And then, to make matters worse, he didn't let go. At least not right away. For about the same amount of time she'd hesitated in taking his hand, he held on to hers, making that melted honey run all the way to her toes. Especially when his thumb rubbed feathery circles on the back...

"Hey, are you guys gonna let me outta here?" Meggie demanded from behind.

Jackson released his grip then, though he didn't actually let go; he seemed to slide away by slow increments that left tingling sparks in his wake. When Ally glanced up at his face she found a crooked, one-sided smile that completely threw her off track because she didn't have the foggiest idea what it might mean. Was he teasing her with that touch? Tormenting her?

Or was he merely enjoying the feel of her skin the way she'd enjoyed his?

Wanting to escape that thought, along with the light of his eyes and the confusion he was wreaking, she spun around to lift her daughter down.

When she'd done that and closed the truck door, she found Jackson standing with his broad back against the store's door, holding it open, too.

He was just being extra courteous as payment for her obstetrical services, she decided, because that was the safest answer and what she needed to think in order to fight her susceptibility to charm that could be very potent when he chose to show it.

"We'd better say hello to Kansas before we do anything else or we'll hurt her feelings," he said then, waiting for them to go in ahead of him.

Ally sent Meggie in and then followed, hating that she was so aware of the pure power and simmering sensuality of the man as she passed in front of him, and trying not to breathe too deeply of his heady after-shave.

Once inside, Ally made a concerted effort to concentrate on something besides Jackson and his sudden show of good manners. With Kansas nowhere in sight, that left the place itself as her only diversion, so she developed an instant interest in it.

She wondered if Jackson's sister-in-law intentionally kept it looking like a turn-of-the-century country store or if it just hadn't been changed since then. Either way it had a great ambience.

The smell of spices and fresh-brewed coffee wafted around wood-and-glass display cases, oak shelves that climbed all the walls to the ceiling, and even a pot-bellied stove in one corner.

But in spite of the old-fashioned atmosphere of the place, it offered most of what could be found in any of Denver's grocery stores, including some gourmet items.

"I'll bet that's Jackson, Ally and Meggie," Kansas called to them from what sounded like the back of the store even before they could see her. Then she came around one of the freestanding aisles of shelves. "Figured it was you all since I just heard Bucky say you were on your way into town,'' she said as she joined them up front.

''You figured right,'' Jackson answered her. Then he added, '''Mornin'.''

''Another hour and it'll be afternoon,'' she said with a laugh. Then she lowered her gaze to Meggie and grinned more broadly than she had at Ally and Jackson. ''There are fresh doughnuts on the coffee cart near the cash register. You can help yourself if your mom says it's okay.''

Ally nodded her permission when Meggie looked to her for it, and the little girl left them.

''How about you two? Coffee and doughnuts?'' Kansas offered.

''None for me,'' Ally declined.

''Have any of those cream puffs?'' Jackson asked, not waiting for an answer before trailing after Meggie.

The thought of the big, gruff man munching a cream puff made Ally smile and she considered pointing out to him that there weren't many things more froufrou than that.

But when he came back with one and offered her a bite, she actually took it, a little surprised at the familiarity that he was fostering between them and a lot surprised at herself for so willingly accepting it.

''Have you talked to Beth or Ash today?'' Kansas asked then, as if the exchange had been an everyday event.

''I called,'' Jackson answered the same way, ''but the switchboard said they were with the baby for feeding time and wouldn't put me through. How 'bout you?''

"Linc and I drove in to Cheyenne last night to see them all,'' Kansas said, going on with reassurances that Beth and the baby were doing well, and marveling at Ally having performed the delivery.

When that subject had been exhausted, she said, "How about coming to our house for supper tonight since you're already in town? Or won't you be here that long?''

The questions were aimed at both of them but it was Jackson who answered. "We were planning on spending the day,'' he said first. Then he looked to Ally. "What do you think? Want to stick around into the evening?''

"Sure,'' she answered, hating that she sounded confused, except confused was what she was.

"How 'bout you, Miss Meggie? Want to eat with Kansas and Linc and Danny tonight?'' he called.

"Okay,'' she said with her mouth full of doughnut.

Ally would have reprimanded her, but she was more focused on Jackson and wondering what had gotten into him. Helping her out of the truck, holding doors for her, including her in a decision...

Not that it wasn't an improvement. But it was disconcerting to have him acting as if the three of them were, indeed, the family the disc jockey had at first mistaken them for.

"We'll just barbecue,'' Kansas was saying. "I close up at six but if you guys get tired of walking around town earlier than that go ahead and go over.

The front door is unlocked, so just make yourselves at home and we'll throw something together when I get there.''

"Sounds good." Jackson had finished his pastry by then and clapped the crumbs off his hands. "I'm treatin' these girls to lunch in an hour or so. Want to meet us over at Margie Wilson's café and I'll buy yours, too?''

"I'm waiting for a truck full of ice cream that should get here about then or I would.''

"Well, we'd better take off," he said. "You ready for some gen-u-ine cowboy boots, Meg?" he called over his shoulder again.

"Yes!" the little girl called back excitedly.

This was the first Ally had heard of cowboy boots for Meggie, genuine or not. "What are you talking about?''

Meggie had skipped to her side in time to hear that and answer it before Jackson could.

"Jackson said for doin' such a good job paintin' he'd buy me some cowboy boots. *Real* ones, like him 'n' Hans 'n' the hands wear.''

"No harm in that, is there?" he asked Ally.

"I guess not," she answered, surprised yet again by the way this day was playing out.

"Let's get to it, then," Jackson ordered, accepting the hand Meggie slipped into his as if it happened all the time, and once more holding the shop door for Ally to go back outside.

The cowboy boots Jackson bought Meggie were much more expensive than Ally approved of. But

Meggie clearly wanted the turquoise ones with the tassels on the sides and Jackson indulged her in spite of Ally's protests.

"This is a deal between Meggie and me, so you just don't have any say in it, Ally. Sorry," he said as he told the salesgirl to wrap up the shoes Meggie had been wearing so she could wear the boots out.

But Meggie taking Jackson's hand and his buying her the cowboy boots weren't the only signs Ally had that he and her daughter had already formed a bond she hadn't been aware of. As the day progressed, she began to realize that the two of them were very relaxed with each other, as if they'd known each other forever.

They shared a surprisingly similar sense of humor and tastes in things like ice cream—butter brickle— and snow cones—grape and cherry mixed. And they were cohorts and coconspirators in more than just the cowboy boots. Ally learned of the practical jokes they'd played on Hans, the teasing they'd done to Marta, and some trick they were trying to teach Mutt.

Basically, they seemed to have formed a fast friendship. And seeing how good Jackson was with Meggie helped soften Ally's opinion of the man even more than the pleasantries and the good time he was offering.

And it *was* a good time.

Jackson insisted on buying their lunch and, while they ate, telling stories that made them laugh, about a Fourth of July pig stampede that had ruined the annual parade one year; about a man who kept his horse in the living room; and various other anecdotes about some of the people he introduced them to.

Then he took them browsing through Elk Creek's shops, filling them in on more town tall tales, history and legends, and basically just entertaining them with his quiet, understated wit and a wryness that was yet another facet of him Ally hadn't seen before.

But then, he was showing her a lot that she hadn't seen in him before. Gone was the gruffness, the intensity, the stern taskmaster, and in its place was a man with a capacity for relaxing and enjoying simple pleasures.

There was nothing about him that was demanding or authoritarian; instead he seemed carefree, flexible, and interested only in spoiling both Meggie and Ally by catering to their every wish and whim. And all while he seemed to delight in doing it, which made it that much better.

They spent the end of the afternoon at the honky-tonk with Linc and Danny.

While Danny showed Meggie the mechanical bull, Linc led Ally and Jackson to the kitchen where Linc told her that anytime she wanted to give up ranch life she could have the job of chef for The Buckin' Bronco.

She expected Jackson to add his encouragement to that idea but it never came. Instead he merely followed along quietly, though she thought she caught him paying extra-special attention to her decline of his brother's open-ended invitation.

At six o'clock they drove to Linc and Kansas's house. Danny and Meggie wanted to ride over together so Meggie went in Linc's truck. That left Ally and Jackson temporarily on their own.

Ally wondered if his mood might be different then, if this lighter side of him had been for Meggie's benefit.

But as they drove the short distance to the small white clapboard house, his attitude didn't alter at all. In fact, he confided to her that Kansas couldn't have kids and that it was a sore subject, so Ally wouldn't accidentally venture into it. And the way he shared that confidence gave her a sense of the closeness she'd seen him sharing with Meggie all day. A closeness she'd been slightly jealous of, if she was honest with herself. It was a heady thing, and Ally was sorry to have it end when they pulled into Linc's driveway and had to rejoin Jackson's brother and the kids.

The evening passed as pleasantly as the day had. Linc and Kansas were good company. But by ten o'clock Meggie and Danny were both visibly worn-out and the grown-ups called it a night.

"We're having a sort of slumber party here tomorrow with my sister's kids and Danny," Kansas said as she and Linc walked Ally, Jackson and Meggie out. "The oldest is about Meggie's age. Do you think she'd like to come? Ashley would be thrilled not to have only her smaller brothers and sister to play with."

Meggie's enthusiasm revived a bit at that. "Can I?" she asked.

"I don't know why not," Ally answered, thrilled that her daughter had agreed. Overnights were not something Meggie was usually open to.

"Great." Kansas ruffled the little girl's hair. Then to Ally she said, "How about if I come out to the ranch around two and pick her up? I'm turning the store over to a friend for the afternoon so we can start the party off with some running through the garden hose."

"Sounds good," Ally assured her, watching for signs of Meggie changing her mind. But they never came.

Instead her daughter said, "See you tomorrow, Danny," and went to climb into the truck while the rest of the good-nights were exchanged.

She was curled up, asleep, in the center of the seat by the time Ally and Jackson got there.

"That was quick," he observed with a nod at Meggie as he started the engine and backed out of the driveway.

"She had a big day," Ally said, smoothing her daughter's forehead. Then she looked up at Jackson, wondering if, now that this informal holiday was over, he'd go back to his gruff persona.

He still *looked* congenial enough.

He'd taken his hat off when they'd arrived at Linc and Kansas's house, and left it off, but there was a slight indentation from it in his espresso-colored hair. That was the only thing about him that wasn't perfect.

He sat there, tall and strong, the features of his profile sharply defined and ruggedly handsome even in the deep shadows of the truck's interior. He exuded pure, raw masculinity that was earthily sensual, something innate rather than consciously manufactured. So much so that he seemed completely unaware of it and the power it wielded to set off a twittering in the pit of her stomach.

"Meggie and I both had a great time today," she said, as if silence might give away the feelings that were stirring inside of her.

"Me, too," he answered simply enough.

"You're really good with her...to her.... I can't tell you how much that means to me."

"Nothin' special," he grumbled a little, obviously uncomfortable with Ally's gratitude and praise.

She knew she should stop looking at him, stop keeping up friendly conversation, face forward or maybe toward the passenger window, and let things between them go back to the way they'd been before she'd delivered Beth's baby.

But she didn't do it. The day and evening had been too nice. *This* was too nice—the quiet intimacy of the truck as they found their way back to Center Street and headed for home.

He was dangerously appealing at that moment, and no matter how firmly she told herself to resist that appeal, the time they'd spent together had gone too far in making her even more vulnerable to him and she just couldn't make herself turn away.

"I thought that being on the ranch was what was improving Meggie's frame of mind," she said. "It seemed good for her to be in the fresh air, around the animals—all the things I brought her here for. But I didn't realize until today how big a role you'd played, too. It's all been a sort of small miracle to see the sudden change in her.''

He turned his face to her. ''You think all this little girl's hurts are solved with a couple of days here?'' he asked kindly, quietly, as if venturing carefully so as not to too harshly shatter any illusions she might have.

''No. But I think she's better.''

''And it hasn't occurred to you that it's just the novelty of it all? That that novelty will wear off and when it does, nothin' miraculous will have really happened?''

''It's occurred to me, but I have to hope it isn't true. Or at least that when the novelty has worn off maybe she'll be on a better footing to deal with the bad feelings when they crop up again.''

He watched the road once more. ''This life can make a person stronger, all right,'' he conceded. ''Or break 'em. But even if it doesn't break 'em, it always takes a toll, one way or another.''

Was there an underlying sadness in his voice? Ally couldn't be sure. ''Are we talking about Meggie or about me, now? Or maybe about you?''

''Me?'' That made him laugh softly.

''Living the life you do has taken its toll on you, hasn't it? No wife, no family, not even a lady friend…''

He didn't answer that, and Ally thought maybe she'd gone too far, so she backtracked. ''But what you're really saying is that living here will take its toll on me, aren't you?''

He shrugged slightly. ''It'll send you back to Denver. Sooner or later.'' There was confidence in that statement, but none of the challenge or smugness that had been in earlier comments of that ilk. In fact this time she thought she heard that quiet note of sadness again.

''What makes you so certain?''

''I've seen it before. Up close and personal.''

''Your ex-wife,'' she guessed.

That got her the front view of his face again, but for just a moment. ''Shag told you about her, did he?''

''Only that you were married young and that it didn't last long. I just assumed—''

''Her name was Sherry,'' he said as if Ally had asked. ''She came up here with the same stars in her eyes that you have about livin' a country life. But that changed fast. The heat and bugs. Not having a mall to run to at the drop of a hat. Folks too busy workin' dawn to dusk to socialize much. A winter of being snowed in for days on end. My gettin' stuck out in a blizzard and nearly freezin' to death before I was found. Her seein' a man thrown from his horse and paralyzed. It all took its toll,'' he repeated the phrase.

''And she left you,'' Ally said quietly, seeing the pain the memory etched into his face. ''How long were you married?''

''First day to last? One year and three months. I came in from a week-long roundup and thought the house seemed too quiet, too empty—more than if she'd just gone visitin'. And I was right. Her closet was cleaned out. All her stuff was gone. There were divorce papers with a note attached to 'em on my pillow."

"Just like that? She didn't tell you or even hint before that that she was unhappy or leaving or divorcing you?"

"Just like that," he answered quietly. "When I looked back, I saw things that were more important than I'd realized. Remarks and complaints I guess I hadn't taken seriously enough. But mostly the plain truth was that she didn't belong here. She wasn't suited to the life. I thought she'd get used to things. Instead it seemed like livin' on the ranch just kept on taking its toll until she didn't want to pay up anymore."

There was a message in his words, but beyond that, there was a simple statement of fact that told Ally he was only recounting the truth, not making anything up to frighten her away. And her heart ached for him and the echo of disillusionment in his voice, because he'd had to come to accept that not everyone loved the ranch and small-town life the way he did. Or could even tolerate it.

Then, with a wry sigh and a tilt of his head, he added more to himself than to her, "I don't ever want to be the last to know a thing like that again."

"So instead you'll drive people out of your life to be the first," she said much the same way.

Once more his head pivoted on his broad shoulders

so he could stare back at her. But his good mood was still in place, because a slow smile crooked up one side of his mouth. "Got it all figured out, do you?"

"Deny it," she challenged.

But he just let the other corner of his mouth join the first and went on pinning her in place with his cornflower blue gaze, leaving her to wonder whether or not she really had figured him out.

Then he looked straight ahead again just in time to pull into the garage at home, ending the drive Ally hadn't paid any attention to and the conversation, too.

He stopped the engine, got out and came around to her side, opening the door and handing her the keys. "You take those and I'll carry Meggie in," was all he said.

Ally didn't move immediately. Instead she stayed where she was—eye to eye with him—still wondering about him, hurting for what he'd suffered even though he seemed to have gotten over it.

His wife must have been crazy, she thought fleetingly as she took in just how handsome he was and considered how kind he could be when he put his mind to it, how sensitive in dealing with Meggie, how sexy...

He took her hand but not for anything except to urge her out, disappointing Ally, who hadn't realized until that moment that she'd been wanting him to kiss her the way he had the night before. Right then and there.

Out of the truck she turned to watch him lean inside and scoop her daughter into his arms.

"Shut that, would you?" he asked with a nod at the door before he headed for the house.

Snapping herself out of her reverie, Ally did his bidding, following behind and trying to keep her gaze from hooking itself to the back pockets of his jeans.

As they went into the house, she couldn't help imagining what it must have been like for him to come home one day expecting to find his wife and instead finding divorce papers.

It helped keep that unwelcome desire that had risen up inside of her at bay.

For the time being, anyway.

He carried Meggie upstairs and gently set her on her bed, pulling off the cowboy boots he'd bought her and lining them up where she could put her feet into them by just swinging her legs over the edge of the mattress.

Then he straightened up and left Ally to do the rest of the undressing.

"Guess it wouldn't do any harm to have another seven-o'clock morning tomorrow," he whispered from beside her, putting what felt like an abrupt end to the evening. "See you then," he added, and before Ally could even respond, his long legs took him out of the room.

It was for the best, she told herself as she eased her daughter into pajamas and under the covers.

But still she couldn't help wishing that, like the night before, he'd invited her to have one last glass of wine.

And just a few more minutes of him.

His door was shut by the time she went to her room, but her desire to be with him was still so strong that Ally knew she couldn't just get into her bed and fall asleep. Instead she decided a swim might be relaxing and help her work such silly longings out of her at the same time.

She put on her one-piece bathing suit and pulled her hair to her crown, keeping it there with an elastic ruffle that matched her plain black tank suit. Then she grabbed a bath sheet from the towel bar beside her shower and silently retraced her steps through the dark house and out back again.

Dropping her towel onto the first lounger she passed, she walked straight to the pool, descending the steps into the water, shivering just a little in its coolness before she became accustomed to it. She hoped it would have the same effect as a cold shower in calming thoughts and longings she didn't want to have.

She did laps in that pursuit, too. Back and forth across the length of the pool. Again and again. Trying not to think of Jackson. Of that extraordinary body of his. That to-die-for face. The kisses they'd shared…

But there was no distraction in swimming, she realized. The monotony of it left her mind wandering as wickedly as lying in bed trying to sleep would have. It didn't even do much in the way of tiring her out.

Where are hay bales to stack when you need them?

She'd probably finished thirty laps by then, and when she began fantasizing about knocking on Jackson's bedroom door, it occurred to her that this was doing more harm than good, and she headed for the pool steps again.

That was when she saw him.

He was standing in one of the open sliding glass doors, his chest bare, his jeans riding low on his hips, his thumbs tucked into his waistband. He leaned against the jamb, dusted only in moonglow, watching her.

She felt her nipples go instantly hard and hated to rise up out of the water and show him—as surely the tight, wet suit would. But she'd already begun to climb the stairs and she couldn't slink back now. Her only hope was to get to her towel in a hurry, before he could see.

"Trouble sleeping?" she asked as though she hadn't a care in the world.

He didn't answer her. He just pushed away from the door at the same time she stepped onto the pool's edge.

The lounger she'd dropped her towel onto was much closer to Jackson than to her. He reached it first, picked up the towel and held it open for her.

And he did notice her nipples, because she saw his eyes lower for a brief moment before lifting to her face again.

Why was he here? she wondered. Had he just come down to the kitchen for something to eat or drink and discovered her? Or had he heard her leave her room and followed her?

The possibility that he'd come down purposely to be with her tightened her nipples even more.

But to get to that towel she had to walk right up to him.

Resisting the urge to hunch her shoulders, cross her arms and huddle over her chest, she went to stand before him. But just as she was about to grab the towel, he took a step forward, flipped it over her head and caught her with it from behind.

The movement brought them closer together, facing each other, Jackson still holding the ends of the towel in his fists in a U around her.

"Did you enjoy your swim?" he asked then in a husky voice for her ears alone.

"It's a nice pool," she answered, feeling silly and inane, and alive and excited at once. "If you can't sleep, maybe you ought to go for a dip."

He smiled the way he had earlier in the truck, with one side of his mouth, as if the dip he wanted to take had nothing to do with swimming. "You're pretty good at it," he commented, closing some of the gap between them by moving nearer at the same moment he pulled her forward, too.

"It's great exercise." Small talk. But what else could she do to hide the race of her pulse, the quickening in her stomach, the urge to press her kerneled nipples to his well-defined naked pectorals?

"I'd have thought I'd been giving you plenty of exercise. Didn't know you needed more..."

There was suggestiveness in that, and Ally knew

the exercise he was thinking of at that moment had nothing to do with ranch work or swimming.

Again he eased her toward him with the towel, and this time they ended up so close together that the tips of her breasts did nudge his chest. But just barely. Just enough to tease, to torment her with the surge of desire for so much more.

He gazed down into her eyes, searching, holding her with his, frowning as if something troubled him. Then he shook his head. ''It's already going to be hard for me when you leave,'' he whispered, as if he didn't mean for her to hear it. As if he were telling himself. Warning himself.

His chin reared back all of a sudden, his eyes closed, and Ally knew he was fighting the same battle she was. She told herself to solve the problem for them both, to snatch herself from the grip of the bath sheet and go inside.

But then he sighed, shook his head yet again and let his chin drop. ''But I can't help this,'' he said just before his mouth covered hers in a kiss that was hungry from the start.

Ally was barely aware of his letting the towel fall around her feet. But she was very aware of his wrapping his arms around her, holding her pressed to him the way she'd longed for, his skin hot against hers.

His lips parted, his tongue thrust in and he plundered her mouth forcefully. But not so forcefully that she didn't welcome it, that she didn't answer every parry, every circle, and chase it with her own.

Waiting barely beneath the surface was a passion

that was combustible and that kiss lighted fire to it. Ally let her hands travel where only her eyes had gone before, up from the small of his back to the widening V of work-honed shoulders; into his hair, surprisingly silky and soft; down again to that thick, corded neck; into the hollow of his collarbone; and even—before she realized what she was doing—to his chest, easing herself slightly away so she could get there.

Because now it wasn't enough to merely have her breasts pressed to him. She craved the feel of his hands there, exploring her nipples the way she was exploring his.

His mouth left hers then, kissing a scorching trail across her cheek to her ear, along the side of her neck to her shoulder, where he slipped the straps of her bathing suit down and with them, the front, too.

It dropped only as far as the crests. But one of those glorious, big hands did the rest, answering the need inside her to feel it covering the whole sensitive mound and working a magic more incredible than she'd imagined, taking her breath away on a sigh of exquisite agony.

His mouth came back to hers, even more hungrily, more urgently, as he filled his other hand with her other breast, driving her mad with a desire more intense than she'd ever felt before. She wanted this man. Wanted him to make love to her. And at that moment nothing—*nothing*—else mattered.

"Jackson," she breathed, meaning to tell him so.

But suddenly he tore himself away as if something

had stabbed him. "I can't do this," he groaned as if stopping were killing him. "I can't put my heart on the road out of this place again."

He jammed his hands through his hair so hard it must have hurt. Ally saw his jaw clench, saw every muscle in his face tense up, saw him swallow so fiercely his Adam's apple punched the sky.

She slipped her suit back in place and somehow, though he'd seemed lost in his own battle again, he noticed that, yanking his head lower and looking at her as if she were stealing something from him.

"I'm sorry. I shouldn't have come down here," he said, stepping around her and striding on long, determined steps toward the barn.

Through the glow of moonlight, she watched him hop over the paddock fence and then leap onto the rear of the nearest horse, landing perfectly on the slope of the animal's back.

And then, with a clicking sound that carried to her through the silence of the night, he set the horse to a gallop, clearing the far side of the fence as if it were no more than a low-lying hurdle and disappearing into the distance.

Ally stood there watching, enduring the ache of disappointed desires even as she told herself it was for the best.

Because deep down she knew something she didn't want to know.

That her own heart was just as much at risk as his was.

Chapter Seven

If the water in the pool had started to boil, Ally wouldn't have been surprised. That's how hot the next day felt to her. In reality, by eleven in the morning the temperature was just shy of one hundred degrees.

Hans and Marta had gone into Cheyenne to visit Beth's small family in the hospital, the ranch hands were all out on the range, and only Ally, Meggie and Jackson were close to home. But even the heat didn't keep Jackson from working or from again expecting Ally to keep up with him.

He set Meggie to polishing his saddle, making sure she kept to the shade, but he insisted he and Ally unload a truck bed full of feed by hand, scooping the dried corn and oats into four-gallon buckets and then carrying them to the bin in the barn.

The heavy buckets nearly pulled Ally's arms from their sockets and even the few minutes in the shade of the barn each trip did nothing to cool her off. She pined for the air-conditioned house and wondered how Jackson could keep at this himself.

But the new day had brought with it yet another change in him. Gone, still, was the gruff, goading tyrant, yet the pleasant pamperer had disappeared, too.

To Meggie he was just as warm and friendly as always, but working with Ally he was even more quiet than usual. Oh, he was civil enough, and polite. But very serious. Very sober. And there was an air of stronger determination about him, as if, sometime during the night, he'd decided he needed to use even more punishing tactics to drive her away.

Or maybe Ally was just projecting that. After all, what had been on her mind since their encounter at the poolside was that maybe she should throw in the towel herself and go back to Denver before she got in any deeper emotionally.

Because no matter how reluctant either of them was—and there was no doubt they were both reluctant—something was happening between them. Something powerful. Something beyond their control. Something that smacked too much of caring for each other.

They stopped for lunch when the truck was finally empty, and Jackson informed Meggie that he was going to teach her how to halter-break the filly afterward.

Meggie was delighted and hurried through her sandwich so she could go out to the barn to tell the horse.

When her daughter was gone, Jackson turned to Ally. "What you need to do this afternoon is climb up and oil the windmill."

He had no way of knowing what he was asking of her. But just the mention of such a thing sent a wave of fear through her. And for the first time since she'd come here and been taking his orders to do every smelly, heavy, dirty, difficult chore, she refused. "I won't be able to do that."

Her answer cocked his head to one side and raised his eyebrows. "Sure you will. You just climb up the back side of it and—"

"I'll do something else."

"It's oiling the windmill that needs to be done."

"You'll have to do it yourself."

"It's an easy job."

"No."

He stared at her, boring into her with eyes that could be surprisingly hard in spite of their soft color. And suddenly, as they were locked in a stare-down, she watched the goading tyrant return.

"What are you thinking, Ally? That delivering Beth's baby took care of your part around here forever? Or that just because we had a nice day yesterday, every day's going to be a party now? Or maybe that a few kisses bought you—"

"I don't think any of those things." She cut him

off, angry at where he'd been headed with that. "I'll do something else, but I won't oil the windmill."

"That's what needs doing."

Back where they'd begun. Stalemate.

Why did this have to come up today, of all days? she wondered. He seemed to be seizing any reason to push her even more than he had been before.

"If you want to live here, you do the work it takes to keep things going," he said with a clear note of threat in his voice.

She considered confessing why she just couldn't be expected to do that, but somehow, admitting she was terrified of heights at a moment when he was looking for a weak link to yank on seemed like handing him the very tool he needed to do the yanking. Maybe reasoning with him would help.

"Jackson," she began very calmly, "I know what you're doing. I know what's been happening between us has raised a lot of bad memories for you and shaken you up. It shakes me up, too. And I know—"

"The only thing you need to know," he said so softly it sounded dangerous, "is that the windmill needs oiling. Right now." He pushed back the stool he was sitting on at the butcher block and stood, taking his plate to the sink.

"I won't do it," she said, giving up trying to reason with him and instead opting for belligerence.

"Yes, ma'am, you will," he countered, more obstinate still. "If you stay here, you work. And you work at what I say you work at."

"I will work. But I won't—"

"If that windmill isn't oiled by the time Kansas gets here to pick up Meggie I'll personally load her car with your belongings, and with you and Meggie, and it'll take a battle in court for you or your daughter to set foot on this place again."

"You'd lose."

"But I'd fight. And by the time you won any kind of order to get back on this ranch I would have told every person in this town that you came here, earned your keep for a few days and then, after I showed you a nice time in town, decided you didn't want to work like that anymore, that I could do it all while you sat around on your duff and reaped the benefits. Folks here don't take kindly to laziness or people who don't do their share. You wouldn't find this such a friendly place to be then."

She met his stare, this native son of Elk Creek, and knew all it would take would be to tell that story into a few well-chosen ears and it would indeed turn his lifelong friends and neighbors against her and Meggie. And she didn't doubt that as nice and friendly as these small-town people could be, they could also be just as unpleasant, cold and aloof, if they chose to ostracize them.

Still, she might just have to risk it.

But at that moment Meggie came bounding back into the kitchen, as excited as if it were Christmas morning. "We're all ready," she announced to Jackson. "Do you think, maybe, if I do a reee-ally good job trainin' li'l Sunshine—that's what I been callin' her, Sunshine—that maybe she could be mine? 'Cuz she reee-ally likes me. I can tell. And I reee-ally like her.''

Jackson's eyes didn't budge from pinning Ally to the spot even as her daughter's happy voice chimed around them, an inescapable reminder of how important the little girl's improved state of mind was to her. A state of mind that wouldn't stay improved if being here meant a court battle and a whole town of people who let it be known they weren't wanted.

"What'll it be?" he demanded.

"I'll oil your damned windmill," she said through clenched teeth in a voice so low it was a wonder even he heard it.

"The can's in the toolshed," he informed, turning to escort Meggie back out to the barn, sparing Ally a glance that warned he'd be watching to make sure she kept her word.

There wasn't much of a lunch mess to clean, but as Ally rinsed plates and put them into the dishwasher she gave herself a pep talk.

"I can do this," she muttered aloud. "It won't take long. I'll just climb up, squirt some oil and be on the ground again before I even know I've left it. No big deal. If I only look up at the sky it won't be a problem. People work from scaffoldings dangling from rooftops and walk along open frameworks for skyscrapers. People climb mountains for fun. If they can do that, I can do this."

As she left the kitchen and went out to the shed, her gaze was trained on the windmill. It seemed much taller than it had ever before, but she tried not to think about that.

"I can do it," she whispered to herself on the way out of the shed with an oilcan that looked like a small flask except that the spout was a long cone that narrowed to a precise tip.

She forced it into the back pocket of her jeans, freeing both her hands, which were so wet with nervous perspiration that no sooner had she wiped them against her thighs than they were damp again.

The windmill was near the barn, just off the corner of the paddock fence. As Ally stood at the foot of the giant thing, she considered going into the barn, where Jackson was, and calling his bluff.

Except that she knew he wasn't bluffing, because she had a hunch that what was happening between them on a personal level gave new impetus to his wanting her off his ranch.

"You can do this," she repeated to herself. "Just get it over with."

She swallowed the lump of fear in her throat, once again dried her palms on her pants, grabbed an eye-level rung of the built-in ladder with clenched fists and took the first step.

The pep talk started again, only this time it was silent, urging her to the second step, and then the third.

You can do this. You can do this. You can do this.

And she did, too. She made it all the way to the top.

The trouble was, once she got there, even taking

her own advice not to look down didn't keep her from realizing just how high up she was.

High enough to look over the barn roof.

And that did her in.

Her heart was pounding so loudly she could literally feel it.

Her throat was dry as dust. Too dry to let words pass through it to even call for help.

Her head felt light.

And every muscle in her body was frozen stiff, from her hands in their white-knuckled death grip on the top wooden slat, all the way down to knees that were locked tight and toes that were curled inside her shoes as if that would give her a better hold.

The voice in her head that had urged her up there suddenly began to ask questions instead.

Was it really worth dying to be on this ranch? With a man who didn't want her here and would force her to risk her life just to oil this stupid contraption? Wouldn't Meggie enjoy other places? Other people? Pets that weren't bigger than she was? Surely there was something else, somewhere else, that would brighten her daughter's spirits. Someplace safe. Someplace where they could spend more time together. Someplace where Ally didn't have to work like a slave to "earn their keep." Or climb windmills...

And she meant it, too, at that moment, when pure terror made the blood race through her veins. She agreed with Jackson—she and Meggie didn't belong here. And Ally definitely didn't want to be here.

She wanted to be on the ground! Safe on terra firma again. Relaxed. Cool. Calm. Enjoying what Shag had meant to ease her burden, not increase it....

"Mom!"

Ally heard Meggie's cry from below, but she could only assume her daughter had just come out of the barn and spotted her up there; she couldn't so much as lower her eyes to see. And the ring of horror in her daughter's voice only made Ally feel worse.

"Jackson! My mom's on the windmill," Meggie shouted then. "She can't be up there! She's afraid of high places! *Bad* afraid!"

"Ally?"

That was Jackson's voice aimed up at her a moment later. She tried to open her mouth to answer him, but she couldn't do that, either. She couldn't do anything but hang on for dear life.

"Why the hell didn't you tell me that was the reason you didn't want to do the oiling?"

Did he expect her to answer him? Because she couldn't.

And when she didn't, he called up to her again. "Just come on back down."

She'd have laughed hysterically at that if she was physically able.

"I think she's stuck. Or dead!" Meggie shrieked, clearly on the verge of panic herself.

"She isn't dead," Jackson assured in a calming voice. "I think she's just too scared to move."

"She can't stay there forever!"

"I'm going up to get her. I want you back in the

barn with Sunshine. Brush her mane the way I showed you, and by the time you're finished I'll have your mom down. Now scoot. There's nothing to worry about. Everything'll be fine in just a few minutes.''

Ally knew his words were intended for her, too, because even though they were calm and reassuring, his voice was loud enough to carry to her. But it didn't help.

''I'm comin' up, Ally,'' he called when, she assumed, Meggie had done as she'd been told and was no longer standing down there watching. ''Just hang on.''

Ha! As if she could do anything else.

''So this is why you didn't want to oil the windmill,'' he reiterated with some amusement in his voice, the idle chitchat of a rescuer distracting a ledge jumper as he climbed up after her. ''Would have been a lot easier to tell me you're afraid of heights. I thought you were just bein' contrary and lookin' for a fight for some reason.''

He reached her then, and although it seemed like an eternity to her, it couldn't have been more than a few minutes before he was carefully placing his booted feet on the same rung hers were on and easing his big body around her from behind, his hands on either side of hers.

More panic freed her throat in a hurry. ''Will this hold us both?'' she demanded in a choked whisper.

''I wouldn't be here if it wouldn't,'' he answered

easily enough, his breath against her hair. "You aren't hurt or stuck on anything, are you?"

"No." But her jaws seemed to be immobilized again and it came out through teeth that were clamped together.

"You really are going to be okay, Ally," he said. "I've got you and nothing's going to happen to you. Now I want you to put an arm around my neck."

"Can't."

"You're gonna have to let go sooner or later, darlin', or we won't be able to budge." He covered her left hand with his, rubbing it soothingly. "Now, come on, let this one relax a little and it'll give."

Having the strength and power of his body around hers was beginning to allow her somewhat of a sense of security. She believed he could handle anything, even getting her safely back to the ground, and though it didn't quell her terror, it did give her enough oomph to slowly open her grip, one finger at a time.

"That's it. Now turn just enough to reach around my neck."

A tougher proposition, but after two false attempts she finally managed it.

Jackson chuckled. "A little looser, Ally, or you're gonna strangle me." He took his right hand off the rung and wrapped it around her waist. "Okay now, can you feel that I've got you?"

She nodded shakily.

"And you know I won't let either one of us fall?"

Another shaky nod.

"Then we need to start down. One step at a time. Think you can do that?"

"No."

"Sure you can. Come on, now, give it a try. And in one more minute this'll all be over."

Finding a dram more courage in the feeling of him holding her so tight he was bearing at least half her weight, she forced herself to take that first step back the way they'd both come. Then he talked her through the second and the third the way she'd talked herself into climbing up there.

It seemed like much longer than one minute but they finally made it all the way down, and the moment they did, the fear that had welded her joints gave way to watery knees and violent trembling that Ally couldn't stop.

"It's okay," Jackson said yet again, keeping his arms around her, holding her close and steady, stroking her hair. He went on murmuring soft, comforting words, letting the strength of his body recharge hers, and little by little her shuddering stopped. Yet even when she gained some semblance of control, he still held her. And as he did, something else took the place of terror. Something much more sensual that lighted tiny sparks in her.

And maybe in him, too, because he pressed a kiss to her temple, leaving his lips there too long for it to be merely an act of solace.

She tipped her head back to look into his face, meaning to thank him, but somehow the words didn't come. Instead he gazed down into her eyes for a moment and then kissed her mouth. A soft, sweet kiss that nevertheless set those sparks on fire.

But the blaze was short-lived, because just then Meggie came running out of the barn, shouting, "Did you get her down yet?"

Ally ended the kiss abruptly at the sound of her daughter's voice, but Jackson was slower in taking his arms away.

"I got her," he answered the little girl in a husky voice that didn't seem to raise any curiosity in Meggie but told Ally just how affected he'd been by that oh-so-brief kiss.

Meggie took Jackson's place at a full run, hugging Ally's waist and hanging on almost as desperately as Ally had hung on to the rung of the windmill ladder.

This time it was Ally who did the soothing and reassuring, and the stroking of Meggie's hair, too.

But over her daughter's head, her gaze followed Jackson as he walked away.

She couldn't help marveling at what had once again ignited between them, almost instantly and all on its own.

And the fact that it had come even at a time when she'd just had the living daylights scared out of her.

As if her attraction to him, her feelings for him, had even more power than that....

Kansas came to pick up Meggie about an hour later. Her car was full of her sister's kids—none of whom Meggie had met before—and between that and the windmill fright, Ally expected her daughter to change her mind about the overnight.

But at Kansas's urge to hurry so they could get to her house, Meggie ran inside and then ran out again with her backpack, kissed Ally goodbye and hopped into the rear of the station wagon with the oldest of the other kids—Ashley—as if they were best friends eager to get together.

And Ally was left as surprised as she was glad to see it.

Still she said to Kansas, "Meggie doesn't always do well sleeping away from me. If there's any problem, even in the middle of the night, just call and I'll borrow Jackson's truck or something and come get her."

"I'm sure she'll be fine," Kansas answered without any concern at all, and somehow Ally sensed she was right.

The other woman got behind the wheel of the car and with parade waves from everyone, off they went.

Ally watched until they disappeared from sight and then turned to go through the house and out back once more where Jackson still worked and expected her return to stack the wood he was chopping.

That was when it occurred to her that for the first time since her arrival here she and Jackson were totally alone on the place.

Not that it mattered, of course. The presence of other people on the ranch hadn't kept them from kissing, from more than kissing, the past few nights. And other people hadn't been the cause of the abrupt endings to most of those occasions, either. So what difference did it make?

None at all, she told herself.

Except that, for some reason, she felt a little unnerved by it.

Her trip through the cool, air-conditioned house only made the blast-furnace heat feel all the worse when she went out the sliding glass door and headed for the chopping block.

Jackson was a workaholic, she decided as she passed the pool. She considered trying to persuade him to take the rest of the afternoon off for a swim but she knew he'd never do it. He'd say the wood had to be cut and it had to be cut right now. And they'd probably have a rerun of the power struggle they'd already had over the windmill. So she rejected the idea and merely went to work.

But Lord, it was hot.

Sometime while she was seeing Meggie off, even Jackson had succumbed to it enough to remove his shirt, leaving his chest and back bare as he worked.

That was well and good for him, she thought grumpily, but what was she supposed to do for some relief? She couldn't strip down to the waist.

Hot and bothered, that's what she was, though not in any sexual meaning of the phrase, she was quick to reason. She was literally hot. Steaming hot from stacking heavy logs in the kind of heat weathermen warned of.

And what bothered her was that Jackson was forcing her to do it just out of pure orneriness to prove a point. And to get rid of her, not only because she was trespassing on his precious territory but probably also because he had some idiotic notion that a few kisses meant something.

But they didn't. At least they didn't have to. Not a few kisses or even more than a few kisses. Or some sleepless nights longing for a sober-sided man in another room. Or even the fact that one of her worst fears could be wiped away with a moment in his arms....

No, none of it had to mean anything.

So what if she couldn't help being affected by the sight of him half-naked, each time she set the logs on the pile and returned to where he was chopping more wood. After all, there wasn't a woman alive who could have looked at him that way and not been affected.

His muscles bulged and flexed and rippled beneath tan skin that glistened with sweat as he wielded the ax in a kind of determination that suggested he was more intent on working something out of his system than on doing the job for the sake of getting it done.

But no matter what was behind it, there was a sensuality to his every movement that made Ally's nerve endings slither to the surface of her own skin, leaving her too aware of her perspiration-soaked T-shirt clinging to her as if it had been hosed down.

How could wood-chopping be a sensual act?

She suddenly began to wonder if her overheated state didn't owe more to the woodchopper than to the weather.

A glorious sight, he worked with a seamless rhythm that looked as if it barely tapped into the full measure of his power and strength.

Each whack of the ax into the wood began to answer a beat of Ally's heart and reverberate through her, enlivening more and more inside of her with every blow, rekindling those sparks that had started at the foot of the windmill.

It was crazy, she knew, but she started to see Jackson's woodcutting as something incredibly erotic. Her nipples puckered up in response and tightened a cord that stretched right through to the center of her. And each fall of the ax raised her body temperature even higher, thrumming that cord, awakening her every sense, her every desire, her craving to slide her palms along that sweat-slickened skin, to press herself against the steely wall of those muscles, to feel his mouth on hers once again, his hands on her body...

"I have to go inside," she blurted out all of a sudden, sounding as if she were in more of a panic than she had been before, *feeling* in more of a panic.

Jackson stopped what he was doing and his eyes did a slow roll down to her toes and back up again, as if searching for the cause. But she didn't wait for him to say anything. She threw the split log she had in her hand onto the pile and headed for the house as if her tail were on fire.

A cold shower! She needed a very cold shower or else she'd either die of heat prostration or jump that man's bones!

It was just too hot outside, she decided on the way.

The sweltering temperature had made her a little nuts. As soon as she cooled off she'd be okay again.

She tore off her clothes the minute she was in her bedroom upstairs and charged into the shower. She didn't even touch the hot-water knob but only turned on the cold full blast, gasping when the chilly spray hit her.

It was a welcome agony.

It just didn't work.

Oh, sure, her body temperature began to drop, but her nipples were still kerneled and straining for Jackson's touch. That cord was still stretched to her lower reaches where an achingly empty need cried out for him. And never in her life had she wanted anyone as much as she still wanted him....

Then, suddenly, a silhouette fell across the frosted glass of the shower door, two sets of fingers curled over the top of it, and she saw what looked to be Jackson's head pressed to the outside.

"Tell me to get the hell out of here," he ordered in the passion-husky voice she was coming to recognize.

All she could think of at that moment was that it didn't look like he had on any clothes on the other side of the door.

And the last thing in the world she could do was resist what she wanted most, what her whole body cried out for.

She pushed on the shower door to open it and there he stood—naked and so gorgeous her jaw dropped. She couldn't help letting her gaze rake down his glistening body, the most magnificent male physique she'd ever seen in person or anywhere else.

And he wanted her as much as she wanted him. It was right there for her to see—long, thick, hard proof.

She swallowed back a rise of overwhelmingly potent desire, forced herself to look him in those oh-so-blue eyes and watched him step into the stall with her.

Once he was there and the door was closed behind him, he took her by the shoulders and pulled her to him, instantly capturing her lips with his, insistently, hungrily.

The heat they'd both suffered outside still emanated from him, and sweat mingled with the water that rained down on them, making his taut skin just as slick as she'd imagined as she slid her palms up those solid, bulging biceps.

His mouth opened wide over hers, his tongue thrust inside and Ally answered the urgency in it because she felt it, too.

Almost frantically they each explored the other's body, like lovers kept too long apart by forces other than themselves, learning and arousing at once. And every caress of those big, callused hands raised Ally to a new level of yearning.

He kneaded her breasts, gently tormented her nipples, reveling in them and tightening the cord inside her even more with the wonders he worked, the tenderness of the restrained power, the adoration of his touch.

She nearly cried out in protest when his mouth deserted hers and those talented hands abandoned her breasts. Except that before she could utter more than a groan, he'd cupped her derriere to lift her slightly, holding her between the shower wall and his hips so his mouth could replace his hands at her breasts, suckling, nipping, tugging at her nipples, flicking them with his tongue in heavenly torture.

Ally closed her eyes, buried her hands in his hair and gave herself up to the miracles the man was working, to the heights of pleasure he was driving her to.

His hands slid from her derriere down the backs of her thighs, lifting her effortlessly and wrapping her legs around his waist so that the long, hard shaft of him barely introduced itself to the spot between her legs that cried out for so much more.

Her breath caught, suspended in anticipation, in a craving so intense she didn't know if she could survive it.

And then there he was, easing her down, sliding up inside of her, filling her so completely there was no room for her to breathe.

Except that couldn't have been true, because she heard herself moan, "Oh, Jackson."

He kissed her again, slowly this time, only pulsing inside her, claiming her, blissfully teasing her, until she flexed back and arched her hips against him.

She felt his smile, accepted the thrust of his tongue as a prelude, and then, finally, he began to move. Delving deep and then retreating. Deeper still and out again.

As good as he was at everything else, he was a master at that, guiding her, setting just the right pace, increasing it at the very moment she needed him to, until, together, passion exploded in them both, driving him to the very core of her. Wave after wave of ecstasy washed through her and seemed to echo in him until the pace calmed, wound down to where it had started and finally stopped completely.

Jackson dropped his forehead to her collarbone. Ally let her head rest back against the tile wall. And as the cold water went on pummeling them, they stayed that way for a moment.

Then Jackson turned off the water and let Ally slide down to stand on her own two feet again. But she was only there for a split second before he scooped her up into his arms and carried her out to her bed, where he laid her down and joined her, pulling her against the length of his side.

He chuckled a little and, with a note of amusement in his voice, said, "Are you afraid of anything besides heights that I should know about?"

"This," she whispered, meaning what was happening between them.

He smiled down at her, though it was slightly hesitant. "Me, too," he answered very quietly, apparently knowing what she'd meant.

But fear of the feelings they shared didn't stop him from kissing her again. Or from reaching one of those now-familiar hands to her breast.

And it didn't stop her from laying her palm on the side of his neck, or sliding her thigh over his to press herself against him as passion took them on yet another ride.

Instead those feelings welled up to overwhelm the fears and carry them both away....

Chapter Eight

It was ten o'clock the next morning when Ally woke up to a clap of thunder so loud it seemed to strike in the bedroom. A big, callused hand lay on her breast.

She was lying next to Jackson, her body perfectly fitted to the length of his, her head on his chest, their legs entwined, her own hand curved along the side of his thick, corded neck, with nothing but a sheet covering them.

"We overslept," she told him in a sleep-husky tone when she'd opened her eyes and could see the clock on the nightstand beyond him.

"It's rainin'," he answered.

It wasn't just raining. A torrential downpour pounded the house, and thunder and lightning cracked like whips all around them while his slow hand at her breast kept up a titillating massage.

"Do you just stay in bed all day when the weather turns bad?" she asked with a smile in her voice for what he was awakening inside her.

"Not usually."

"You just sleep in a little?"

"Not usually."

But after a night that had included a stand-up supper in the kitchen, another round of lovemaking in the pool, then another on one of the loungers, it was no wonder even Jackson hadn't been bright eyed and bushy tailed before now.

His hand slipped from her breast to her side and around to her rear end, pressing her more firmly to his hip. "How you holdin' up?"

"Well enough," she answered, ignoring the soreness that made that a lie, because he'd already raised anew the now-familiar desire they'd shared into the wee hours of the morning.

He chuckled, a seductive echo from deep in his chest. "I don't think I've ever known anyone quite like you, Ms. Brooks."

She did a slow, tantalizing rub of his chest with a feather-light stroke that kerneled his male nibs almost the way her nipples were. "How am I different?"

"You just never fail to surprise me. Every time I think I have you pegged one way, you up and prove me wrong."

"Is that bad?"

"No, ma'am, it's not. It's not bad at all. Except maybe that I'm enjoyin' it altogether too much." He paused a moment, and when he went on, it was in a tone that was quiet and sincere. "Enjoyin' *you* altogether too much."

His hand slid back the way it had come, but bypassed her breast to cup her chin and tilt her face up to him so he could kiss her, chastely, sweetly, lovingly...

"Ah, Ally..." he nearly moaned in what sounded almost like sorrow, leaving her lips to kiss her brow, her eyes, her nose and then her mouth once more.

Somehow she knew what he was lamenting. It was the feelings she knew he had for her even though he'd expressed them only with his body, with his touch, with the tenderness and care he'd shown all through the night.

And she understood, because she shared not only the feelings, but the fear of them, of the pain they could cause. She was very much afraid that she was falling in love with this man. That maybe it was too late and she'd already fallen...

"Mom? I'm home!"

Meggie's call from downstairs, accentuated with the slam of the front door, was like a bucket of cold water thrown on them.

Then Linc's deeper voice sounded, "Could be they're out workin'. You take your things upstairs and I'll go look in the barn."

"Oh, my god!" Ally said, jumping up and making a mad dash for her bathrobe. "Hide!" she whisper-shouted to Jackson as she did.

But he just lay there, grinning at her, and clamped

his hands behind his head. "Tell her to get an umbrella and go collect the eggs," he said calmly.

Ally opened the door only enough to squeeze her head through, just as Meggie tossed her backpack into her own room and headed for Ally's.

"Hi, sweetie!" Ally said much too brightly, garnering a chuckle from Jackson that she was relatively sure Meggie didn't hear. "How was your slumber party?"

"It was good," her daughter answered. "How come you're not dressed yet?"

"I guess my alarm didn't go off. Why don't you go out and collect the eggs and I'll be down in the kitchen by the time you're finished?"

"I could do that later. I want to tell you what we did last night. It was so fun."

"Go do the eggs first and then tell me while we have breakfast."

"I already had breakfast."

"You can tell me while I eat." The desperate note that was overtaking her tone brought another chuckle from Jackson. Ally amended it to motherly firmness. "Go on now. Use one of the umbrellas from next to the hall tree in the entranceway and don't get wet."

Meggie looked at her as if she'd lost her mind but finally conceded, and Ally ducked back into the room, closing the door and falling against it.

"Caught in the act," Jackson said softly as he got out of bed and came her way in all his masculine, muscular, gorgeous glory.

When he reached her, he slid his hands inside her

robe, laying it open to pull her naked body up against his, and kissed her again, playfully this time.

But when that playfulness turned more heated, he stopped and propped his chin on the top of her head. "Beth and Ash are bringin' the baby home today. What do you say to cookin' a special dinner for tonight?"

"Instead of mucking out horse stalls or slopping pigs or—"

"Instead of all that."

Was he letting her off the hook for the hard chores just for the day, or had last night made such a difference in their relationship that he was telling her a permanent change was in order? And if it was a permanent change, what did that mean?

"I'd like to cook for them today," she answered, meaning it but sounding a little tentative just the same.

Jackson didn't seem to hear the tentativeness. "Good. Then I'd better get out of here before Miss Meggie comes snoopin'."

He kissed Ally's forehead and reluctantly took his arms from around her, clasping her shoulders to move her away from the door. "See you downstairs." Then, with a cautious glance to make sure the hall was clear, he left.

Ally felt an instant disappointment to have him gone and had to fight the urge to follow him.

But it wasn't only thoughts of Meggie coming back and catching them that stopped her.

There was also a little wave of panic about where things between them were going from here.

"Mighty fine food," Linc said for the dozenth time that evening as he, Kansas and Danny, and Ally, Meggie and Jackson were leaving Beth and Ash's house.

Everyone added their praises, even Jackson—with no comment about the chateaubriand being froufrou.

"I enjoyed doing it," Ally assured them. "I had a day full of my three favorite things—rain, cooking and Meggie as my assistant chef."

Jackson's expression seemed to deflate slightly, as if he'd expected—or maybe just hoped—to be one of the three. Not that he'd spent much time with her. He'd popped in periodically but had mainly kept to the barn.

Still, Ally hoped she hadn't inadvertently struck some sort of blow. He'd been warm and funny and nice when they had been together during the day. And he'd passed the evening helping her with the food and tossing her secret glances and intimate smiles that had set off sparks to dance along her nerve endings. The last thing she wanted to do was answer all of that with anything that would hurt his feelings.

"Remember," Linc said as they all stood at the door to go, "anytime you want to come cook at the honky-tonk—"

"And make Jackson hire six men to do my job around here?" she joked.

That made everybody laugh, including Jackson.

A loud clap of thunder interrupted this exchange and when it passed, the good-nights really did get said, along with a reminder about the Native American ceremony Ash had scheduled at dawn the next morning to name the new baby.

Outside in the yard, Linc and Kansas said a second set of farewells to Ally and Jackson and then went to where their car was parked near the garage.

But rather than heading for the house, Jackson looked up at the starless black sky with its low-hanging, ominous clouds, obviously assessing the weather to come as Ally and Meggie waited for him.

The rain had stopped about an hour before they'd gone to Beth's place, so Jackson and Meggie had taken the horses from the barn to let them loose in the paddock beside it. Now he went from checking out the sky to studying the animals.

"This storm is going to start up again. We can't leave the horses out in it. If they get anxious enough they're liable to try jumping the fence," he said as Ally and Meggie followed the direction of his gaze to where five of them were in various states of agitation. "We'd better get 'em back inside."

Ally had her hands full of the platters and bowls she'd used to cart food. She lifted them just enough to remind him. "I'll set these in the kitchen and be right out."

Jackson nodded and then squeezed Meggie's shoulder. "Come on then, Miss Meggie darlin', you and I will get started ourselves."

They headed for the barn while Ally went on her

way to the house, smiling at this latest version of one of Jackson's pet names for her daughter. First it had been *Miss* Meggie, in an old-fashioned courtliness, and now it was Miss Meggie *darlin'*.

She could tell it tickled her daughter, because every time he said it, Meggie flashed a tiny smile that illustrated how special it made her feel. A feeling Ally understood completely.

Jackson might be slow to show that quiet, understated charm of his, but when he did, it was potent and irresistible, and all the more flattering because it wasn't something he did readily or in an offhand manner or to just anybody. It was as if it came from the core of him and was shared only with those he let in that far.

Another crash of thunder hit so hard and close the house rocked as Ally quickly put the dirty utensils into the dishwasher. The first drops of rain were beginning to fall again when she went back outside, but in just the time it took her to reach the paddock where Meggie and Jackson were, rain was pouring once more in heavy sheets that made it hard to even see through.

"Go on up to the house, Meggie," she heard Jackson call to her daughter as Ally climbed the rail fence and hopped to the ground on the other side.

Lightning lighted up the sky so brightly it was blinding, and not a breath later, thunder hit with the force of a cannon. The horses that were still out in it whinnied and snorted and moved jerkily, as if they didn't know where to go to escape what was frightening them. The gelding Jackson had a hold of by the cheek piece of the harness shied even from him, but he held on tight and tugged the animal into the barn.

Ally didn't know if Meggie was ignoring Jackson's order or just hadn't heard it, but she was still hanging on tight to the reins of the filly she called Sunshine, trying to pull her into the barn. Sunshine was clearly the most scared of the lot and the small child was having trouble keeping her grip on the harness the animal was new to.

"I'll take her in. You go up to the house like Jackson said," Ally shouted from across the paddock through the noise of thunder and rain, as she headed in her daughter's direction.

But Ally was still some distance away when another boom struck. She saw Sunshine rear back on its hind legs, yanking Meggie's arm sharply, jerking her nearly off the ground. Even through the noise of the storm, Ally heard her daughter's gasp of surprise and pain.

"Let go!" Ally shouted, breaking into a run.

Meggie did, falling to the ground just as the animal came back down, catching the little girl's temple with a front hoof.

And then Sunshine reared again.

Everything appeared to happen in slow motion for Ally, who couldn't seem to run fast enough through the pounding rain and muddy earth as those hooves hovered in midair, directly over Meggie, pawing at the rain like a kitten at a dangling twine ball. Only this was no kitten. This was a terrified animal with a great deal more weight and power behind it, even if it was only a very young horse.

"No!" Ally shrieked as those hooves began to lower.

And then Ally slipped and fell flat.

She scrambled back to her feet but still she was yards short of her child when, again, Sunshine's front half lowered.

This time a hoof clipped Meggie's elbow, where the little girl had curved it over her face to protect herself.

"Roll away!" was all Ally could think to advise as she again rushed to help.

But just then Jackson came from out of nowhere at a full run, his boots maneuvering the mud better than Ally's slippery-soled loafers. "Hya-hya!" he shouted along the way, the words and the deep, loud voice finally shooing the animal to veer in the opposite direction just as Ally reached Meggie, dropping to her knees beside her.

Meggie's cut arm shook as she took it away from her face. Her eyes were wide, her skin ashen with fear, and blood from her temple had already flooded her hair.

Without thinking about the wisdom in moving her daughter, Ally grabbed her up into her lap and held on tight, mindlessly rocking her as if she were a baby whose minor fussiness could be soothed that way.

But Jackson took command and cut it short. "Let's get her inside," he said through the din of the storm, bending over and taking the little girl from Ally's arms to head for the house.

Within an hour Ally knew Meggie wasn't seriously hurt.

Jackson had called the emergency number and the town doctor had come out to the house. After a thorough check he'd declared Meggie cut and bruised, but okay.

Ally gently cleaned her up, gave her a pain reliever and tucked her into bed—her and the entire contingent of dolls and stuffed animals that her daughter had once again situated all around her. She also made sure Mutt was at her feet before she'd close her eyes and go to sleep.

For a few minutes Ally stayed by her bed, watching her, working to believe everything really was okay, trying to stop the internal shaking that was still rumbling through her like her own private earthquake.

Maybe being here wasn't what was best for Meggie after all, she thought.

But she knew now was not the time to consider it. She was too jittery, too scared to make any kind of decision.

And standing there studying the rise and fall of her daughter's chest to make sure she was breathing wasn't helping anything, so she finally pressed a soft kiss to Meggie's brow, tucked in the already tucked-in covers and left the room.

"How's our girl doin'?" Jackson's question greeted her as she carefully closed the door behind her. He was waiting in the hall, his arms crossed over his chest, his back against the wall.

She knew the doctor had to have filled him in before he left, but as if Jackson actually might not know what was going on, she said, "We were lucky. Both her head and elbow were only grazed. And her shoulder wasn't dislocated, just wrenched. It'll be sore for a few days, but she won't even need a sling. She has quite an egg on her head, though. Living on a ranch might be helping the inside of it, but I'm beginning to wonder how dangerous this place is for the outside of it."

Ally had intended that to be a joke, but neither of them laughed. Probably because it had too much of a ring of truth to it to be funny.

Instead, Jackson's brows dipped down in a frown, and somehow she knew what he was thinking—that just when he let his guard drop with her, she'd take off the way his ex-wife had.

And suddenly Ally realized that he might be right. That somewhere during the time since Meggie had been hurt, the thought of leaving here had begun to seriously tease at the fringes of her thoughts.

Jackson pushed away from the wall and stood up straight, tall, proud. And distant. "Life here isn't only hard, it's hazardous, too," he agreed, though not in the warning, ominous way he'd said it before. Just as a matter of fact. "That's something you'd better take into consideration."

Before either of us gets in any deeper, Ally added mentally. "Did Meggie do something wrong?" she asked, searching for a reason, for a way to convince herself that the hazards could be avoided.

"Nope, she didn't," he answered, instantly dispelling that hope. "Meggie's good with Sunshine. She's also right about the horse liking her. That animal responds to her better than to anyone 'round here. These things just happen. Could have been me as easily as it was Meggie if one of the bigger horses had shied. We're dealin' with unpredictable animals that outweigh us ten times over. And with the power and force of Mother Nature. With wide-open spaces where help is faraway. With equipment that can be treacherous. It's all part of this life, Ally."

Take it or leave it.

He didn't say that, but Ally heard it, anyway, in his tone. And it sent a renewed shiver up her spine, bringing with it more of that internal shaking she'd just managed to stop.

Jackson seemed to sense it. He took a step toward her and his arms unlocked from across his chest. But that was as far as he got. He didn't actually reach for her the way she thought he was going to. The way she wished he would. He stopped short and only jammed his hands into his pockets.

"Guess you'd better think about some things," he suggested, his expression resigned, sad, knowing.

Then, as if he were leaving her to do just that, he turned and went into his bedroom.

It wasn't as if Ally could think about anything else as she went into her own room, into her bathroom and peeled off her muddy clothes.

The sight of Meggie lying on the ground like a rag doll with that horse above her, on the verge of stomping her, kept flashing through Ally's mind in every vivid detail.

An inch more to the center of Meggie's head and her skull could have been crushed or her face shattered. She could have been killed. She could have been scarred for life.

Standing in the shower, thinking about it, Ally felt her heart begin to pound, and the shaking started yet again, this time not only internally but externally, too.

Images of Meggie hurt and bloody kept flashing themselves at her. Thoughts of losing her stabbed like knives. Her whole body quaked uncontrollably, and even the warm water of the shower didn't chase away the chill that felt as if it were bone deep.

She turned off the water and stepped out of the stall, under the heat lamp in the ceiling, thinking maybe that might help. But it didn't. And neither did drying off.

She knew the shock, the full impact of what had happened, of what *might* have happened, was striking. The same thing had occurred when she'd been involved in a car accident—she'd functioned while she'd needed to and then fallen apart after the fact.

The delayed reaction, the fear, was insurmountable and the tremors went on running through her, leaving her shivering, shaking, weak-kneed.

And into it all came a craving for Jackson. For his strong, steady presence. For his calm in the storm that was ripping at her from the inside out. For his comfort. For him....

She told herself it wasn't wise even as she slipped into her bathrobe and headed out of her bedroom. Jackson was the very person she'd leave behind if she opted not to stay here. And they were both already in so deep it wouldn't be easy for either of them if she took Meggie and left.

But her feelings for him were stronger than any reasoning she could come up with. Her need for him was more powerful. And at that moment she was too weak, too vulnerable to put up a fight with herself.

She crossed the hall to his door and knocked softly, still trembling, on the verge of tears she couldn't explain.

"Come in," he called quietly.

She opened the door and there he was, standing in the middle of the room, shirtless, his feet bare, the waistband button of his jeans unfastened. His dark hair was finger-combed carelessly; his mustache added a seriousness to his expression, the dent in his chin caught shadows. And just one look at him lighted a tiny ember of much-needed warmth deep inside her.

Ally wasn't sure what to say and so just stood there in the hall, staring at him and shaking like a leaf. Finally she murmured, "I don't want to be alone..." when what she really wanted to say was, *Hold me, please, just hold me, close and tight....*

But he seemed to know.

He came to her and pulled her through the doorway and into his arms, against that broad, hard chest of his, the way she'd wanted him to before. His arms wrapped around her in just the solid embrace she yearned for, letting the heat of his body seep into her pores.

She circled his waist with her own arms, pressed her palms to the expanse of his back and laid her cheek to his chest.

She could hear his heartbeat and she closed her eyes and gave in to her other senses as they drank in the nectar that was Jackson, feeding her bruised spirit, reviving her.

For a long while that was how they remained. He didn't do anything but hold her, comfort her, massage her tense shoulder blades with big, capable hands, cocoon her body with his magnificent one, and press soft kisses to the top of her head.

It was all the perfect balm.

Little by little her trembling stopped—first on the outside and then even on the inside. She could feel the tension leaving her by degrees, feel the stiffness draining out of her, feel her lungs taking in more than just the shallow breaths that were the best she'd been able to manage since Meggie's accident.

And then solace gave way to something else.

Her body molded itself to his, softness to hard, curves into valleys, and his touch was no longer merely comforting but had a slower, more sensuous feel to it.

His hands trailed up into her hair, cradling and guiding her head away from his chest so he could peer down into her eyes, searching them with a troubled gaze and yet clearly as unable to fight this as she'd been.

"I love you, Ally," he whispered as if it hurt him somehow to say it. Or maybe to feel it.

"I love you, too," she answered, her voice no louder, for as great as the fear he'd just quelled in her was another, a fear of the feelings they'd just admitted to and what could come with them.

But then he lowered his lips to hers in a kiss too sweet, too deep, too forceful to resist.

Ally gave in to it. To the freedom it allowed her from all thought.

With his mouth still covering hers, he picked her up in his arms and carried her to his bed, where they made love with a wild abandon that kept rhythm with the thunder and lightning that still raged outside, swept away on a passion greater than everything else at that moment, wiping away all reason, all inhibition, all worries and fears.

Ally truly lost herself in the exquisite sensations Jackson bestowed, carried on the tides of pleasure that came with the contained power of his hands on her breasts, on her stomach, lower still.

His mouth enraptured hers. His tongue played, teased, fenced with hers, and then went on to explore for other, even more sensitive spots on her body to delight and bring to life.

She reveled in her own exploration of him, too— hard, honed muscles and deeply cut vales; massive, sinewy legs; that tight derriere; and the long, steely shaft of his masculinity and desire—need—for her.

And when he slipped that glorious shaft inside her and drove them both to a new and higher peak, she knew not only a blind ecstasy but a completeness, a sense that what they'd found together was meant to be. And for a brief, explosive moment, she couldn't imagine being anywhere else or ever leaving him behind.

But then they crossed over the crest and came back to earth.

And even though lying in Jackson's arms was still bliss, fear crept back into her consciousness. And though he stroked her hair where her head rested on his chest, though he held her close and their legs were entwined the way they'd been when she'd awakened this morning, the fear didn't lessen.

Then, in a passion-raspy voice he said, "Do you ever think about getting married again?"

Fear turned to the same kind of terror she'd felt at the top of the windmill, but she fought to hide it. "Sure, I think about it," she answered quietly. "Do you?"

"Not until lately." He paused a moment and then, almost hesitantly, said, "Would you think about marryin' me?"

Ally didn't answer that immediately. She couldn't. How could such a simple question strike such disparate feelings in her? But it did, as fear warred with happiness.

Then she realized that agreeing to think about marrying him was not the same as saying yes. So, as if she were venturing out onto thin ice, she said, "I'll think about it." She wouldn't be able *not* to think about his quiet, solemn proposal.

Then, out of the blue and completely taking Ally by surprise, came a flashback of her daughter under that horse. And that much more reasonable and rational fear pushed aside the unreasonable and irrational one she'd just been feeling as she was washed in an intense memory of her own helplessness in doing anything to save Meggie from that danger.

And Ally knew that she'd be thinking a lot about that, too.

Chapter Nine

The storm of the day and night before had stopped and given way to a clear sky for the naming ceremony that was to take place as the sun first rose above the horizon. The hundred or so guests began arriving just before dawn.

Everyone brought a dish for a potluck breakfast, leaving it on the picnic tables, and birth gifts stacked up in a considerable pyramid in one corner of the patio.

Ash's grandfather, Robert Yazzie, had arrived late the previous night and in the predawn haze, Ash introduced him around.

The two tall Native American men were dressed in dark slacks and white shirts, but beyond that, their attire spoke of their own culture.

Each wore soft white deerskin moccasins that wrapped around their calves nearly to their knees, and beaded necklaces and wristbands that lent festivity and dignity to the event. And both men, whose hair reached well down their backs, wore it loose today— something Kansas confided to Ally that both Ash and his grandfather did only for sacred rites, otherwise keeping it tied back.

As the sun's first rays lighted the sky cotton-candy pink and butternut yellow, family, friends and neighbors gathered near a small stand, on which rested a wooden cradle that looked like a section of hollowed-out, halved tree trunk.

"This has been handed down from generation to generation in my family," Ash explained as Robert carved a triangular notch in the edge of the cradle, where seven other, similar gashes had already been made in the age-old wood that was as smooth as sueded silk.

"We cut into the frame," Robert continued as he worked, "to leave a mark for each child who uses the cradle. As you can see, it belonged to Ash and to his father before him and to me and my two brothers, as well as to our father and his before him."

"And yes," Ash added with a laugh, "this baby is the first girl born to our family in quite some time."

Robert finished the job by sanding the edges smooth. When that was done Ash went to his house, where Beth stood in the doorway, holding the baby and watching from there.

He took his daughter from her, offered his wife his arm and carried the child out into the dawning light.

When they reached the stand he laid his daughter in the cradle and with tender care placed a soft leather cummerbund across the infant's swaddled middle, wrapping thin leather strips around that and the wood at once to hold her secure.

Then he picked up the cradle.

That was the cue for Ally and Kansas to step forward.

"We've chosen Ally and Kansas to be our Corn Mothers—the Blue Corn Woman…" Beth gave Kansas a flawless ear of blue corn. "And the White Corn Maiden…" An equally perfect ear of white corn came to Ally. "The Corn Mothers symbolize the original mothers of our people and they will offer the earth's bounty to the sun and also in six other directions— north—" he paused for them to comply "—west… south…east…nadir…and zenith."

Ally and Kansas held the ears of corn on either end and, with each turn, extended them as was befitting the giving of a gift.

"And now they will present our baby the same way."

Ally and Kansas each took an end of the cradle and did as they had with the corn—holding the child out to the sun, the other four compass points, down to the earth, and finally straight up in the air, before handing the cradle back to Ash.

There were tears in the big man's eyes as he kissed the baby's brow and announced, "Beth and I have decided to call her Marissa Morningdove.'' Then, to everyone watching, he said, ''Thank you all for coming out so early to be a part of her beginning.''

Beth hugged her husband's arm, stood on tiptoe and kissed him. Then she said jokingly, ''He's only slightly proud of her,'' making everyone laugh and break into applause.

Ally felt Meggie step to her side just then and take her hand. She glanced down at her daughter, finding the little girl staring teary eyed at the scene in front of them.

Or more specifically, at Ash and the obvious love he exhibited toward his daughter as he took her out of the wooden cradle and began to show her off to his guests.

Meggie had awakened in good spirits this morning and insisted she felt fine in spite of the huge lump and angry purple bruise on her forehead, the matching set on her elbow, and the bluish tint to her shoulder. She'd been anxious for the Indian ceremony and the breakfast party.

But the child Ally looked down on now was a world away from that. Instead she was every bit as morose as she'd been before they'd come to the ranch.

''Did my daddy used to hold me that way?'' she asked in a quiet voice that broke Ally's heart.

''Sure,'' she answered as glibly as she could manage, hoping to defuse the depression that seemed to have made a resurgence.

"I'm too big for him to hold like a baby now, though," Meggie said bravely.

"That's true."

"But maybe if he came back pretty soon I wouldn't be too big to sit in his lap, do you think?"

"Meggie…"

"I know. You don't want me to get up my hopes that he's gonna come back. But *if* he did?"

"You can sit on *my* lap anytime you want."

It's not the same.

Meggie didn't say it, but Ally read it in her expression as her daughter glanced longingly back at Ash where he cuddled the baby in his arms and rubbed her nose with his while he made silly noises to her.

Doug, you bastard, Ally thought, fighting tears of her own.

And then all of a sudden Jackson came up from behind them and clasped both of Meggie's shoulders. "Here's my girl!" He claimed her heartily.

Ally didn't know if he had any idea what was going on with her daughter, but she could have fallen at his feet in gratitude just then as he went on to use his special charm on the little girl, saying he had breakfast steaks to cook and needed *his* Miss Meggie to help him to do it.

Meggie's smile wasn't as bright or carefree as it had been the past few days, but she mustered one for him and that was something. And when he offered her his hand to hold, she blushed with pleasure and took it.

There was no substitute, Ally realized, for what Meggie was really starved for—the love and affection of her own father—but at least Jackson's attention seemed to stave off some of it.

The trouble was, Ally thought as she watched the two of them head for the barbecue, until now she'd hoped that coming here would be more than a mere distraction. That it would be the cure that would let Meggie accept that she might never see her father again and go on from there.

But now, seeing that the despondency was just lurking beneath the surface, ready to spring back to life at the drop of a hat, she felt as if these hopes had been dashed.

And she couldn't help asking herself if the weaker-than-she'd-believed merits of being here outweighed the much-greater-than-she'd-known dangers.

It was something she most definitely had to factor into her thinking about marrying Jackson.

Once Jackson had finished his cooking duties, he stayed close to Ally the rest of the morning. It wasn't only that he wanted to be near her—which he did—but he was also answering a feeling that if he left her side for too long, she'd disappear.

He tried to believe the feeling was irrational. After all, he'd thought the same thing the night before, that Meggie's accident had done what all his tactics had failed to accomplish—it had scared Ally so badly she'd hightail it out of here at the first opportunity.

Instead, she'd come to his room, made love with

him. And he'd convinced himself he was imagining things.

But this morning the feeling had returned and he couldn't stop the overwhelming sense that she was shying away from this place. From him. That he'd seen the same look in her eyes that had been in Sherry's just before she'd left.

It didn't help matters that Meggie's bumps and bruises brought questions from nearly everyone at the celebration and that Ally had to relive the incident in answering them. Or that too many times once her answer was given the response was a horror story about accidents or injuries or mishaps that someone had had themselves or witnessed or known about.

Jackson watched Ally every time it happened and although no one had said anything to purposely frighten her, nevertheless each tale drained a little more color from her face. He couldn't blame her for feeling frightened for her little girl. Frightened enough to leave here, maybe?

No. She'd been determined enough about staying here to put up with all he'd dished out, he reminded himself. To turn down his every offer to buy her out. She'd been convinced this was where they belonged. So why would she leave now?

And yet, as much as he tried to convince himself otherwise, he just couldn't shake the sense that she would.

By early that afternoon all the guests were gone, leaving behind the kind of mess a gathering of that size engendered. Ally, Jackson, Marta, Hans and Ash comprised the cleanup crew, but they'd barely gotten started when Jackson received a call that several head of cattle were down on one of the outlying pastures. It was something he had to see to and, when he hung up the phone, he went to announce it to everyone in general.

Then he took Ally aside.

"I'll have to take the helicopter out—this herd is at the farthest edge of our property. Want to come along?"

Her smile was wan and still it had the power to heat up his insides. "The helicopter?"

"I'm a good pilot, if you're worried about it. The view is incredible and you'll get to see the whole ranch at once. We can even take Meggie, give her a ride."

Mistake. He could see it the moment he said it. It was apparent Ally wasn't enamored of his favorite toy, but add Meggie to the equation and Ally's face turned the color of the rail fence her daughter had whitewashed.

"I don't think that would be a good idea," she said, those terrific Irish eyes of hers growing wide.

"She'd love it."

"She'd love to eat her way through a candy store, too. That doesn't mean she knows what's good for her."

"Okay, then we'll leave her here with Hans and Marta, and just you and I will go."

Her head shook with enough vigor to set her long

curly hair shimmying. "If you're giving me a choice, the answer is no. I'm basically the only parent Meggie has and—"

And she really was spooked. Suddenly he saw just how deeply.

"And I forgot you don't like heights," he said, more to himself than to her when he remembered it. He could have kicked himself for no doubt reminding her of yet another unnerving incident—the windmill.

Trying for some damage control, he made light of it all. "I don't suppose surveying your kingdom from a helicopter would be a lot of fun for you, would it? It doesn't matter. You don't ever have to fly in the 'copter if you don't want to."

She looked relieved but only marginally.

He couldn't resist reaching out to her, rubbing her arm. "It's okay, really. No big deal."

But he could see that she wasn't comforted and that it was a big deal to her. As everything suddenly seemed to be.

"I'll be back in a few hours. Why don't you and Meggie go for a swim, relax the rest of the afternoon?" *Lounge around the pool the way I accused you of wanting to do. But now, if only you'd stay, I wouldn't care if that really was all you ever did....*

"You'll be careful?" she answered, clearly as concerned for his safety as for her daughter's, for her own.

"Sure. Nothing to worry about," he said confidently, squeezing her arms and even venturing a small kiss in spite of the fact that they were in plain sight. "I'll be back by suppertime," he assured.

Then he headed for the helicopter.

But she really was worried. It was the last thing he saw as he lifted off from the helipad. It was etched into her beautiful face, lining it, pulling her full pink lips down at the corners, creasing a spot between her eyes as she watched him go.

That was when he knew he was just kidding himself to think history wasn't repeating itself. And in that instant Jackson Heller hardened his heart.

Ally was a city girl through and through. She didn't belong living a rancher's life. She wouldn't be happy in the long run. His feeble hopes that they could have a future together, a good marriage, a family, were unrealistic.

As unrealistic as thinking his love for Sherry would have been enough to keep her here all those years ago.

This wasn't the place for Ally any more than it had been the place for his former wife.

The best thing would be for Ally to sell out and go back to Denver.

Best for her. Best for Meggie.

Best for him, too.

Because as he returned home at dusk, just the way he had so long ago at the end of the cattle drive that had taken him away from Sherry, he remembered much too vividly how anxious he'd been to see her, and how hard it had been to find, instead, an empty house.

So damn empty it had echoed.

Empty closets.

Empty drawers.

And just a note hooked onto the divorce papers saying she couldn't take living here anymore....

He didn't ever want to walk into that kind of emptiness again. To feel that fist of pain jammed into his stomach. That shock. The agony that went on and on....

Better that he lost Ally and Meggie face-to-face. Better that he watched them go.

So before he'd even reached the sliding door to the kitchen where he could see her setting the table for supper, he'd made up his mind.

One more night.

He could have one more night with Ally.

And then he'd send her away.

"You're sure you don't want all your dolls and stuffed animals around you like last night?" Ally asked Meggie as she tucked her in.

"No, not tonight. I only wanted them then because I had those dumb ol' butterflies in my tummy like before, but they're gone now."

"And how about the sad feeling? That was back this morning, too, wasn't it?"

Meggie frowned. "I wish I was the new baby and my daddy was here with me."

"I know, sweetheart." Ally smoothed her daughter's forehead and waited for the tears that this conversation was likely to bring on.

But they never came.

Instead Meggie yawned and snuggled into her pillow.

"Hans said the momma pig was havin' her babies tonight so we'll get to see 'em tomorrow. They'll be so cute...."

Meggie's eyes had closed as she talked and Ally watched her drift off to sleep, amazed that the subject of her father had been so easily passed over. But that single comment seemed to have been the sum and substance of it.

Grateful for that, at least, Ally kissed her daughter's tiny, bruised brow and silently made her way out of the room, carrying with her the knowledge that no matter how substantial the improvements in Meggie were, they could be reversed in the blink of an eye.

She eased the door shut after herself and found Jackson waiting for her in the hall the way he'd been the night before.

Tall and muscular, he was dressed in a black T-shirt that fit him like a second skin, tight blue jeans whose pockets sported his thumbs, and his ever-present boots—one crossed over the other at the ankle, the pointed toe spiked against the floor. He looked heart-stoppingly handsome. And Ally wished she weren't so drawn to him that she felt complete only when she was with him.

"You're not lookin' happy tonight, darlin'," he observed in a lazy drawl.

"I'm just a little tired," she answered. He didn't

need to know that the weariness was more emotional than physical.

"Too tired for some wine and stargazin'?"

Never too tired to be with you, she thought. And even though she knew she should decline the invitation, she said, "I could probably stay awake for that."

She turned in the direction of the stairs, but he caught her arm and pulled her the other way. "Best place for it is on the deck off my room. Less light."

But lots of privacy.

Again Ally knew she shouldn't be doing something that could only make ending her time here more difficult if that's what she decided—and it *was* what she was thinking she needed to do.

Yet how could she refuse herself what might be the last time with him?

She couldn't. No matter how strong the reasoning, her feelings for him made her will too weak.

So instead she went to his room.

It was dimly lighted by only his bedside lamp. The French doors on one wall were open to the balcony beyond, and a small table there was set with crystal glasses and a silver bucket of ice that chilled an open bottle of wine.

"Pretty sure of yourself, aren't you, cowboy?" she joked as he closed the door behind them.

He only grinned at her, a grin that sent sparkles all through her.

She loved him *so* much.

So much it scared her....

He took her hand and pulled her out onto the balcony that faced the wide-open countryside, away from the pool and patio, the barn, the bunkhouse, the garage, the caretaker's cottage, so that the glow of the moon and stars was undisturbed.

Then he poured them both wine and handed her a glass, taking his own with him where he went to prop a hip and one thick thigh on the railing.

Ally joined him there, but while she looked up at the sky, he watched her.

She couldn't help feeling as if he were waiting for her to say something, *expecting* her to say something, and she felt obliged to address the subject she believed was on his mind.

"I can't give you an answer about getting married," she said quietly, even though she knew what she *should* say. She *should* say that quite likely she'd turn him down, because staying on the ranch just seemed too dangerous. That even if Meggie's mental state was improved, not only was it merely a temporary thing, it seemed more and more possible that her physical well-being was threatened.

But just then she couldn't make herself say any of that, any more than she'd been able to keep herself from accompanying him to his room.

But Jackson solved the immediate problem for her, if not the longer-range one. "We don't need to talk about marriage," he said, sounding as if that were the last thing on his mind. "In fact, we don't need to talk about anything. We just came out to do some stargazin', remember?"

She glanced over at him, at the small smile that

peeked out from beneath his mustache as he went on studying her as if to memorize her face.

"It isn't stars you're looking at," she observed.

"Sure I am. It's just that I'm lookin' through that extra set of eyes I have out of the back of my head."

"Funny, I never noticed them before. Where are they exactly?" she teased, giving in to the urge to slide her free hand up into his hair as if in search.

"Careful you don't blind me, now," he joked back, dipping to allow her better access and kissing her lightly at the same time. "Find 'em?" he asked a moment later.

"Lumps, maybe. But no eyes."

"You complainin'?"

"Who, me? I'm wild for men with lumpy heads."

He kissed her again, smiling as he did. "And I'm crazy for a sassy woman."

"I guess that makes us wild and crazy."

"Yes, ma'am, I guess it does." He chuckled and kissed her yet again, longer this time.

Then he reached over and set his wineglass on the table so he could rest a hand on each of her hips and guide her to stand between his legs. Once more his mouth met hers but there was nothing wild or crazy in it. Instead it was leisurely, languorous, as if they had all the time in the world.

Maybe she should warn him that they might not have, Ally thought. That this could actually be the end for them...

But his lips were so soft over hers, so warm, so wonderful, that somehow when words found their way out she said, "Lumpy head or not, you kiss better than anyone I've ever known."

He smiled through another one and she couldn't be sure if it was because he was glad she thought so or because he already knew it. "Don't wait for any complaints from me, because you won't be hearin' any," he said between the end of one kiss and the beginning of another as he took her glass and set it on the table with his.

Ally gave him a lazy smile of her own and slipped her other hand into his hair, too, and that was the last of the talking they did as Jackson drew her close, into powerful arms that wrapped around her and a kiss that was so deep she drifted away on it.

There was something different going on between them tonight that Ally couldn't quite put her finger on. Not that it was bad. Not at all. Just different. The hunger, the urgency that usually drove them both was suppressed, and in its place was a sense that these moments, this closeness they shared, needed to be cherished.

They stayed on the balcony a long time, just kissing, before Jackson took her to his bed. And even then there was no intensity. Instead, when their bodies entwined, their hands explored, caressed, aroused unhurriedly. Their mouths and tongues did the same, learning the secret spots to delight and delight in, discovering that even nuances could awaken passion.

All with a pace so slow, so tender, it savored every moment, every touch, every sensation. A pace that allowed them to revel in each other, in the magic their bodies made together, in the emotions that were so strong they were nearly tangible, in a poignancy so sweet it almost hurt....

Hours later, when Ally lay in Jackson's arms, replete and exhausted, he whispered very, very solemnly, "I love you, Ally."

"I love you, too," she whispered back, meaning it with all her heart, believing that he did, too.

And yet, as sleep pulled her toward it, somehow she couldn't help feeling that it was as if they'd each just said goodbye.

Chapter Ten

It was after seven when Ally woke up the next morning. She was still in Jackson's bed. But she was alone. He was nowhere in sight and the room was too quiet for him to be even in the connecting bathroom.

Ally got up in a hurry, both because she didn't want Jackson to accuse her of being a slugabed and because she didn't want Meggie—who could be waking up anytime—to catch her there.

In her own bathroom, she took a quick shower, gathered her hair onto the crown of her head with an elastic ruffle, applied a little mascara and blush, and slipped into a pair of jeans and a sleeveless chambray shirt.

Then she went downstairs, expecting that Jackson had already gone outside for the day.

But the kitchen was where she found him.

He was sitting on a stool at the butcher block, his forearms resting on either side of an untouched plate of biscuits and gravy. But apparently he hadn't just sat down to his breakfast, because the gravy was beginning to congeal.

"Jackson?" she said as if she weren't sure it was really him behind an expression that was as sober, as remote, as what he'd shown her when she'd first arrived at the ranch.

"'Mornin'," he answered in a low rumble of a voice.

She was about to ask him what was wrong when the place setting across from him caught her eye. A plate, a juice glass, a coffee mug, a napkin, silverware, and a check attached to a handwritten note.

"What's this?" she asked instead, on her way to see for herself.

He didn't say anything. He just waited for her to pick up the papers and read them.

The check was for ten thousand dollars. The note was an IOU for the rest of the best offer yet to buy out her share of the ranch.

Ally propped a hip on the bar stool on her side of the counter for the support she suddenly needed and stared at what she held in her hand.

"You and Meggie don't belong here," he said before she could wade through her thoughts and feelings. "You aren't right for this life. Neither one of you knows what you're doing, you get yourselves into trouble, get hurt, could get hurt even worse. A lot worse. It's time we faced up to reality and did something about it before that something worse happens.''

''Guess this is your way of telling me to stop thinking about your proposal,'' she countered, incensed, hurt, and letting it all sound in her voice.

''It isn't marrying me you've been thinking about, anyway,'' he countered. ''You're leaning toward leaving, proposal or not. Don't deny it.''

How could she when, for the most part, it was true? But it shocked her to learn that he'd realized it.

''That's a fair offer,'' he said with a nod at the check and promissory note. ''I won't take no for an answer this time. What's best for both you and Meggie is to get the hell out of here.''

''Is it what's best for you, too?'' she demanded, challenging him.

''I think it is, yes,'' he answered very solemnly and without missing a beat.

''And it's what you want?'' And *she* wasn't what he wanted, a little voice in the back of her mind said bluntly. Just like she hadn't been what Doug had wanted in the end.

''What I *don't* want,'' he nearly shouted, ''is to come home one day and find you gone. And it'll happen, Ally. If it doesn't happen now—because of Meggie's accident—it'll happen after the next fall from the hayloft, or the next kick of a mule, or the next snakebite. But I know damn good and well that it *will* happen. So let's just get it done.''

"I'm too much like your ex-wife, is that what you're saying?"

"You're nothing like my ex-wife."

"But you're sure I'll do the same thing."

He confirmed that with silence.

And, much as she wished she could, there was no arguing with something he was right about.

Oh, she might not have made up her mind completely about whether or not to leave here, and she would never sneak away behind his back with no more of an explanation than a note and some divorce papers. But the truth was, she had been thinking more about leaving than about staying and marrying him, and that told her it was the likelihood.

"I can't lie to you and say I haven't been wondering if the bad of being here didn't outweigh the good," she admitted. "But—"

"But nothing. Once you start thinkin' that, you never stop. You'll be seeing dangers and hazards and hardships and things you can't abide lurking everywhere. You already are, if the truth be known, and don't bother denying that, either."

"What is it you want me to say, Jackson? That yes, you're right, I have been wondering if I should take Meggie away from here before something else happens to one of us? That maybe Meggie and my leaving *is* for the best?"

In spite of all he'd said to push her to it, the words seemed to hit him like a thunderbolt.

Had he been testing her? Just wondering if she'd fight him down? If she'd still stand her ground about staying even now that she'd seen the worst he and this life had to offer?

But this was no game, she told herself.

Any more than it had been a game when Doug had rejected her. When she'd tried to believe that eventually he'd come to his senses, that he didn't really mean the hurtful things he'd said and done, that he couldn't possibly be throwing away all they'd worked for together, all they'd shared, all they'd been to each other...

No, the bottom line here was that Jackson didn't want her. Just the way Doug hadn't wanted her. And at that moment she knew that she was facing the most real danger of being on this ranch—Jackson. And her feelings for him. And how she could be crushed beneath them if she didn't run as far and as fast as she could.

He stood, taking his uneaten breakfast to the sink. "You put a good effort into living here. I poured on the work thicker than I should have, but you kept up. Don't feel that you didn't give it a good try," he said as if to put a kinder edge to firing a ranch hand who hadn't been able to do the job. "It just wasn't meant to be."

"Funny, but it felt like it was," she murmured sarcastically from the part of her that was hurting.

He turned to face her again. "Yeah, well, things can seem that way even when they aren't."

"I should have just been smart enough to have taken your offer from the start and saved us both a lot of trouble," she added for him.

His eyes stayed on her but suddenly they softened. "I wouldn't change anything," he said quietly. "I'm grateful for the little we've had. There just can't be more of it. Get your things together and I'll drive you to the train station."

Then he headed for one of the sliding glass doors, each boot step firm, final, and leaving Ally with nothing but the view of his broad, proud back.

Ally didn't know how much or how little time passed as she sat on the stool at the butcher block, staring at the door Jackson had walked through. But when she heard the sounds of Meggie stirring upstairs she realized she had to rise out of that limbo and go to her daughter.

She felt numb as she moved back through the house, and between that and focusing on how Meggie would accept the news that they'd be leaving the ranch, it helped keep the horrible pain that lurked on the fringes at bay. Somewhat, anyway.

Meggie was just dressing when Ally knocked and slipped into her room.

"Good morning," she said, hating the shakiness in her voice when she'd wanted to sound cheery.

"Hi," Meggie answered as she pulled a T-shirt over her head and tucked it into her shorts.

Her bumps and bruises were better, and just before the shirt covered her completely Ally noticed her daughter had put on a pound or two and wasn't as emaciatingly thin as she'd been when they'd arrived.

Keeping her fingers crossed that the good that had

come from being here wouldn't be lost in leaving, Ally sat on the bed beside Meggie while the little girl put on her socks.

"I have something to tell you, sweetheart," Ally began.

"Did the momma pig have her babies?" Meggie guessed excitedly.

"I don't know. That isn't what I have to say."

The sober tone of Ally's voice seemed to register just then. Meggie stopped short of pulling on the cowboy boots she was so proud of and looked directly at her mother, waiting expectantly.

"Jackson and I had a talk this morning and we've decided it would be best if you and I didn't live on the ranch after all. If we went back to Denver."

Meggie's face fell. "Why?"

"Well, since we've been on the ranch all you and I seem to do is get into one scrape after another. Things that are pretty scary. Things that get us hurt or could." Ally smoothed a curl of her daughter's hair away from the wound on her brow. "I just think it's too dangerous for us to be here."

"I'm not scared! I don't want to go back to Denver. I like the ranch and the animals and Jackson and Hans and Marta—"

"I know you do. I do, too. But—"

"I promise I'll be more careful and next time Jackson tells me something I'll do it right then, I won't pretend like I didn't hear him."

"Honey, it isn't as if you did something wrong." Ally addressed the sound of guilt in her daughter's voice. "It's that right or wrong, the ranch is a dangerous place."

"But I can be careful. Like when I ran out in the street after my ball at Gramma's and about got hit by the car—I was more careful after that and I never did it again. And I stayed away from Grampa's lawn mower like you told me to, and I didn't ride my roller skates down the big hill after I crashed and got all scraped up, and I never talk to strangers or nothin' like I'm not s'pose to. I can learn about stuff I'm not s'pose to do here, too, and then it'll be okay. Okay?"

"Meggie—"

"No!" her daughter shouted, jamming her feet into her boots and making a dash for the door. "I'm gonna go talk to Jackson and tell him I'll be good so he'll let us stay."

And out she went, leaving Ally to helplessly watch her go, much the way she'd watched Jackson just a little while before.

Ally took a deep breath and blew it out in a frustrated, forlorn sigh, resting her elbows on her knees and dropping her face into her hands.

The last thing she'd intended to do was make Meggie think she'd done anything wrong. Sure, maybe she'd been overeager to help with the brushfire and hadn't stayed away from it the way she'd been told to, and she'd ignored Jackson's telling her to leave Sunshine and go into the house in the storm, but she was only a little kid and little kids did things like that.

Just the way they did things like running out in the street without looking for cars, going out of control on roller skates, trying to help mow the grass. Kids didn't always think about how dangerous something might be and Ally didn't expect Meggie to. Not on her own, anyway. Not without being warned first and sometimes barreling in even then. Whether she was here or…

Or in the suburbs.…

That thought suddenly struck Ally, and with it, something she hadn't considered in all of her thinking about how dangerous the ranch was—that there were plenty of dangers in living where they'd lived before, too. Or in living anywhere for that matter. That the dangers might be different, but they were dangers just the same.

And yet, somehow, the near-miss accidents and scrapes and bumps and bruises Meggie had had during the years before, even the more dire possibilities like kidnapping or any of the perils she'd warned her daughter of, had never seemed like *dangers*. Just the stuff of everyday living that a child either got into or needed to be made aware of. They didn't loom like ominous dark clouds over every moment, the way Ally had begun to think of things around the ranch.

And Ally had never been in a panic over them. Or ready to move at the drop of a hat to try avoiding them.

So what had gotten into her now? Why, in the past few days, had she been so lost in fear and worry over living here that she'd hardly been able to think about anything else, even Jackson's marriage proposal?

Ally straightened up and stared into space as light began to dawn in her mind.

What had she thought in the kitchen just a little while ago? That Jackson and her feelings for him and her attraction to him were the *real* dangers here...

Ally shook her head in amazement at herself.

Sure, the things both she and Meggie had encountered here had been unnerving, but it suddenly seemed very suspicious that she'd been able to take the first ones in her stride. Her fears and worrying had only grown out of proportion at about the same time her feelings for Jackson had blossomed, when she'd begun to lose the battle against her attraction to him, when she'd let down her guard completely and made love with him.

"Camouflage," she muttered, wondering if it was possible that rather than confront her very real and potent fear of a new relationship, a relationship with Jackson, and maybe a repetition of what had happened with Doug, she'd focused all of her fear on the ranch itself.

It was not only possible, it suddenly seemed more than likely.

Not that there weren't real perils in living here. Things and situations that needed more care than she or Meggie had given them. But life-threatening danger didn't wait around every corner as she'd begun to think.

Only Jackson did.

And the truth was, she realized, she was really

afraid of being let down by love, by another man, more than she was afraid of anything else.

"Really smart, Al," she said out loud. "And while you were hiding it from yourself you walked right into it."

The numbness receded and a wave of pain as powerful as what she'd felt at the end of her marriage washed over her.

So much for protecting herself.

Then it occurred to her to wonder if protecting *himself* was what Jackson was doing by sending her away.

But she didn't have to wonder long, because too much of what he'd said in the kitchen told her that was exactly what he was doing. He'd seen her waffling about staying on the ranch and, before she could walk out on him the way his ex-wife had, he was ending it himself.

Or was that just wishful thinking?

What if he really didn't love her?

But how could that be with all that had happened between them the past few days...and nights?

At the end of her marriage Doug hadn't touched her. Not for months before. He hadn't even had a kind word for her or a moment to spare to spend with her.

But with Jackson the exact opposite was true. He'd wanted her—as urgently, as intensely as she'd wanted him. His attitude toward her had vastly improved from what it had been when she'd first come here, not deteriorated the way Doug's had. Now kind words were all he had for her—even this morning when he'd been rejecting her. And as for spending time together, he'd wanted more of that, not less. He'd barely left her side at the naming ceremony and he'd even tried to get her to go with him in the helicopter afterward, just to have her company.

And more than all of that, just this past night together, when he'd made such sweet love to her, told her he loved her and held her close as they'd fallen asleep, there hadn't been anything in one moment of it that said he didn't really love her, didn't want her.

No, there had been tenderness and care. He'd cherished her with every caress. And though he might have been saying goodbye to her, savoring what they'd shared and filling up on memories to carry with him, there hadn't been a lack of feelings for her. And nothing he'd said since could convince her otherwise.

So where did it leave her?

Could she assure Jackson she was here for good? That nothing would ever drive her away?

Thinking about Meggie's accident still had the power to send a shiver up her spine. As did thoughts of the brushfire and all the other things that had happened during their time on the ranch.

But then she thought of Meggie's state of mind, and how her little girl had taken to life on the ranch— and to Jackson. Ally had thought the improvements in Meggie's mood had been only temporary, but since they'd all reemerged after a single day and night of what had looked like a relapse, now it seemed that it was the relapse that was only temporary. Country life suited her little girl. And if anything would ever allow her to get over her father's desertion, Ally suddenly admitted that being here had the best chance.

Which only left the bottom line. The real issue.

"Okay, so what about me?" she whispered, wondering if, when it came down to brass tacks, she could face what actually frightened her most—loving Jackson, giving herself, her heart, completely, freely, to a man again. Committing herself totally to a future with him.

Because that was the real question.

She could find another countrylike environment in which Meggie would thrive—this ranch wasn't the only solution to her daughter's problems. But giving in to her feelings for Jackson, taking a chance on another relationship, on love again, that was the more daunting prospect.

Daunting or not, she realized that she was coming to this question too late. Because no matter how much it scared her, she did love him. Completely, with all her heart and so deeply that the thought of not having him in her life was too awful to bear, fear or no fear.

So she'd actually already taken the risk.

And lost.

Unless she could repair the damage.

"But why is it best?" Meggie's voice echoed in the barn as Ally went in in search of Jackson.

"It just is, darlin'," she heard him answer her daughter, sounding every bit as morose as the little girl as Ally headed for where they stood near a pile of hay. Jackson held a pitchfork in one hand; he was stroking Meggie's hair with the other to comfort her.

Jackson noticed Ally first, looking up at her as she reached them. But it was to her daughter that Ally spoke. "Meggie, honey, I want you to go into the house and fix yourself a bowl of cereal."

"I'm not hungry."

"Do it anyway. I need to talk to Jackson."

"Will you make him let us live here?"

"Just go up to the house."

"I want to stay."

"I'll be up in a minute."

"I mean I want to stay on the ranch. With Jackson. Forever."

"Meggie..." Ally said only that, but very firmly, in a motherly warning tone.

Her daughter pouted and hung her head and kicked at the hay on the barn floor, but finally sulked off.

For the time it took her to get out the great door, both Ally and Jackson just watched her go.

Then Ally turned to Jackson and gave his shoulders a mighty shove. "That's just to let you know that I won't stand for you making my decisions for me."

She'd surprised him, but he recouped quickly and frowned at her. "What decisions did I make for you?"

"That it was too dangerous around here for Meggie and me. That I was selling my share of this place. That I was not marrying you." She shoved him again. "And while I'm at it, I'll tell you another thing. I'm a person who knows a thing or two about commitment, and riding through rough patches, and working hard and sticking with things and people.'' Another shove. ''Now, tell me you don't love me. Tell me you don't want me in your life—not on your ranch—*in your life*. Say it right to my face. Because that's the only reason I'm leaving this place today.''

''That so?''

''Yes, that's so because I *do* love you. It just took a kick in the pants for me to see *that's* what's been scaring me more than anything around here and that I've just been using the other things as an escape hatch to protect myself. Just the way you're ready to push me out the door to protect yourself rather than risk going on with what's started between us.''

''You have it all figured out, do you?''

''Yes, I think I do. Or at least I have it narrowed down to two possibilities—it's either that or you don't love me and don't want me and just proposed in some weak moment when passion had sapped the sense out of you.''

A small smile tugged at the corners of his mouth. ''When passion sapped the sense out of me?''

She ignored the amusement in his voice. ''Tell me you don't love me. That you don't want me,'' she repeated. ''Because all you said before is that you don't want to come home one day and find me gone. And that's not the same thing.''

He sobered. ''But it's the truth.''

''But not wanting it to happen, being afraid of it, doesn't mean it's *going* to happen.''

''Doesn't it?''

"No, it doesn't. I like it here. And Meggie likes it here. But more than that, I love you enough to do anything I have to do to be a part of your life, even to go through the rest of my days working like a dog if that's what it takes—"

The smile came back. "You wouldn't have to work like a dog. Or even a ranch hand. That was just me being ornery. You could cook at the honky-tonk if you wanted, or just stay around the house and raise babies."

"So what are you telling me, Heller?"

He sobered yet again. "I guess if I was tellin' you anything it would be to be sure about what you're sayin', Ally. And about what you're thinkin' about doin'."

"I'm sure that I love you. I'm sure that I want to be your wife and live here on the ranch with you, no matter how far away the next neighbor is, no matter how bad the weather or how much work. No matter how many new safety precautions I need to learn and teach Meggie. Because the only thing that really does matter is that I have a life with you." She gave him one last shove for emphasis, but this time he saw it coming, let the pitchfork drop and caught her wrists.

Still, she went on, just closer to him now. "Unless you tell me you don't love me or want me. Or Meggie or—"

He gave a tug that brought her up against him and cut off her words with a fierce, hard kiss even as his arms went around her and held her to him.

And then, as abruptly as it had begun, he stopped

kissing her. "I can't tell you I don't love you, because I do. And I want you—everywhere and every way—more than I've ever wanted anything or anyone as long as I've lived. And as for Meggie? Well, you know better than to think I don't care for her as if she were my own. But—"

"But nothing," she repeated his earlier phrase to her. "Does that mean I can start thinking about marrying you again?"

His blue eyes searched hers and Ally could see the thoughts running through his mind, the temptation to believe her, the fear that if he did he might be hurt the way he'd been before.

"You said yourself that I'm nothing like your ex-wife. And I'm here to tell you that I'd never do what she did to you. I might fight to change something I don't like, but I won't run away from it."

"No, I don't think you will. Not once you've made the commitment," he agreed quietly. And then his expression eased into another smile and she knew.

She knew he was taking the risk again, too.

"So. Shall I start thinking about that proposal of yours or not?" she asked.

"No, ma'am," he answered in a slow drawl. "I think you just ought to pick a date so we can do it."

It was Ally who smiled then, but only for the moment before he kissed her once more, softly, sweetly, this time.

"I won't ever leave you, Jackson," she promised very solemnly when it was over.

"Good, because I figured we were both signing on for life."

"Unless of course you ever make me climb that windmill again. Then you may find yourself kicked off my ranch," she joked.

"*Your* ranch now, is it?"

"Mmm."

"I'll try to keep it in mind," he said with a crooked grin that went straight to her heart. "Unless of course you ever come shovin' me again. Then you just might find yourself up that windmill quicker than you think."

Ally gave him the same kind of grin as he kissed her a third time, only this one was deeper than the others and much, much longer.

But just when sparks of that passion she'd mentioned before began to light, Jackson stopped. "Much as I'd like to give you a taste of a real, live roll in the hay, I think we have a mighty upset little girl in the house who doesn't need to be mighty upset anymore and we'd best see to her."

Ally reached up and kissed him one short peck, loving him enough to burst, wanting him, but so, so grateful that he cared enough about Meggie, too, to think of her even at a time like this.

"What was she saying to you before I came in?" Ally asked.

"That she wanted me to convince you to stay."

"Well, you have," she teased.

"I'm just irresistible," he agreed, keeping one arm around her as they headed out of the barn.

On the way to the house that Shag Heller had built, Ally knew she was doing the right thing. The right thing for herself and for her daughter—she and Meggie and Jackson would be a family.

And in her heart she thanked the old man who had left her so much.

So much more than he'd ever known.

For over and above the money and land, the holdings and assets, Shag had given her the gift of his son.

And a whole lifetime of love.

* * * * *

Presenting three tales by bestselling author

VICKI LEWIS THOMPSON

URBAN Cowboys

Cowboy #1: **THE TRAILBLAZER**
Businessman T. R. McGuiness thought ranching would be a breeze—
until sexy cowgirl Freddy Singleton showed him how
much more he had to learn....

Cowboy #2: **THE DRIFTER**
Trucker Chase Lavette was looking forward to having time alone
on the range—until his former lover showed up with
a little surprise....

Cowboy #3: **THE LAWMAN**
Cop Joe Gilardini had decided to give up law enforcement—
until mysterious "accidents" started occurring at the ranch...
and he found himself falling for his primary suspect.

Coming August 2001

Every woman loves a cowboy...

Visit us at www.eHarlequin.com
BR3UC

When California's most talked about dynasty is threatened, only family, privilege and the power of love can protect them!

THE COLTONS

Coming in August 2001

I MARRIED A SHEIK

by **Sharon De Vita**

When honorary Colton son Sheik Ali El-Etra's investment firm hired a new consultant, Ali was infinitely intrigued. Faith Martin was wary of high-handed "princely" types like Ali, and she would have liked to take the sheik down a notch or two. Had this sultan and plain Jane finally met their match?

Available at your favorite retail outlet.

Silhouette ®

Where love comes alive™

Visit Silhouette at www.eHarlequin.com
PSCOLT3

Available in August from

JOAN ELLIOTT PICKART

A brand-new, longer-length book
in the bestselling series,

The Baby Bet

Party of Three

He was a hard-boiled cop with a child in his care.
She was a woman in need of his protective embrace.
Together they were a family in the making…

Available at your favorite retail outlet.
Only from Silhouette Books

Silhouette®
Where love comes alive™

Visit Silhouette at www.eHarlequin.com

PSBB

DON'T MISS OUT!

MONTANA MAVERICKS: BIG SKY GROOMS
Three brand-new historical stories about the Kincaids, Montana's most popular family

**RETURN TO WHITEHORN, MONTANA—
WHERE LEGENDS ARE BEGUN AND
LOVE LASTS FOREVER BENEATH THE BIG SKY....**

Available in August 2001

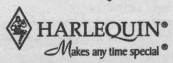

HARLEQUIN®
Makes any time special®

Visit us at www.eHarlequin.com

PHBSGR

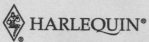

HARLEQUIN®

makes any time special—online...

eHARLEQUIN.com

your romantic escapes

━Indulgences━

♥ Monthly guides to indulging yourself,
such as:
  ★ Tub Time: A guide for bathing beauties
  ★ Magic Massages: A treat for tired feet

━Horoscopes━

♥ Find your daily Passionscope, weekly
Lovescopes and Erotiscopes

♥ Try our compatibility game

━Reel Love━

♥ Read all the latest romantic
movie reviews

━Royal Romance━

♥ Get the latest scoop on your favorite
royal romances

━Romantic Travel━

♥ For the most romantic destinations, hotels
and travel activities

All this and more available at
www.eHarlequin.com
on Women.com Networks

HINTE1R